PRAISE FOR *THE EN*

"Rao gifts us a soaring and he
about grief, rage, and the en g power of love."
Sunyi Dean

"Powerful, intricate, and raw – a richly satisfying and riveting conclusion to the Rages trilogy."
H. M. Long

"A mind-blowing close … As always, Rao's prose is lush and poetic."
S.B. Divya

"An explosive conclusion to the Rages trilogy … Fans will be anchored in their seats through the last page … If you haven't picked this series up yet, what are you waiting for?!"
M. J. Kuhn

PRAISE FOR THE RAGES TRILOGY

"Riveting … an instantly immersive epic that expands the boundaries of what fantasy can be."
Library Journal

"A powerful, sweeping story; epic science fantasy at its best."
Sunyi Dean

"A powerful epic of heartbreak and hard-bought triumph, of anguish and enduring hope."
Melissa Caruso

"Breathtakingly inventive … This is a book to get lost in."
TASHA SURI

"Intensely imaginative and heartbreakingly human."
ANDREA STEWART

"Extremely original and thought-provoking …
I utterly loved it and couldn't put it down."
SHANNON CHAKRABORTY

"Wildly imaginative … Don't miss it!"
LUCY HOLLAND

"[An] utterly creative, heady and mysterious
tapestry of love, duty, and discovery."
H.M. LONG

"A prodigious gift best slowly unwrapped …
Rao has offered us a world like no other."
SUYI DAVIES OKUNGBOWA

"An immersive and original epic fantasy."
GAUTAM BHATIA

"Brimming with fascinating lore
and dangerous magic."
CHELSEA ABDULLAH

"[A] brilliant, gorgeous debut."
FRAN WILDE

"Everything I hope for in a novel."
JOSHUA PHILLIP JOHNSON

THE ENDURING UNIVERSE

Also by Kritika H. Rao
and available from Titan Books

The Surviving Sky

The Unrelenting Earth

THE ENDURING UNIVERSE

KRITIKA H. RAO

TITAN BOOKS

The Enduring Universe
Print edition ISBN: 9781803365299
E-book edition ISBN: 9781803365305

Published by Titan Books
A division of Titan Publishing Group Ltd
144 Southwark Street, London SE1 0UP
www.titanbooks.com

First edition: September 2025
10 9 8 7 6 5 4 3 2 1

A CIP catalogue record for this title is available from the British Library.

EU RP (for authorities only)
eucomply OÜ, Pärnu mnt. 139b-14, 11317 Tallinn, Estonia
hello@eucompliancepartner.com, +33757690241

Printed and bound by CPI Group (UK) Ltd, Croydon CR0 4YY.

To those seeking.

PROLOGUE

In the airborne nest, the falcon found him.

Its massive silver wings cut through the air. Its black eyes glinted in satisfaction, for there was fear and recognition in the man's eyes. The falcon slammed into the floating nest, ripping it apart. Earth and trees fell away, disappearing into the jungle below, as the nest tilted, plummeting a hundred feet before righting itself. Where was the man-thing? It would not be denied again. It saw him emerge onto grass, holding a female body. It saw his indecision as he looked to the female, as if he would choose her.

The falcon screeched in outrage, unleashing its power. Vines grew around the woman, strangling her. It would take her out of the reckoning. It would *destroy* her.

It swooped down, clutching the man's body between its talons, leaving behind cries of fear and shock. The jungle screamed below, and the falcon turned its power into the globule of stars, exerting its will. Shards of earth pierced its wings but as the falcon pushed its power, the storm relented. To navigate carefully through the storm was necessary. The human would not survive the jungle.

The falcon despised the man-thing, but it needed him safe, and so he remained alive for now. The falcon flung him away in disgust once they arrived at the safe-nest. It returned to the darkening caves where others of its kind slumbered. *Awake,* it called to the other survivors, but it had tried before. These creatures—its kin—were lesser still, unheard by their halves. For thousands of years, the falcon had tried to awaken them, to corral them into action. They were too dull. Too lost. Exhausted, it tucked its head under a wing to tend to its wounds.

The next time it awoke, the man had arrived, accompanied once again by the female. The falcon fluttered its wings warily. In the velvety darkness, it saw the man's jagged shape, and felt a rush of relief as it realized the human wished to finally unite their powers. Thousands of years, it had waited for this moment.

It mimicked the man's light, creating a spiral vortex of great power, and wrapping the man and his female within its wings. Power coursed through it, and it wove among the stars, guided by the man, just as the man wove through the Deepness guided by it. They felt *completion.* Its voice burrowed within the man, and the falcon thought, *Peace. There is peace.* Words and language flowed into its mind, slowly at first, then with growing rapidity. The remembrance of such sentience was so beautiful, it ached.

But despite months of unity, the man did not give in.

He did not learn. He refused to see purpose. His heart was too full of anguish. The falcon studied the shape of him, the angst and infinity, the shame and guilt, and its rage mirrored back. Its purpose bled in the man.

Amends, he heard the man say.

Destroy, the falcon returned.

And the man agreed those meant the same thing.

The falcon laughed, a feral sound even to its own ears. In the velvety darkness, it attacked the man over and over again, trying to take him over—this small, foolish creature that should have acquiesced in seconds but had resisted for years. It felt the man's terrible purpose and it screamed in panic and terror as this small creature performed a subsummation—*no, no, no*—

It dissolved in a final relief, its presence a shadow inside the man's heart.

And within that shadow, an understanding.

A waking.

A learning.

1

AHILYA

In the silence of the jungle, the mutters of the architects echoed loud and restless. Ahilya moved to distance herself from them, her tread quiet yet careful.

The care was ingrained in her after a lifetime of exploring the unpredictable jungle, though there was hardly any need for such caution anymore. It had been three months since the last earthrage devastated all the ashrams. Now those storms were over. Despite the thriving foliage, the jungle lay still, unnatural and quiescent, as though dead.

No, Ahilya thought. *Not dead. Merely resting. Merely watchful.*

There were no animals in the jungle, but the Virohi seemed to watch her from between leaves that stirred in the breeze, tracking her footsteps. The architects with her couldn't sense the creatures, she knew, but she could feel the Virohi in the whispers of the trees, in the endless dark depths that even her bright sungineering torch could not pierce. The cosmic creatures studied her with longing and rage. A deep familiarity emanated from them, filling her with dread.

<*Ahilya*>, they whispered. <*Come back to us. You belong to us.*>

Her hands slowly shook in terror. *This isn't real,* she thought. *The Virohi are in Irshar. They are not in the jungle. They cannot be.*

Leaves stirred. People murmured behind her. Evening sunshine fell in dappled shafts, intersecting with the light of her torch, illuminating a patch of grass here, a thick bush there. She swept aside a branch, cut a small notch in a passing tree, and hacked away the clustered vines in front of her. She tried not to give in to the fear that always arose when the cosmic creatures called her.

The Virohi had been silent when she left the habitat three days ago, but leaving was still a risk. The habitat—Irshar, as everyone had taken to calling it—had grown unruly, beyond her control.

A couple of months before, the Virohi-imbued pathways, roads and walls had listened to her persuasion by settling into fixed forms when she'd asked them to. Lately, they had begun changing with more frequency. That the Virohi were reaching to her so easily, beyond the confines of Irshar... It was a sign of her weakening hold over them. It was a sign of their control of *her.* They were growing agitated. She was needed in Irshar to stabilize the architecture.

Yet she was needed in the jungle too. It was why *she* was in charge of this mission. Councilor or not, her true vocation was to be an archeologist, and her task was to find a new home away from the ever-changing habitat. That was why she had been sent here, leading ten people into the dark, guided by nothing but her intuition.

Ahilya ducked under a heavy branch, her cheek brushing stray vines. Moisture hung in the air, heavy and oppressive. Dark green moss silenced her footsteps. She trod over fallen branches and roots, the undergrowth as still as the rest of the forest. Twice, she had to circle back—something she had never done in a moving jungle.

It unnerved her, this stillness.

Irshar's council had expected life to return to the jungle, as the small creatures of the landed ashrams expanded into this new ecosystem. Yet though leaves susurrated in hushed tones, the bursting green was grim and devoid of chirrups or birdsong. It made the hairs rise on Ahilya's neck. This was still an alien jungle, one that all of them had abandoned for thousands of years. No living creature was used to it, not even the squirrels and mice that had undoubtedly climbed up the trees and burrowed into the earth. They were waiting, and wary. Just like humanity's survivors. Just like her expeditionary team.

A glance behind confirmed this. Irshar's architects marched in formation, yet their voices were growing louder, laced with bitterness at their inability to traject the jungle. Sharp words filtered to Ahilya, whispers of her name, skepticism regarding her authority to lead them. This expedition was unlike any of the others she had undertaken before. In the past, she had circumvented obstacles, split the vines that had reached for her, danced through the landscape like she was one of the plants herself. What little she had not managed had been managed for her by an accompanying architect. Yet none of the ones with her now trajected the jungle at all. Instead, each of them wore a bracelet made of seeds, remnants of the once-airborne ashrams. Tendrils curled from the seeds, wrapping around the architects' arms, all the way up to their shoulders.

Pari, an architect who had once belonged to Reikshar, twisted; the vines she was trajecting strangled her, and a scream formed behind terrified eyes—

Then the light shifted, and Ahilya blinked. Pari shrugged, muttering under her breath, her imagined strangulation still echoing in Ahilya's mind.

Ahilya tried not to stare. *Not real,* she thought again, in a slow building panic. *Not real. See with your eyes. Hear with your ears. Notice what is real.*

The tattoos on the architects' faces were dim, a mockery of the power the architects had once had. Trajection in the jungle had always been difficult, but now it was impossible. The earthrages had always been tied to trajection and in ending one, Ahilya had unwittingly damaged the other. There was only one place the power truly worked anymore—Iravan's Garden.

She had slowed without meaning to. Eskayra, who had been marching with the rest of the team, caught up to her. "You seem uncertain," she said, her voice husky. "Are we lost?"

The other woman was shorter than Ahilya by a head, her build muscular, her delicate features exceedingly beautiful. Clipped dark hair framed a dewdrop face, and her perfect white teeth glinted in the beams of the torchlight. A few months ago, Ahilya had found Eskayra with the citizens that had stood against the cosmic creatures. They had reforged their friendship, but in Eskayra's light brown eyes now, Ahilya could see the same desire from years before, when they had been more than friends. She shook her head now, as much in answer to Eskayra's unspoken proposition as to her question.

"No," she replied. "We're not far. This is the route Irshar told me to take."

"You mean the Virohi told you."

Ahilya didn't reply. They both knew the answer to that question. The habitat was Irshar; it *was* the embedded Virohi.

Eskayra touched her arm and spoke in a low tone. "My dear, are the Virohi leading you right?"

The others clustered around to listen. Ahilya might be leading the way, but Eskayra was the one the expeditionary team answered to. *She* had mobilized them all to the cause, insisting that finding alternatives to Irshar was a priority. It was Eskayra who had become the voice for every non-trajector in Irshar. Eskayra who even the architects of Irshar obeyed, because she was neither an architect, nor associated with one. She was, in all ways that mattered, a complete being.

Once Ahilya had thought she was a complete being too, but she had changed against her will. She had battled with the Virohi, but she had invited them into herself inadvertently. Iravan had warned her the Virohi would corrupt her, and for the last several months she had become lost in her mind. The image of Pari being strangled, the delusion that the Virohi were in the jungle somehow, the constant voices in her head, all these were mild examples of the distortions she endured. Horror and grief snuck up on her when she least expected it. Eskayra was right to doubt her.

<*Ahilya*>, the Virohi said in the Etherium. <*You belong with us. You're one of us.*>

Ahilya felt the sungineering torch in her hand tremble violently, flashes of light dancing in the rich darkness. Terror overtook her as a mirrored chamber glinted between her brows without her consent. She blinked rapidly until she was looking at the assembled archeologists in the dying sunlight within the jungle once more.

The unseen map in her head vanished. "We're here," she said, breathless, raising a limp hand.

Relieved sighs and nods rippled through the expeditionary team, though a couple of people looked skeptical.

Pari frowned. "Are you sure?"

"This place looks like everywhere else," a non-architect called Ranjeev added. "How do you know—"

"She knows," Eskayra cut in. "This is Ahilya-ve of Nakshar you're talking to. She controls Irshar. More working, less questioning, if you please. *We're here.*"

The members of the expedition exchanged glances, but no one objected. At Eskayra's gesture, they began fanning out and hacking at the vegetation with their machetes and axes.

Ahilya watched them, saying nothing.

Ranjeev had asked a fair question, but there was little more to the answer than they already knew. For months, the team had tried to find a site for a new city in the jungle. Irshar was solely dependent on Ahilya's will; it was why finding a new home was imperative, but every mission had ended in disaster. All the sites where Eskayra's team had begun building had failed—one destroyed by a strange forest fire, another crumbling to ash, and the third collapsing on top of the team, who barely escaped with their lives. No one had been able to explain the strange phenomena, though Airav suggested it was the remembered instability of the jungle, passed down seed to seed, a legacy of constant earthrages. Eskayra, and the council, despaired over ever escaping Irshar.

Eventually, out of desperation, Ahilya had asked the cosmic creatures for potential habitats, and a map had formed in her head like a nebulous idea, revealing bit by bit. Charged by the rest of the council to follow this lead, Ahilya had woven her way in the jungle for the last three days, turning at that tree, going past this waterfall, following not a sungineering tracker but a vague sense of rightness in her head.

She had told the team as much when they camped at night, but she was met with blank stares. To non-architects it sounded like madness. She thought the architects on her team would understand at least, but *they* saw the entire path to their trajection before they built it. What Ahilya was doing was strange even by their esoteric standards. She ought to be grateful people were continuing to work with her despite her communion with the cosmic creatures. The non-architects had nowhere else to go, but the architects of Irshar could have easily defected to Iravan's Garden, driven by their abhorrence of the Virohi. Her husband, after all, wanted to claim all architects. It was mere fortune, twisted as it was, that these remaining ones feared Ecstasy more than they feared the Virohi.

She sat down silently on the closest rock, her fingers worrying at the torch. Hushed words came to her as the rest of the team discussed the cosmic creatures among themselves. Sunlight beamed through the trees, and citizens plunged spades into the moist earth, removing weeds and brambles, lighting fires to burn the brush away.

Her mistakes had brought their entire civilization to ruin, survival become forfeit. Thousands of people had died in the crash of the Conclave. She had read the reports of Irshar's council, and she had attended the mass vigil. Like every other citizen, Ahilya had held a burning ember cupped within a clay pot, an ancient tradition common to all the sister ashrams when there was no body to return to the earth. Irshar had blazed like fire that night, each ember signifying a death, yet Ahilya knew the tradition could not encompass humanity's loss. Cities she did not even know the names of had crashed in the skyrage. Men, women, children, families… Mothers and little ones, the disabled and the elderly, innocent lives who had done nothing wrong except exist in the same time as she and her husband. Ahilya shuddered, the weight of this knowledge crushing her.

She had no defense. She did not deserve Eskayra's kindness. She deserved nothing.

Eskayra crouched next to her. "I'm sorry. I shouldn't have questioned you in front of the others. Not about the Virohi."

Still wretched, Ahilya waved away the apology.

"Do you see them now?" Eskayra said.

Ahilya shrugged. She was always aware of them in her mind, though true communication took place in the Etherium—but were the two things really very different? A shift of her vision—that was all it took to see the Virohi in the mirrored chambers.

<Ahilya> they crooned, and she wrenched away. The mirrored chamber was where she attempted to persuade the Virohi to stay bonded to Irshar. Without that persuasion, pathways in Irshar became underwater caverns. Homes split into two, falling into chasms. When once a playground had changed into green rock, Ahilya had wrested control of the architecture back from the Virohi to save several children from being buried alive. It was a close thing—the children had escaped with their lives, though several were severely wounded. Irshar continued to suffer casualties, embedded as it was with the Virohi.

She tapped at her citizen-ring, a crude approximation resembling a rudra bead, a product of the sungineering they still had in the ashram. The bead chimed and Chaiyya's face formed over Ahilya's hand, the hologram flickering in and out. Once the Senior Architect of Nakshar, now one of the many councilors of Irshar, she looked tired as all of them did these days. Her round face was wan, her braid almost entirely gray.

In another time it would have been incongruous to see her dressed not in her regal architect uniform but in expeditionary clothes, a head lamp on her forehead and devices strapped to her wrists. Yet Chaiyya had been waiting ever since Ahilya had left Irshar. Along with Kamala and Meena, members of Ahilya's personal medical team who hovered behind her even now, she was prepared to follow the expedition into the jungle as soon as given the signal.

"Ahilya," Chaiyya said. "Did you find the site?"

"Just now. The builders have begun working."

"Good, that's good. Send us the coordinates immediately, please. We are worried about you."

"Transferring now," Eskayra replied. She tapped at her sungineering beads, and Chaiyya nodded in satisfaction.

It was bizarre that Ahilya needed her own medical team, to watch for her health every single day. When had she deteriorated so much? Or was it that she had always been in this space, but for once was getting the help she needed all her life? A part of her wanted to deny this assistance—she did not deserve such care, not after what she had done—but she could not even summon the will to fight this mandate from the council. Everything had changed. The ground beneath her feet was unsteady even while the world grew still. She could barely believe she was surrounded by so many people out on an expedition, where once she had fought to conduct one alone. Eskayra was sending latitudes and longitudes to Chaiyya—a method so archaic it was only remembered by sungineers. They had all returned to lost ways of living. Ahilya had no way to measure anything anymore, least of all the chaos of her mind.

Over the hologram, Chaiyya frowned. "You are not far at all. We could be there by sunset. Yet it took you three days from Irshar?"

The question was not meant as an accusation, but Ahilya still felt compelled to explain and smooth any impending trouble.

"We did not travel in the most efficient manner," she said softly. She did not give voice to her mistrust of the Virohi—there was already too much suspicion within the group, indeed all of Irshar, regarding her and the cosmic creatures—and what would speaking of that achieve? One way or the other, to trust the Virohi and arrive here had been their only option. Chaiyya knew not to push further. The architect merely *hmm*ed, raising her eyebrows.

"How is the ashram?" Ahilya asked into the silence.

"Undulating all day," Chaiyya answered.

The image over Ahilya's ring wobbled into a map of the city. Several parts of the design glowed crimson, indicating architecture ready to break.

"We're monitoring it," Chaiyya said tiredly. "It looks worse than the last few days, but it ought to keep until you return."

"I can get to it now. I just need a few minutes to rest."

"No," the other woman said at once. "Don't start until I get there, Ahilya. That's the entire point of us coming into the jungle. You're tired already and you can't make mistakes. Let me guide you through it. Just practice the initial exercises until then."

"I don't—"

"Promise me, Ahilya," Chaiyya said, her voice hard. "You won't attempt it until I arrive."

Ahilya looked from the hologram over to Eskayra who watched silently. She sighed. "All right," she said. "I'll wait."

Chaiyya relaxed, her relief palpable. "We'll be there soon." She cut the connection.

For the last three nights, Ahilya had resisted the call of the cosmic creatures, trying not to be pulled into the mirrored chambers, but she did not know how long she could avoid it, how long she *should*. Earthrages were not a threat, but what did it matter if the last survivors of humanity could be buried under their homes at any moment? Ahilya had invited the precursors of earthrages into their homes—a worse thing than being plagued by the rages themselves. Now there was no more time to waste. No more time to rest.

She tried to school her features and contain her shivering, but a shadow fell on her and Ahilya knew any subterfuge was useless.

"Do you need to return to Irshar?" Eskayra asked, touching her hand. "I can send you to Chaiyya instead of her coming here."

Yes, Ahilya thought. *It would be easier.* The persuasion—and any exercise to calm her mind—was easier closer to Irshar's core tree, the vriksh. But she shook her head. "We've only just gotten here. It'll take you days to assess if this site works for a city. I can't ask your architects to waste their energy on me."

"None of us want you burdened anymore than you are. If Chaiyya knew how hard this has been for you, she would suggest one of my architects take you back too. I could have them make you a nest. Return you to Irshar within hours."

Eskayra was being kind. Ahilya took in the locked shoulders of the architects and the stiffness of their jaws. It was not from exhaustion, she knew; it was from the idea of answering to her, of changing their plan for *her*, she who had brought humanity to its knees.

"Can you afford to waste the few seeds we have left to traject me back and forth?" she asked. "Making a new city is our only real hope for any future. This mission is more important than me."

"Is it?" Esk said skeptically. "What will happen if you cannot convince the Virohi, my dear?"

If she lost control of the Virohi, they would try to escape their form within Irshar. People would get hurt, more than they did now, and who knew if Ahilya would ever be able to lock the cosmic creatures back into the architecture. It had taken all of the everdust—an element they no longer had—the first time. If she lost control, then every day could be filled with tragedies.

Worse, the Virohi could affect their world again, both in the jungle and in the skies. If humanity was lucky, it would endure a slow decay filled with failing architecture, but if not, a massive final storm could erase the fragile life the survivors had attempted to build. The last of humanity would become extinct. It was what they'd faced only a few months ago, when Ahilya had made the fateful decision to wrap the Virohi into Irshar.

"It would be awful," she relented. "But the council chose this option for a reason. We all have our duties. These architects are meant to build with you, and Chaiyya is supposed to guide me."

"She should have joined the expeditionary team, then," Eskayra said, frowning.

They'd had this conversation before; Irshar could not afford for two councilors to go on this expedition, and Chaiyya's infant daughters needed her. It was decided that Ahilya *needed* to go, while Chaiyya did not. Did Esk really expect Irshar to bow down further to Ahilya's needs? It was stunning how she refused to see how much Ahilya was disliked. How badly she had made mistakes. *That* was the real reason Ahilya had been asked not to overextend—to not make any more decisions without anyone else at the helm. She should have been tried as a criminal, but here they were, dependent on her, and the council was now doing all it could to control her.

"Why do you insist this?" Ahilya asked softly. "I agreed to listen to the council. To act in a manner they see fit."

"Did you agree because you think they are right? Or because you think you deserve punishment? Chaiyya is supposed to take care of you, but how are you to do your job if she recuses herself whenever it is convenient for her? The council makes its calculation, but being away from Irshar has been hard for you. Every day you suffer more."

"You expect me to fail," she said, uncomfortable. "You're insisting because you don't expect me to be able to convince the Virohi without Chaiyya."

Eskayra drew back at that, hurt on her face. "Never. I am concerned about the toll this is taking on you. That doesn't make me *him*."

Ahilya said nothing. Cataclysms aside there were other costs that only she cared about. If the cosmic creatures escaped, Iravan would unleash war in his attempt to finally destroy the Virohi. It was what he was counting on—the failure of her will. Left to themselves, the councilors of Irshar would have her relinquish the Virohi to him too. The only reason they had not commanded

Ahilya to do so was because removing the cosmic creatures would hurt Irshar.

It was a terrible stalemate. Irshar was as much a hostage to Ahilya's actions with the Virohi as it was to Iravan's desires. Though he had resources in his Garden, Iravan had refused to share them. It was another reason Ahilya was here, looking for city-sites.

Eskayra glanced at her, shaking her head. "He is not a good man."

He is trying to be, Ahilya thought, but she couldn't defend this erosion of trust, and how she and Iravan found themselves over and over again at opposite ends of a fight, counting on and waiting for each other to fail. When had that begun?

She wanted to explain how she saw Iravan to Eskayra. This was the same man who had once wanted to change things within Nakshar. Once, both of them had planned for how to raise non-architects to the council. Though Ahilya had accused him of corruption, she had since understood the difficult task he'd faced.

In his own way, Iravan had challenged sacred laws. In a society that revered the tradition of marriage he had first risen to his status without children, then wished to raise Naila to councilor, a woman who was not even married. He had circumvented laws with the force of his charisma and his position, but despite that he had always been driven by his morals. Now his morals told him to make amends, and he was going to do it. No more politicking, no more asking, simply one foot in tyranny and the other in hatred, whether or not it hurt them all in the process.

Ahilya had decided to be subservient to the council, but Iravan did not have such compunctions. He did not care to be accountable—not in the same way she did—but they were not so different. Ahilya wanted to release her burden, and Iravan did too. She looked to her council to guide her, to tame her, and Iravan looked to his past and his capital desire. In a way, neither of them trusted themselves anymore, relinquishing control to someone else, now when they had destroyed everything so badly. So what if their defeats manifested in different ways?

She understood him, just as she understood his suspicion of the cosmic creatures. Who better than her to see what the creatures were capable of, when it was she alone who could communicate with them? She knew they'd destroyed life, not just on her planet, but on several others. Yet buried within her terror of them lay a sickened intimacy. Despite what she knew, she could not help but see her own desperation to be acknowledged, to be free, within the Virohi. She had fought against erasure, and so had the cosmic creatures, and they had warped her into giving them insidious compassion. In Iravan's eyes it was simply more evidence of her corruption. Perhaps the council of Irshar thought similarly too, though none had said so to Ahilya.

The truth was that while the councilors of Irshar feared him, they were wary of her too, a woman who controlled humanity's survival, who was fast becoming part of the creatures they all wished to destroy. If he was not a good man, could she even think of herself as a good woman? They were both the same. Terrible versions of what they could have been, perverted reflections of each other.

"You can see him, can't you?" Eskayra said. "In your Etherium?"

Eskayra spoke the word with unfamiliarity. Ahilya had explained what she knew of the realm, the third vision of an architect, a vision that non-architects had as well, but Eskayra had never fully understood it.

Truthfully, Ahilya barely did too. The Etherium was where she communicated with the cosmic creatures, and a burst of combined desire had made it possible for her third vision to become intertwined with Iravan's when they'd stopped the earthrage together, so long ago. Yet despite knowing this, the Etherium itself remained a strange place to Ahilya. All she knew was that she could command her third vision—and his—in a way that he could not.

"What do you see when you seek him?" Eskayra asked.

"Must I spy on my husband as a matter of course now?" Ahilya replied quietly.

"Is he your husband, still?"

He was. In name alone, for he kept to no rules of any ashram. Where did her loyalties lie when he had chosen to abdicate his own?

Ahilya opened her connection to Iravan.

He appeared behind her eyes: a tall dark man with thick silver hair, cut in a close-cropped way that suited him, and his face clean-shaven. He sat on a tree trunk, a glistening blade hanging around his neck held by a thin vine. His skin was lit with silvery-white tattoos, eyes glinting with rings around the pupils as he stared ahead in contemplation. Iravan no longer looked like the man she had married. Yet the husband, the lover, the friend, and companion still remained, lurking in the angles of his face, the slight tilt to his mouth, the dark skin she wanted desperately to touch.

"He's building," she said.

"Building what? A weapon?"

"I don't know. I think he is looking for an alternative to Irshar and the Garden too."

Iravan stirred, and then he was looking directly at her. Just for an instant, his silvery eyes hollowed with guilt and regret. Iravan stared at her, and unbidden images flashed in her mind, of when he had kissed her while she held him after Bharavi's Ecstatic attack; when he lay spread-eagled while she took care of him in the habitat; when he shielded her after she lost their child. She saw both of those men together, the Iravan of her past and the one in her present, who could see the very same things she was seeing.

He flinched as her memories and longing washed over him.

His jaw trembled then hardened. He tilted his head as though in acceptance of a punishment, and sudden rage grew in Ahilya at his gesture, at this convoluted path he was taking to make amends. If he wanted, the two of them could atone for all they'd done by working together, find ways for life to flourish, even back away and let someone else take charge for once. They could have a future. They could have peace between themselves. They could have *love.*

Yet he chose this senseless war. He chose to fight her, alienate humanity, and destroy the man he had once been, all because he wished to save them from something they had already accepted. How could he be this blind to his own devolution?

Look at what you have done to us, she thought savagely. *Look at* us, *Iravan. Do you remember what we'd wanted once? Children? A home? What about amends to* me*? How dare you let yourself go down this path? How* dare *you?*

Iravan blinked as though he could hear her.

They stared at each other for a long moment.

Her thoughts skittered around her mind, images of her and Iravan preparing to speak at the Conclave; throwing their wedding garlands around each other, promising to travel the same path or none at all; the both of them believing the best of each other and of humanity, once. She couldn't take it, the loss that engulfed her on beholding him like this.

Ahilya collapsed their connection, her breath catching in a soundless sob.

The sounds of the muttering architects returned to her. Eskayra still watched her, chewing her lip. <*Ahilya*>, the Virohi called. <*Return to us.*>

"Enough," she said, half to herself. "I need to calm my mind before Chaiyya gets here. We all have our duties."

"Remember yourself," Eskayra said, squeezing her hand. "Remember you are not alone. We are here. *I* am here."

Ahilya nodded. Her mind still full of Iravan, she braced to find a version of herself to hold onto.

2

IRAVAN

The shock of the connection with Ahilya rippled through Iravan. Bharavi, Nakshar, the children he would never have, flickered in his mind. He shivered, trying to stabilize.

These encounters with his wife were always sudden and out of his control. He had become better at concealing his reactions, but the pain Ahilya had shown him today, the rage, pulsed under his skin, flooding his veins, itching. He willed himself to silence, letting the stillness of the jungle seep into him.

Under a large banyan tree, darkness ate away at his silvery light. Trees stood like sentinels in the shadows, vines hanging off them, motionless. Shafts of dying sunlight illuminated a trunk with gray moss, and a heavy carpet of undergrowth. Iravan had cleared a very precise quadrangle in front of his rock where lush grass grew. Slowly, still reeling from Ahilya, he began trajecting again.

Soft earth flew upward in a gushing waterfall that solidified into the likeness of a carved door. Wood shards scraped into the shape of a thousand jasmines. Iravan flexed his fingers, and the carvings on the door bloomed into true flowers that released an intoxicating scent.

The everpower flooded him. He called the use of it trajection, but it was not that, not truly. He had no language for it yet. When he alone wielded it, what did it matter what it was called? He understood this power beyond articulation. He wielded it as naturally as breathing. In the act of subsuming the falcon-yaksha, in *becoming* the yaksha, Iravan had forsaken trajection and embraced this new everpower, one so intimate that it *was* him. He did not intend for anyone else to ever get such dangerous, intoxicating control that could shift the planet should he desire it.

He did not desire it. Not now. Not yet.

Iravan desired to build. So he cosseted the remains of the architect he had once been—and more dust flew in a small contained tornado, leaves and earth gently swirling and combining with substances sucked from deep within the planet. The structure in front of him took shape, a shrine, a temple, a grave for what he had lost.

Had Ahilya seen this? The thought shamed him, as though he had shown her a weakness. In that itself was a quiet grief. Since when had being weak in front of Ahilya become a bad thing?

Grief was too painful.

He clung to the other emotion, for shame, at least, was familiar.

It had been three months since he had last seen his wife outside the Etherium. He had gathered—*stolen*—hundreds of architects and nearly all the sungineers from the landed ashram of humanity. Neither he nor Ahilya had said a word to each other as the exodus occurred. Instead, he had bowed to her in solemn gratitude for allowing her citizens to leave. Even if he had given her little choice, he owed her that much respect as he contradicted her wish.

She was no longer just a councilor. She was *the* councilor, the only one who could control the architecture of Irshar. The only one who stood in his way.

Tiredness overwhelmed him. He missed her so much that it

ached. *I am getting old,* he thought, rubbing his eyes. *I need it to end.*

The structure in front of him continued to form. Wood chips stacked atop each other, the walls deckled. Water turned into glinting icicles to hang like crystalline lamps along the door. Phosphorescence shone everywhere, and furniture formed within the home, a desk, a closet, a bed, visible through the shimmering ice-windows. Chairs grew out of the soil, not high-backed and carved like his seat in the Garden, but comfortable, low, meant for household tasks and ease.

A bitter smile formed on Iravan's face at the suggestion of this domesticity. If survival had not been the cost, Iravan would have found his battle of wills with Ahilya a diverting challenge. Instead, fury rose in him. They had come so close to reconciliation and understanding. They had come so close to finally ending the Virohi together.

And she had chosen them.

She alone knew the pain of separation. She had seen his fight with the falcon-yaksha, and experienced the way complete beings had been treated. She had campaigned for change once. If she wanted to, she could simply will the Virohi out of the architecture—give them to him so he could destroy them once and for all. How could she put him in a position where he had no choice but to alienate Irshar, despite his desire to make amends? They could have given the survivors new life if not for her stubbornness. But she had left him alone… with himself.

His resentment found expression in the construction. The chairs began to decay. The carved wooden door began to warp, and the jasmines on it grew dark, withered, fell away. The tiny icicle lamps and delicate ice windows burst into silent shards, whipping toward Iravan's cheeks like sharp tears. The home he was building shook as though an earthrage was imminent. Iravan took a deep breath, and mastered himself with an effort. The decay paused, then shook once, before the construction bloomed anew.

He could not afford to rage, not with the everpower.

This ability, that was neither Ecstasy nor trajection but superior to both, was connected deeply to his emotion and his capital desire. The Moment, the Deepness, the Etherium, even the silence where the falcon-yaksha once lived, had all combined into a singular evervision. It had been this way ever since he fully embraced his Ecstasy to build the original Irshar in the skies. Then, he did not understand it. He stumbled through it blindly, merging all the ashrams together.

Since he subsumed the falcon though, he'd realized that in reality there were never three separate visions. He could manipulate them all at once, like he could move his hands and feet though they were separate parts of his body. Now he understood: there was very little that lay between himself and sheer possibility.

The only mystery that remained was his lack of control in the Etherium he shared with Ahilya.

In a futile test Iravan called for the connection to her, but nothing happened.

It irked him to distraction that she alone had that control. Was this some sort of balance? Everpower for him and the Etherium for her? He thought the Etherium a place of guidance, a place that could not be controlled, and there had been a deep relief in that, even joy. But if she could do it, could he? Was this only available to complete beings like her, or perhaps only to her?

She was so much more than just a complete being. She was… she was *Ahilya*. She had let him into her mind many times during the last three months, sometimes when surrounded by others in Irshar, other times to see what he was doing, at all times aloof and cool.

Her aloofness terrified him. He was so scared that the cosmic creatures were corrupting her beyond hope that the glint of her rage today was a relief, a gift. *Oh my love,* he thought in sudden despair. *We have come to an ending we were headed for all along.*

The house had become a multi-storied thing of beauty, its roof slated to allow rainwater to slough off, its ice windows glazed and glittering. Jasmine bloomed on all the walls, a rich tapestry of tiny white flowers. Stone statues of falcons in mid-flight ornamented the front door. Iravan hadn't consciously built any of this, yet the house formed due to a buried intention, a stream trickling in the front, a verandah, trees that grew in the shape of a playhouse, a yard and swings and a slide. His hand drifted to the blade of pure possibility he wore, and just for an instant he thought of whether he could do with it what he intended. Whether he could… *return.*

"Iravan-ve," a voice said.

He turned to see a young boy stand by the trees, staring in wonder at the construction.

With his tousled hair and wide eyes, Darsh looked younger than fifteen, but that impression swiftly left Iravan as the boy neared him. An air of seriousness hung around the child, one Iravan had noticed that first time he had met him back in Nakshar's deathcage. In the past few months, Darsh had grown taller by several inches and now reached nearly to Iravan's shoulder. A rush of pride and affection filled Iravan on seeing him. This young man was one of the best, most skilled Ecstatics of the Garden. Iravan's lieutenant.

"What are you building?" Darsh asked, coming to join Iravan on the rock. "Is this for the Ecstatics? For after we've united with our yakshas?"

What *was* he doing? Building a home for Ahilya—for his children—despite knowing everything he did? It was pathetic. He had returned to this project often, no matter where he and Darsh stopped in the jungle, building and rebuilding idly, almost as a form of meditation. But for the first time, the pointlessness of it hit him. He had seen Ahilya's anger. In destroying the Virohi, he would destroy any future with her.

His hand dropped from the blade around his neck.

Enough, he thought.

The house exploded into tiny shards.

Mulch, wood, bark and leaves spun silently around them in a gust of wind. The falcon statues splintered then dissolved into gray dust. Jasmine putrefied, its rotting stench smothering the air as the flowers disappeared.

The clearing lay bare as though there was never a home, never this indulgence, and Iravan thought in grim acceptance, *What purpose this building? What need for such a construction?* His marriage to Ahilya was meaningless now. This house was a dream, a foolishness. It was truly over between them.

He answered Darsh's question with his own. "What did you find?"

"Nothing," the boy said, a sullen twist to his mouth. "The presence in the Deepness has not returned. Maybe I am not releasing Nakshar's Constant when I traject."

"That's not possible. All trajection, Ecstatic or otherwise, releases the raga. Each time you traject you call out to your yaksha."

It was one of the earliest things he and Ahilya had discovered together, all those months ago in Nakshar, when they could never have contemplated where life would bring them. They'd hypothesized, along with Dhruv and Naila, that within trajection lay the seed of its demise, but none of them could have known how true that statement would be. Ahilya had ended the earthrages and tied all the cosmic creatures to this dimension, effectively ending any split of a Virohi. She had ended the rise of new architects in the future, and because of her in time trajection would die—something Iravan ought to thank her for.

But that would only occur if Iravan completed his part of the task.

Unless all architects alive united with their yakshas, they would be reborn with the power to traject, Virohi or no Virohi.

What would occur to civilization then? Everything Iravan had achieved could be erased away. Ecstasy could be outlawed once more, years from now. Or perhaps architects would rise again, returning to what they once had been. Perhaps they would be imprisoned, the very power of trajection disdained, and all architects become slaves.

It did not take too much imagination to consider the many paths civilization could take if a few people continued to have incredible power. Whether oppressors or the oppressed, nothing would really change for the architects, their destinies controlled by the power they were born with.

Iravan could not allow that. The only way to ensure equity was to take the power away once and for all, and give architects the hope of one day becoming complete beings.

The architects of the Garden were counting on this. They had joined him to learn to unite with their yakshas. The fact that the Garden was the only place they could traject anymore was important not because of trajection, but because without the power they could not release the raga that would signal their presence to their yakshas.

But the yakshas were missing. Iravan had not seen any for months. The last time he had seen any was when several aerial yakshas joined the falcon—the falcon that he had subsumed. Is that why the other yakshas eluded him? Because he had absorbed their leader? He needed to find them, and he had been lucky that Darsh of all people felt an inkling of a presence in the Deepness. Since the boy had told him of it, Iravan had visited the jungle with him as often as he could to track the creatures down, hoping to be led by the boy's signal.

"Tell me again what you experienced in the Deepness," he said.

Darsh made a face. Iravan had asked him this already several times, and the boy's tone grew annoyed, though he did not refuse to answer.

"When Reyla and I were trajecting, I sensed a presence in the Deepness. A fluid one, and only briefly, and the both of us saw it. It was unfamiliar to her, but I felt like I'd seen it before. We followed it to the Moment and I could see it there too, though Reyla couldn't. That's when we told you about it."

It was very similar to Iravan's experience. Only he had been able to see the falcon in the Moment; that was how he knew Darsh was witnessing his own yaksha. Since then, Darsh had received impressions of different parts of the jungle in his Etherium, in the same way that Iravan had once because of the falcon. Of course, *he* hadn't known back then what was happening, but these Ecstatics would receive the benefit of his experience. Iravan understood the boy's yaksha was likely leading him into the jungle to unite.

In reality, his problems were not finding the yakshas or assisting other architects in completing themselves. Those were minor aspects of his capital desire. His task was to end the Virohi—the source of all ill. Ahilya had embraced the cosmic creatures, and it was already affecting her. In time, they would affect all the other citizens of Irshar, in ways none of them could comprehend. He needed to axe the root of the tree, wrench it from its depths and remove all presence of it. Only Ahilya stood in his way.

In desperation, he sought the Etherium within his eversion for a clue again. The darkness between his brows flared. His many forms cycled in front of him, weaving in and out of his vision. Iravan flitted between them: he swept his spouse, Mara, into a dance; he became Agni who beat the drums in their ashram in celebration; he was Mohini, and he—she—was asleep between her spouses, Taruin and Radha; he kissed Vishwam, tasting his husband, the slight dryness of his lips, no, not his husband, *Nidhirv's*, the man who he had once been in another lifetime. And even as that thought occurred, Iravan became aware that he was sitting differently, his shoulder sunken like Nidhirv's, the muscles moving in unfamiliar memorable ways.

Iravan held this awareness, as if to fix the image of Nidhirv even though he knew he had no control in the Etherium. Ever since he'd subsumed the falcon-yaksha, the memories of his past lives had become more easily accessible to him, to a point where he could reach out and submerge in one of their lives for long hours, understanding who they were. It was a dangerous balance—to not lose himself within them. Iravan had finally found a method to separate his past lives enough to study them. Everpower swirled within him and dust rose, leaves churning in the shape of a man, a memory.

The shape coalesced on the forest floor like a ghost. Nidhirv appeared made of wind and tree bark and dust. Unlike in the Etherium, the projection's eyes glowed silver. He looked more real than the wisp in Iravan's mind, but more feral too.

Nidhirv stalked forward, a strange smile on his face, his silvery eyes flashing, and Iravan thought, *What are you trying to tell me?*

Had he been alone, Iravan would have strengthened the projection, trying to understand the edges of his capital desire. But Darsh's mouth fell open. The boy staggered back from Nidhirv, tripping over himself. Iravan knew he was scaring the child. He dropped his sight in the third vision, and Nidhirv disappeared in a huff of leaves, inches from Darsh.

The shape drifted away, carried by the breeze. Iravan clenched his fist then released it. Frustration was futile. He would not learn secrets from them today, and did it matter at all? He had learned to work with what he had.

Iravan turned to Darsh. "When you call your yaksha now, are you trajecting the same pattern as when you saw it before?"

Darsh shook his head, confused. "No. You said all trajection releases Nakshar's Constant, so I didn't think it mattered what or how I trajected."

"It shouldn't," Iravan confirmed. "But if the yaksha is being so elusive, then it won't hurt to try what you did before again." He gestured to Darsh to enter the Deepness. "Traject that pattern," he said. "Let's see if we can lure your yaksha out."

3

AHILYA

The sun had set by the time Chaiyya arrived.

The Senior Architect appeared in a rustle of leaves, brushing twigs off her hair and clothes as she entered the clearing the builders had made. Her dark skin shone with the light of trajection, but though Chaiyya was now an Ecstatic, she still worked only in the Moment. Ahilya knew Chaiyya had never been curious about Ecstasy, and her encounter with Deepness had been unnatural.

Chaiyya smiled tightly at Ahilya as she picked her way through Eskayra's team toward her. Two other healers accompanied her, Kamala and Meena, both of them non-architect nurses. They had both been studying the mind, a nascent field in the airborne ashrams, at least with non-architects as the mind had always been the purview of consciousness-experts like Iravan.

Now, when people couldn't trust architects, when Irshar barely had any left, these nurses had become more important than ever, helping people with their grief and loss. Kamala and Meena were specifically assigned to Ahilya, assisting Chaiyya in guiding her through the interaction with the Virohi.

While Meena went to work on arranging a delicate medical instrument, Kamala greeted Ahilya with a nod. A young woman, perhaps Naila's age, her long angular face cut by apple-cheeks, and a certain cold wariness in her eyes, Kamala had once belonged to Nakshar. She had perhaps known Oam who had been a nurse studying the mind. If he were alive, Ahilya's case would have been handled by him, but perhaps if he was here, Ahilya wouldn't have found herself in this situation. It was such a circular thought that Ahilya choked, unable to follow it.

Under Chaiyya's supervision, the two nurses began to sort the medical instruments, uncoiling thin glass tubes, and tinkling sungineering equipment. Chaiyya trajected the seeds around her wrists and neck to power the equipment but, if the slow blinks on the devices were any indication, she was having trouble in the jungle, just like the team of Eskayra's architects.

Perhaps it would have been wiser to return to Irshar, but all they had were bad choices. Ahilya suppressed a wince as Kamala inserted an intravenous line, strapping a few bands around Ahilya's wrists and chest to read her vitals. Another line infused saline and herbal medicine directly into Ahilya's bloodstream. A surge of clarity rushed through her, and the jungle became brighter, more present. Chaiyya and the others sharpened, as her own Etherium receded. Ahilya breathed a sigh of relief.

Encounters with the Virohi always fatigued her. This was why for the past three days, she had been instructed by Irshar's council not to attempt the persuasion, no matter the call from the Virohi. To do so without her team of healers was practically suicidal—not just for her but for all of Irshar.

It had not always been this way, of course. In the early days after the Conclave had crashed, Ahilya had entered the Etherium to conduct the persuasion easily, following her instincts. The Virohi had appeared as smoky forms then. Ahilya spent hours in the mirrored chambers, showing them a life in the ashram, conjuring images of her sister Tariya and her nephews, Arth and Kush, feeding Virohi parts of her memory. Laughter and love, pain and joy, grief and regret—she gave the Virohi everything. They listened at first. She thought that would be the extent of her interaction with them.

But then the shivering had started, followed by incessant vomiting. Once Ahilya had fainted in the middle of the persuasion, and Irshar had wobbled, buildings crashing, people trapped and injured and dead, all while she lay unconscious. It was sheer luck that the Virohi did not escape then. Nearly twenty people had been buried in the wreckage.

The council agreed Ahilya's loss of control was unacceptable, and all of them imagined it was the stress finally manifesting in her. But the diagnoses didn't indicate anything out of the ordinary—nothing that other non-architects were not experiencing. Then Chaiyya began using methods usually reserved for architects. They'd realized then how Ahilya had become more like an architect with her awareness of her Etherium. In treating with the cosmic creatures so intimately, in offering them her consciousness as meat and fodder, Ahilya had gone too deep. She had given unknowingly, and they had taken, and taken, and taken.

The medical devices began to whirr and beep. The two nurses moved away, monitoring Ahilya's progress on their beads. Chaiyya stepped in their place, kneeling in front of Ahilya. She withdrew a slim retinoscope and shone it into Ahilya's right eye. Ahilya remembered how she herself had used such an implement on the elephant-yaksha on another expedition.

"Did you practice?" the Senior Architect asked, peering into the lens then switching it to the other eye.

"Unsuccessfully," Ahilya muttered.

Chaiyya drew back, returning the lens back into her pouch. "These practices have worked on the most recalcitrant of architects, but you have to believe in them working. *That* is key."

"I don't doubt them."

"Then what? You doubt yourself? Us?" Ahilya stilled at that and Chaiyya's face drew into a frown, and the woman sighed. "You don't believe that you can count on us," she said flatly.

"I do," Ahilya replied automatically, but she could hear the lie in her voice.

Once, Chaiyya had thanked her, said that she'd saved everyone's lives—but that was before they'd understood the full extent of what Ahilya had done. When the architecture started shifting again, becoming more and more unstable, Chaiyya and the rest of Irshar's council had begun to fear Ahilya.

They began to treat her differently after that. Part hate, part fear, part abject pity—the people who were her friends became her hostages and her tormentors. They were walking a tightrope—keeping her sane enough to commune with the Virohi, yet knowing that each communication only corrupted her further. Even their speech to her was more careful than ever, as though anything they said would push her over the edge. How could one count on people like that?

"Have you considered that this was never meant for me?" Ahilya mumbled. "These powers, these experiences, they were always the province of the architects."

"It doesn't matter if you are a non-architect," Chaiyya said, but a tone of distress entered her voice. "These practices are foolproof. They are meant to anchor you into yourself. The architects would once use them in order to enter the Moment, but my adaptations consider that you are a complete being. You have to trust that."

Ahilya's mouth twisted. Surely Chaiyya did not really believe her own words? How could one be a complete being, and split at the same time? Either Ahilya was becoming like the architects—lost to herself beyond her imagining—or she was a complete being, her consciousness unmolested. She could not be both at the same time, and after her encounters with the Virohi, she knew which one she veered toward. *I have become what I've always hated and desired,* she thought. *An architect, a tyrant, a monster.* In her mind, the Virohi whispered for her to join them again.

"I trust that you're trying to help me," she said, but she left her true feelings unsaid—that none of this would make a difference, not in the way Chaiyya expected.

Intentions aside, the architect's knowledge was theoretical. Chaiyya had never entered the Etherium. She had not spoken with the Virohi. She did not know the danger, the lure, the sheer *power* of the cosmic creatures to obliterate any defense Ahilya built against them. Chaiyya could not comprehend what Ahilya contested with each time she went to persuade the Virohi. These exercises would never work for her. What architect had seen the mind of the Virohi? Even Iravan had not; he had only jumped to conclusions about the creatures, driven by his hate for them. Ahilya couldn't help her streak of resentment—for Chaiyya, Iravan, for the rest of Irshar, and mostly for herself, knowing she had no right to feel this way, not when she received a perverse delight in speaking to the Virohi, not when she had brought them all to this destiny.

She gestured at the builders and the other members of the expedition. "Do you think this place will work?" she asked, changing the subject.

From her expression, Ahilya knew Chaiyya was not about to let her deflect that easily, but before she could say anything, Eskayra spoke.

"It is holding for now," Eskayra said.

She marched over from where she was standing and pointed at the image on her solarnote. Diagrams glittered there, of low-lying buildings shaped like nests, and shelters imitating rocks. Roofs used the existing canopy of the jungle, and vines were tied to weight-supporting pillars. There was something almost architect-like about it, and indeed the architects on Eskayra's team had their heads bent together as they trajected precious seeds to form the foundations of the structures on the solarnote tablet.

Yet this construction was different too. Grubby hands, mud beneath nails, faces streaked with dirt… Architects once used sophisticated methods, but this was earthier, laborious, more *alive*. Eskayra was using her own style here, one that equated non-architect methods with trajection. Already the beginnings of an outpost were visible in the construction.

Chaiyya made an approving sound, but Ahilya watched Eskayra silently. Long ago when they had courted in Nakshar, Eskayra had been resentful of the architects because her talent in building had been considered useless. It was why she had left for another ashram on the same travel route which had brought Iravan to Nakshar.

Their faces wove in and out of Ahilya's head, Iravan and Eskayra shifting one into another. Eskayra was streaked with mud, brushing her hair back with an impatient gesture and smearing her cheek with more dirt. Iravan's tattoos glittered in Ahilya's mind, his pristine architect uniform from the past, and his suave, careless handsomeness. Ahilya nearly opened her Etherium again to watch him, needing him to reassure her that she'd made the best choice in marrying him. She forced herself to notice the details of what Eskayra had done instead, the way she used fire to melt glass and supplement the construction, the way non-architects carried axes and machetes, tools that architects had never used. Sweat dripped down the builders' skin—so different to a time when architects had trajected whole ashrams from the cool comfort of an Architects' Disc. She had to take comfort from this change. Believe that humanity was building something better.

"Maybe the Virohi led us right, after all," Ahilya said softly.

"Maybe," Esk said, though she sounded skeptical. "All this could still break apart, though. Last time, the second we started building the constructions began to misbehave, and the jungle started to attack us. If Airav is right, and the jungle has retained a memory of destruction, then all our attempts here are doomed, and—No," Eskayra called out to a builder. "Not like that!"

She marched over to correct them, leaving Ahilya. Eskayra had disdained a councilor's position in Irshar—and never fought for one in her airborne ashram—but she was a natural leader. How would Ahilya's life have been different if Eskayra had never left? Ahilya had never harbored the same strength of passion for Eskayra as she had for Iravan. For better or worse, she had found her reflection in him, but would time and proximity with Eskayra have changed a lukewarm feeling of fondness into deep love? <*Ahilya*>, the Virohi sang, and Iravan shone in her mind, callously brilliant. A stab of pain went through her, at the unknown possibilities of lost chances.

"Your blood pressure is rising very quickly," Meena said from her devices.

Chaiyya frowned. "What is it? What are you thinking of?"

"The Virohi," she said. "They called again. I need to confront them now. There is no more waiting."

"Then let's practice," Chaiyya said.

Ahilya tried to clear her mind as she had been taught. The mirrored chambers beckoned to her, and she conjured the strongest picture of herself—a necessary exercise before talking to the Virohi. She saw an archeologist laughing with Dhruv as they planned to become councilors. But the image darkened, and Dhruv said to her, *You two deserve each other.* She saw a wife, throwing the wedding garland over her husband's neck. But Iravan smiled at her, a dark cutting smile. *You will find me a difficult enemy.* Tariya flashed in her mind, memories of growing up together—but they had not spoken in months, and the very thought of her sister was a knife to the heart. Ahilya gasped, wrapping her arms around her, staring at the jungle floor, breathing hard.

Chaiyya dropped to her knees. Her concerned face swam in Ahilya's vision. "What happened?"

"T-too much," Ahilya stuttered. Her entire body was cold. She couldn't stop shivering. Where was her cloak? Chaiyya was still looking at her, waiting for an explanation and Ahilya tried to contain the stutter in her voice. "Everything we've lost," she said. "Everything—all the people—*I* have lost..."

"But those you've gained too," the architect said softly. "Focus on *us,* Ahilya. On me and Airav and Eskayra and Naila and all those who stand behind you."

"Because you have no choice," Ahilya said. "Because I have forced you to."

A range of emotions passed over Chaiyya's face, from resentment to anger to sadness, but she did not deny it. Ahilya waited for Chaiyya's censure, almost wished for it—would it not be better to confront her failure, rather than tiptoe around it simply because she was unwell? Simply because she held their survival in her hands? But all she had were these vague hints of her friends' true feelings, these imagined vapors of hate and terror. At least Iravan's anger was honest. The others thought so little of her, expecting her to be fragile, her mind ready to break at the slightest instance. They had stripped her of her dignity with this treatment, and in the end she was alone.

"Your blood pressure," Meena squeaked. "Ahilya-ve, it is out of control."

Chaiyya's eyes grew wide in alarm. "Stop," she said. "Stop, Ahilya, whatever you're thinking, stop."

In her mind, the Virohi laughed, and she heard Iravan say, *They will corrupt you.*

"Say the words," Chaiyya commanded. "Ahilya, say the words out loud."

"I feel foolish."

"Do it anyway."

Ahilya raised her eyes to Chaiyya. "Architects really did this in their training?"

"Young ones and even Maze Architects." Chaiyya's face grew earnest. "I myself have done this when my Two Visions have merged accidentally. Ahilya, I do this everyday since Iravan jerked me into the Deepness against my will."

The words should have been comforting, but implicit in them was an undercurrent that Ahilya still cared to compare herself to the architects. She had been envious of them once, and now that she was like one, her body was weakening and her mind shattering. They had always been the source of her inferiority, but worse, she finally understood them—and by extension, everything Iravan had endured—now when she was so removed from him. She was trying to hold onto *any* familiarity in this alien terrain, and architects and trajection and their history were her history too, no matter how much she'd fought it. For so long those things had given her identity as they had Iravan, and it was such a twisted realization, so full of contradiction—

"Ahilya?" Chaiyya asked, her voice heavy with worry.

Ahilya watched the rising terror and alarm on Chaiyya's face. "I am an archeologist of Irshar," she said mechanically. "I am a non-architect, a complete being. I am a councilor. There are other councilors too. We work together to ensure survival. I am not alone." She breathed deeply. "My name is Ahilya, and I am not alone."

Chaiyya nodded in approval, and opened her mouth to speak, but a series of soft sounds emerged from her beads—a signal from other councilors in Irshar that the deterioration of the ashram was beginning. Ahilya saw her own anxiety in Chaiyya.

"We can wait a few more minutes, if you need time," Chaiyya offered.

"I'm as ready as I'll ever be," Ahilya said. Besides, she could sense the agitation of the Virohi.

Chaiyya did not protest. She simply stepped back, joining the nurses in order to monitor Ahilya's vitals.

The Etherium beckoned. A great sense of inevitability filled Ahilya. She closed her eyes and entered the mirrored chambers.

4

IRAVAN

Within the Deepness, Iravan and Darsh floated next to each other.

Embedded though he was in the velvety blackness, Iravan could still sense the other realms. The jungle was visible to him in his first vision, the reality of his physical surroundings clear as it always was while trajecting. He saw Darsh too, standing next to him, his hands clenched into fists. But though Iravan was not in the Moment, he could sense it as well. It hovered in his mind, a part of the evervision and its unchanged reality. The Moment, the Deepness, his first vision—these were not separate realms, but he could focus on any one of them at a time, like experiencing sensation in one part of his body while still inhabiting the rest. For now, he let the other realms subside from his attention, and nodded to Darsh. The boy's dust mote flickered in the Deepness, more jagged than before.

Vaguely, Iravan wondered if Darsh's form was an evolution of his growing familiarity in the Ecstatic realm. Iravan's own manifestation had developed since his very first time. Where once he had been little more than a speck, now he took the shape of an enormous silver-winged falcon, in a crisscrossing of glittering light. He flapped his wings and felt the rush of wind on his face within the jungle.

"Begin," he said quietly.

In the Deepness, Darsh summoned the Moment. Iravan felt sucked in by Darsh's intention as the boy began to traject a thin filament of light into the quivering, fragile-looking Moment. Once where it had appeared as a shining globule of stars, the Moment was now shrunken. No matter whether Iravan saw it from the evervision or from the Deepness, or inhabited the Moment proper, the universe remained distorted, like a withered grape that had lost its juice. Lights still glowed within it, but hesitantly. This was another infection of the Virohi—the Moment was not the same since those creatures had infiltrated it to mutilate the architects. This realm had been his home once, his peace. The cosmic creatures had taken that away from him.

Iravan buried his hatred of the Virohi, and watched as Darsh's filament of light split in the Deepness, then became four, eight, and then too many to count. It was a form of supertrajection the boy had come up with—what he had been doing when his yaksha had first appeared. This particular one created tiny thorny plants in the Garden. They used it to make blades that were near indestructible.

But as Iravan watched, the Ecstatic trajection changed. It started to shake, the way it had for the past fifteen minutes while Darsh had undertaken this exercise. Lines disconnected from the trajection, whipping into darkness, disappearing. One ricochetted into the Moment, aimed at a stray star. Another struck close to Iravan's wing, and he felt the wind of its passage. Iravan thought, *This is why they outlawed Ecstasy. Architects always did lose themselves in this realm.*

He slashed at Darsh's power and instantly the beams of light dissipated. His movement was harsh, akin to pushing the boy down to stop him from hurtling into danger, but Ecstasy was not a subtle power. There was no other way to stop Darsh while he held so much trajection energy. It was clear Darsh could not summon his yaksha right now, and there was no point in the boy remaining in the Deepness unnecessarily. Iravan had to get to the root of the problem, instead of making Darsh repeat the same exercise fruitlessly.

He raised his hands in a gesture of pacification, but Darsh stared at him, breathing hard. Anger gleamed in the boy's eyes. For a second, Iravan thought Darsh was going to attack him; light seemed to glow in his dust mote, and he knew that if the boy struck at him in the Moment, it would hurt.

But Darsh took a step back and suddenly Iravan was alone in the Deepness.

They stared at each other in their first visions.

"If you ever want to find your yaksha, you need to control yourself," Iravan said, dropping his hands.

"I know."

"If you keep losing focus, you will never be able to unite with it."

"I know."

"It all begins there, Darsh—"

"For fuck's sake," the boy said, throwing up his hands. "I said I know!"

Iravan paused. Darsh continued to breathe heavily for a moment, then finally met Iravan's deadpan gaze.

"I apologize, sir," the boy said at last, his voice tight and formal.

Iravan waited until Darsh had mastered his breathing again. "You are driven by anger when you traject, or seek your yaksha," he said at last. "But you cannot find your counterpart in such a state."

"Can't I?" Darsh challenged. "*You* did. How is my anger different from yours when you seek to destroy the cosmic creatures?"

This time Iravan raised an eyebrow. He did not allow anyone else to speak to him this way, and Darsh was pushing the line, but he had already given the boy too many liberties. He reminded him too much of himself. In a way they only had each other, the last true relationship Iravan maintained with anyone. How ironic that this material bond had arisen without his control when he had been ending all others. Darsh had carved a place in his heart, a place he'd saved once for his children. Perhaps for that alone he owed the boy an explanation.

"I am not led by anger," Iravan said. "Not *only* by anger," he amended at Darsh's skeptical look. "There is reason here too. Tell me, what do you think will happen to the Garden—to all the architects within it—once they unite with their yakshas?"

Darsh blinked, confused. "We will gain powers. Like you."

"Yes," Iravan said gently. "You will know yourselves. But you will have no more lives or reincarnations, not in the sense that you have been taught. When architects die after unity, it is a final death—yet our entire culture is built on rebirth. I don't think it is even *possible* to have a final death; one presupposes the other. Then what will occur to us?"

Darsh frowned. Iravan had taught the boy to think of these events in the last few months of patronage, but this question had haunted Iravan for so long that it was hardly fair to expect Darsh to answer it.

"We'd return to becoming the Virohi in some capacity," Iravan said, answering himself. "*That* is what the final death would achieve. Can you imagine that, Darsh? Everything we have done, all that we hope to achieve in the Garden, all of it for nothing? Can you imagine us condemned to ultimately return to becoming the worst of us over and over again in a cycle of imprisonment? Would you want that? Would any of the others?"

Horror grew on Darsh's face. Iravan suppressed a sigh, half-satisfied half-regretful, to make Darsh feel this way.

In truth, he did not know if this was the path his consciousness would take. All his searching within his past lives was to learn for certain whether he would die and turn into a Virohi, or if another kind of rebirth would present itself. There had, after all, been a time when Ecstatics had fulfilled their capital desires and disappeared, during Nidhirv's life. What had happened to them? Surely they did not return to a Virohi-like state? And what of those who never completed their capital desire? That question was even more important.

But it was not something Iravan needed Darsh to know. He needed Darsh's compliance, and he had made the right calculation.

Anyone else would have preferred life—even life as a Virohi—over complete death. Ahilya certainly had argued for it. Yet Darsh and all the others in the Garden were *architects*. They were trained from infancy in the culture of the ashrams, in believing themselves superior, in serving their community with their power. The reason so many had come to join Iravan was because they abhorred the Virohi, and Iravan was offering retribution and redemption. They came to him because the cosmic creatures had mutilated their powers during the Conclave's crash. They saw their own helplessness.

The architects hated the Virohi. As far as Iravan knew, the citizens of Irshar did too.

Only Ahilya was attempting to find common cause with the cosmic creatures, trying to forgive the Virohi, turning *him* into the enemy. That alone showed how corrupted she had become. His heart tore at the thought of how much he had failed her in allowing this.

"Why do you think you're unable to make this pattern of trajection now?" he asked quietly.

"I don't know," Darsh said moodily. "I can try again."

"No. I want to figure this out first. You've made this pattern a dozen times before in the Garden, but for some reason you can't do it now. Why?"

Darsh merely shook his head.

"It is because of Irshar, isn't it?"

Darsh frowned, but did not reply. He hardly needed to. Iravan knew he'd guessed right.

When they'd left the Garden to come to the jungle today, they'd passed Irshar. Ordinarily, Iravan would not have picked that way, but it was the fastest path to get to this part of the jungle. He'd noticed Darsh's lingering gaze on the ashram, noticed the tightening of the boy's mouth. It was hard for Darsh, this alienation of the Garden from Irshar, this renunciation of material bonds. Irshar was meant to have been a sanctuary for Ecstatics, but ever since the Conclave Darsh's world had turned upside down. Iravan had caught him looking wistfully toward Irshar more than once, as though hoping to return there. After all, *Irshar* was where Iravan had promised Darsh a new life, safe within an ashram-like society, the only society the boy had ever known.

In the ever-cycling vision of the Etherium, Iravan saw Mohini pick up her child, and nuzzle the baby to her.

"Everything we're doing," Iravan said softly. "From finding our yakshas, to training in the Deepness, to the war with the Virohi... it is all for those we love. For those whom we disagree with, and those who are left behind while we forge a new world in the Garden. Because even if they don't see, *we* do. *We* know what is right. I know it is not easy."

Darsh's mouth trembled, and his gaze fell. "My parents," he said haltingly. "They will never be convinced."

Iravan wanted to pull the boy into a hug. Darsh's parents were architects of Nakshar. They'd written him off when he was found an Ecstatic. They'd supported the council's imprisonment of him in a deathcage with the intention of excising him. Even the events since the Conclave's crash hadn't changed their minds. They had refused Iravan's personal invitation to join him in the Garden, and though they had been civil enough their politeness had been forced, intimidated by his power. Even if they hated the Virohi, they likely blamed Iravan and his Ecstatics for it all. They weren't the only people.

"I'm sorry," Iravan said. "Is that why you cannot retain control? I can speak to them again, convince them to come—"

"Don't," Darsh snapped. "They're as good as dead to me."

That kind of thing was so much easier to say than to live. If they *had* died, Darsh would have blamed himself, and Iravan too—though there was no telling the boy's reaction. He changed from grief to anger to moodiness like quicksilver, emotions hurtling through him in the throes of adolescence. Iravan had been around too many angsty teenagers in Nakshar's Academy, teaching them about their role in survival, to expect any different. Combined with everything Darsh had endured, it was no surprise the boy retained fleeting control.

Or perhaps it was the boy's yaksha. Darsh was more unpredictable since feeling his counterpart. The falcon had made *Iravan* more prone to emotional outbursts, a full-grown adult and a Senior Architect. It had slipped past his self-awareness to embed him with its emotion. He didn't understand it fully on his first unity with the falcon, but through the subsequent months it became more and more apparent that the lines separating him from the creature were blurred. He was always an angry man, but the falcon had ripped apart any veneer of calm, infecting him with its thousand-year-old simmering rage.

Even now, he could feel its form in the Deepness replacing his. Here, Iravan *was* the falcon, his wings glittering in magnificent fury. Here, he acquiesced to the yaksha's superiority, for this realm had always belonged to the creature. Here, the falcon's rage was indistinguishable from his own, for the falcon showed him just how much there was to rage about. In a way, it was like Ahilya. They both awoke something in him he had been unaware of. In his head, he could hear the falcon's laughter. He had subsumed the creature, but Ahilya had warned him that all he had done was absorb the creature's hate. What she didn't understand was that they had always been inseparable.

As though in summons, his Etherium flickered. Ahilya flashed between his brows. She had opened their connection again and he saw through her eyes, architects staring, and a short-haired woman shaking her head, while Ahilya argued, horrified.

The connection ceased.

Sudden silence loomed over Iravan. Ahilya hadn't opened the connection to him deliberately, but her sheer horror and panic… What had caused it?

His heart raced as his eyes traveled to the beads looping around Darsh's wrists.

Darsh understood. They had both rendered their beads inactive in order for the communion with the yaksha to remain uninterrupted, but now they tapped at their sets together. A burst of static greeted them, before a hologram formed over Iravan's wrists: Dhruv's face barking out commands, sungineers working around him. Over Darsh's wrist, another image flickered: Irshar wobbling, making ready for another change, viewed through the drones Dhruv had floating over the ashram.

"Dhruv," Iravan said. "What is going on?"

"Finally!" The sungineer turned to face him, his face now clearer.

"For fuck's sake, Iravan, you can't just up and leave whenever you want to. We've been trying to reach you. You have responsibilities, and you've given me no leave to act on your behalf. Especially in a moment like this—"

"What," Iravan asked again, injecting calm into his voice, "is going on?"

Dhruv's voice thrummed with suppressed anger. "It appears Irshar is collapsing. We can't tell from the Garden, but we've been hearing screams from all directions. And the architecture—we can see shapes and movements. Pranav thinks the Virohi are coming alive."

Images from the drones replaced the sungineer's face. Iravan watched as the sprawling ashram within the jungle shook like a water droplet. Roads and alleys, buildings and playgrounds, shivered as if they were little more than toy structures before an approaching hurricane. The last city of humanity, this oasis of massive proportions spreading out for miles and miles, caved, hollowing out from the inside. Buildings crumpled like paper, arches collapsed, and a substance leached out of the city like dark smoke. It took the shape of half-formed limbs, of hands outstretched, and faces with features eerily like Ahilya's.

The sungineer's words reverberated in the jungle. Iravan bent his head, his breath coming out in shallow heaves. Out of the corner of his eyes, he saw Darsh freeze.

Ahilya had finally failed, after months of resisting. This was it then. The end of it all.

A dozen thoughts chased him. He had anticipated this. Irshar's construction was flawed. Ahilya, despite her strength, would never have been able to hold it together. That she had done it for three months was beyond astonishing; the Virohi had destroyed whole planets in the pursuit of immortality.

Had she suffered through those months? Had she lost bits of herself like he had?

He would relieve her now, but the thought of fulfilling his capital desire after so many lifetimes brought tears to his eyes. Would she see he did it to make amends? That he did it for her as much as himself? Would she understand? Would she forgive? It had always been about saving her. From the very beginning, even during the earthrage that had swallowed Oam, Iravan had done everything he could to protect Ahilya. This was no different. His fingers tightened over the blade around his neck, and its smooth texture was like touching Ahilya's skin.

"What do we do?" Darsh whispered.

Iravan raised his head, his grief giving him purpose. "Ready the architects and the sungineers," he told Dhruv. "I'm on my way."

5

AHILYA

Behind the darkness of closed eyes, the Etherium overtook every other sensation. A circular chamber full of mirrors appeared.

Ahilya tried to anchor herself, but smoke coalesced, took form, and she was surrounded by a hundred Ahilyas. The Virohi were dressed exactly like her, in loose kurta and trousers, with expeditionary equipment strapped around them and a satchel to match. But they were not-her too, their expressions varying from sorrow to watchfulness to hunger, always the *hunger*.

The not-Ahilyas moved sinuously, and approached closer in the mirror. They tossed their hair behind a shoulder. It unnerved her how human they were now. If she shared this with any of the councilors, they would take it as a sure sign of her madness. Yet she had seen the Virohi evolve before her eyes. This was a way for the cosmic creatures to communicate. From buildings, and streams, and pathways and walls, to smoke-like entities with tentacles and vines, now the Virohi reflected her own image, the one thing they knew to be closest to the form they desired. Iravan's warning reverberated in her head, *They have already corrupted you.*

<*Ahilya*>, the Virohi said. <*Did you think you could escape us?*>

I never wished to escape you, she replied. *I know it is impossible.*

The Virohi threw their heads back and laughed, because there was truth in her statement, but fear too. The joy and freedom of seeing herself in these infinite forms, of being allowed to... She had always sought this, though she had not known it. After all, hadn't that been the reason she had compared herself to architects once? Why she had sought the same equity? It had all been in the pursuit of freedom—not merely a political one, but the freedom to *be.* The Virohi were showing her all the possibilities of everything available to her, beyond the limited measures of architects.

The thought was so twisted, her journey to this so convoluted, that her body shook. She forced her mind back to the task. She could not allow the Virohi to take control of her so stealthily. *I have given you everything of me,* she thought to them. *Is it not enough?*

The Virohi smiled at her. <*You have given us your memories, your fear. But we still live trapped within Irshar. You must know it already. This form will not last.*>

Irshar is made of pure possibility, Ahilya thought back to them. *Remember how it was created. Remember what you needed.*

On the mirrors, she began to project a vision of a civilization, but the not-Ahilyas paced back and forth, dispelling it before it could form.

Nothing is more eternal than the ashram, Ahilya continued, a familiar litany. *It has lasted thousands of years. It is the most abiding form there is. Even now, when we are in the jungle, an ashram survives. Our world has endured.*

<*We require*>, the creatures said, <*an enduring universe.*>

And the mirrors changed.

The Virohi-Ahilyas sparkled, some with stars, some full of rocks, others with turbulent oceans. A memory came to Ahilya of what Iravan had said, that her planet was only one of the many the Virohi had infiltrated in their fear from erasure.

< *We were rich of life once.* > A wistful sigh.

You have that here, Ahilya argued. She enforced her will, and the mirrors changed into scenes from Irshar: Airav and Rajiv tending to a meal; Tariya laughing as Arth pulled her hair; Chaiyya nestling with her wife, Lavanya. There was life in Irshar, the sweetness and pain of the citizens, their conflicts, their love, their joys and sorrows, a richness.

< *To witness*>, the Virohi chafed. <*But not to experience.* >

To be immortal, Ahilya countered. *That is your greatest desire, is it not? To live forever? Is that not why you seek form in us, carried by our endless cycle of birth and rebirth?*

A considering weight grew between her brows. In the jungle, she was aware of the delicate trajection the architects were doing, but her focus remained in the Etherium, as the Virohi paced back and forth.

Remember what you were escaping, Ahilya said. The mirrors reflected her memory of the first time she and Iravan had learned of the destruction of the Virohi's planet. Terror had rippled through the minds of the cosmic creatures at their erasure.

You have already won, she went on. *Being Irshar is eternity. It is immortality. This ashram is the sum total of every experience of every human being. We are the last of humanity, and we are yours to see, to learn from, to watch.*

<*IT IS NOT ENOUGH*> the Ahilya-shaped creatures in the mirror shrieked.

She had no more warning.

Sudden emptiness. Splitting apart like fragments. Creation at the moment of birth, and blue-green tattoos that decohered… and she—*they* felt the pure rush of relief.

Ahilya was dimly aware that she was within the jungle, that the architects were building their structures, that Chaiyya and the nurses were monitoring her. Chaiyya was holding her hand, and Ahilya noticed that the healers' equipment was beeping alarmingly, and the Senior Architect looked stricken.

But that awareness was a faint thing, like the hazy reality of a dream.

She could taste the circular room like a bitter tang. Smoke filled her nose, but it was not the clean scent of scorching wood. This was a decay of sorrowful partings. This was the burning of betrayed friendships, of thwarted expectations. It was not an alien scent, but her own familiar one. Why did she feel such fear and aversion? This was a confrontation with herself.

Complete, Ahilya thought frantically, fighting this realization. *I am a complete being.*

She began to make a keening sound.

She was flying.

She was falling.

She was *failing.*

Was she a complete being? What was happening to her?

She needed a tether. She needed a strong memory, but the strongest ones were filled with pain. Oam dying, flung away from her. Bharavi strangled with the spiralweed. Iravan walking away, abandoning her for seven months.

<*It did not need to be like that*>, the Virohi murmured.

You two deserve each other.

<*You do not need to be that person anymore.*>

You're leaving me, too.

<*Think of the possibilities.*>

Ahilya's imagination betrayed her.

Nakshar, Dhruv, Iravan, and all that she had lost flashed in her mind. A vision unfolded, of things unsaid and almost dreamed, of shameful desires and unacknowledged regrets. Of what would have happened had she and Iravan never fought. How Iravan might have been had they borne a child. How her life would have been if they had never discovered the cause of earthrages, and she had simply submitted to the architects' will like everyone had told her to while they'd all lived in the skies.

Tears ran down Ahilya's cheeks as the visions of these half-spun fantasies bloomed.

They will corrupt you, Iravan said.

Are you sure you can trust them? Eskayra whispered.

A part of her knew that even thinking of a different life was a betrayal of everything she had achieved, and everything she had learned of her history. Her regret was a betrayal of *truth.*

But another part of her knew that, manipulation or not, the Virohi were right.

If she had made different choices, this would not be her life now. If she had not been this person, survival would have been different. For months now, Ahilya had fought this battle with the Virohi, their desire against hers. The others had tried to help her, but in the end this was her battle.

She was so tired now. It would be so easy, so very easy to let the cosmic creatures break from Irshar as they wanted. Would it truly be so bad? They would be free, and so would she. Each time she trapped them in Irshar, she only trapped herself. How sweet the release would taste.

The desire to end this carried her inexorably forward, and horrified, she let it, following it like a temptation. The Virohi-Ahilyas moved in the mirror, coming ever closer.

She remembered saying to Airav, *How does having so much power make me different from Iravan?* She remembered warning Iravan of becoming a tyrant. She had never wanted to be like that. If she allowed the Virohi out… If she did this…

<*If we did this.*>

She alone would no longer have the crippling absolute power she had now. She would not be so hated. She alone would not be responsible—not for Irshar, not the Virohi, not the architects and the citizens, not the rest of humanity, not *anyone*. Survival would become everyone's duty. It was what the rest wanted.

The Virohi glinted, smiling. <*Freedom from this. Is this not what you want?*>

I…

<*Is this not what you desire?*>

But…

<*This is what we desire.*>

And Ahilya thought, exhausted and truthful. *This is what I desire too.*

Glee filled the cosmic creatures.

Ahilya wrenched away from the mirrors, but the seed was planted. Relief seized her, even as horror climbed into her throat. The Etherium winked out, and she was back in the jungle. Chaiyya was holding her hand, nearly crushing it. The nurses' devices were chiming loudly. All activity from the builders and expedition team had come to a standstill. Everyone was staring at her, and Eskayra was marching toward her with concern on her face.

Ahilya realized she was sobbing.

"What happened?" Eskayra demanded of the others. "Ahilya only closed her eyes a minute ago."

A minute. She had betrayed them all—betrayed *herself*—in only a minute. Chaiyya was speaking, trying to ask her questions, but Ahilya's gaze drifted to Kamala and the hologram hovering above the nurse's wrist. It was an image of Irshar. Misty shapes emerged from the construction. Eskayra's eyes widened. She knelt down, her face twisted in worry.

"Ahilya?" Chaiyya whispered.

"I lost. I lost, Chaiyya. We have to…"

Citizen rings all around her began chiming. Every single person was connecting to the ashram to check on their loved ones. Holograms flickered everywhere, and the one above Chaiyya showed an image of the council chambers, Basav and Airav's worried faces flickering. Their voices were distorted, the words unclear. Sinuous smoke entered homes. Pathways changed, as dark fog overtook the habitat. Screams echoed, and distorted views flickered. Trees lurched, swaying dangerously, and a crack echoed from the sungineering devices, a sound that must have been deafening in the ashram.

"What does this mean?" Pari shrilled, pointing at Ahilya. "If the Virohi are infiltrating the city, do we need to return her to the ashram? Are earthrages going to begin now again?"

"What did she do?" Ranjeev said, panic on his face.

Leaves and branches creaked around them. The expedition closed in on Ahilya. The Virohi screamed at her, and she glimpsed Iravan between her brows, a dark shape moving above the jungle toward Irshar, war and purpose in his mind.

Chaiyya arose, stepping away from her, speaking urgently into her bead.

Eskayra lifted Ahilya's chin up, looking at her anxiously. Of all the people here, only her focus remained on Ahilya. Only she had neither hate nor fear distorting her features. Eskayra wore calmness like acceptance, in what could be their moment of death and extinction.

"I have to go back in," Ahilya breathed to Eskayra, gripping her hand. "I have to persuade the Virohi to return to the architecture. It's the only way."

Eskayra's eyes grew wide. "Is that even possible without everdust?"

"I have to try." Full of anguish, Ahilya stared at Eskayra. "Esk, he knows. He's going to attack them. If I tell them it's for their safety, surely they will listen?"

"Wait, let me call Chaiyya. We need to talk about this for a minute."

But Ahilya closed her eyes. Ignoring Eskayra, she plunged back into the mirrored chambers.

6

IRAVAN

He flew toward Irshar, the jungle flashing underneath him.

Wind rushed through his silver hair, slicking it back. The feather-cloak he wore streamed behind, making him appear half-a-bird. Iravan glanced below to see trees and smoke, wood and dust. Green landscape chased his flight. The jungle was motionless, ignorant of the Virohi's escape from Irshar, but it was only a matter of time before it was destroyed. The cosmic creatures' escape would have consequences for their world. He knew Ahilya was somewhere down there. Iravan put on a burst of speed.

Darsh flew next to him, sustained by Iravan's everpower. The boy flew inelegantly—this was only the second time Iravan had allowed him to rise with him—yet there was a raw delight on his face that warmed Iravan despite his grimness. When they had arrived in the jungle from the Garden, Iravan had used Ecstasy to create a nest to wheel them to their destination. The events in Irshar now warranted more speed—but seeing the wide-eyed smile on Darsh, and how infectious it was—perhaps he should have allowed this innocent joy more frequently. Darsh had so few chances at joy these days.

"*This*?" Darsh screamed incredulously. "This is what I can do if I gain the everpower?"

Iravan merely smiled, tight-lipped.

The first few times he had flown, he had struggled to understand the falcon inside him. Flight had been precarious, subject to his moods, careful and precise one day, a disastrous misadventure the next where he'd crash to the jungle. Over the last few months, he had learned how to manipulate the air with everpower, how to turn his body to the changing wind currents, how to direct the particles around him so he could breathe and hear and see while flying.

The knowledge of flight came from the falcon-yaksha and Iravan embraced his shape in the Deepness: massive wings, glinting eyes, an awareness of profound and complete loneliness. The yaksha's rage at the cosmic creatures pounded at him, *erase, destroy, never split, never again*, the emotion spurring him faster.

Dhruv's face hovered over the black beads around Iravan's wrist. "The Ecstatics are ready."

Iravan could see his army in the Deepness, a hundred different architects arrayed in battle formation. The deep, velvety darkness of the Deepness flickered, and beyond that a million worlds blinked in and out, worlds the Virohi had tried to contaminate too.

The Ecstatics couldn't see those worlds, but they didn't need to. They continued to bind themselves to each other in the manner he had trained them. Brilliant lights of a hundred different hues zoomed past each other, their rays crisscrossing in complex patterns around Iravan's falcon. Some of the shapes in the Deepness reverberated as they lent each other their power, fastening to each other with tight, unbreakable knots. Somewhere in the Garden, the Ecstatics were waiting, their skins glowing blue-green. Iravan's skin shone with silver tattoos. No matter which realm he used the everpower in, such was the effect of the evervision.

"The sungineers are ready as well," Dhruv reported.

Briefly, Iravan's bead flickered. Arrayed around the bone-white battery that had once brought Ahilya to him in the habitat stood a dozen sungineers. Massive golden holograms enveloped them from all sides. Iravan had found the battery months before and kept it with him as a memento of both Ahilya and Nakshar. Darsh's face darkened when he saw it; he had once been tortured by a similar one. The Garden had never used it for that purpose, but this evolved version would help Iravan destroy the beings that had trapped him in this existence.

As though reading his mind, Dhruv spoke over the bead. "I know you are committed to this, Iravan. But I want to reiterate that I still haven't built safeguards around the device."

"We must act," Iravan replied. "Ahilya might be trying to coax the Virohi back into the architecture even now."

"I disagree with her on many things, and for better or for worse you have my allegiance. But think of what happened the last time we used the battery."

Memory flashed. Ashrams wobbling. Lightning storms. A face with jagged teeth and fiery eyes. Skyrage. The battery had weakened the Moment before, allowing the cosmic creatures to break through into the world.

"This time it could be worse," Dhruv warned. "You could damage the Moment irreparably."

Did it matter if the Moment *was* damaged? The Moment was useful only to a rare few, and trajection was nearly dead. The architects of the Garden used Ecstasy to traject *into* the Moment; very rarely did they use constellation lines to build anymore. Even the architects left in Irshar who could use the realm couldn't truly traject their precious ashram to manipulate its architecture. They could only use it on seeds left over from the crash.

Iravan did not voice this. It was callous, even for him. "We will not be in the Moment this time," he said instead. "We will be in the Deepness, and the Deepness is immune to damage."

The original battery had broken Airav's mind, and the Ecstatic battery had tortured Ecstatics. All batteries were dangerous to consciousness, which was why a battery was the only way to ensure the true death of a vast consciousness such as the cosmic creatures. Dhruv had taken the technology from those early prototypes and created a bomb, a remarkably ingenious invention that would suck the consciousness of the Virohi into itself in the same way that a battery had once sucked Airav's. Then instead of using such an energy, the bomb would explode the Virohi out into the Deepness in a species-destroying cataclysm.

Iravan had no doubt that it would work exactly as intended. He and Dhruv had tested it already on the Virohi Iravan and Ahilya had trapped in the Moment when they'd stopped that first earthrage in the habitat. Iravan had gone hunting for the creature, and seen the effects of the bomb. This time, the bomb was more powerful, aimed to obliterate not just one cosmic creature but all of them.

Darsh's face was thoughtful and full of questions, but he didn't speak. Iravan was hardly modelling the restraint he'd advised, but he did not anticipate anything occurring to the Moment or the Deepness. The entire point of removing the Virohi into the Deepness was to ensure no damage could occur to the Moment.

He'd tested the bomb in the Moment, but had known it would not be a viable option to destroy the species. The cosmic creature he had tested the bomb on was weak, imprisoned as it had been by the maze Ahilya and Iravan had constructed. But the others who were embedded in Irshar would be able to affect the Moment; they would try to infiltrate the architects again, making them burn crimson like they had during the skyrages. Iravan could not afford to leave his Ecstatics vulnerable. He had to take the cosmic creatures to a realm they had no power in, and that realm was the Deepness. Besides, the Deepness was a realm which superseded architect-control. A realm where other planets existed, where Iravan could see those planets, this was a place of a thousand worlds, far vaster than a single universe, too immense for a minor explosion to have an effect. Iravan had calculated the risks carefully.

"You're certain you want to do this?" Dhruv said quietly.

"It's either them or humanity," Iravan said grimly. "What choice would you have me make?"

Dhruv did not reply, but the answer was likely clear to the sungineer, in the furious cascades of dust rippling over the ashram, the terrifying gusts of wind howling like enraged beasts. The sounds were miniscule, coming from Iravan's beads, but in the Garden Dhruv would be able to feel the rumbles of an impending storm, the very same one Ahilya had delayed by interring the Virohi into Irshar. This time Iravan was prepared.

He was going to commit genocide, but what else could one do when faced with such parasites, such a plague? The Garden had superseded the need for ethics. This was about survival.

An image hovered over Iravan's bead from the drones Dhruv kept positioned over Irshar. Molten stone-like entities dragged themselves out of the architecture. Chunks of green rock lifted into the air and crashed, smoke and fog overtaking the city in thick tentacles. Screams echoed through the device, breaking into static. Nausea built in Iravan, merging with the falcon-yaksha's vengeance. He willed his body to fly faster.

In the Deepness, the Ecstatics stood ready. Ten-year-old Reyla hovered, her binding to a dozen Ecstatics making her light brighter than everyone else's. Beside her the other Senior Ecstatics, Pranav who had once belonged to Nakshar, Theria who had sworn allegiance from Kinshar, and Jyaishna who had once been of Reikshar, all waited for Iravan's signal.

Each of them was an Ecstatic he had trained. Once, there had only been four, but since then nearly three thousand architects had come to his Garden to learn of their destinies. Each of them would undoubtedly have their own capital desires once they reunited with their yakshas, but for now he was conditioning them so deeply with his own that their only purpose would be to make amends.

That reality was minutes away.

Giddy laughter built within Iravan, and he spun mid-air, flying faster. Within the Etherium, Nidhirv, Mohini and Agni stared at him across time and space, their eyes glinting silver. The falcon reared back in the Deepness. The lives inside of him waited, their eagerness and confusion a sharp reminder of how long he had delayed the fulfillment of his capital desire, how this one fateful action was the last thing needed before true freedom was his. Bhaskar shifted his weight. Mohini rang out in desperate laughter. It was dizzying, to hold so many lives. The desire was like the sweetest rasa, forcing him to react. And he yearned—oh, how he yearned.

"Watch closely," he said to Darsh. "You can't make a mistake. Everything hinges on today, and all your training has led to this."

Thin filaments of silvery light shot out of Iravan's falcon in the Deepness. His skin radiated silver, coiling patterns blinking in an amazing tapestry. In the Deepness he knotted himself to the five Senior Ecstatics, and through them to a hundred other architects.

A surge of power filled Iravan.

A hundred voices burst into his mind. He could sense the architects in the Deepness, their terror, their excitement, their adrenaline. A part of him wondered what they would feel when he unleashed his wrath. He could sense their strain, how they attempted not to fight his leash, and how they attempted to acquiesce. Their motes flickered and steadied, long lines of power weaving through a complex trajection of knots to feed him their Ecstasy.

"I already know how to do this linking," Darsh said. "Teach me about the everpower. You're going to use it now, aren't you? To destroy the Virohi? Let me help you."

"No," Iravan said. "You have your task."

Darsh made a face, but did not argue. They continued to fly in silence until they could see the Garden in the distance, its cave mouth and open clearing visible through the foliage.

Carefully, Iravan manipulated the wind stream around Darsh. He slowed long enough to jettison the boy down to the clearing, watched to make sure he was safe, then accelerated again. Darsh would take his command from the Garden, directing other Ecstatics in the Deepness the way Iravan had just now. He was going to act as a general in the war, helping the other Ecstatics with their trajection, while Iravan took the battle to the enemy. Dhruv had disapproved, both for using Darsh in this way and for the fact that *he* did not have that control though he was Iravan's true second, but this was a matter of trajection. The sungineer would not be able to help. Iravan could feel his simmering annoyance over his communication bead.

But then Iravan forgot about Dhruv's irritation, for he had arrived.

Irshar spread out below him, a lone city in the jungle with spires and columns sprawling far into hills. Even as Iravan watched, a massive tower cracked in two, falling in slow motion, bodies hurtling through it as the Virohi escaped in streams of smoke. Several buildings surrounded a huge central plaza, each of them caving in, sucked from within. Roads and paths snaked in and out of each other, massive stone slabs rising in the air then crashing in balloons of dust. Arches and orchards crumbled. Dust rose everywhere, as if many tiny earthrages were beginning. Within the city, shadowy tentacles swam, appearing almost human-like in their imitation of arms, and legs, and bodies. The single massive core tree shivered in the center of the plaza, rearing back in agony.

Next to this, the Garden remained untouched. Existing a few miles away, far enough from Irshar to stand as its own dwelling, the Garden was separated by a large swathe of hills. A massive tower made of bark and moss rose within a central courtyard, leaves curling and uncurling with the power of trajection. Glinting glass windows trembled in their panes, their chinking sound coming to Iravan through his beads. This last final storm would surely destroy the Garden too, but for now it stood strong, uncontaminated as it was by the Virohi.

Grim laughter bubbled in Iravan as he looked back to Irshar. He had created the Garden in purity. He would purify Irshar too. He hovered, surveying the landscape for a long second.

Wind buffeted his feather cloak. A thousand lives within him radiated their terrible fury, their desperation, their will. Voices thrummed in his head, echoing from the architects in the Deepness. Even from so high up, he could hear the screams of the citizens within the ashram.

I am going to save you, Iravan thought, but he did not know who the words were for—himself, the citizens, Ahilya, or humanity.

His wings flapped in the Deepness as a signal he was about to enter the Conduit.

Iravan pulled the Ecstatics with him into the Moment, and a billion stars surrounded him. In the Moment, the possibilities of the cosmic creatures glittered at him. Some shaped like irregular stars, some like rocks tapering off into waves, others like smoke-filled chambers that thrummed and vibrated—all were possibilities of the Virohi, blinking in and out. All living creatures were reflected as possibilities within the Moment, including the Virohi now that they had become so fully part of this dimension, but consciousness existed on a scale of sentience and awareness, and one could only sense an awareness less than their own in the Moment. The Ecstatics—advanced though they were, and capable of sensing a yaksha—were still not sensitive enough to feel the consciousness of a massive entity like the Virohi. None of them had the capability—not even now when so many of them were tied to him. Iravan almost wished he could show them what the Virohi looked like. Unlike regular stars and frozen possibilities, the cosmic creatures existed as movable pieces—so advanced and alien that even the Moment could not contain their infinite possibilities. They were alive here, in the same way architects were.

Iravan had found these strange stars of the Virohi long ago. He had prepared for this instant. He had simply not trajected the creatures so far, ignorant of how he would harm Ahilya or Irshar in the process, but with Ahilya's failure, there was no need for such deep care.

They were here. They were accessible. They were finished.

Iravan dove from the skies, launching his attack.

7

AHILYA

The Etherium was out of control.

The mirrors in the chamber cracked and bled, smoke and mercury leaking from them. Ahilya slipped in the chambers, and her reflections rebounded in every direction, shards of smiles, splinters of grief. *Stabilize,* she thought frantically—but the mirrors only multiplied further, a hundred of them, more and more until she could discern no sense between any images. Her form grew meaningless. Only fragments of the Virohi remained.

Frantic, Ahilya retreated from the chambers. She opened the door in her mind that connected her to Iravan's Etherium, and saw him flying, his feather cloak billowing behind him, a silvery birdlike creature glinting in the evening sun. Her eyes flickered to Eskayra in terror.

"Help me," she said, her voice a sob. "Help me, Esk. What do we do?"

"Ahilya, please." Eskayra threw a look at Chaiyya. The Senior Architect hurried over from the other architects and took Ahilya's hand again.

"Take a deep breath," Chaiyya instructed.

Ahilya noticed Meena increase the dosage of the medicines entering her bloodstream through the intravenous glass. Someone draped a cloak around her, but Ahilya couldn't stop shivering.

At Chaiyya's instruction, Kamala opened up another connection to Irshar. The image flickered, flakes of stone rippling down the walls in a crumble. Chaiyya crouched down and pressed Ahilya's shoulders. Her voice was low, her eyes deep pools of concern.

"I need you to be calm," Chaiyya said. "Look at this, Ahilya. Tell me what you see."

Smoke rose and curled from Irshar. The cosmic creatures were pulling away from the architecture. A rooftop cracked, citizens screamed, and the smoky form of the Virohi shimmered. The cosmic creatures extended a tentacle from the walls, then the tentacles morphed into arms. Ahilya thought she saw her own hand, but it withered into smoke, scaly fingers turning ashy.

The jungle beyond remained motionless. Underneath them, the ground was firm, as if to mock her with its steadiness. Ahilya was an archeologist—she knew what was occurring. Irshar was where the Virohi lived, but Ahilya was in the jungle, and she had control of them. She was the eye of the storm. In her absence the storm would hit the city first. The citizens—her sister, her nephews, her friends—would all be buried under the avalanche of her failure and hubris. Then, and only then, the storm would spread to the jungle, trees ripping apart, dust and earth exploding, until nothing remained. Until it washed over Ahilya and finally took her.

Would they feel pain? How long would it take the Virohi to fully extract themselves, and to destroy the planet? They would do what they'd always done, break the world in order to find form as architects, but such a thing was no longer possible, not now they had been brought into this dimension fully, no longer operating as creatures outside of the Moment. They would end up destroying the earth and themselves, for no reason. They would mutilate the architects, making them bleed crimson like they once had, and it would all be for nothing. She should have told them that. She had been foolish not to already; her persuasion in the Etherium had always been disoriented, with logic a fleeting weapon.

She could feel their confusion now as they emerged from Irshar. No doubt the Virohi sensed something amiss in their plans but the hive evolved fast. What would they do in their loss and confusion? Would it take time, or be a terrible slow decay? She rocked herself, because this is what it was always going to come to—ever since she had stepped out of Nakshar with Oam. The destruction of her world and of humanity, all because of her foolishness, her arrogance. Ahilya stared at the holograms, a horrible gurgling sound emerging from her throat.

"She can't," Eskayra said, her voice hollow. "She isn't focusing. She is in shock."

Chaiyya nodded grimly. "Basav," she said. "Tell us what is occurring. Tell us clearly, so Ahilya can hear and understand."

Basav's voice floated out from Chaiyya's citizen's ring. "Irshar crumbles, and the Virohi are making ready to attack. We cannot see Iravan-ve, or the Garden. No one is sending aid." Terror was palpable in the Senior Architect's trembling voice. "We are alone," he whispered in disbelief. "This is how it ends then." He trailed off, a soft sob.

Around Ahilya, the members of the expedition were silent, in shock themselves perhaps, or in grim, defeated acceptance. Oam flashed behind Ahilya's eyes. Between her brows, Iravan's face was forbidding. He was still flying through the forest, the form of another Ecstatic next to him. They would arrive in Irshar any moment. Tears choked her throat.

She raised her eyes to Chaiyya. She did not have to speak—Chaiyya understood.

"Listen to me," Chaiyya said quietly. "If Iravan is going to attack the cosmic creatures, then we need to allow this to happen. It is the only way for the ashram to endure."

Eskayra bent down as well, capturing Ahilya's chin between her fingers. "She's right. I know it is not what you want, but if it saves all of us, would it be so bad if he kills the cosmic creatures?"

A part of Ahilya knew what they were saying was true. That Iravan was right, that *they* were. That anything she said now to the contrary would simply show her corruption.

Another part of her remembered the Virohi reflecting her image.

Her gaze fixed on the Senior Architect. "I can try to put them back into the architecture," she whispered. "Is it not worth the attempt?"

Chaiyya did not even bother to reply. After all her talk of choosing life, faced with such a horrible choice, what else did Ahilya expect of the Senior Architect? This had always been a war for survival. It was what Iravan had done in letting go of Oam. What the architects had done in erasing non-architects. Ahilya turned to Eskayra, whose gaze grew gentle.

"I'm sorry," Eskayra said. "I agree with Chaiyya. We do not have the time."

Ahilya waved a limp hand. "The storm has not yet come to the jungle. Look around you—everything is still. We don't know what Iravan's assault will do the planet. Experimenting with consciousness has ripped our skies apart before, and to attempt to destroy creatures of such massive consciousness could tear the planet fully." Her voice grew beseeching. "Please. I don't think we *need* the everdust to put the Virohi back into Irshar. Not when I can communicate with them directly."

Eskayra frowned and exchanged a glance with Chaiyya. Consideration grew on Chaiyya's face—Ahilya's point about experimentation on consciousness could not be denied. Chaiyya had seen it with Airav only too clearly. But Ahilya's motivation in saying this now? All of them knew that she defended the Virohi. That her fight with Iravan was because she refused to hand over the cosmic creatures to him. Ahilya could see the calculation on Chaiyya's face. Could Ahilya be trusted to act in humanity's best interests? Between saving the Virohi from Iravan, and saving humanity from the Virohi, what would she choose? Ahilya herself could not say. To her, one was the other, but the rest of them would not see it that way, and Ahilya knew that time was running out.

The architects around them watched the three women silently. Ahilya took in their tense shoulders, their pinched mouths, the sheer *otherness* of their faces. They obeyed Eskayra, and they considered Chaiyya one of theirs, but where did that obedience come from? The architects all hated the Virohi. There were no more secrets regarding an architect's origins. Each of these trajecting architects had experienced the mutilation of their very beings when the Virohi had seared through them, turning their trajection against the people they had sworn to protect. There was no room for self-forgiveness.

But this guilt. Its performance. Its exploitation. Look where it had brought them. Look at the *amends* Iravan wished to make. Coldness spread through Ahilya's bones.

"Chaiyya, please," she whispered in a last desperate attempt. "You helped me build Irshar. If you help me keep my mind now, we could do it again. We could work together."

It was the wrong thing to say. An expression of great hostility flew across Chaiyya's face, as if in reminding her she had once helped to inter the cosmic creatures, Ahilya had implied Chaiyya's culpability in Ahilya's own failure.

She raised her hands, wanting to take it back, wanting to explain herself, that she did not mean to manipulate Chaiyya. That she only meant to speak from her heart. But screams echoed from sungineering devices again, and Chaiyya blinked, as if recalling she had family back in the ashram; children and a wife she loved.

"I'm sorry," Chaiyya said. "If it is between your method or his, I choose his. He is more practiced. He has sungineers aiding him. He knows and understands the Virohi."

Eskayra nodded. "I see how the Virohi affect you. Whatever you do now, they cannot be trusted. They are inherently evil."

Are they? Ahilya thought in anguish.

It's what Iravan said too, and he had been one of them, once. Yet now when Ahilya saw them she saw her own shape, her own shame. The cosmic creatures reflected both of them. Her erasure and his loneliness. Her desperation and his guilt. Her future and his past. *We do not even know them. Just as we do not know ourselves. How can we call them evil?* She wanted to say those words out loud, but it was not the way to convince Chaiyya. She would just be pushing her away further.

Ahilya clutched her stomach, feeling sick. "And Iravan?" she asked softly. "He is the one fighting them. What if he dies?"

"We are all dead anyway," Chaiyya said, her voice flat. "The storm will spread from Irshar to the jungle. If he dies to save us, it will be no different from when he was a Senior Architect."

Ahilya stared at her. Chaiyya had already sacrificed Iravan once in choosing to imprison him in the deathcage after his trial during the Conclave. He had once been her friend, but so many bonds had been destroyed now.

"If we are lucky, the Virohi and that man will end each other," Eskayra said. "We could be rid of two threats. If we win this, we *survive*."

But that thinking, Ahilya thought. *That has always been the problem, hasn't it?*

Behind her eyes, Iravan's image spiked as he dove from the sky. His rage, his satisfaction, his grief pounded at her. His mouth moved in instruction. She could almost hear it, the command to Dhruv to power the battery that had brought her to Iravan once. The one Dhruv had made to save Nakshar, which had destroyed all the flying ashrams.

Panic grew in her, and she closed her eyes, rapidly examining and discarding possibilities. She had asked Chaiyya for permission to intervene because she did not want to act alone anymore; she had no faith in her ability to do so. Was she to obey, and watch this happen now? Do nothing? She had no more energy to argue with the others, and the thought of making another colossal mistake terrified her, but she could not allow herself to believe that she had failed so spectacularly. That she had led these cosmic creatures to extinction and killed all of them with what she had done. If she chose not to act now, death was the only thing to await them.

Behind her eyes, Iravan's face grew relieved. The others murmured to themselves as another rumble echoed in the jungle.

Frantic, Ahilya closed her eyes and re-entered the Etherium.

8

AHILYA

What was the Etherium? Ahilya had never truly understood.

Iravan had once explained it as a place of guidance, a third vision where he had seen probabilities of the future convert into true possibility. To Iravan, it had looked like a maze, a mountain-path, and a way to see behind the falcon-yaksha's eyes. He had seen events occurring far from him, and looked into his past by focusing within it. As Iravan changed, so did the imagery of the Etherium, evolving at the pace he evolved. He had tried—desperately and failingly—to explain it and fit it into his world vision.

Ahilya had always thought of it like a many-chambered house.

She was familiar with only two chambers—one where her vision merged with Iravan's, and another where she met with the cosmic creatures. One had been created out of an explosion of her desire with Iravan's, and the other with her acquiescence to let the Virohi take her. She had not understood the Etherium, but she had relied on it to understand her changing world.

Yet now all the chambers of the Etherium, even those that were unknown, were out of control, and she ran through a crumbling edifice, all meaning crashing around her. She slipped and fell, and shards of mirrors scraped her as she righted herself and moved over uneven ground.

Something beckoned to her, the leaves of a core tree within a chamber she recognized.

Ahilya lurched and grabbed a passing branch. She skidded to a halt—and there she was, in the chamber where she had once spoken and understood the rudra-tree's command.

Awe filled her, momentarily eclipsing her terror. Memory rushed into her of a time when she had returned to Nakshar after Iravan had transformed the Conclave into a many-spoked wheel. Back then, she had communicated with Nakshar's rudra-tree to return the architects their permissions by channeling her desire into the core tree. When the Conclave had crashed to the jungle, Nakshar's rudra had merged with all the core trees to become the vriksh. The vriksh had always anchored her communication with the Virohi, and it bloomed now in the chamber. Ahilya found herself touching its great trunk, staring up at the foliage, only to see a sky full of stars peeking between moving leaves. The Etherium still wobbled, but she held on to the tree, planting her feet.

If it was an explosion of her desire that gave her control over her connection with Iravan, and the mirrored chambers to speak to the Virohi, then could such desire help her commune with the vriksh too? After all, she held all the tree's permissions. She tried to ask the tree to help her again, and as if sensing this, the writhing of the cosmic creatures stilled. The rumbling of the earthrage shivered, pausing for a brief instant. The Virohi watched her, reading her intent.

Ahilya's heart leapt in hope. *Return*, she thought to the cosmic creatures, inviting them back into Irshar. *Return.*

The cosmic creatures pulled at her, hovering around the tree, feeling her call them. Iravan snarled, yanking them toward him. He could see what she was attempting, and she felt his attack as if it was on her body and mind. She felt his fury with her.

Ahilya did what she had always done. She anchored herself in the tree, rooting herself to become immovable, and desired for the cosmic creatures to bind themselves back into the ashram. They filled her mind, swirling toward the vriksh. Above, the universe spun with a million stars. *Hold*, she thought to herself, as Iravan attempted to pull the cosmic creatures from her grasp. *Hold.*

9

IRAVAN

Iravan circled the expansive city of Irshar, noting each crevice from where the Virohi seeped.

A thousand links whipped out of him like arrows as he drew on the combined power of all the Ecstatics. He flew through the Moment, converting pure Ecstasy into hair-thin constellation lines. He leapt between the stars of the Virohi, tying the lines to each other, drinking in the power coursing through him.

His trajection manifested like the most intricate web. When he had trajected plants in the past, he had always felt their life. Now the instant the trajection rendered toward the cosmic creatures, their voices filled his head, <*RELEASE US*>, they screamed, and his rage spiked, sweat coating his skin. The falcon within him snarled in response.

His constellation lines *burst* with power.

The Ecstatics cried out. They strained within the Deepness, their power filling Iravan, coursing through his veins, turning his skin translucent. Iravan tugged at the trajection lines. He could see Ahilya trying to anchor the Virohi and return them to Irshar, but

Iravan pulled them toward him by trajecting their stars within the Moment, and they collected out of the architecture in a swarm, swept up in his storm. Their howls echoed in his ears, but he paid them no mind.

The Virohi gathered to him, forced to obey his will. Within Irshar, their snaky foggy forms shuddered, paused, and shuddered again.

The creatures had destroyed Nakshar, weakened the very universe. They had infiltrated the Moment and ruined it. They were going to eradicate life.

He would *erase* them.

With all the power of the Ecstatics tethering him, Iravan roared as he pulled the Virohi to the tunnel of the Conduit. His plan hinged on taking them through the Moment and obliterating them with the bomb within the Deepness. Inch by inch, the Virohi seeped into the Conduit, their shrieking loud in his ears, and Iravan cried out a command to Dhruv, to begin the extermination.

Dhruv obeyed, and a blinding flash that lasted an eternity reverberated in Iravan's eyes, filling the evervision. The first of the explosions launched, and he sensed Ahilya's panic, but a wave of jubilation rose in him. It was working.

He beat his wings, and form by snaky form the Virohi were yanked from the Conduit into the Deepness where they did not belong, explosions attacking them as soon as they arrived in the velvety darkness. It was a manifestation of his imagination, he knew, but Iravan saw the scaly bodies of the cosmic creatures squeezing through the tunnel of the Conduit, only to be met with destruction. He saw massive black holes erupting across their bodies, breaking them down. He saw their alien mouths open in an endless scream, viscous blood oozing out. Their skins burned in a cleansing fire, and he thought grimly, *Yes. Destroy.*

Sweat broke out over Iravan. Tears blurred his eyes.

Irshar trembled in the jungle, shaking like a leaf in a storm. Dhruv shouted over the communication bead, but Iravan could not hear beyond the roar of the falcon. The Moment shuddered and dust motes within it whizzed around in confusion and anxiety. All trajecting architects could see his actions. They could feel the effects even if they could not understand what he was doing.

The yearning burned in him, pressure from a thousand lifetimes. The Ecstatics swayed in exertion. Irshar cracked underneath him, a whole section of rooftops exploding into powder as the cosmic creatures leached out of the architecture toward him. Their destruction was rendering in the first vision even as they burned in the Deepness; Iravan saw their snaky, misty forms distort like a fabric rent with holes, as they fluttered toward him.

The effort from the tethered Ecstatics pierced his ears. Dhruv's hologram flickered over his wrist, and the Virohi screamed *<save us, help us>*, as he pulled them into the explosion, puncturing their consciousness repeatedly, breaking them apart as they hovered over the ashram.

Ahilya's will grew in his heart as she attempted to stop him. He felt her alarm and despair, her desperate attempt to bind the creatures back in Irshar. They both knew that he was the stronger of the two. She had only just learned of her power. He had been aware of it—conditioned within it—since birth.

Iravan thought, *Is it really just this easy?*

Relief made his muscles weak. A few more minutes until the bomb reached its full potential and then it would be finished.

He pulled the Virohi, one final tug as smoky forms filled the sky, pouring toward him. Irshar wobbled, debris falling as he sucked the cosmic creatures away.

And in that instant when he felt Ahilya's hold slip, the precise instant when the last of the Virohi were pulled in the Deepness, Iravan reared his wings. "*Now*!" he screamed.

Dhruv pulled the switch on the bomb, blasting all the remaining sungineering power of the device into the Deepness with maximum prejudice. The explosion blinded Iravan momentarily. All three realms shuddered, slamming into each other. The connection with the Ecstatics broke.

Architects fell out of the Deepness, their lights winking away. Their power severed from Iravan, and he spun in the darkness all alone, tumbling head over heels. He floated in his first vision, and saw through the bead on his hand the battery sizzling, sparks flying, Dhruv's frantic gestures as he attempted to contain the device.

The Virohi had been exploding only a second ago, but with Iravan's power severed, they slammed into his mind, escaping the Deepness to return through the Conduit, weeping.

The battery detonated into sudden fire.

The universe shook, stars and possibilities turning to powder.

The Moment shattered.

10

TOGETHER

The Moment shattered.

They watched it happen in every realm.

11

IRAVAN

The Moment shattered.

A thrumming overtook the Deepness, reverberating from the fracturing Moment. Iravan felt a horror unlike any other.

For a long, interminable instant, the Deepness stilled, waves of a silent supernova pouring through it. Iravan watched, spinning.

In the Etherium, all of his past selves recoiled. Nidhirv began to scream in the forest, holding his head, the tattoos on his skin turning black, turning crimson, like blood pouring out of his body. Askavetra flinched as a tiger-yaksha attacked her; she was an intruder, she had always been the intruder. Iravan stood within Nakshar's temple, staring after Ahilya, but before she could leave he reached her, he apologized, he never found Ecstasy. Bharavi patted his cheek and smiled, except her teeth cracked and her skin bled, and the Moment shattered again.

What had he done? Tears of fright streamed down Iravan's face. He had lost. Humanity was obliterated. He had thought his plan was foolproof, a bomb that the Virohi could not escape, but it was over for all of them. The ricochet of the Virohi's return into the Moment, the use of the bomb, the terrible explosions had all broken the universe. He drifted in the shattering Moment as stars crumbled one after another, limestone powdery, constellation lines collapsing and disappearing, the entire maze of traps he had constructed falling apart. The stars of the Virohi that Iravan had been squeezing through the Conduit shimmered in the broken Moment, one second there, the next gone, on and on again as if the creatures were attempting to return to the universe fully but were unable to do so. The cloud of Virohi that had been hovering above Irshar grew larger, stronger in Iravan's first vision. The cosmic creatures sobbed, and it sounded like confusion.

Outside Irshar, the jungle finally began to shake.

The skies thundered as all over the planet, mountains burst into being, trees turned into humanoid shapes, mud turned to quicksand and quaked. Irshar wavered, and massive jagged mountains erupted all around it. The ashram shrunk, hills displacing, people dying. In a corner of his mind, Iravan knew that his perception was failing; that while reality was unravelling, he was too.

Particles flaked from his skin. Bhaskar became him became a corpse became a child. He was Nidhirv and he never met Vishwam, never became an architect. He was Iravan and he lived with Ahilya, their children living in a desolate world as around them earthrages came and went.

Desperately, attempting to hold onto his mind, Iravan tried trajecting with the everpower to stabilize himself and the environment, but the cosmic creatures surrounded him from all directions like a flock of birds. He felt their manic terror and rage, their utter insane derangement. Like injured animals, they were more dangerous than they'd ever been, and he spun, recklessly, his feather cloak whirling, trying to use the everpower to change the air currents, warp them away from him, make sure they didn't touch him. An air shield built of shards of dust. The cosmic creatures attempted to pierce it; it cracked, and Iravan twisted, fought off the swarm of shadows, diving and dodging, horrified. Within the Moment, he saw their possibilities flicker, attempting to find anchoring, failing to do so.

In a slow, rational part of his mind, Iravan understood several things. The Moment was destroyed, and the Virohi's consciousness would not find purchase there. The cosmic creatures would attempt to embed themselves back into the realm, but it would only result in the destruction of the planet. It should have surprised him how the Virohi could affect him so materially now, flocking toward him, trying to break him, but he knew that by containing them in Irshar, Ahilya had allowed them to affect reality directly. They were tied to the planet now in profound ways, and their destruction of everything would come from many avenues.

There was no more hope. Nothing to stop this.

Iravan saw only shadows in front of him, vestiges of smoke that became Ahilya, Bharavi, Arth, and Kush. He knew those were tricks of the Virohi. Each time he moved to dissipate them, they reformed. If his air shield broke they would destroy him from within, burst his body, choke him. They knew he was their enemy. Their destruction of him would not be personal, it would simply be logical—before they destroyed themselves and everything else in their rage and confusion. He almost welcomed his end, but instinct made him fight harder, the falcon within him shrieking in madness.

He pushed with his everpower, but his strength was failing.

He broke.

12

AHILYA

The Moment shattered.

Ahilya sheltered under the tree, crouching as a gale whipped through the chambers of the Etherium. Chaiyya had dropped to the forest floor, writhing, her eyes rolled back into her head. Eskayra looked wildly toward her, reaching a hand as all sungineering blinked out.

Fissures opened in the clearing, another new city destroyed before it could begin, Ahilya held onto consciousness with a fingernail, as the foliage lurched suddenly, trees waving, a gigantic trunk swaying so close that she thought it might hit her. Eskayra cried out, throwing herself over Ahilya's body, and Ahilya closed her eyes, breath heaving.

Between her brows, she saw the Virohi swoop around Iravan, consumed by their insane grief. She caught a startling image of them in her mind, reflecting her own face but burned and pock-marked, deep holes cut into her skin, black tears running down her cheeks. The Virohi had been damaged in Iravan's attack. Injured and in pain, they would have no restraint. They would retaliate.

Iravan's skin flaked, becoming gray. The blood in his body was freezing. The planet was rupturing, and so was he. She had been warned about this, that the Virohi were evil. She had brought them to this, not just humanity but the cosmic creatures too, in dealing out this fate to them. In that moment of startling clarity, Ahilya saw how deeply corrupted she had become.

Sap cracked and bled down trunks. Dust churned the jungle. Ahilya squinted, trying to see, but all was mayhem. Eskayra was yelling, and Chaiyya and the architects were lost to their terror. The non-architects in their expedition huddled together, as twigs scored their skin, and wind beat against them. Ahilya knew they only had moments before the full power of the storm hit them, before the ground under them caved. She saw herself, and she saw Iravan unmoving in the sky, cosmic creatures attacking him from every side. When the Virohi were done with him, they would turn their attention to the rest of the planet. All the consideration and life she had given them had been useless. They had gone mad, and soon they would raze the planet in a storm Ahilya had delayed for three months. Iravan was all that stood between them. And he was being destroyed.

Ahilya anchored in the tree, pleading,

Slowly, languidly, an attention overtook her consciousness, a gravity to it, a terrible old age.

Visions came to her of flying in the sky, of people living in her boughs, of purpose being embedded into her. Men, women, children, and creatures of all kinds grew and died within her limbs. She flew into the air, she landed in the jungle, she responded to the desires of life.

Awe filled her, bringing tears to her eyes. Iravan had once changed the permissions of all the core trees to obey her above anything else, and the core trees of the landed Conclave had amalgamated to become the vriksh. Now the tree was responding to her desperation, as it had ever since.

The vriksh's attention—the consciousness of all the core trees of the Conclave—encompassed her. Roots spread their tentacles into her chest and heart, gripping tightly. Her back arced.

Determination surged through her. The vriksh recoiled like a branch whipping in the storm. Above Irshar, the Virohi continued to hammer at Iravan. She could see him, suspended mid-air, his feather cloak billowing behind him, arms spread out like a bird while smoke surrounded him, wrapping him in thick corded swarms. His panicked breathing echoed in Ahilya's ears, his mind searching for escape—and behind it she felt his desire to be eradicated. This would not just be an end, this would be his final end. *Their* final end.

Would it be so bad? Eskayra said.

Ahilya closed her eyes, bringing the power of all the core trees with her.

13

IRAVAN

Iravan fragmented.

He remembered a night under a star-filled sky.

Glim~~mered~~

~~Gone~~

Explosions in shadows of light.

How was he alive?

<Not much longer>

Did I win?

Shards pierced his skin, lulled his consciousness.

Blood turned sharp. The pain was excruciating.

He withdrew, watching.

A grateful thought. *Finally.*

He drifted

  his bubble of protection waning

He waited

  relieved

for his end.

14

AHILYA

Her desire amplified by the vriksh, Ahilya reached into the earth.

She did not know what she was supposed to do, only that she had to find a way to protect Irshar and the planet, protect Iravan before the Virohi destroyed him, and the Virohi before they unleashed chaos. The vriksh listened to her unspoken commands and obeyed on its own.

Massive roots, each as thick as a house, plunged into the soil, crisscrossing the jungle and intertwining into tight nodes as deep as the planet. The planet wobbled, and held, tightening around the tree.

Iravan's voice flickered in her mind, *Let me go.*

Ahilya shook her head, unsure if she could really hear him.

In her mind's eye, she saw the tree rear back, whipping in all directions, leaves raining down, branches creaking. It expanded within Irshar, the trunk growing massive, shooting upward to blot out the sky. Roots rippled out, curling all around Irshar's broken architecture, supporting roads and bridges where they fell apart, and wrapping thick tentacles around buildings that had caved in.

Before, the vriksh had been a gigantic tree, but it had limited its reach to Irshar's plaza. Now, it exploded, swelling and surging all around the ashram, catching fragmenting structures, wrapping itself gently around huddling citizens in protection.

Sluggishly, Ahilya watched the tree looming inside and beyond her. Branches burst into existence, and the jungle shrieked.

The vriksh waited coiled with her heart. *Please,* she begged, gasping. *Please.*

The tree gave all of itself to her.

And, knowing what to do, Ahilya directed the Virohi toward the vriksh. The Virohi were one of her; they could not deny her call, not when they were a hive mind and they had learned to see themselves as her.

They responded against their will, and their voices merged with the memories of a thousand years, screaming, weeping, grieving.

Ahilya pulled her many selves together. She saw the vriksh rising higher and higher, binding the Virohi to itself as she desired. Branches wrapped around the trunk in tight coils like a human hugging their own body. Roots curled, like fingers closing. Underneath Irshar, more roots secured the planet, clutching with hair-thin fibers, straining, containing the Virohi within themselves.

A cry, and the mirrored Ahilyas shrieked, mouths wide open, eyes wild.

The vriksh bound itself. It shook, and Ahilya sank to her knees with the effort, her entire body quivering.

Iravan cried out, a sound of wretched despair and sorrow—

Until—

Silence.

She snapped back to her reality, eyes focusing on Eskayra and the architects. Her mind buzzed like she had a fever. Her breath came out in heaves.

The voices of the Virohi whispered, but it was in a manner of an aftershock, a phantom presence in her mind. She started to shiver.

Between her brows, she caught a glimpse of Iravan still floating above the ashram, head tilted back, arms spread out like wings. The feather cloak continued to flutter, and he was a picture of both stillness and motion. There was shock in his posture, a deep amazement that bordered on agony. Could he see the vriksh? It was tall enough to shelter him too. What was he thinking? Would he stop now?

The glimpse shattered, and Ahilya retched, throwing up. Eskayra bent to her. "What in rages happened?" the woman asked, frantic. "What did you do?"

I won.

"I trapped the Virohi," Ahilya sputtered, wiping her mouth. "They're in the vriksh now."

She cut off, only now realizing the eerie silence surrounding her. The jungle had stopped rumbling. The storm that had begun suddenly had ended, just as abruptly. Trees were motionless again, in strange postures of pain, caught midway toward being destroyed. Sap seemed frozen, amber stuck to trunks like honey, and the earth was torn, great gaping crevasses riven with a thousand tiny streams.

But all was still, and Ahilya couldn't believe that only a few minutes ago, she had been lamenting that stillness. It was so precious. The alternative was so much worse. She could *see* how much worse.

With Eskayra's help, she straightened. The architects had stopped screaming. Chaiyya was still on the forest floor, but she was sitting up, half supported by Kamala and Meena, the two non-architect nurses who had evidently revived her. Other non-architects of Eskayra's team were helping their architect comrades, but all of them looked around them at the broken jungle in deep shock and horror. Perhaps they knew how close they had come to death.

"A-Ahilya," Chaiyya said trembling. That was all she could get out before bursting into sobs.

Eskayra pulled Ahilya aside. "What happened to them?" she asked in a low voice, gesturing with her head toward the architects.

Ahilya met her gaze. "The Moment is gone."

Eskayra's eyes grew wide. She tapped at her citizen ring but it did not respond. With the Moment gone, all sungineering in Irshar was dead.

"How long will it take us to get back if we go now?" Ahilya asked.

"If we don't stop to rest at all, and with no trajection from the architects..." Eskayra considered, and Ahilya tried to make the same calculation.

It had taken them three days to find this city site, but they had meandered through the jungle, finding the path. Chaiyya had reached it in only a few hours using a trajected nest. Without architects it would take them...

"Maybe by dawn?" Eskayra said. "Or tomorrow afternoon? If we do not stop at all."

"We won't stop." Ahilya said. "Gather them all, Esk. We must go."

15

IRAVAN

He searched for her.

He had come to himself still hovering in the air above Irshar, but Iravan did not return to the Garden to check the damage there like he should have. Gathering the everpower to him like a cloak, he forced his battered body to fly back over the jungle, his heart racing with a deep, slow terror that built within him like a choked scream.

Where are you? he thought frantically. *Where are you?*

He tried to infiltrate her Etherium. If he could only sense her—if he only knew that she was alive—that she had been unhurt—

His attempt was futile. He'd never had any control in the third vision.

A sob built in his chest, hurtling out of him in turbulent breaths. His trembling hand grasped the blade of pure possibility hanging around his neck. He could not accept it. He would not believe it.

Had the destruction of the jungle hurt her somehow, when the Virohi had escaped Irshar—when he'd failed in his attempt to kill them? She had forced the situation in attempting to pull the cosmic creatures into Irshar again. He was certain the Virohi would not have bounded back into the Moment with such force, precipitating its destruction, if she had not fought him. But he did not care about any of it. All he knew was that she needed to be alive. That if this had killed her, he would go mad.

The stone blade felt sharp against his fingers. He could use it now to bring her back to him. Surely possibility could be used in such a way? He had been saving this last bit of everdust for a last secret mission—secret, even from himself, for he could not afford to acknowledge what it meant. But if Ahilya was dead, the reason to save this last everdust became moot.

Below him, the jungle was a ruined mess. Tree trunks lay haphazardly, smashed into chunks. Dust and earth ballooned everywhere, and rivers of mud cascaded like avalanches. Hills and valleys formed unnaturally, and wet earth snaked up Iravan's nose even through his air shield. At one point, he saw a whole section of the jungle cut off, leading into a massive yawning crevasse so black that he could not fathom how deep it went. It appeared as though a gigantic creature had taken a bite out of the jungle, and Iravan shivered, his eyes scanning for movement and light within the torn landscape.

Despair curdled within him. The everpower burned his skin. He saw his failure in the utter stillness of this terrible jungle where life had been erased. His power scored his own body, the shards of his air shield inflicting pain, and he felt the planet shudder as if it could feel his intention. He would bury himself, and everything else in his rage and grief. It would not be a conscious decision. It would simply… be.

Light flickered in the depths of the dark green.

Iravan blinked.

He saw them. Archeologists of Irshar, looking miniscule from up where he was, but alive, walking one behind the other in single file. Amidst them he found the shape he had been looking for. He would recognize her anywhere, the bent of her body, the soft trudge that had memory of a lilting walk. His vision sharpened and he saw her face. Ahilya—in shock, and barely conscious, but unhurt. Alive.

Iravan made to fly down, to rescue her and the rest of them, and bring them back to Irshar with the everpower if he needed to. But his vision trembled, and within his constantly cycling Etherium, another voice spoke, Agni, then Bhaskar, then Mohini, his past lives overlaying one other in an awful echo.

She is corrupted, they said, their eyes glinting silver. *She is sympathetic to the Virohi.*

Iravan struggled against the voices, but it was as if his limbs were locked. He was imprisoned within his body, staring down at the line of archeologists, his wife at the front. The group had to traverse a dangerous jungle—it could take them days to return, and they could injure themselves. They could sicken of thirst and hunger, perhaps become lost. He spun the everpower, forcing it to respond to him, but his mind blazed with pain and Iravan retched.

And he knew.

He could not save her. He could not interfere. Not when doing so was against his capital desire. His past lives were right. She had supported the Virohi. If not for her, the cosmic creatures would be destroyed. In going to her now, he would be betraying all of his lives, his very consciousness.

A howl of anger and grief escaped him—but there was no one there to hear.

Return, Nidhirv/Jeevan/Bhaskar/Mohini/Askavetra and a dozen others commanded him, their bodies blazing in silver light, their eyes glinting.

Iravan diminished against their combined strength.

And obeyed.

16

AHILYA

They moved through the jungle in a blur. Eskayra kept a brutal pace, marching without break. Ahilya trudged behind her, then moved alongside her, trying to keep her attention only on the architects who would periodically break out in sudden tears. They seemed physically fine, yet they displayed none of their earlier alacrity. Several couldn't be roused at all. Pari had to be carried on a makeshift stretcher, dragged through the forest floor. Chaiyya refused to walk, simply staring into nothing and weeping. It was only the mention of her children that made her blink and follow, her steps faltering.

Non-architects were faring no better. They had seemed to escape the fate of their architect friends, but two days into the march, Ranjeev complained of terrible headaches that brought him sinking to his knees, gasping for breath. Meena vomited all over herself, her skin breaking out in hives, and Teertha and Manogna, builders from Eskayra's team, had to be asked the same question several times before a response was forthcoming, as if they had trouble hearing.

There was enough to be troubled by. The jungle had changed, and though they took the shortest path Eskayra could map, the devastation that Ahilya's battle with Iravan had unleashed was everywhere.

Hills had arisen where once there had been none. Trees lay sunken across their path. Massive, gaping holes with water streaming down them created chasms they could not circumvent. Eskayra stopped often, consulting the paper maps she owned, muttering to herself before leading them on. Sometimes, she consulted with Ahilya, and though Ahilya tried to help, she knew it was fruitless.

The jungle was dense, and it was impossible to chart any sense of direction. Even before this destruction, Ahilya had needed the help of the Virohi to reach the city-site.

Ahilya tried to understand what had occurred. The jungle had been still, until the Moment had shattered. All this change was a result of that cataclysm. Or maybe this was the Virohi's doing? Had she brought this about by letting the cosmic creatures escape Irshar? She attempted to speak with them, hunting for them within the mirrored chambers of her Etherium, but they were no longer there. They were silent, curled into a tight ball within her heart like they were nesting within the core tree. Nothing she said to revive them made a difference. She remembered that haunting image of them that had filled her mind after Iravan's attack. Her own face, perforated and pocked, as though Iravan had attacked *her* consciousness with his bomb. Her mind swam, and for Eskayra's sake she tried to focus, but she had trouble thinking.

Eventually, Eskayra stopped consulting her. They traveled past landscapes they had not seen before, and though her friend did not say it, Ahilya knew that their earlier estimation of how soon they would return to the ashram had been a joke. Neither of them could have known the scale of devastation the battle had unleashed.

Ahilya lost track of how many hours passed. The canopy of the jungle lifted, and they moved in a surreal dimness, unable to tell whether it was day or night. No one spoke, and the architects had to all be helped with water and waste.

At one point, Eskayra tied a rope around everyone's waist, keeping them connected lest they lose an architect on the march. At another she passed around dry crackers, forcing everyone to eat. Ahilya's mouth felt like bark but she swallowed the rice biscuits that tasted like sandpaper. One foot in front of another, it was all that mattered. The landscape echoed on, trees rippling, breaks in the sunlight, twilight descending. Ahilya blinked when a light caught her eyes—dawn? How many dawns had come and gone?

Eskayra had led them over a small hill. The expeditionary team huddled together, breathing hard.

"Rages," Eskayra breathed, her voice coming out cracked. "What has happened here?"

Ahilya stared. Eskayra took her trembling hand in her own. Ahilya couldn't think, exhausted with hunger, but the longer she stared, the more the dim shapes began to make sense.

Gigantic arms and legs frozen in shadow. Curving vines that looked like monstrous tentacles. Misty shades of smoke made solid. This was Irshar, but it was starkly different to the ashram she had left. Ahilya could barely comprehend it.

When they had left Irshar all those days ago, the ashram had spanned miles in the jungle, a flowing, beautiful city, with valleys, hills, orchards, and roads constructed with care and finesse—a refuge of civilization within the alien jungle. Now the city looked like a monstrous, leviathan creature frozen in pain.

At its center stood the vriksh, but its trunk loomed so wide that it blotted out anything beyond it. When Ahilya craned her neck, she could not see the canopy. She was certain they had been walking under the vriksh for a long time before reaching the city, for it rose hundreds of meters high, the darkness of its shelter absolute.

She could almost hear it speak. If she returned to the broken Etherium, perhaps its heavy breath-like susurration would echo in her ears, mingled with the trapped cries of the Virohi. Its roots rippled out, capturing buildings between them, each tendril taller than her, creating a maze of natural pathways. The city lay nestled within the vriksh's embrace, licking its wounds.

Her fingers fumbling, Ahilya untied the rope from around her waist. Architects clustered around her, some collapsing wordlessly, others weeping in relief and horror as they noticed the city they'd returned to. Her instinct made her want to comfort them, but what could she say? Ahilya stumbled away from her expeditionary team, climbing down the hill, clambering over thick roots of the vriksh, dirt caking her palms, fibers tearing her clothes. She made for what she hoped was the direction of the council chambers, but all was dark, and the pale indigo of daylight was muted under the vriksh's deep canopy.

A few lights burned here and there, visible to Ahilya between the thick roots. From the flickering glow, she could tell it was not sungineering but a primitive fire created with pieces of wood and flint. The deeper she went toward the center, the more recognizable the structures became. She walked past one of the schools, and a group of houses that were untouched by the devastation. She came across a residence raised unnaturally in the air, the roots of the vriksh spearing it, like fingers holding up a smashed toy. All was silent and dark within. Ahilya shuddered and kept moving, her only thought to find her sister and nephews. Footsteps thudded behind her, and she noticed that the others were following her. Chaiyya's face was listless, but Eskayra looked mutinous, directing her expeditionary team to the infirmary when they came upon it.

By the time they reached the center of the plaza, only the three women remained. Ahilya paused, her eyes widening. Encrusted by deep boulders riven from the earth, the council chamber stood within the plaza, wrapped in a tangle of brown roots. Light shone through the windows fitfully, and the chamber was broken everywhere, foliage bursting through gaping holes. Still, miraculously it stood, and there was no mistaking the arched roof, which had somehow retained its shape. Followed by Eskayra and Chaiyya, Ahilya stumbled past debris and fallen walls into the chamber.

Inside it was no better. The chamber had been a long hall when they'd left, with offices for different councilors housed within it, but except for the round center table, little remained. Ash and dust lay thick in the air, and sounds of voices filtered toward Ahilya past her coughs.

She trudged further into the light. Shadows resolved into the shapes of councilors, in the middle of a conference, though the hour was early. Basav looked like he had been weeping. Airav's wheelchair seemed broken, then hastily fixed. Garima and Weira were speaking in low, tense voices, and Kiana sat with a few sungineers Ahilya didn't know.

Several chairs were unoccupied, the other councilors presumably roving through the city to see to the citizens. Ahilya heard snatches of conversation, "…healing…" "…injuries…" "…must speak with him…"

Their mutters stopped as she approached. Silently, Ahilya righted an upturned chair and sat around the lopsided remains of the round council table. Chaiyya stumbled over to Airav, who took her hand in his. She pulled up a chair too, then leaned her head on his shoulder, tears leaking from her eyes. Someone asked Ahilya a question but she did not hear. She could only stare at where the roof that had caved in like a cascading wave.

A hand emerged from the rubble and her bile rose. She forced herself to remember it was just the cosmic creatures' attempt at escape. That hand did not belong to a citizen, trapped in the architecture. She had stopped the destruction. She had saved humanity *and* the cosmic creatures. Right?

She could not fool herself. The damage to the ashram was as bad as in an earthrage. If her war with Iravan had levelled the jungle and created whole hills, it was a miracle Irshar had survived. Yet how many had died? Was Tariya all right? Were Arth and Kush? She wanted to ask about her sister, and about the rest of Irshar, but she was so tired. With a trembling hand, she reached for the bowl of nuts that was usually kept on the table, but of course, this time there was nothing here. Her stomach growled, her mind blurring.

"Ahilya-ve?" Airav said.

She blinked.

They were all looking at her. Someone had spoken.

"We asked what happened," Airav said, not unkindly.

Ahilya tried to clear her head. "My sister," she rasped. "My family."

"They are all right, Ahilya-ve," Airav said. "By some miracle, they were unhurt though their neighbors were not so lucky."

There was no accusation on his face, but the words hit Ahilya like a slap regardless. She knew it was not a miracle that Tariya and the boys had survived. The vriksh was encoded to Ahilya. It must have kept her sister safe because of Ahilya's desire for her family's safety. A part of her had *known* Tariya was all right, before Airav had confirmed it. This was exactly why so many of Nakshar's citizens had survived—because of her buried intention.

But other citizens from other airborne ashrams… Ahilya's mind conjured an image of a thousand airborne ashrams that had once existed. Inkrist, Carran, Erast—these had been cities that had once floated in different bands to Nakshar and her sister ashrams. But Iravan and Ahilya's consideration had extended only to the Conclave, and in the end only the Conclave had survived. Now, of the Conclave… perhaps only citizens of Nakshar had survived, because in the end, that is where Ahilya's memories lay. The bodies were undoubtedly cleared away in the days since the battle, but death had overtaken the rest of them once more. Ahilya had thought herself capable of extending compassion and care even to the Virohi who were so alien, but she had failed them all. She felt smothered by her shame. She could not hold Airav's gaze. *What have I done?* She thought. *What have I become?*

Airav leaned forward. "Ahilya-ve, will you tell us what happened in the jungle?"

Ahilya tried. Slowly, her voice hoarse, she explained what she had experienced with the cosmic creatures, the visions they had shown her, how she had failed in her desire and then fought with Iravan in a cosmic tug of war.

"The Moment—" she said.

The architects in the room flinched, but her eyes were for Basav, the seniormost of them all.

"I can still see it," he said, and his skin flickered blue-green. "It is shattered. I can float in it, but all the stars are broken, and several of them are g-gone." He paused, his mouth trembling. "I-it is as though glass has fractured, and I remain with the splinters. The only possibilities that are intact belong to the Garden, but it is only a matter of time before those crumble too." His eyes filled with tears, and he pinched the bridge of his nose. "Trajection is over. This is what one Ecstatic's capital desire has wrought. Him and you—you stupid, selfish girl."

Ahilya recoiled, and despite her grief Chaiyya flinched too, casting a disturbed look at Basav. By common understanding everyone had been polite to Ahilya—they'd had to be, she held their fates in the palm of her hand—but with the Moment gone, Basav's last reserve had broken.

She wanted to defend herself. But how could she? A voice, her own, whispered in her head, *You wanted this.* When she had been a naïve, lonely archeologist, she had looked for a different way of survival. She had thought that survival without trajection would allow for everyone to be equal. Now her desires had come true, yet humanity still only existed at the brink of survival.

"Perhaps it can be repaired," she said helplessly. "If it isn't completely gone—if you can still see it and feel it."

"Not by us," Basav replied, wiping his eyes. He took a deep breath, then another, clearly fighting for control, and it was clear from the nods of the others that they'd already spoken of this. "Only an immensely powerful Ecstatic Architect, could do it. One who was united with their yaksha counterpart. And it would have to be their deepest capital desire, one they could pour their whole will into."

"So, Iravan then," she said.

Who else was there? Irshar had only one Ecstatic Architect—Chaiyya. All the others had sworn to Iravan. And Chaiyya had not found her yaksha yet. As far as Ahilya knew, no one else except Iravan had managed that.

"Does it need to be repaired?" Eskayra spoke.

All of them turned to the doorway where Eskayra stood, leaning against the frame, her arms crossed over her chest. Ahilya had forgotten that her friend had followed her, but Eskayra gave her a small smile and walked over to stand next to her.

Ahilya expected Basav to tell Eskayra to get out, or to demand to know what she was doing here—she was no part of the council—but he knew her power and popularity.

"I beg your pardon?" he asked.

"The Moment," Eskayra repeated pointedly. "Does it need to be repaired at all? It is only an architect's reality. It has always been invisible and inaccessible to us complete beings. Why must we waste time repairing it?"

"The Moment is our most sacred place," Basav said coldly. "Without it, we cannot traject. We cannot do anything at all. With it gone, architects have no purpose."

"Yes, the *architects*." Eskayra sneered. "But there are more of us than there are you, and *we* have purpose. We can help you redefine who you are."

"We know many architects follow you, but—"

"Isn't that what we're doing here?" Eskayra demanded of the room at large, turning away from Basav. "The cities we are trying to build, the future we are hoping to have—I thought we all agreed that, unlike flying ashrams, we were finally going to make something that was not dependent on trajection. That trajection was weak and dying and unsustainable. Believe me, it gives me no pleasure in defending *him*, but that man in his Garden has done us a favor. He has taken away the temptation to keep using this power. Or has everything just been lip service for you people?"

The chamber erupted into cries and snarls. Ahilya's head began to pound. She needed to eat. She could not take another altercation.

"What Iravan-ve has done is an abomination—" Basav said, rising out of his chair, tears still glittering in his eyes.

"The Moment was sacrosanct," Weira said.

"—you would not understand, a non-architect—"

"—a place to see consciousness—"

But Eskayra remained unperturbed and contemptuous. Watching her, Ahilya felt a kinship. Her friend's words and attitude were not far from what she herself would have said, once upon a time.

"The power was already dying," Eskayra said, interrupting the cacophony. "But now our sungineers can actually try to invent something new. You cannot see it now, because you have lost something precious, but this is an opportunity. Is that not right, Kiana?"

The once-Senior Sungineer of Nakshar blinked, her mouth thinning. "That puts a lot of pressure on the sungineers, Eskayra. We are struggling, especially after everything that has happened in the last few days."

"Yes, but now with Irshar finally safe—"

"Irshar is not safe," Basav began.

"Ahilya said the cosmic creatures have been removed from Irshar's architecture," Eskayra countered. "It will no longer morph arbitrarily. Wasn't that the whole reason we were looking to make cities? But we no longer have that threat to Irshar, to *humanity*. We need to recover, certainly, and this grotesquerie is a reminder of what we have endured, but our city doesn't need to be pretty. It needs to be functional, and we can stay here for years, for decades, while our sungineering evolves and finds a way, before we need to make new cities. My team will no longer have to work with the pressure of survival breathing down their necks. And Ahilya will not have to fight the Virohi to make them stay within the city."

"Do you think yourself so unaffected?" Basav sneered. "I cannot speak for your builders but *complete beings* in the ashram have fared no better than architects after this calamity. Many have experienced debilitating migraines, others have difficulty breathing, and still others have such trouble with their vision that they cannot see their hand in front of their faces. It is all the result of the Moment breaking, and the infirmary is full, with no real help available because everyone suffers to some degree. The only reason we here have escaped it is because of our training through the years to manage disaster." He gestured with a head toward where Kiana sat. "Ask her how she feels. It is her store of medicines that keeps her functioning now."

Eskayra glanced at Kiana, but then her eyes flashed to Ahilya, as if looking for a way to dispute Basav. Both of them could remember the journey back to the ashram, and how non-architects had fared.

Ahilya stayed silent. Perhaps in a different time, before Oam's death, before her councillorship in Nakshar, she could have supported Eskayra. But she had seen the similarity of different identities too closely. Her allegiance, such as it was, no longer encompassed only non-architects. *This is why we could never have been together,* she thought. *We are too similar.* Iravan, with his architect sensibilities had been an opposite, completing Ahilya in ways Esk couldn't.

Eskayra's face registered mild disappointment. "These effects on non-architects are sure to dissipate," she muttered. "Even if the Moment's destruction affected them, Kiana—and *I*—are proof that we will recover. Distribute the medicines, and after recovery, the rest of us complete beings will build something anew for all of us."

"And what happens when the medicines run out?" Basav replied scornfully. "We have been dependent on trajection for more than a thousand years. Landing in the jungle has not changed that. How will we make medicines if we cannot traject the few seeds we have left from the crash? Where will we get food? We have terrible injuries among us, which we cannot heal without trajection. We will starve before the year is over, if we aren't all wiped out by disease. Without the Moment, we have no technology, and while I applaud your dream for the sungineers, they have not been able to invent an alternative to trajection when we had all our resources and were flying in the skies. Now when we have nothing?" He shook his head, and his gaze took them all in. "We are dead people walking. These two have doomed us."

Another silence greeted his words, this one heavier. Eskayra opened her mouth to argue, then closed it, frowning. Kiana stirred, and one of the other sungineers made to speak, but Ahilya noticed Kiana's imperceptible shake of the head.

Eskayra was speaking thoughts she herself had thought once upon a time, the very thing she still thought in her heart of hearts, but to hear from Basav how impossible the dream had been…

"So, once again, our only solution is to change his mind?" Eskayra said, making a disgusted sound in her throat. "We make ourselves hostage to his whims again? Haven't we learned anything? We've sent emissaries to the Garden, and invited him to treat with us. We asked for his sungineers. What has any of that achieved? He told us he will refuse to help us build anything as long as we harbor the Virohi, and whether in the vriksh or in the architecture, the Virohi are still here among us. He is not going to help us—if he were going to, he would be here already. He is probably out there celebrating the Moment shattering."

Was he? Ahilya thought. His shock still rippled in her. Whatever else he had meant to do, Iravan had not wanted to destroy the Moment. But Eskayra was not wrong, and Basav was nodding too.

"You should have let Iravan-ve destroy them," he said, his eyes flat on Ahilya. "You have been trying to save that man, but there is nothing left of him to save. He has long since died and now you have doomed us all with your desperate desire to retrieve your husband."

Ahilya's shame caught in her throat like a sharp bone. She could say nothing to refute him.

Basav had never seen Iravan as a man, only known him as an

Ecstatic, a monster, a rabid creature that had to be feared, controlled and eventually, put down. But as her eyes moved over the rest of the council, Chaiyya, Airav and Kiana averted their gazes too. Eskayra frowned as though unsure what to think, and Weira and Garima looked disturbed. All of them agreed with Basav's estimation to some degree. She should have forsaken Iravan.

In her guilt and shame, she had seen all of their points of view, even agreed with them, but it hit her now how separate she and Iravan had always been. Why it had been fine for them to let her suffer alone with the weight of the cosmic creatures, and sacrifice Iravan. For all that she and her husband had been trying to save everyone, their own destruction had always been acceptable, because that was the easiest and the best solution.

Her mind spun, and she saw Iravan on one side, her on the other—except the image shifted and they stood together, the world opposing them. She did not know if this was her thought or another corruption of the Virohi. The cosmic creatures had been trapped by the vriksh, but they were still a part of her as much as she was of them. They had given too much of themselves to each other. Eskayra looked at her with concern, reaching over a hand, but Ahilya pulled away. The other woman flinched, hurt on her face.

Eskayra turned back to the councilors. "How long until we run out of resources?"

"We're still assessing," Kiana replied, shuffling some papers in front of her. "Sungineering is dead though, so it will take time to know the full effects of this."

"Nothing we do will make a difference," Basav said. "Only they can do something." He gestured limply between Ahilya and toward the Garden, to where Iravan was.

Eskayra glanced at Ahilya, but her words were for the room. "If we tell him all this, will he help?"

"Will he?" Airav said skeptically. "He wants to destroy the Virohi, and an Ecstatic Architect's capital desire cannot be changed this easily. You said it yourself—he hasn't helped us though we are the last survivors of humanity. He wants to make amends but he wants to make it on his terms. I don't believe that Iravan can *breathe* anymore, unless it is in service to his capital desire. It controls him now, more than he knows."

A wave of loneliness washed over Ahilya. She had never felt so far away and so close to her husband before. Wasn't this exactly how she felt about the cosmic creatures, and why she couldn't trust herself? "The Virohi aren't a threat anymore," she mumbled. "Attacking them now would be akin to attacking innocents."

"They broke planets once. They are not blameless. The way you talk of them..." Basav turned away, disgust all over his face.

His revulsion poured off him in waves, and for an instant, Ahilya could see how abhorrent it was for him to work with her. That he had not defected to the Garden was a miracle—but then again, what was his choice? She and Iravan had taken it away from all these people. Either her folly or Iravan's; either this perverted form of an ashram or the company of Ecstatics. Those were the only options left to humanity's survivors.

She saw this realization on everyone's faces in a way she had not seen before. No wonder they wished for new cities so desperately. Not just for humanity to endure, but for all of them to no longer be prisoner to two tyrants. It would be best for them if Iravan and Ahilya were dead, but that freedom was not theirs either.

Something within her broke at this realization. How terrible it must be to be trapped within someone else's delusion. She sympathized with them. She *was* them, caught in her mind and that of the Virohi. Was Basav wrong at all?

"Speak plainly," she said softly, her gaze roving over the others.

"You want me to extract the Virohi from the tree, don't you? You want me to turn them over to him. Let him commit genocide, now when it is not necessary anymore. Is that it?"

"It would prove your allegiance," Basav said softly, his eyes glittering in the candlelight. "And your sanity."

None of the others refuted him, but Ahilya saw her desperation reflected in them. These were architects. They had grown up revering life and consciousness—all life and consciousness. In their hidden histories, architects had only stopped the Virohi from breaking the world. What Iravan was planning was beyond anything anyone had ever done.

Chaiyya trembled—she who had always been the healer, who despite her call to allow genocide of the creatures knew how wrong it was. Kiana's mouth was pursed—the sungineer who had been the only one so long ago to question the ethics of draining a yaksha for its Ecstatic energy, when Nakshar stood on the brink of destruction.

But what place did ethics have when they were contemplating the end of everything? What place did morals? The two women avoided Ahilya's eyes. Only Eskayra watched her impassively, and her voice echoed in Ahilya's ears. *Would it be so bad?*

Abruptly, Ahilya stood up. She swayed on her feet, but her hands clutched the table. "If this is what the ashram needs," she said tightly, "then I will speak with Iravan."

Eskayra moved closer. "Now? Ahilya, you're exhausted."

"You heard what Basav said. We have no time. I'm going to the Garden."

"Then I will come with you."

"No." Ahilya tried to make her voice gentle, but it cracked under the strain. "You heard Basav. This is between me and Iravan. It is not war he wants, nor destroying the Virohi. I know what he is after and I will give it to him."

"And what is that, Ahilya-ve?" Airav asked warily.

The chamber swam in front of her eyes, the broken promises, the phantom emotions, the heartbreaking echo of Iravan's voice, asking her to let him go.

Ahilya gritted her teeth.

"Erasure."

17

IRAVAN

The bodies were shrouded in black.

The Junior Ecstatic, Shayla, uncovered them one by one, and Iravan gazed upon the faces of the architects who had been in the Deepness with him, his first line of defense, the ones who had needed his protection the most.

Shobha had been from Auresh, with such a quick wit that it had made Iravan chuckle. Aachal had been serious, one of the first to come to Irshar; they had come to Iravan's aid long ago when he had fought the falcon-yaksha in Nakshar's sanctum. Uma had been one of the most promising Ecstatics he had ever worked with; she had discovered the method to combine and tighten Ecstatics' bonds that had been instrumental in the recent battle.

Iravan forced himself to remember the architects for who they had been, not the mere bodies they were now.

"We are still assessing casualties," Shayla said softly. "There might be more dead."

Next to Iravan, Dhruv shifted on his feet and adjusted his glasses. His face was grim.

The Senior Ecstatics following Iravan exchanged uncomfortable glances. The original four—Pranav, Trisha, Darsh, and Reyla—said nothing, but Kamal, Nagesh, and Mukthi muttered nonsensical words of sympathy and despair.

They were the most skilled in Ecstasy. Their loyalty was unquestioned; they had come to Iravan first and stayed with him through the last few months of upheaval. They had been his generals, and commanded the power of the other Ecstatics to feed it to him. Other Senior Ecstatics, Jyaishna, Theria, Vineet, had trained with Iravan only after landing, but these ones he had known when Nakshar was in the skies.

He could feel their confusion now. How could this have happened? They had followed his commands. Iravan-ve knew what he was doing. Didn't he?

These trusted architects of his retinue were little more than children. Darsh and Reyla *were* children at fifteen and ten. The only one who had ever been in a true position of power was Manav, once a Senior Architect of Nakshar. The man stood with them now, his eyes vacant, staring into the distance, his fingers playing with the edges of his kurta.

All of them had accompanied Iravan to the medical ward of the Garden. Iravan's home had escaped the physical devastation of the battle with the Virohi. Compared to what Iravan had seen of the ashram from the skies, it was almost obscene how untouched the Garden was.

Keeping true to the design of the Garden, the medical ward was built like an enclosed terrace, with several wild copses growing in clusters, benches rising out of fragrant wood, and streams running haphazardly through the growth. Healbranch grew in profusion, along with mediweed and yararoot and amelaus. Individual chambers were partitioned with trellises, but the effect was still of a wild forest made partially tame.

It was nothing like a sanctum, yet it reminded Iravan of an ashram—neither Nakshar nor Yeikshar, the two ashrams he had lived in, but of Uparesh, a skyborne city that had long been subsumed more than a hundred years ago. An image flashed in his head, laughing with his friends as he performed shift-duty in Uparesh's sanctum, while he tended the plants with his bare hands, a practice long gone out of fashion, but one that had persisted in Bhaskar's time. The Garden had taken shape out of Iravan's memory, except it wasn't truly his memory, but one belonging to his past life. He shook the memory away.

Shobha, Aachal, and Uma had been popular. They had been teaching the others. They had been part of this fledgling community that the Garden was building. Mutters and whispers came to him like a breeze through the leaves. The chamber was full of architects who were in the battle with him, and those who came to pay respect to the dead. All of them sounded disgruntled, and quietly frightened.

Hostility reverberated through the gathering, and Iravan slouched, the way Bhaskar would when trying to hide his overly tall frame; he shifted into Mohini's frown, his face scrunching. With an effort, he banished his past lives.

"The Ecstatics were arranged to fight in the same chamber," he said. "What do you mean there might be more? How do you not know who is dead, and who is not?"

Shayla fidgeted nervously. "Aachal succumbed to their injuries only a few minutes ago. They seemed fine, but then death took them. I believe it was delayed shock, Iravan-ve. The shock of whatever happened."

The shock of the shattering Moment, Iravan thought.

Or perhaps they had finally seen, finally felt, the cosmic creatures.

Had they all seen what they were up against? The battle was confused in his mind. Iravan could not remember if the Ecstatics had disappeared from the Deepness before or after the Virohi had attacked. The Virohi's consciousness no longer blinked in the Moment attempting to anchor, as if Ahilya had taken them from the broken realm and restored them fully by wrapping them in Irshar's core tree. But even if the Ecstatics did not see the Virohi in their second vision, they must have seen the creatures in their first vision. A feeling of wretchedness climbed over him, terror and amazement in equal parts, making his palms sweat.

He could not fully remember what had happened, only that Ahilya had somehow intervened and the cosmic creatures had retreated to where he could not follow. If he could only feel them in the Moment again, perhaps he could find a way to destroy them, but how was he to fulfill his capital desire now? It burned in him. He could almost feel it sloughing off of his flesh, as if by taking stock now he was only delaying acting against the creatures. Had Ahilya made it back to the ashram safely? His feet fidgeted, wanting to go to Irshar, but though he thought it, his body froze, reading his intent.

Ahilya's survival meant little to his capital desire. To his past lives, she was the clear enemy—not only one who had thwarted his attempt to wreak vengeance on the Virohi at every turn, but one who had taken the Virohi to a refuge he could not follow at all. He tried battling his body, tried to make it swerve toward Irshar to check on his wife, but he knew that unless his actions served the destruction of Virohi, he could not act at all—not without fighting the will of the many inside him. And the flight over the jungle, searching for her, had already shown him how difficult that was. He had not been able to rescue her then. He would not be able to reach for her now.

Iravan stared at the dead laid in front of him. His body was not the only one which was failing to follow a command. Ecstatics healed, that much was known. How much damage had these three sustained that their bodies had not instantly recovered? These limits he pushed himself and the others beyond… how would he be able to conquer them? *We deserve to be punished,* Bhaskar whispered. *We need to make amends.*

"May you be reborn in better times," he murmured. "May your desire be pure and just, and may you fulfill it to make amends."

He willed it, and flowers bloomed on the grass. He picked up the three lush wreaths, placing one on each architect's body. The flowers would remain fresh for days, he had used the everpower. This much at least he could do, before his desire waned.

Iravan looked up to see the mutters had stopped. An uncomfortable silence lingered, a dozen pairs of eyes on him. He met their gazes levelly.

He had added to the traditional epitaph with his wish for amends. Iravan had been blatant with his desire; these were Ecstatics he was dealing with, not mere architects. Once, he had been more discreet with his agenda, but those had been the games of a Senior Architect. Such a thing wasn't necessary with Ecstatics.

Ecstasy was brute force, not a delicate maneuvering of constellation lines like trajection. The power changed the people using it. The everpower had changed him too: he had become more single-minded. But the falcon screamed in his head, and Mohini laughed, a tinkling sound, and Iravan grimaced, an action made by Nidhirv in the twist of his mouth, and thought, *Can I really be single-minded when I have so many minds inside me?*

"They have—*had*—family in Irshar," Shayla said.

"Inform them of this," Iravan replied. "These three were Ecstatics of the Garden. They will be returned to the earth here. But their families can say goodbye and find closure for their grief."

Shayla nodded and covered the bodies again.

"We have not communicated with the ashram yet," Dhruv pointed out softly. "They will ask for aid. What is your decision regarding that?"

Iravan did not like this line of questioning. He knew he needed to send resources to Irshar—everything he did here in the Garden was to make amends to the complete beings of the ashram, and already so many had died there,

But he could feel the resistance the Ecstatics had to being answerable to the ashram they had escaped, especially when their own lay injured and dead. Iravan could not allow them to think that they were above the non-architects. If anything, he needed them to be subservient to the complete beings. He had not opened communication with the ashram before because he did not know how much the Virohi had infected the citizens through the architecture, but though that was no longer the concern, he had done nothing yet. Matters were shaky in the Garden. He had to find a politic way to help Irshar.

Without answering Dhruv, Iravan stepped away from the bodies and exited the medical ward, taking one of the many pathways that led around the Garden. Dhruv and some of the others followed him back to the main hall without a word.

Outside the ward, it was more obvious how the Garden had escaped the battle. Iravan had arrived to see that, apart from sungineering blinking out, the rest of the Garden functioned much like before, with hallways lined with plumeria-lined bushes and residences rising beyond the central courtyard. A massive central tower rose above the courtyard, standing on long tree-trunks and spearing into the sky. Iravan lived there alone, in his quarters on the topmost level away from the others, though one chamber in the tower was carved for Manav. From his vantage point earlier, he had seen the vriksh's assault on the ashram, but the core tree did not encroach his space, though its canopy sheltered part of the Garden.

Perhaps the tree knew it was not welcome here. Unlike the ashram, the Garden had been built with Ecstasy, and Iravan had examined the shattered Moment, seen the stars of the Garden almost indecently untouched, while other possibilities crashed and crumbled. It was what he had been busy with, bolstering the Garden's possibilities with everpower, while Dhruv undertook the Garden's administration.

The Garden still bloomed, trees and hedges intact, and pathways crisscrossed like trails in a forest, some leading to the main attendance hall, others to the solar lab and the practice yard. It was a matter of time before those broke too, but for now, glowglobes glittered, hidden like stars among the foliage, whirrs and hums coming to him from behind dark passageways as sungineering began again, as if the calamity was but a small interruption.

Dhruv gestured at the glowglobes. "We'll need to build more medprobes. Those were destroyed in the explosion. We will have to divert from other inventions to do so."

Iravan nodded but did not comment. Sungineering was Dhruv's affair, as the Garden's Senior Sungineer. Everything related to the technology went through him, and Iravan did not need to know the details. It was enough that things worked. After the battle, Iravan thought he had broken sungineering—and had scared him more than anything else—but on his return, he put his reserve Ecstatics to work and the devices had begun again. Now, Ecstatic Architects were in the solar lab, powering the Garden in a delicate, devious trajection.

The sungineers had come a long way in the last three months. Much had been damaged in the Conclave's crash to the jungle, and the Garden's sungineers had built all this with the materials Iravan had provided. Now the Garden flourished with the technology enough to rival any ashram of the sky.

He had been right to place his faith in them, in understanding that they were the future of humanity. Especially now with the Moment gone, the Moment *gone*—and a part of him gibbered in shock at that—with trajection effectively dead, there was no other way forward except sungineering. Everything in the Garden used Ecstatic energy, built on the model of an energex. It was something Irshar would never have.

Iravan picked up his pace, heading for the main hall.

Dhruv fell in beside him.

The sungineer's voice dropped. "The battery is long gone. We do not have the materials to make another one. We could trade with Irshar, but I don't know if their battery has survived."

"It doesn't matter," Iravan said. "We will need to think of another way."

His plan had been dependent on the Virohi's unfamiliarity and distaste for the Deepness, and the bomb's all-consuming power. He had searched for the Virohi's stars and trained himself to lure them into the Deepness, and it had taken the better part of three months simply to make that plan. With the Virohi embedded in Irshar, Iravan had known it was only a matter of time before Ahilya's will failed. But now that they were in the vriksh… he could not even see them in the broken universe. They were out of his reach completely.

The tree would hold them far longer than the city could have, years upon years perhaps, outliving Ahilya. Iravan saw the way the tree expanded. He saw the roots plunging into the earth. The Virohi were safe, and he could not touch them. Could he perhaps train his Ecstatics in a way that their capital desires manifested as hate for the Virohi too? Perhaps they would find a way he could not.

It was a risky thought. He was already conditioning them to make amends, but if he changed that toward war, who knew how each architect would interpret it. War—despite the fact that he was pursuing it—would be disastrous if each Ecstatic desired it from the depths of their consciousness. Ahilya had told him about the bloodshed Ecstatics had once unleashed, when humanity had barely crawled back from the brink of extinction. Iravan had no memory of that time—perhaps his consciousness had been reborn after the war, his two lives falling on either side of the event, but he could well imagine it. With such hate, Ecstatics could break the world. There would be nothing remaining to make amends to.

The lack of answers frustrated him. Apart from not knowing a part of his own Ecstatic history, a part that could have helped him in his pursuit now in conditioning and taming the Ecstatics, it irked him that he did not know what happened to Ecstatics who had died in that war, their capital desires unfulfilled. Iravan had told Darsh that fulfilled Ecstatics, after achieving their capital desires, would return to the Virohi form in some way. What he hadn't shared was how he feared unfulfilled Ecstatics returned to such a state too. In their last life, what else would happen to their consciousness? If this were true, he was doomed no matter what he did. *I cannot go back to that,* he thought. *Never again to become something so filthy.* All his knowledge, he could barely believe that he would still need to rely on obscure architect histories to tell him more.

Either that, he thought, *or the skills of an archeologist.*

Dhruv seemed to be following the same train of thought.

The sungineer's voice dropped further. "Did you find any yakshas in the jungle?"

Iravan did not reply.

He had not looked this time. He had wasted his time building and destroying a home that he would never have with Ahilya.

And if he found the yakshas—what then? In conditioning the Ecstatics, he was already skirting the edge of morality to ensure they did not damage Irshar. Iravan himself was a prisoner to his capital desire, and he had once been a Senior Architect, with a Senior Architect's discipline. How would these children react when their capital desires manifested? War aside, it would be calamitous for the world if there were united Ecstatics running amok, each with their capital desire building for lifetimes, ready to be released without any rationale or control. A race of super beings beholden to no law, no power, no ethics… He shuddered, contemplating it. Such a reality could not be allowed to happen. He had to control it.

His strides grew longer, fueled by his nervous energy. Dhruv glanced at him but said nothing, matching his pace. Behind them, the others hurried too, a retinue of the most powerful Ecstatics.

They entered the main hall, and it flickered in front of Iravan's eyes, to appear as it had been when he had first made it. He could almost reach out and touch the memory: Ahilya sitting next to him on the stairs where now there was a heavy highbacked chair with carved armrests; a tapestry of dark damaged jasmine leaves draped on the wall, walkways sluiced with water where now a courtyard served as an assembly place for the Garden.

The architecture was different from only a few months before, but the ghost of the original design still lingered under the modifications, ready to become apparent if only it were acknowledged. Where Ecstatics would have loitered, either discussing plans for the battle, or comparing methods for supertrajection, they were now busy with repairing the architecture. Iravan and his retinue walked past torn earth, and upturned grass, to the chair on the platform.

Eschewing the chair, which he reserved for more formal audiences, Iravan took a seat on the stairs, and the others joined him. Darsh picked at the grass by his feet, his face expressionless. Trisha and

Pranav exchanged one of their usual glances, laden with meaning and friendship. Reyla placed herself down serenely, saying nothing. Kamal, Nagesh, and Mukthi sat haphazardly around, taking seats where they could.

Dhruv alone chose to remain standing. The sungineer glanced at Manav, who had begun to wander, then raised his eyebrows at Iravan.

"Ahilya has trapped the Virohi in the vriksh," Iravan began tiredly. "Anything I attempt to do to the Virohi now would damage the vriksh, and the core tree is a part of Irshar. I cannot perform such a direct act of war against the ashram. It will defeat any purpose of making amends to the complete ones. I'm open to suggestions."

It was what had stopped him from initiating war with the Virohi until now. Iravan's fist thumped on his knee, an action from Bhaskar within him. He regained control and smoothed his hand out, slowly, deliberately.

"You changed the permissions of the trees once," Kamal said. "Couldn't you do it again with everpower?"

Iravan had not tried to meddle with the vriksh using the everpower. The vriksh was an amalgamation of all the core trees of the landed Conclave, and when he had changed the permissions of the core trees before, he had done it using Ecstasy.

Even then, it had been tricky. He recalled laying back in a bed next to a sleeping Ahilya, while she recovered from losing their child. His grief and pain were still fresh, and inside him the falcon howled in agony. Iravan had changed the permissions of the core trees in his fury and vengeance, but had not expected the vriksh to form. What might the everpower do to Irshar if he meddled again? What if he accidentally destroyed the tree altogether? Now when it was rooted so deeply into the planet, such a thing could be calamitous. The truth was he did not know the limits and consequences of his power, and a part of him shirked from attempting too much.

"It's a possibility," he began—but then paused, raising his head.

A commotion emerged from the corridor. There were no raised voices, no shouts, but strains of consternation, questions, and dismay.

The architects around him began to glow without being told. None of them were trajecting Ecstatically yet but somehow, to Iravan's surprise, the architecture began to change. The grass grew lusher, the damage to the slender trees knitting. Along the walls, the dark leaves changed, almost as though it were a veristem garden blooming into a lie, except instead of those flowers, the walls bloomed with intoxicating jasmines.

Ahilya, Iravan thought.

His heart skipped a beat.

He had expected her to come.

He was surprised it had taken her so long.

How had she fared? Was she hurt? He had wanted to find out, but each time he had tried, Bhaskar or Agni or the falcon had gripped his mind until the intention passed. It meant something—this control of them over him, unto making his very body still. His past lives were telling him he could not succumb to the temptation of her material bond. Still, relief bloomed in him. She had come. She was all right. His hands shook with how much he had needed to know this.

Wearily, Iravan rose from the staircase and approached his chair. Though he did not command it, though he barely desired it, the rest of his council took their places as well. Dhruv stood by his right shoulder, crossing and uncrossing his arms nervously. The others arrayed themselves on Iravan's left, their gazes watchful. Reyla and Darsh guided Manav to stand by them, and the excised architect met Iravan's eyes, his stare startlingly astute for one second.

Black-uniformed Ecstatics began to pour into the hall, taking up room around the chamber. Nearly a thousand architects found their place, muttering and murmuring, filling up the space in a few minutes. A ripple of movement occurred between them and a lone figure strode in, her head held high, eyes trained forward, straight toward Iravan.

Ahilya had clearly just arrived from the jungle, despite the days that had passed since the battle. She no longer wore her expeditionary equipment, but she was dressed in a plain kurta, severely muddied and crumpled. Her hair was in disarray, curls falling loosely around her shoulders, dark eyes proud and angry. She looked tired, and determined, and utterly glorious.

Iravan stirred, his fingers dancing, an action from Mohini. He wanted badly to meet Ahilya halfway, to submit to her, to kiss her, be kissed by her, but she walked through the gathering Ecstatics with deep disdain.

Iravan flexed his hand, trying to stay present.

"Ahilya," he said, his voice carrying. "Welcome."

She stopped in front of him.

Her gaze took in all of them, his council behind him, the muttering Ecstatics, the sungineers peppered here and there, the glass of their instruments glinting in the phosphorescence. Her eyes passed over the glowglobes, and her lips thinned.

Then she stared directly at Iravan.

He returned her look unflinchingly.

With a wave of his hand, Iravan drew her a chair next to him, the same one he had trajected when she had last visited him in the Garden. That time, he had only just subsumed the falcon-yaksha. The two of them had been alone, and the Moment had been unbroken. His trajection now was a waste of resources, taxing an already shattered Moment, but he would be damned if he treated her like an enemy. He could not afford to disdain Ahilya, not if he wanted them *all* to make amends. The rage grew in him suddenly, at how little he had achieved, at how little time he had. The falcon roared, and Agni shrieked, and Iravan clenched his teeth and tamped them all down.

Ahilya did not take the seat.

"You owe me a debt," she said, stonily.

The chamber grew silent, each person listening intently now that she had spoken.

Iravan sat down, and the chair he had created for her dissolved. "You have suffered," he said quietly. "Irshar needs help. This I already know."

"Do not mistake me for a petitioner, Iravan. I am here to claim what is rightfully mine, what is rightfully ours in Irshar."

"And what is that?"

"Our place in this world the way we see it, not the way you do with your desire for amends."

The silence in the chamber grew tenser, a tautness to it like a vine stretched tight ready to snap.

Iravan felt Dhruv stir behind him.

Anger simmered within him, that Ahilya took no responsibility for her part in it, but he kept it contained. Whatever transpired in this conversation would affect the Ecstatics. He needed to sway them toward his capital desire, but he couldn't afford to look weak, not when he had caused the death of their comrades and presented no yakshas to them.

"Your war with the Virohi has damaged Irshar," Ahilya said. "Listen well to me, Iravan, for my demands are clear. You will help us remake the ashram. You will send your Ecstatics to help us with our designs, to repair our architecture, to grow food and medicines—and not just until Irshar comes back to where it was, but until *I* determine their service is over. You will do this not merely for Irshar, but for all the cities in the jungle that we are building. You will see this done, and done again, now and for the rest of your years. You will enter into a binding contract with me, as strong as an unbreakable healbranch vow, Iravan, and you will find a way to enforce it."

There was another silence, a breath taken in and held.

Behind his veil of inscrutability, Iravan felt a rush of relief, relaxing his shoulders.

This was shockingly perfect. Ahilya had given him an easy way to mold the desires of the Ecstatics toward making reparations to the complete ones. Still, he leaned back and steepled his fingers.

"Is that all?" he asked, injecting irony into his voice. "You exact a heavy price."

"I am not done," she snapped. "You will also send your sungineers to make our equipment work, to help with our inventions, and to make us independent of you and the Garden. This, you owe us."

Dhruv shifted behind Iravan, and he imagined the sungineer open his mouth to speak, but Iravan raised his hand and Dhruv subsided.

Iravan knew what his objection was going to be.

All the architects of the Garden were Ecstatics now, even if they had not come to him so. Iravan had wrenched them into the Deepness through the Conduit in an unnatural awakening. Ecstatics usually supertrajected into the Moment, but the devices of the Garden were working because Iravan had taught his most reliable architects to traject into a dark, velvety Deepness the way the falcon had once shown him.

They were trajecting into other worlds though none of them could see those other worlds. Such knowledge was potentially disastrous. It was what the cosmic creatures had done—affecting worlds that were not theirs. Iravan still did not fully know the effect of such a trajection, and only the most critical sungineering was being powered right now.

Ahilya was right in that he owed her a debt. But giving her this would take a heavy toll, one he still could not calculate.

"Anything else?" he asked.

Ahilya bolstered herself visibly, and her eyes bored into his. "You will repair the Moment," she said, and at that, Iravan finally exhaled.

There it was.

Her real demand.

He met her gaze. "No."

"You *will* repair the Moment, Iravan," Ahilya said furiously, taking a step forward. "And you will do so personally. No one else has that power, and it was your capital desire that wrought this."

"Why would I want to?" he asked. "Why would you want me to? Do you, of all people, want the world to be dependent on trajection again?"

"You don't need to know my reasons. You will need to see this done. You owe me this. I saved you from the cosmic creatures."

For a second, Iravan did not say anything. The hall was so quiet that he might have been able to hear a leaf growing.

"And what about what you owe me?" he asked quietly at last.

She had been prepared for the question, he saw. Ahilya's jaw tightened, and she said, "Make your demands."

"You know my demands," he answered. "All architects belong to the Garden. We will help you remake your ashram, we'll even help you make your jungle cities. You have no need for architects—you have nothing to traject anymore. They belong with me."

"No," Ahilya said, crossing her arms. "I told you I will not force anyone to leave Irshar just so you can fulfill your mission to destroy them. I will not separate families."

"Then we have no bargain."

"What if I offer you something else in return?"

"This is what I want—"

"The Virohi," she said. "Access to them."

And Iravan paused.

Color heightened Ahilya's cheeks. Her fingers crept to hold herself closer.

For the first time since she had come to the Garden, her lips trembled in uncertainty. She was afraid of what he wanted to do to the Virohi. Because of how she saw them as herself? It terrified him, what she had become, and how she could still remain the same.

Iravan pressed his hands together, an action that was wholly his for once. He wanted very badly to soothe away the wrinkle on her mouth, to comfort her, and it was unnerving how much he wanted to reach out. His past lives retreated, became quiescent, and watchful, waiting to see what he would do. What was this hold she had over him?

He took a deep breath to clear his head, and with a rush, Nidhirv, Mohini, Bhaskar, Agni and the rest returned to him, crowding his mind.

"How do you intend to do that?" he asked.

"That is not your—"

"It is my affair," and this time it was he who snapped. "Do not expect me to take you at your word, Ahilya, especially if you do not intend to take me at mine."

Ahilya glanced at the surrounding Ecstatics and seemed to come to a decision. "You saw what I did," she said. "The Virohi are contained by the vriksh, but I believe I can reverse my action with the core tree. It will take time, but I think it is possible. And I will release the tree's hold on them for you."

"To do as I want with them?"

A dozen expressions flew over Ahilya's face, anger, fear, worry, shame. Iravan forced himself not to react as she closed her eyes in obvious pain. "Yes," she whispered.

Iravan leaned forward again, staring at her. "Why would you do that? Do you no longer think it is genocide?"

Her eyes flew open. "Would you agree to any other terms?"

Slowly, Iravan shook his head.

"I will need all information about the Virohi that you have," he said. "Not just access to them, but anything in the architect histories. I know there are people in Irshar, Basav, Garima, others—they will need to give us those records. As will you—anything you discover through archeology."

Ahilya nodded tightly.

"Should you learn how to destroy the Virohi," Iravan went on, "you will give me that information as well. Our contract is for everything, including news you deem dangerous."

Once again, she nodded curtly.

The assistance of the Ecstatics was easy. He had planned to do that once he found a way, regardless of Ahilya's demands. The assistance from the sungineers was harder—but something that he and Dhruv would figure out somehow.

But the Moment…

Even if he'd wanted to repair it, could it be done at all?

He knew that he couldn't simply will the universe to return into existence. There was a hierarchy to what he could do with his will alone, and the changes he made with the everpower did not endure too long. Nothing endured long unless it was tied to his capital desire, and the voices of Nidhirv, Askavetra, Rajesh, and Mohini reared back at him, to destroy the Virohi. They had waited for so long.

Iravan saw a thousand pairs of eyes watching him. Ahilya stared at him, her chin lifted slightly.

"Kamal," he called out. "Nagesh. You are to go with Ahilya-ve and assess the damage to Irshar. Make a detailed account of what the ashram needs, and what the Garden can provide."

The two architects stepped down from the platform and flanked Ahilya. She didn't bother to look at them. Her eyes were only for Iravan.

He inclined his head. "It appears we have an agreement."

"Then enforce it," Ahilya said.

"How?" he questioned. "A healbranch vow will have no effect, not when there is no Nakshar and no rudra tree."

"Yet the principle stands," Ahilya retorted. "Make a bracelet that will poison the wearer should the vow be broken."

Iravan cocked an eyebrow. "I am an Ecstatic. I am more than an Ecstatic. I will heal."

"But I will not," Ahilya said.

Shock ran through him, and for a second, he remained utterly still.

No, he thought immediately. He could not allow her to do that. He knew what she was asking—he could not harm her, not a complete being, not *the* complete being. Ahilya, who had ended an earthrage, who had supported the architects, and told them the truth about themselves. He could not harm her, not *Ahilya*. It would eviscerate him. If anything happened to her, because of him and his actions—he had wanted to rescue her, not destroy her—

The others were watching.

She had planned this. She had come prepared.

He had no choice. If he did not agree, the Ecstatics of his own Garden would know him for a hypocrite. They would never follow him to their destinies of making amends to the complete ones. They would never hold themselves accountable to complete citizens if he did not show that he was willing to be accountable to Ahilya.

She alone had ever been able to maneuver him without trying.

Slowly, without dropping his gaze from hers, Iravan trajected using the everpower.

Two dark heartpoison vines grew from the floor, curling in his hands, their surfaces smooth and shiny. The vines formed into bracelets, and Iravan spoke, loud enough for everyone to hear. "I vow to fulfill our contract to the best of my ability, Ahilya, if you fulfill yours. Let this heartpoison incapacitate the wearer if either of us breaks our vow."

The vines glinted in his hands and solidified.

Iravan held up the dark bracelets for everyone to see, and heard the collective sigh that went through the gathering. Heartpoison was so toxic that a single thorn from it could fell the strongest person in seconds. A bracelet like this could fell a yaksha.

Iravan wore one, then climbed down the platform. He extended his hand, and Ahilya stretched hers.

Her fingers were cool against his skin. They trembled once, then stilled. She gave no other sign of her fear.

Very gently, Iravan slipped the other bracelet onto her wrist.

For a second, they stood there, their hands entwined. He could feel her pulse under his wrist. He could feel her heart beating inside his chest.

Then, Ahilya stepped back and pulled her arm away.

"I expect to see resources pouring into Irshar immediately after the assessment," she said. "I will be waiting to hear from you."

"As will I," he countered.

With a tight nod, and a final glance at everyone, Ahilya turned around. The Ecstatics surged around her, muttering as some of them followed her out, while others lingered, waiting for Iravan's order.

Dhruv stepped up next to Iravan. His voice was very quiet. "What do we do?" he asked.

Iravan studied the Ecstatics. Remembered the hostility he had felt. "We do exactly what we promised her," he said grimly. "And we find a way to finish the Virohi."

18

AHILYA

She was on her bed in the infirmary, Eskayra asleep next to her on a makeshift cot. Even in her half-aware sleep-befuddled state, Ahilya could hear Eskayra's breathing. When she cracked her eyes open, she could discern the shape of Esk's body in the darkness. Her friend had eschewed her home ever since Ahilya had been transferred here as a permanent patient after their return from the jungle. It felt like an imposition at first, but Ahilya was now glad for the company.

Ordinarily, the infirmary would have been quietly alive with the soft whirrs and beeps of sungineering devices. Ahilya would have been strapped into machines that would monitor her vitals constantly. With the Moment gone, however, only flickering candlelight gave any illumination, and all was still and silent. Ahilya closed her eyes, rolled her shoulders, and thought of what she had promised Iravan in return for fixing the Moment.

She had promised to give him the cosmic creatures. How was she to begin? Not too long ago, she was not allowed to speak to the cosmic creatures without the council's explicit permission, but those instructions had been for when the Virohi were tied to the ashram. Unlike the city, the council did not control the core tree. Who did, then?

Tentatively, Ahilya focused between her brows.

A sharp pain overtook her, and her vision *tilted,* like falling headfirst into a mirrored pool. Her third vision still resembled a broken house, full of several chambers. The mirrored chambers where she had once spoken to the Virohi were shattered, and she retreated from that room. She imagined something else, a familiar landscape, and the third vision changed, opening not into the chamber of the core trees, but transforming her Etherium completely.

She dropped on all fours within a forest. It surrounded her in all directions—not the jungle she was accustomed to, but a verdant, watchful presence that whispered to her, tugging at her attention. *The vriksh.*

It was everywhere. At her command, the Etherium had coalesced into this one chamber, and the chamber was infinite.

Branches drooped down, whispering to her. Leaves curled, caressing her face. Roots writhed around her toes, cushioning, and moss grew everywhere, as if inviting her to breathe, to rest. Still on her knees, Ahilya nearly wept, her chest rising and falling in soft, unheard gasps.

What have we done? she thought. *What have we done?*

She could not believe it, how much she had missed this moving architecture, this life, this familiarity. Humanity had adapted, they'd had to, but she could not believe that the airborne ashrams were finished forever. For this brief moment, in this space of soft imaginings and remembered safety, she was home, and it was terrible that she had destroyed it for everyone. Never again would they experience the joy of shifting leaves, of morphing architecture, and grand views of their planet, all because of her insecurity and Iravan's callousness, and their combined arrogance.

Leaves drifted down to her, soothing her face, each one touching her skin briefly. Memory flashed, of running with her sister, the both of them young girls. Hunching within Nakshar's library beside a tower of books. Speaking with Naila on a curved, latticed balcony. The images lasted just for an instant before the leaves floated to the ground, but Ahilya understood. Each leaf was a memory that she had once fed the rudra tree. The vriksh was returning them to her in these glimpses.

She rose unsteadily to her feet. The forest glowed, scented with the sweetness of wet bark. The foliage stroked her cheeks, other images flashing behind her eyes too fast to catch. As she walked, more roots seeped into the earth, growing from the branches above. She could not see beyond the few feet in front of her, except for leaves and the glimmer of twilight, but she was surrounded by humanity and the memories of every one of the survivors. This was the amalgamation of all the lives remaining, desire that had fed itself back into the core trees through all of their civilization's history. She breathed in the scent of the rudra, tears burning her eyes. The tree was doing this, of course. Presenting itself to her in the Etherium in this way, though outside in her first vision, it remained a towering immobile being.

Beyond, in the forest, other shapes moved. She heard someone weeping, a horrified, grieving sound that reminded her of a funereal dirge. The melody crept into her bones, making her shiver, and Ahilya's heart responded with deep sorrow. When she touched her cheeks, they were damp with tears. She moved forward through the forest, her footsteps becoming faster, trying to reach the sound.

When she pushed aside a branch, she saw *them.*

They looked like her, a dark shape that was half-silhouette half-shadow. Their body hunched like hers would have, the outlines fuzzy. The Virohi sobbed, the simulation of their face in their hands, and a chill dread climbed Ahilya. The Virohi-creature's body was covered with dark holes, each so deep that it made her dizzy to look at them. There was a wrongness to this creature. She had promised Iravan she would turn the Virohi over to him, but she had not thought finding them would be so easy. She had hoped for more time, yet here they were, wrapped within the tree, reminding her of what she was to do to them.

She could not walk any further. A part of her wondered if she should try to extract them now somehow, but the thought was tinged with horror. She was not prepared to seize them. To exterminate them, no matter the heartpoison bracelet around her wrist. She wanted to speak to them, give them the kindness they so clearly needed. But their shape revolted her, so much like the worst version of herself, and she was disgusted with herself for balking, for being so weak and shallow now. Their shape fuzzed again, as if they were a swarm of black bees instead of one single shadow, and the weeping intensified.

Alert and unsettled, Ahilya tried to remember. The events were confused in her head—it had all happened so fast—but as far as she could make it, she had released the cosmic creatures from Irshar, the Virohi had clustered around the vriksh, and then—

The Moment had shattered.

They'd gone insane then. Why? Why had the Moment's breaking affected them so? In that there was the key to understanding them. She knew it in her gut.

She took a step forward, stretching out a hand.

The hive-creature looked up. Hate, grief, terror, sadness—all the emotions she'd gifted to the Virohi—warped the creature's face. It screamed, a high-pitched sound that made the hair rise on her neck. The hive burst, billions of black bees rushing past her in a swirl, leaving her alone again.

Ahilya clutched a branch, breathing hard. Memories of some citizen cascaded over her, like wind on the surface of a pool, but she held onto herself. She would have to fulfill her promise—or find a way not to—but not yet. Not yet.

She continued moving. The forest grew thicker, and more shapes became apparent. She thought she saw Dhruv, and Chaiyya, and men and women whose names she did not know, a hundred silhouettes, a thousand. Their shapes were indistinct, and they appeared not human at all, just wisps of shadow, yet a familiarity ached in her as though those shadows were simply doorways.

The cosmic creatures were physical shapes here, trapped as they were in the tree. The leaves growing from the trees were memories of humanity.

But these others shadows and shapes… could she talk to *them*? Were they real? She was in the infirmary and was only present here through her Etherium. The vriksh had become her third vision, but the vriksh had always belonged to all of the citizens. Each person's Etherium was unique to their consciousness, and consciousnesses were connected. The architects had seen such connection in the Moment, but perhaps for non-architects, the Etherium was where the third visions connected. Perhaps all of these were doors into everyone else's mind, and the house of Etherium that she was used to was not just her house, but that of everyone else's.

There was only one way to test this theory. Only one person's consciousness she had ever been able to peer into.

If she saw him, she did not know what she would do. He had acted so indifferent in the Garden when she had come with her demands. So proud, and hostile, and othered. Still, she parted the leaves in front of her, and in the manner of stepping from one chamber to another, opened her connection to Iravan.

She saw him laying back on a carved bed, the collar of his shirt splayed open, moon-like eyes staring up at nothing, silver tattoos winking restlessly on his dark skin.

Her heart wrenched, and Ahilya thought of when he had brought her to an airborne Irshar. While she had been recovering from her miscarriage, Iravan had stayed with her, tending to her, cleaning her, loving her. Tears burned in her eyes. After all this time and in all the ways they had changed, he could still remind her of the man he had once been. She reached out a hand unthinkingly, making to touch him.

Iravan blinked, and his eyes widened as he became aware of her.

Then he was in front of her, his Etherium merged with hers. He was a shadow within the trees approaching her, parting the leaves. He was coming to her, with his questions and demands. Coming to her, with that look on his face, as if half-lost half-in-love. He would ask her about the Virohi again. He would demand she turn them over. She would not be able to lie or prevaricate this time. Here in this space, she would have no defense, her heart laid bare.

She would have to admit that she had seen the Virohi, that she could assist him with genocide.

Startled, Ahilya opened her eyes. She banished the Etherium.

19

IRAVAN

Iravan blinked.

Shapes called out to him, and suddenly she was there, staring at him past thick leaves. His heart raced as he approached her.

He saw her mouth drop open.

Before he could move, the Etherium collapsed, and abruptly Iravan came to himself.

For a long instant, he stayed still, his vision spinning.

He was in his room in the Garden. All around him was stillness, though if he focused he could hear the quiet hoot of a night bird roosting somewhere in the cross-beams of the ceiling. Hours had passed since he'd retired to his bedroom to attempt to sleep, knowing full well rest would elude him. This was the chamber he had lived in ever since he'd expanded the Garden to accommodate all the architects, but the chamber looked like a strange amalgamation of all the homes that he had lived in with Ahilya.

The balcony resembled the very first one they'd had after being wed. The bed was like the one after an anomalously long lull. The rushes were half-flowers, half-clover like he'd always trajected for her so her feet would be cushioned. Everything here reminded him of her, and clearly he had begun hallucinating, overwhelmed by tiredness. What had that image of her been? Had that really been her, caught inside a forest? Was it a memory?

His breath grew uneven.

He had been circling through his past lives, hoping to find answers to the destruction of the Virohi. Hidden amidst so much mundane life, Iravan had finally found a useful memory, but before he could study it, the Etherium had twisted. He'd found himself hurtling into a forest, staring at his wife.

Iravan searched his mind for the forest again, but could no longer detect Ahilya. Whatever that glimpse had been, it had gone as fast as it had come. He pressed his hand to his eyes, squeezing his lids with a forefinger and thumb. *I'm losing my mind,* he thought. *I have descended into darkness.*

He arose from his bed. Slowly, Iravan walked over to the stone basin at one corner of the room. Cool water waited in a jug, and he splashed some over his face, resting his palms over the basin. He stared at his face in the glass mirror above the stone.

The mirror was a luxury, a remnant of what Dhruv had salvaged from the Conclave's crashing. It was just a shard, only big enough to reflect part of his face from this angle. The shard was useless to Dhruv, but it was enough to show Iravan how much he'd aged.

Haunted dark eyes, graying stubble, hair that was completely silver. Had he always looked this terrible? How old was he now? Forty? Older? He had lost count, and whatever number he thought felt too young.

It was hard to look at himself when behind his eyes all he saw were images of his past selves. Of Bhaskar, who had died in a freak trajecting accident, and Nidhirv, who had been surrounded by his loved ones, and Askavetra, whose death was a mystery to him. Their moments of death were fleeting in his memory, yet their lives were easily recalled. Each of them had chosen their material bonds, but he sensed their revulsion with themselves within him for making that choice, and it was his own.

It was not always this way. Iravan could remember vestiges of something else, a time when his past lives had not sought vengeance against the Virohi. Surely Nidhirv had known of the Virohi—in his time, Ecstasy was encouraged and legal. He had simply chosen not to pursue it. Instead, the man chose to live with Vishwam, wanting to be born again, to find the same kind of love he shared with his husband again. Then how could it be that Iravan's capital desire had manifested into this? How could it be that he felt such disdain from the man's memory about his own choices made in love, as if Nidhirv himself had changed? *Could* the past change? Iravan had seen himself through Nidhirv's eyes, and the eyes of his other past lives, back when he and the falcon had fought to subsume one another—but he had always thought that a twisted vision of his own fears. If the past itself could alter in some way, he had descended into true meaninglessness. He could count on nothing and no one, not even the knowledge gained by everything he had been through.

It was so convoluted. He was fighting the very same people he was meant to protect. What was he doing fighting Ahilya? Why did his past lives suddenly view her as an enemy, when it was their task to make amends to her and those of her kind? He had left her in the jungle, his past lives telling him not to find her even unto knowing if she were alive. If they had sought their material bonds always, why did they push him away from her? It was so wrong.

The answer came to him on the heels of the question. *Because I am their last chance. I am all of our last chance.*

Each time he watched Nidhirv and Vishwam together in his mind, each time he saw Mohini with her children, or Askavetra with her daughter, all Iravan saw was how they had succumbed to architect society. Tied themselves in bonds of marriage, borne children, tethered themselves to trajection, and never found Ecstasy or their yaksha. He—they—had once had so many opportunities. And they had all ignored the call. Now it lay up to him, the last life of this consciousness. Amends or not, complete being or not, Ahilya was still his wife—and that meant a material bond, the thing that had trapped him forever. He had to separate her identities, if he had any hope of getting through this with his mind intact. Ahilya, his wife, was his enemy. Ahilya, the complete being, was his salvation. He could not afford to conflate the two.

He felt the clarity of this thought, but a growl escaped him, and Iravan gripped the stone basin tight to keep from shaking. The stone blade of possibility dangled from his throat and he stared at it, resentment shooting from him, making his body itch. A part of him could not believe what he was doing—dissecting his wife's personality and motivations so minutely, walking on a tightrope with every intent, hoping to maintain control over himself while functioning in the world with his mind such a maze. He had only been in the jungle building a house for her a few days ago. All of his other lives had gotten what they wished, but what about what *he* wanted? Children, a family, domesticity. He wanted to rail against the unfairness of it, of the fact that *he* had to sacrifice everything while his past lives could walk away freely, but the thought was such a betrayal of his capital desire that he physically choked, his body rebelling against it.

We could have been better, he thought, staring into his eyes, but seeing Mohini behind them within the Etherium. She laughed as she wrote something in a scroll. *We could have been so much better.*

We had the choice. The opportunity. The power. The rest of you could have done this before. Why didn't you?

It was a foolish question. He knew why. With all his knowledge, he still found himself wanting to return to Ahilya. Of course, his other past lives would not have had that chance—most of them had lived in a time when Ecstasy was prohibited, when material bonds were sacrosanct. It was Iravan's destiny, his treasure and his misfortune, that he had learned so much in his lifetime.

He had been born to become a hero, trained as a savior of humanity, as a Senior Architect of an airborne ashram. When he'd finally confronted his own past, he had seen his shameful history. What else would be his path, except to find a way to make amends, no matter that it meant fighting the very people he wanted to make amends to? Ahilya—as much as she wished to deny it—was a creature of an architect-ruled world. They all were, conditioned into it, unable to see past the prisons of thousands of years of culture.

Only Iravan had gained clarity. It was why he disdained the rules of that culture now. Why he could not afford to be weak, like his past lives. He ought to be grateful that his body knew the truth of this even if his mind conspired to seed doubts. It should be a relief that now, finally, his past lives were giving him the strength he needed to tear Ahilya from his life. He should not question why they took him over each time he wished to show her consideration. He should rejoice in the help he was finally getting.

The architects were raised in a culture of supremacy, their entire lives considered a responsibility, to be sacrificed for in a duty of care. He was finally living those principles. Darsh was wrong. He was not motivated by rage. He was motivated by disappointment and clarity, warped now into this thing he had become.

Shaking hard, Iravan looked up again. A grimness entered him. The mirror reflected his eyes, gray like the falcon. His past lives only showed him fleeting images of material bonds. But it was the falcon-yaksha that had always been clear-eyed. The falcon-yaksha was within him now, and it was helping him in its subsummation as it never had in reality. It was orienting all of his consciousness, past, present, and future, toward the only thing that mattered.

Destroy, it whispered from a lifetime ago. And Iravan thought, *Yes.*

Yes.

20

AHILYA

Irshar's solar lab glittered with whispers and shadows. Ahilya moved through the chamber like a ghost.

Instruments lay across her path, silvery and silent. No whirrs, no clicks, no hums. No sounds at all except for the quiet murmuring of the sungineers and other councilors at one end. Glass crunched underneath her feet as she stepped over a mess of optical fibers. Ahilya swept her eyes over the uneven ground, and picked up a shattered magnifying glass, then continued on, stopping only to retrieve some other wayward device. Sunlight streamed in through broken windows—windows which were hardly more than holes in the wall. From one of them, she could see the vriksh's massive trunk, partly obscured by twisting foliage. She looked away from it, shuddering. She could not think of the cosmic creatures and her task to extract them now. She could not think of the price of her failure, and all that it had already unleashed on Irshar. No, today was about something else, and she forced herself to be useful here, to be attentive to her role as a councilor as she was expected to be.

The rest of the council did not pay her any mind. They clustered by the giant inventions table on the other side of the lab. Sungineers made up the bulk of the gathering. Kiana in her mud-stained clothes, leaning on her cane. Umang, a citizen-scientist who worked closely with her, light reflecting on his glasses. Anusha and Ratan, who had been Senior Sungineers of other ashrams once but were willing to work under Kiana now. Compared to the sungineers Ahilya had seen in the Garden, this was a sorry number, but she was thankful they had stayed. More torches and glowglobes lay on the table between them. A soundless spark flickered in the devices, purple ricochets of light. The others murmured in confusion and wonder.

Architects collected around the sungineers, keeping a few steps away as though to not interfere. Chaiyya exchanged a look with Airav, who shrugged in a private communication Ahilya had gotten used to. Garima, who had once belonged to Yeikshar, watched the sungineers without expression. They had all debated Basav joining them, and in the end decided that no matter his expertise, his presence would be construed too antagonistic, even if he attempted to be subservient to Iravan. Irshar could not afford to derail the conversation today, the same way Ahilya could not afford to be distracted.

She paused as another architect strode into the chamber. Naila, the once-Maze Architect of Nakshar, now one of Ahilya's closest friends, broke into a smile, seeing her. She was not a true part of the council, but she had been summoned from her regular duties at Irshar's school. Naila circumvented the sungineers, and hurried over to Ahilya, enveloping her in a tight hug.

"I've missed you, Ahilya-ve," she said grinning.

Ahilya hugged her back, a wry smile on her face. "I've missed you too. How many times must I ask you to drop the suffix?"

"Maybe when we finally destroy ourselves," Naila said cheerfully.

Ahilya smothered a laugh and pulled away. The two of them studied each other, searching for signs of injury. Ahilya had no illusions about what she looked like, with lines under her eyes, her skin tired, grief and strain etched into her every movement. Yet Naila had never looked more beautiful.

With her hair cut short now, and laugh lines—*laugh* lines—curling around her mouth, the younger woman looked like she was part of a thriving airborne ashram, not a citizen of this last refuge of humanity. She had even found kohl from somewhere to line her eyes. It was as though with extinction staring at all of them in the face, Naila had simply grown more confident. Is this what those belonging to Naila's generation were embracing? To be free and irreverent and furious? Ahilya envied them. How she wished she could associate with them more. Perhaps that would remind her of who she was, and the possibilities of who she could be.

She had spent most of her time in the infirmary since meeting with Iravan. A steady stream of architects and non-architects had entered and exited the infirmary, still reeling from the effects of the Moment shattering, but until now Ahilya had not seen Naila. She had heard from her nurses that Naila was still teaching the children, trying to manage their fear, healing them in her own way so the infirmary did not become inundated. With sungineering no longer reliably working, neither of them had known how the other had fared. Ahilya had received reports about Irshar's reconstruction, of food and medicines being brought to the council chambers for easy access and distribution, and of Chaiyya using Iravan's architects to convert this last ashram into a refugee camp. Lying on her cot, Ahilya had not attempted to break the routine that had been prescribed to her by her healers and friends. She had no wish to fight them. She was theirs to command. It was the least she could do—even if it meant the caging of her freedom.

Still, old habits were hard to kill. Every night, while most of the city slept, Ahilya had crept out of the infirmary, walked to the vriksh, and pressed her hand against the trunk. She had vowed to the council she would do as they said. She had told Iravan she could extract the Virohi through the core tree. But in the secret honesty of a few stolen hours, Ahilya sought her fragile freedom, resting her forehead against the tree, breathing it in, searching for peace.

The council had asked her to be here today to indicate their control of her to Iravan. To show him they were ready to cooperate with him, and leash her as he undoubtedly wished. They wanted him to see that they appreciated him keeping his end of the bargain; that they were willing to keep their own. Would they put her in a compromising position, asking her to bend to him? Would he demand answers from her today? She had not told any of them that she'd seen the Virohi in the Etherium. She had not even looked for them again, too afraid to follow through with her appointed task.

Naila's face softened, reading her. "He cannot object to our arrangements. No enemies here."

Or only enemies here, Ahilya thought, but she allowed Naila to lead her back to the others. Nervousness rippled through the gathering, all of them looking up at the doorway every now and then, while they chatted quietly. Everyone here had once been friendly to Iravan, or at best, indifferent. Would he see through it? If he read the council's control of her, would he be satisfied? Happy that Irshar finally supported him? Or would he be aghast, seeing her brought down in this way?

She could not know. The Iravan she had married would have made the council pay, but this man now could not be predicted. Once, Iravan had rebelled against his own caging by Nakshar's council. He had found it difficult to navigate the council's maneuverings with their marriage, though he had tried to leash her too. At least this time, their marriage was no longer a factor. Ahilya tried not to stare at the debris swept away to the corners of the lab.

When he finally arrived, she was the first to notice.

Her husband did not come with any fanfare. One moment the doorway was silent and empty, the next he stood there in his black uniform and silver tattoos, his retinue surrounding him. She had not expected him to come alone, but was surprised by the people he'd picked.

Dhruv was anticipated; Irshar had specifically invited the Senior Sungineer of the Garden, to discuss the technology they were to inspect today. But Manav, an architect Iravan had excised, and Darsh, a child… The two of them flanked Iravan, dressed in similar black kurta and trousers. Manav, his gaze wandering, seemed unaware of his surroundings as he so often was, and Darsh stood, arms crossed, surveying all of them with disdain. The similarity between the three architects was unnerving. It was like seeing Iravan from his past and future. Manav's skin was as dark as Iravan's. Darsh had cut his hair like her husband's. Had Iravan picked his retinue as deliberately as Irshar had? Why these two people?

Ahilya realized the murmurs in the solar lab had stopped. They were all watching Iravan and her, because in the end it came down to them. She felt the energy shift, the quiet tension of the chamber ratchetting into acute danger. She could sense the wariness from her council, at what she would do. If she would betray them now, rebelling against them, showing hostility toward Iravan. What words should she say to make them all comfortable? If she tried to hide her true feelings of humiliation and diminishment from Iravan, he would see through it instantly. He might grow angry with the council, for lying to him about their intentions. He might think they were concealing something, when the only thing the council wished to conceal was their fear of him. If she made a misstep, it would regress Irshar and the Garden back into their cold war.

Should she start with his retinue instead of him—but no. What did those citizens of the Garden know of her, the woman who had brazenly walked in and commanded their king? To Darsh, she was simply another councilor of Nakshar who had once imprisoned him in a deathcage. To Dhruv… well, everyone knew where she stood with him now. This meeting had been long coming, the first of its kind since the creation of Irshar. They had all finally met to negotiate, under the excuse of sharing sungineering technology, but so much had happened between her and Iravan, beyond being representatives of their councils. The loss of their marriage, the fights they'd once had, the reconciliation, the war. All of it political, all of it so personal. She could not forget it. Yet if she and Iravan could not put aside their differences during this dialogue, there was no hope for their nations. She knew this.

Ahilya opened her mind and invited him into her forest.

She expected to see only his shadow, but to her surprise the forest bloomed in both their minds. It was as if in opening the door to her chamber to him once, she had given him access to the vriksh forever. They stood now on opposite ends of the solar lab, and they stood across a small clearing within the twilit Etherium, and Ahilya saw herself walk toward him, in the lab and in the vriksh, while he mirrored her movements. Her eyes couldn't take it, the strangeness of the two visions, the synchronicity. She stumbled and it seemed to happen slowly, but Iravan was there, holding her up. Her head swam, and she clutched his sleeve, breathing hard.

"Let it go," he said quietly. "Let it drop, Ahilya."

"No," she whispered. In the solar lab surrounded by her council, she had no power anymore, but the Etherium was still hers. That is why she had chosen to make this move. This was the only honesty she knew now.

But Iravan looked tormented, his brows creasing, as if ashamed himself that this is the way she had chosen to present herself. "Please," he whispered back, and there was pain in his voice. *Please, my love. You are not an architect. You were always better. Do not seek the Two Visions.*

She jerked up to look at his face, both in the forest and in the lab. The both of them realized in the same instant that though he had not spoken out loud, she had heard him. She saw a swirl of emotion on his face, remorse that this was what they had come to, that she could not even speak with him except in the hidden forest of her Etherium; shock that she *could* speak to him in the forest when such a thing was unheard of before; curiosity whether this forest was to become the only place of sincerity for them, separate from the rest of the world.

What did it mean that they had connected now so intimately in this unseen space when they were driven so far apart in real life? What did it mean about their marriage? Was there any hope of his return? Ahilya blinked, the questions hurtling to Iravan through the forest. He wrapped his arm around her body, tightening his hold.

"You do not need it," he said, softly but slowly, as though to hear his own voice. "Let it go, Ahilya. I am here."

He pulled away, gently in the Etherium, retreating into the shadows, and this time she obeyed.

Lucidity returned to her with a blaze of pain. Within the solar lab Iravan's hand tightened over hers. He straightened her, pulling her close to him, his arm tucking hers under his so they were attached side by side, like they were once meant to be—a farce he was presenting, just like her civility to him, for the betterment of their two nations. A deep exhalation filled the chamber, telling her both their reactions were received well.

They approached the rest of Irshar's council and experts, Iravan's retinue following them. Memory flashed in Ahilya, of the time Eskayra had left Nakshar to find her fortune on the same trade route that Iravan had arrived on from Yeikshar. It had been a conglomeration of three or four ashrams, Nakshar among them. *Don't go,* she had asked Eskayra, and though Eskayra asked her to come with her, Ahilya could not leave her sister. Iravan had blossomed into the void, young and virile, sweeping her away with his love and magnetism, until they somehow arrived here.

Ahilya's grip tightened on his arm. *My love,* he had called her now when their thoughts had met, but that was accidental surely, a mistaken utterance due to force of habit. He had not indicated once in the last few months that he cared to return them to what they had once had. Eskayra had wondered if she had a marriage at all, and Ahilya had not responded, but it was because she was hoping for something long dead with Iravan. There might have been love once, but under the weight of who he was now, it had shattered like delicate sungineering in a storm. Who would either of them have been had they never come into each other's lives? Iravan had said once that he'd never have traveled this path to Ecstasy without her; that she'd made *him* possible. This is what she had wrought?

Ahilya wished to draw herself away, but she forced herself to walk alongside him. Dhruv gave them an inscrutable glance, and walked over to the sungineers and the councilors. Iravan followed more slowly with her, and though she expected him to speak, to take charge when they reached the table where everyone had congregated, her husband lingered back, bearing the furtive glances from the others like she did. He seemed as lost in his own thoughts as she was in hers. They stood there, together yet apart, in this temple of sungineering.

For a while, all of them simply watched as Dhruv wordlessly tinkered with some of the devices on the table, replacing some parts with others he had brought. He gestured to Darsh, and the young boy, his sleeves pulled back just like Iravan, began trajecting.

The instruments on the table began to whirr and buzz. The lab came alive as blue-green tattoos grew over Darsh's skin. Golden light spilled from the sungineering devices, holograms flickering and dying. The residents of Irshar muttered, the sungineers glancing at each other. Airav sat up on his wheelchair.

"How are you doing this?" Kiana asked, intrigued.

"Replaced the transformers with the energex," Dhruv grunted. He gestured to the small rectangular glass pieces he'd removed from some of the devices.

"I can see that," Kiana replied dryly. "But the energex works on Ecstasy, and Ecstasy works on trajecting into the Moment. How are you doing this with the Moment broken?"

Dhruv scowled. "It doesn't matter."

"I only ask because we are doing something similar," Kiana said, her voice smooth.

"Like what?" Dhruv asked.

"Let me show you," Kiana answered. "Darsh, if you wouldn't mind stopping, please?"

The boy looked startled to be directly addressed. He glanced at Iravan, then at Dhruv, who nodded. Darsh left the Deepness, and the solar lab swam in gloom again, the golden light that had been charged with Darsh's Ecstasy quietening.

Ahilya felt Iravan's attention shift. The two of them watched as Kiana gestured to Umang. He reached over to an adjacent table and pulled some of the equipment and torches from the expedition closer. In the darkness and silence, Umang spread the torches out and stepped back. All of them stared at the devices. Ahilya could hear everyone's breaths, too loud in the quiet chamber. *Work,* she willed silently. *Please work now.* It all depended on this.

"Are we waiting for something?" Dhruv finally asked, glancing at Kiana.

The instruments sputtered to life, flickering in purple shadows. Iravan froze, suddenly alert. Dhruv's mouth dropped open. He glanced about them all to confirm that no architect was trajecting, then rounded on Kiana.

"How are *you* doing this?" he demanded.

"We don't know." Kiana resettled her cane, shifting her weight. She had declined a chair. What were they all trying to prove to each other? When had they begun thinking like this? "All our sungineering died when the Moment shattered, of course," Kiana said. "But then some of it began again in fits and spurts. It is not reliable, but it is something, and we thought you might know. These devices were based on the prototypes you once made in Nakshar. After the success of the energex and radarx, I kept those devices close and managed to save them during the crash, but they were your technology. Once they worked on constellation lines, each time our expeditionary teams took them to the jungle, but now they seem to be working without such trajection. What do you think is happening?"

Iravan watched Dhruv closely. The sungineer stared at the devices, deliberately not touching them. Ahilya got the sense that he did not want to claim ownership of them, not until he knew more. Sure enough, he muttered, "My devices always worked on Ecstasy, and this is not it, otherwise, these would react to Darsh too when he gave these other ones life." His fingers nudged the Ecstatic devices he had been tinkering with, then he looked up at Kiana. "You have a theory, don't you?"

Kiana nodded. "Yes. You'll hate it."

"Well?"

"A field."

Dhruv let out a sputter of disbelief. "You cannot be serious, Kiana. You might as well claim the sun revolves around our planet instead of the other way around. The theory of a trajection field was discredited long ago."

"Maybe it was simply misunderstood," Kiana said.

Dhruv gave her a look of disbelief, but Naila cleared her throat, placed a gentle hand on his arm and said kindly, "Would you like to speak down to the rest of us?"

He snorted, but Ahilya saw amusement in his eyes. Naila and Dhruv had maintained their friendship, despite their separate allegiances to Irshar and the Garden, despite their differences as an architect and a sungineer in this new world. How had that happened? When had Naila replaced Ahilya in Dhruv's estimation? The well of quiet devastation that always accompanied any thought of him grew larger in Ahilya's heart.

Dhruv threw up his hands as all of them watched him.

"We have to look back into our history to understand this," he said. "As a technology, sungineering is new, very new. Yes, it began about four hundred years ago, but back then it was simply a few non-architects mucking about trying to see if they could capture the sun's energy. Their experiments were laughed at, and the early sungineers had to prove the worth of their inventions. Even then, their results were not trusted. It took hundreds of years for acceptance of a single idea. The field nearly died out several times. That is what sungineers had to contend with. Because architects could not conceive of a science that didn't involve them."

The architects in the chamber exchanged glances. Next to Ahilya, Iravan remained still.

"It was a technology born out of chaos," Chaiyya said, speaking for the first time, her voice a protest. "Ashrams ascended to the sky a thousand years ago, but the time immediately after was marked by infighting, each ashram unsure of its place. Subsummation, collapse, and crashing of certain ashrams—all of that took place for a hundred years. Sungineering could not be given that much importance then, not when it did not help with survival, not in those times."

"It took hundreds of years because of architect arrogance," Dhruv snapped. "And the only reason sungineering was allowed to exist was because it helped architects—an effect that has lingered into our time."

Chaiyya relapsed into silence, though her eyes did not leave Dhruv. Airav's face was expressionless, but Ahilya saw him shake his head very slightly toward Chaiyya.

Kiana cleared her throat. "In order for sungineering to progress," she said, "sungineers had to appease architects. I think we can all agree to that much, no matter the cause of it. When sungineering was given credence, it occurred because of an accident—a famous one in sungineering circles, where we tapped into trajection as a power. That accident birthed modern sungineering. We took the architects' understanding of trajection as our own. Architects were sacrosanct, each one important above any other life. So sungineering accepted that as a wisdom, and as a limitation. Architects had their mystical understanding of what trajection was, but sungineers translated the importance of an architect into a field. When an architect trajected, they emitted a field of trajection. Every sungineering device in the past, from a tiny glowglobe to the largest heat shields, all contained a key part—the transformer which took an architect's raw and scattered trajection field and converted it into usable energy. We use that technology now... or well, we had been, until all this happened. And for a long time, sungineering accepted architects' understanding of trajection as a field, centered around each sacrosanct architect."

"But everything changed with the invention of the deathdevices," Dhruv said, taking up the explanation again. "Things like deathboxes and deathcages were created so that Ecstatics wouldn't simply be killed, they could be severed from their power. Architects were still sacrosanct, but sungineering's understanding of trajection evolved with these devices. Think of how a deathchamber works. Deathdevices cut off active trajection. But why does architecture not simply fall apart or detach from that of the main ashram, if we carve the Moment out?"

"Because constellation lines still hold," Naila said. "Each time we used those devices in an airborne ashram, we patrolled the lines, and rebuilt them when they frayed."

Dhruv nodded approvingly at Naila. "You can see why sungineering evolved to dismiss the importance of individual architects, no matter what architects themselves preached. We learned through the deathdevices that the energy we were capturing was not from an architect's unique field. It was from the act of creating constellation lines—or in the case of Ecstasy, of trajecting Ecstatically into the Moment. Sungineering cuts out when architects stop creating constellation lines, even if the ashram stays afloat through pre-constructed lines. This is why when a deathcage rises, though architecture remains stable, sungineering cannot work, not unless new lines are created and maintained and an architect is actively trajecting. Our understanding and manipulation of this changed everything."

Everyone fell silent. The whirrs and clicks from the expedition's equipment hummed into whispers before dying. They stood there, all of them trying to understand the implications of what Dhruv said.

Ahilya was not surprised. She knew most of this from her research as an archeologist. To an untrained eye, the effect was the same. Field or constellation lines, sungineering worked the way it always had—on trajection. And architects were revered like they always had been—society's most significant class.

Yet politically, the change was immense. With an evolved understanding of trajection, and architects' role in it, individual architects no longer emanated absolute power. The change in society was undoubtedly slow, spanning centuries, but gradually, the work became more important, as opposed to individual superhumans. Architect Discs came into being, becoming more popular in every ashram—focused on a unified vision. Non-architects were allowed to marry architects, their desire used to augment an architect's trajection. Council structures changed, rules for shift-duty were created, and ultimately, sungineers and architects worked together to keep an ashram afloat, protected from the earthrages. All ashrams—even the most conservative ones like Katresh and the Seven Northern Sisters—understood that, united, their nations had far more power than any one individual.

Until Iravan and Ahilya arrived, to bring humanity to its worst phase yet, dependent not just on individuals, but on two individuals. Two unstable, unreliable, mistaken individuals who didn't know their own minds let alone that of the people they served.

A great panic seized Ahilya. She was close to hyperventilating. Without thinking, she extricated herself from Iravan, chanting the things she had been taught by her nurses in the infirmary. *My name is Ahilya. I am a complete being. I am an archeologist. There are people in Irshar who will take charge when I cannot. I am not alone. I am not alone.*

Iravan didn't respond, but her movement away from him broke the others out of their contemplation. They gazed up from the devices to Ahilya, as she walked away from her husband and closer to Irshar's council.

"The theory of a trajection field," Kiana said quietly, bringing them all back, "was discredited. But if this is working now..." She waved a hand toward the purple sungineering devices, and all of them stared. "Maybe architects are emitting a field."

"Though they are not trajecting?" Naila asked skeptically. "Though they are not in the Moment, not making constellation lines?" She paused, then her gaze flipped to Manav, then darted between Ahilya, Iravan and Dhruv.

They were all thinking of the same thing. In Nakshar's solar lab, only a few months ago, the excised architect Manav had done something similar too. Dhruv had found a weak Ecstatic signature emanating from Manav. But Manav had not been supertrajecting or displaying any tattoos, similar to whatever was powering this device now.

Ahilya looked at the excised architect, the way his eyes roved over the solar lab, fastening on nothing, the slight humming under his breath, the manner in which he clutched a blue ice rose. Manav's excision had destroyed him, but he had fared better than most other excised architects. He was alive, with brief flashes of lucidity. Bharavi had worked with him, trying to understand Ecstasy for her own study. Manav had been Nakshar's foremost expert on the power before her. Had his expertise extended in some way after his excision, enabling him to use Ecstasy beyond what was known possible? What would he tell them now if he could?

Dhruv turned to Iravan, a frown on his face. "When Manav did something similar, you said it was because he had a second yaksha."

Iravan nodded slowly. "An entity related to Manav came to my rescue twice during my challenge with the falcon. I suspected it was a second creature bound to him, an incorporeal one, though I once excised him from his other yaksha. Manav and the creature seemed to be working in concert, both of them supertrajecting to rescue me, but while the yaksha was in the Deepness, Manav himself was not. He was in the Conduit, seeking to join his second yaksha in the Deepness, sending out sporadic signals of Ecstasy toward it, perhaps from the time I excised him. That is why you detected an energy signature from him though he did not glow."

"Isn't glowing a necessary quality of trajection, though?" Naila murmured.

Iravan shrugged. "There are effects of trajection and Ecstasy on the body. This much has always been known. But the precise nature of the effect has always been a guess. We have always thought that trajecting gives us only blue-green tattoos, but my own skin radiates in silver, even if I act in the Deepness or the Moment instead of in the evervision. In Manav's case, he was excised from one of his counterparts. Perhaps that had an effect too, his body continuing to be dark even though he was supertrajecting."

"Supertrajecting while not in the Deepness, according to you," Chaiyya said, frowning. "Is that possible?"

"The Deepness, Moment and the Conduit are inseparable if you know to look at them in that manner. It is simply a matter of perception. Separation is a quality of the Two Visions, it's a learned phenomenon. Once you unlearn it, the realms are really the same. That is what the evervision is—the plane in which I operate."

"You're saying the Moment is not really destroyed," Airav said, interrupting. "That we can unsee it if we only change our perception."

"The Moment *is* destroyed," Iravan said flatly. "That is a fact. But just like you can see the Moment as its own thing from within it, and as part of something greater while outside of it—from the Deepness or the evervision, for instance—you can see all the other realms as unique and different, while still belonging to a whole. Don't fool yourself about the Moment's viability though. No matter which vision I see it from, it has shattered. That remains unchallenged."

"And you know all this for certain?" Kiana asked. "That more than one yaksha can exist for an architect?"

Iravan made a balancing motion with his hand. "How much certainty can one have about these things? We are all walking in the dark here. I stand by the explanation, however. It seems reasonable."

"And what are yakshas, if I can ask?" Umang said, speaking for the first time, his voice diffident.

Iravan looked to Ahilya in deference. After all, she had been the expert on the creatures for a long time.

But unsure of her role, Ahilya remained silent, and Iravan sighed with a hint of long-sufferance at her unspoken mutiny against his wishes.

"Yakshas are split halves of a cosmic being," he said. "Just like an architect. In their corporeal form, they are massive creatures, but in their incorporeal form..." He shrugged. "I would imagine they contain some similarity. The ability to supertraject. A sentience. A loss of memory. A familiarity of their architect halves. In their simplest forms, yakshas are beings of pure desire, without any true agenda or planning—simply seeking their architects as a fulfillment of their nature, like a river running downhill, compelled by gravity. The falcon-yaksha evolved enough to transform from a creature of pure desire into one with an agenda, but that took thousands of years, and it was a learned phenomenon for the falcon. Perhaps its desire to seek me was just that strong, that it evolved from being a passive creature into one with conscious purpose."

"You're claiming the evolution of consciousness and sentience as a function of desire," Airav said, raising a brow.

"Do we have a better explanation?" Iravan countered. "We've debated it in architect circles, but this is the prevailing theory, is it not? What else does our world work on? What else is the substrate of trajection?"

"If that is true, then could yakshas be powering this somehow?" Chaiyya said, pointing at the purple devices. "You said Manav's second yaksha helped you in your time of need. Then could there be similar non-corporeal yakshas, present here now, invisible to our eyes, giving us mysterious energy to use?"

"Corporeal or not, yakshas only do Ecstatic trajection," Iravan said. "Non-corporeal ones might be invisible to us in the first vision, but they reflect in the second vision and I don't see any in the Deepness. I don't even see any in the Conduit or through the evervision. Besides, these devices don't work on Ecstasy, do they? They don't have an energex, and they did not light up when Darsh was supertrajecting just now. You said they worked when your architects were using the Moment during their expeditions."

"I said that they worked even when the architect stopped, and the Moment was destroyed," Kiana clarified.

"Yes," said Iravan. "So what you're really asking us is if we know of any other secret power. One we have been hoarding from you and that could be charging these." His eyes twinkled in morbid amusement at this roundabout way the council had thought to confront him, and he shrugged. "I can assure you we do not have any such resource. I came here in good faith today. I would tell you if I were aware of such a thing."

Dhruv nodded his assent, though his gaze was still fixed on the expedition's device. Ahilya imagined his mind racing. She recognized his look—the same one he'd had all that time ago when they'd been analyzing devices from her own expedition with Oam out in the jungle. How long ago that seemed. How many things they had achieved and lost and learned about their world since then? Yet they did not know all the answers.

Kiana removed her glasses and rubbed at her eyes. "I cannot believe I am asking this. But what exactly *is* trajection? Whether trajection proper or Ecstasy or whatever you are doing, Iravan."

"It is manipulation of consciousness," Naila said.

"It is a usable energy," Dhruv responded at the same time.

"It is the harnessed power of desire," Ahilya said tiredly—and all eyes turned to her.

Chaiyya tilted her head. Airav nodded. Iravan studied her, and a small smile grew on his face.

"It is indeed," he said quietly. "Which brings me to the real reason I am here. I bring you a gift."

At his nod, Dhruv removed a solarnote tablet from his pocket. It buzzed to life with Darsh's Ecstatic trajection, and images filtered on it of trees within a jungle. Captured through Dhruv's drones was an image of—

"A city," Iravan said. "Your city, if you should wish it."

The citizens of Irshar gasped. Dhruv settled the tablet so images on it became visible to all of them, dust rising gracefully from the surface of the earth, columns building as mud hardened. Structures rose from the jungle, as trees whipped, breaking into wood chips and rearranging themselves into houses and apartments, a wall here, a fence there. Ahilya recognized the site, the very same one she had been in a few days ago, the one the Virohi had showed her as a possibility for building a new home. How had Iravan found this? Why had he picked this site, and not any other? And was there no end to his powers, to single-handedly build a new city? She remembered the effort of her expedition, their grubby hands, the rumpled clothes, the dirt streaking their faces.

The others were murmuring, and Kiana leaned forward studying the screen. "This could work," she said approvingly, having forgotten sungineering mysteries for a brief time in light of more pressing issues of survival. She was already contacting Eskayra through her sungineering beads, gesturing to Umang to apparently call others of the expeditionary group.

"I'm pleased you are pleased," Iravan said dryly. "But you will have to excuse me now. Other duties await. You have Dhruv here to answer any other questions you may have. He speaks with my voice."

He made to leave, but Ahilya leaned forward and laid a hand on his arm.

"Wait," she said. "For all of our endeavors to go uninterrupted, and for the Garden and Irshar to continue working together, we need more communication between our nations."

Iravan raised an eyebrow. "I am not going to make regular reports to your council, Ahilya, as entertaining as this has been."

"That's not what I mean. I—we—propose an ambassador. Dhruv will certainly tell us everything you wish him to, and if not him then one of the Ecstatics you've already posted here. But perhaps Irshar can send you someone too."

Iravan's gaze traveled over the gathering. "Who do you have in mind?"

"Me," Naila replied, stepping forward.

Ahilya could see Iravan knew what they were doing. Naila was here for this reason alone, and they'd picked her of all people because she had been his favorite student once, capable of extracting knowledge and truths out of him without being obvious. He was going to laugh at them, call out this manipulation, this subterfuge. He was going to tell them he'd already seen through their clever ways hidden behind their sungineering discussion. He was going to refuse.

"You did want architects in the Garden, did you not?" Ahilya asked quietly.

The implication was clear. Take Naila or have her be sent as a spy.

Iravan watched her for a second, then sighed. "Very well. But if she changes her allegiance—"

"Oh, she already has," Naila said dryly. "Shall we go, sir? Tick-tick. Duty awaits."

21

IRAVAN

He didn't immediately leave the solar lab. He could tell Darsh wanted to look around, though the boy said nothing. Iravan pulled away from Irshar's group, and Darsh and Manav followed him. Darsh kept a supportive arm on the excised architect, ambling through the circular chamber. Irshar's council had not given them leave to inspect the solar lab, but what were they going to do? Deny Iravan and his retinue now, after all the times they'd begged him to come? They knew that sungineering was the only reason Iravan was here.

He could feel their eyes darting between him and his two charges. Undoubtedly, they were wondering why he'd picked these two, but all they needed to do was ask. He might have told them.

With the bargain made with Ahilya, it was only a matter of time before the Virohi were in Iravan's grasp. Once he found a way to destroy them, his capital desire would be finished, the path to his freedom laid bare. Iravan would have no purpose afterward. He had a vague notion of what he wanted to do then—heal with Ahilya, if the chance ever came, help her heal from her encounter with the Virohi, leave the Garden and build a home elsewhere—but he didn't dare think of that too closely. Already he could feel the voices of his past lives infiltrating him, half-deranged, half-furious, as though to think of an *afterward* at all was a betrayal of his capital desire. He kept his gaze on Darsh as the boy explored the lab with Manav.

Someone would need to take Iravan's place in the Garden once the Virohi were gone, to ensure all of Iravan's plans were followed through. Darsh would not have been his first choice ordinarily. The boy was too young, too volatile, too angry. Yet weren't the same things said about Iravan once? Darsh was loyal, and that alone was worth the other limitations. Iravan needed Darsh to be subservient to sungineering, and to Irshar, after it all ended. It was why he'd brought him today.

As for Manav… There was a debt owed. Manav had come to Iravan's aid twice in the past, saving him from the falcon-yaksha. Iravan still did not know why—there was a personal link he was unable to see between Manav and himself—but it was no coincidence that the sungineers of Irshar had discovered a power similar to what Manav had used once. Iravan had excised the man, and it was a reminder of what would come to pass should Iravan fail in his endeavors with his Ecstatics. Should they choose capital desires contrary to his, Iravan would have to excise them. Could excision happen without a core tree? He would have to find a way, and live with committing such an atrocity.

The council of Irshar had not asked him, but he made no secret in the Garden that he kept both Darsh and Manav around for a reason. Darsh, an Ecstatic seeking his yaksha and primed for condition, indicating all that Iravan still needed to achieve; and Manav, an Ecstatic Iravan had excised, one who indicated all of Iravan's failed legacy. They were both reminders of his continued responsibility, and the consequences of making a mistake. Darsh could not be allowed to have Manav's future; Iravan—and Darsh himself—would have to lead the Garden to something better. Too much depended on this balance between the past, present and future. Too much that Iravan had set in motion already.

His preoccupation must have shown on his face. Iravan felt Ahilya in his mind, a questioning presence, but he raised his shield, backing away from her as she attempted to pull him back into the strange forest of her Etherium.

He had been shocked that she'd heard him there. Seeing her there in a place so reminiscent of an airborne ashram, she herself appearing so like the woman he had married, had nearly broken Iravan's resolve. He'd wanted to nestle into her. Beg for her forgiveness. Tell her that the both of them should forget everything, and walk away from all of this to find some peace together, survival be damned.

It had been such a seducing, terrifying thought that Iravan had become alarmed. What could the cosmic creatures make him do, speaking from behind Ahilya? The prospect was chilling, and so he'd created a shield.

He had thought of it only during the recent discussion. If the Moment, the Deepness, and the Etherium really were the same realm in some ways, why should they not work similarly to an extent? It was a simple quality of trajection, to learn to keep the Two Visions separate, something architects learned at the start of their training. All of Iravan's visions had merged after his subsummation of the falcon-yaksha into the evervision, but the principle still applied. He had simply forgotten that basic principle.

He exercised it now, pulling away from his own Etherium and denying Ahilya access to it too. A shield from her, but also in a manner from himself. As long as he did not enter his Etherium, she could not use it to spy on him, or to call him arbitrarily to hers in that endless forest. All he needed to do was be careful while searching for answers within his third vision.

Iravan stopped at a small table, littered with coils of neatly arranged optical fibers. From here, the conversation of the sungineers at the other end of the room was a dull mutter. He watched Dhruv and Kiana in the middle of another explanation, Airav and Chaiyya nodding every once in a while. The people Iravan did not know were finally participating as well, easier now that he had left. A woman with short-cropped hair and a heart-shaped face marched into the solar lab, said something to Ahilya making her smile, then brushed a strand of Ahilya's hair behind her ear. The gesture was so surprising that Iravan stared.

"Eskayra," Naila said helpfully. "She used to belong to Nakshar before she moved away, but of course, we're all one ashram now, aren't we? You know they used to court once. Before you, of course. Ahilya-ve finally seems happy, wouldn't you say? I think Eskayra has asked her to marry her, and I think that's a great idea. Don't you? Though I imagine she would need to divorce you properly first. How does one go about that in the Garden, anyway?"

Iravan said nothing, but looked to the once Maze Architect. She smiled at him, a grin full of teeth.

It was absurd that this news should hurt him. That this knowledge should stab his heart in the way it did, with pain and loneliness and terrible grief, when he and Ahilya did not have a marriage anymore, not really. He ought to be happy for her, that she had found joy again, comfort surely, and perhaps love. That she had found everything she deserved, everything he had been unable to give.

And yet, all he felt was a rush of despair like he was a lovelorn adolescent. He could see the house he had built and destroyed so many times in the jungle, a house for Ahilya and the family that they would never have. A house as strong as their dream had once been for children together. A house as tragic as the way they had gone about it. He had told no one of this structure, but what if he shared such a thing with Ahilya? What if he whispered it in the forest of her Etherium? Would she wait for him? Could the both of them find a way to each other beyond their perspectives on the cosmic creatures? His hand reached for his stone blade of pure possibility, beating against his throat like a noose. He had been saving this last bit of everdust for a purpose, but even he knew it was lunacy.

Naila said nothing more, but a satisfied expression skittered across her eyes. She didn't even bother to hide it. She was furious with him. He had never seen her like that—part-disappointed in him, part-enraged, as if he had failed her personally somehow with everything he'd done.

Absurdly, she reminded him of Bharavi, and for a brief instant, his Etherium opened up without his will and he saw his mentor, with her impatient expression and dry wit. He saw Bharavi as he threw a spiralweed leaf into her cage. Iravan slammed the Etherium shut before Ahilya could pull him again into her forest. He called out to Darsh and Manav, and the three of them left the solar lab with as little ceremony as they had arrived.

Back in the plaza, Iravan took a few deep breaths. It haunted him, that image of Ahilya and Eskayra standing together. Darsh studied him with a concerned expression, but wisely did not ask. Naila strolled slowly out of the lab and joined him, her hands in her pockets. She might as well be whistling.

"Where would you like to go?" she asked, scratching at her short hair.

Iravan gave her a sidelong glance. "You're the ambassador."

He had already visited the places he was interested in. The council chambers to look at food rations. The solar lab. The massive, splendid, unbelievable vriksh. He had examined the core tree from every side, inspecting it with the everpower, hovering above the ground until he was within its boughs, but it had given him no insight. The everpower seemed to have a strange resistance to it, as if opposing him in some way, and the vriksh belonged to Ahilya through and through. He gazed at its trunk now, an enormous thing, blotting out the sun. This core tree that had once belonged to airborne ashrams was now harboring the Virohi, become an obstacle in his way. He had destroyed life in the skies. Would he have to destroy its last legacy in the jungle too?

Naila gestured to him, and they strode silently through the plaza, winding their way past labyrinthine roots. Afternoon sunshine beat down on them, the heat of the jungle stifling here in Irshar, unable to be managed by sungineering. Dhruv's drones had returned images of the entire ashram and how it had changed since the vriksh's transformation. The citizens had cleared much of the rubble, but the city was speared with the vriksh's roots, the tree enclosing it within itself. Never before had this landed ashram resembled one of its airborne predecessors so clearly.

They stopped at a low-lying building, with a courtyard of grass enclosed inside a waist-high wall. Children of different ages sat clustered under smaller trees, with adults who seemed to be lecturing them. There were no solarnote tablets. Instead old-fashioned books made of paper were being passed from one small hand to another. Roots spread here too, but several had been cut to make a sort of clearing.

A school. Iravan was looking at a school.

He had promised to make one for the Irshar he had created in the skies. These people had actually done it. Iravan saw more children through doorways, leading past the verandah into the building proper.

Darsh looked longingly at the clustered children, and Iravan almost asked him if he wanted to join them, but held his tongue. Darsh would not leave, even if Iravan asked.

"These children," he said instead, resting his elbows over the gate. "They are architect children, and complete beings together?"

Naila nodded and joined him. "Any child, regardless of their birth and ability, schools here. It was one of the council's earliest decisions. There would be no more differentiation. That separation is not part of the society Irshar wants to build. The children don't learn trajection either, and that was before you destroyed the Moment. They learn history mostly. Sungineering basics too. Ahilya-ve has taught here sometimes, and others in the council. This is my primary occupation."

A bell rang somewhere, and children rose from under one of the trees. They collected their books and returned within the building, chattering the whole time. In airborne ashrams, every child went to a common school—at least until they displayed trajection abilities. After that, students who could traject were transferred to the Architects' Academy, while the rest continued in the same place. Iravan had never liked the system—it created too much division between the children, too much animosity. With trajection come to an end, the ashram had finally obliterated the need for separate establishments.

"Does Eskayra want children too?" he asked quietly. He had not meant to say it out loud, but the question escaped without his consent, and what did it matter anymore whether he asked it or kept it to himself.

The question seemed to surprise Naila. She watched him a long second as if to judge his sincerity, then her expression softened.

"Maybe," she said in a low voice. "It is easier for them. Children have been a sore subject for architects, not complete beings. I certainly never wanted them, or ever to be married—you know this already. All our attempts to make me a Senior Architect in Nakshar challenged material bonds in a more profound way than your childless seat. Still. I am beginning to think that we've never actually deserved them."

Children were an essential part of survival. It was another reason they were tied to material bonds, and to airborne ashrams fleeing destruction. Iravan's path to parenthood was forever closed; it was the price he and Ahilya had paid for stopping the cosmic creature all that time ago from breaking into an earthrage. But would more and more architects like Naila choose to close that path themselves? What would that do to the odds of survival? To rebirth and reincarnation?

Yet was it not a choice architects *ought* to be able to make? Had he not wanted to give them such a choice? For generations, architects had been trapped by the need for material bonds, made to marry and bear children. Now, when they knew who they were, and the reasons behind the creation of those bonds in the first place, perhaps children would be borne out of love, instead of duty. What better reason to bring a life into the world than that?

He and Naila had discussed it often, though never as openly. The both of them had thought the compulsion to bear children a barbaric need of their society. He had never told Ahilya of it—another secret he had kept from her—not wanting to muddy his desire for children. She had accused him of wanting to have children solely because of his needs as an architect, but Iravan had been unable to refute her; it would only show the council that he did not respect material bonds as he should. Back then, any indication of swerving from the council's line would have been construed as an indication of his Ecstasy. What would have happened if he had been allowed to be honest with his wife from the very start?

Voices drifted toward them, and Iravan and Naila turned to see more people enter the courtyard, chatting quietly to each other. Parents had come to take their children home. Iravan stepped back, following Naila toward a courtyard with a few scattered benches. A shape caught his eye, sitting silently on a bench.

Iravan's breath faltered.

Tariya.

She was studying him, her gaze unflinching. She had been sitting there a while. He had not noticed her. Without thinking, he stepped toward his sister-in-law while Darsh and Naila followed.

Tariya watched him come, her once-bright eyes dull, her beautiful face etched with deep lines of sorrow. This was the first time he had seen her since Bharavi's funeral. Next to her, he could almost feel Bharavi. He could almost see her roll her shoulders and give him an impatient glance, as though to tell him to find his courage. The words were already forming on his tongue, to argue with his dead mentor, the way they had so often. Tears pricked Iravan's eyes. Tariya and Arth and Kush were Ahilya's family, but they were his family, too—more than his parents in some way. He had lived in Nakshar far longer than he had in Yeikshar. He had formed bonds.

Weaving through the moving bodies, he was almost upon her, past the crowd, when something hit him hard in the midriff.

Iravan staggered, more surprised than hurt. He looked down, and there was Kush, a fierce little boy no older than eleven, his face reminiscent of Bharavi. His hand was clenched in a fist. He looked like he was about to cry. Instinctively, Iravan dropped to his knees to capture him in a hug, but Kush reared back his fist again.

"Stay away from her," the boy gasped. "You killed—you killed—"

Stunned, Iravan could form no words. Bharavi's death flashed behind his eyes again, her pacing in her deathcage, coolly telling him he would become an Ecstatic. Movement flashed in the corner of his eyes, and then Kush was sprawled on the ground, Darsh looming over him. Manav hovered behind Darsh, evidently having followed him, but his gaze was uninterested and listless as always.

"Stay away from him," Darsh said coldly. His body was lit with trajection, a terrible intent in his threat, but Kush jumped back to his feet.

"He killed my mother."

"You don't know anything about it—"

"This has nothing to do with you—"

"Break it up, break it up," Naila barked. "Both of you." She darted forward, putting herself between the two boys.

"Darsh, leave," Iravan said, finding his words. The boy shrugged and obeyed, his face expressionless, but he gave Kush a dispassionate glance, and a chill ran through Iravan. Darsh no longer was in the Deepness—his skin did not glow blue-green—but he had intended to attack Kush. The boy was prone to violence; Iravan had not forgotten how Darsh had been deeply interested when Iravan had trajected Viana unto her death. He'd have to keep a closer eye on him, but for now Iravan turned to Kush, who was brushing his clothes. Iravan extended a hand, but Kush gave him a dirty look and walked away too.

Iravan watched his nephew's bent posture, and the fury in the lines of his body. What had life been like for the boy after Bharavi's death? Tariya had clearly told him Iravan had killed his mother, but had she told him why? She had not moved, silently watching all this occurring. Carefully, Iravan approached her, sitting down next to her on the bench. Manav followed but remained standing. The excised architect's eyes widened on seeing Arth, as though amazed to see a baby. Arth extended his chubby arms, reaching for Iravan, and Tariya allowed it. The baby—Bharavi's baby—pulled at Iravan's collar gurgling.

They sat in silence for a time. Iravan's mind swirled with grief and confusion and heartache.

"I miss her," he choked out, finally. "I miss her all the time."

Tariya's eyes filled with tears. He didn't know what to do. Did he have any right to talk to her? Was he simply imposing his presence now, intimidating her with his power? He had become such a terrible monster, he could not tell anymore if he was welcome in any sincerity.

"I can leave you alone if you want," he began in a low voice, but Tariya shook her head, wiping her tears.

"What you did," she whispered. "It was what she wanted. I know this."

Her words were forgiving, but there was fury there, the same fury Ahilya had. Tariya was right—Bharavi had wanted to be killed. Death was a mercy that both she and Iravan had preferred over excision.

But he had betrayed Bharavi too—him and all his other lives. Behind his brows, he saw Nidhirv with Vishwam again, he saw Mohini and Askavetra and Agni with their families. If his past lives had not chosen their bonds, if they had found Ecstasy all that time ago, then perhaps they would have *destroyed* the Virohi long ago. Their capital desire would have manifested in a previous life, and Iravan would have remained unborn, and civilization—and life in the ashrams—would never have outlawed Ecstasy. Bharavi wouldn't have *needed* to die to escape excision. Excision would never have been. The very fact that he lived now—Bharavi had died for it.

Anger curled his fingers into a tight fist. He smoothed it out, patting Arth on the back, trying to keep control of himself.

"He can traject," Tariya said, dully. "He responded to the radarx, when we were still in the skies."

Iravan contained his surprise. Not merely trajection—if Arth had responded to the radarx, he could *super*traject. The baby was displaying Ecstatic energy. Perhaps like Reyla in the Garden, he had found the Deepness before the Moment, a pure Ecstatic who never needed to unlearn the limits of trajection.

Iravan tore his gaze back to Tariya. "You and Arth and Kush," he said. "You could come to the Garden. I could teach Arth. And I would take care of you—the way Bharavi would have wanted."

"What Bharavi would have wanted," Tariya echoed, mirthlessly. "You think this is what she would have done, if she were one of those Ecstatics like the ones in your Garden?"

"Bharavi would have been more powerful than anyone else," Iravan said, his throat raw. "More powerful than me, her desire to change the world more potent than anything I could do. Tariya, she did amazing, powerful things that I could never do. If she were here, she would change everything about how we once lived. She would do more than I have."

Bharavi had landed Nakshar in an earthrage to unite with her yaksha, long before he had ever known any of this was possible. He had never asked her why, or what creature it had been, but in his heart he knew it was the elephant-yaksha he and Ahilya had encountered in that terrible expedition into the jungle. Had Bharavi felt the same familiarity and fury from her split part that Iravan had once felt from the falcon? She had not gone outside in the jungle to meet it, or perhaps she had been biding her time. Perhaps she hadn't known fully she was Ecstatically trajecting. *The first few experiences are mystifying.* Whatever she had endured in those early days, the Bharavi he'd confronted in the deathcage had made her choice. She had been clear about what she'd wanted. Iravan had to trust in that memory.

"I was with her in the end," he said. "Bharavi wanted to recreate civilization. She wanted to raze it all to the ground and rebuild it because she knew how wrong everything was. She understood the lies that formed the foundation of our culture, even before I did."

Tariya turned to him and swallowed. "And would she have left me then, too? Left Arth and Kush? The way you have left Ahilya? The way you left us?"

Iravan recoiled as though slapped. He had thought to convince Tariya now of his own actions, as though seeking her forgiveness and absolution would relieve his conscience and count toward his making amends.

But her words were poison. He had never seen her like this; she had been reverent toward architects before, he'd expected her sympathy, her understanding. Had he misread her so badly all this time?

It was as if Tariya could see these thoughts on his face. She leaned forward and clutched his hand, her gaze suddenly fierce.

"You abandoned us, Iravan," she hissed, giving him clarity. "Not just me and the boys and your wife. You abandoned every one of us to fend for ourselves. Do you know what I endured after the Moment shattered? How I couldn't distinguish between nightmares and reality, watching Bharavi die over and over again, though I had begun to heal myself? Do you know I suffered in Nakshar during the Conclave, our living conditions so poor that I could barely hold together my broken family? And you have the audacity to ask me to come with you? The audacity to tell me you are doing what Bharavi intended? You are what caused this."

Her grip was painful on Iravan's wrist, nails digging into his skin. Kush was watching them sullenly from across the courtyard, and Iravan thought of the words Bharavi had said before he'd murdered her: *I loved them, didn't I?* She had been searching for a way to balance her material bonds with Ecstasy. She had deliberately not gone out to the jungle to the yaksha because she had tried to choose Tariya. She had fought him, not wanting to die. What would her capital desire have been if she were alive? What would she have done if she was here by his side, arguing with him, mentoring him?

He remained speechless, shame, regret, and a profound loneliness throbbing in him. For an instant, the desire to destroy the Virohi wavered.

Because Tariya's words were no manipulation of the council. Her words had no agenda. This was grief, pure and true, and it pierced him like a knife to the heart.

Iravan stood up, handing Arth back, his movements wooden.

Propelled by deep shame and chaos, he trajected, and the air around him twisted and lifted him and Manav up into flight. Darsh and Naila would follow in their own time. Perhaps it was dangerous to leave Darsh alone when he was clearly volatile. But Iravan needed to get away from Tariya now—from Kush and Arth, and the family they reminded him of. He needed to get away from this specter of his past.

Iravan fled back to the Garden, away from Tariya's accusing eyes. Dust swirled behind him in an echo of his cowardice.

22

IRAVAN

He landed gracelessly in the central courtyard, his legs unsteady. Next to him, Manav stumbled, and Iravan shot out a hand to steady him. Ignoring the greetings of the other Ecstatics, who were milling about in the courtyard, Iravan approached an elevator hidden behind a wall of curling leaves. He trajected and the bark opened to let him and Manav in. Silently, they rode the elevator high up the tower.

There, alone except for someone who could not harm him, Iravan thunked his head on the bark, breathing heavily. The Etherium cycled within the evervision, and he saw Askavetra bump her husband's arm. Agni grinned as they reached out to sweep their lover's hair behind an ear. The flashes came faster, but Iravan heard the voices of these people too, in sharp counterpoint to the images. A single message breathed in concert. *Destroy.* Their eyes flashed silver before turning back to their original shade.

I'm going mad, he thought. It was not possible to contain so much conflicting information within oneself. His head was a cloud of meaningless noise, chattering away incessantly. How could one make any sense of anything? How could one live? *I contain lives*, Iravan thought, smiling darkly. *And they are all insane.*

The elevator came to a stop. Manav had been silent all this while, and Iravan grasped his elbow, and stepped off, gathering his purpose to him like a cloak. They marched through together, Iravan escorting the man to his chambers.

This floor lay still, though lights from glowglobes blinked here and there, merged with gleaming blue-green phosphorescence. Iravan had designed it using only Nakshar's plants. The waving, leafy pothos, the bark railings engraved with carvings, the soft chimes that were reminiscent of the landing raga. Iravan had made these decisions deliberately. The chamber smelled like ice-roses, enough to make him light-headed. He wound their way past a small fountain edged with stone, taking care to slow down so Manav would not feel his agitation. Iravan tried to still his turbulent emotions, hoping to feel the peace that he had created for Manav.

In this chamber it was easy to forget that they had all landed in an alien jungle not long ago. Iravan had talked to the Maze Architects of Nakshar to recall this, but this floor resembled the very same luxurious house that had once belonged to Manav, when he was a Senior Architect of Nakshar. Iravan could feel the ghost of his own footsteps echo. In his mind's eye, he watched as he, along with Bharavi and Chaiyya and Airav, marched down the same paths, cornering Manav before taking him to the Examination of Ecstasy. It was the only excision he'd ever done, and it would haunt him for the rest of his days. In a way, this chamber was an attempt at a reparation he could never perform. Manav's condition was a direct reminder of what came from living by the dictates of ashram society. Tariya was welcome to her anger and grief, but didn't Manav prove the sheer number of atrocities that were committed in the name of peace once? Atrocities Iravan had been complicit in, without his knowledge? The Garden was not perfect, but at least excision was completely outlawed. That was because of him. He had to keep faith in himself.

He and Manav reached a small courtyard open to the skies. Ice blue roses littered the floor, and Iravan trajected two benches facing each other. He helped Manav down onto one, then took his place on the other, facing him.

Silently, Iravan withdrew a small notebook from his pocket, filled with Bharavi's tight writing. Every now and then he came here to speak to Manav, to ensure his welfare, to remember Bharavi—and each time was different. Sometimes Manav spoke in halting words, other times he hummed without tune. Iravan could tell that today Manav would stay silent. After the events in Irshar, it was only to be expected. Somewhere, Manav's mind must have registered everything that had happened. Had he heard his name being spoken in the solar lab? It was amazing that the sungineers in Irshar had found another energy source, one so similar to what Manav had done after being excised.

"You knew," Iravan said softly. "You knew about the everpower, didn't you?"

Predictably, the man did not respond.

Iravan opened the book to a familiar page, with creases borne out of constant use. He did not need to read the words. *Two roads in sleep,* he thought, but his tongue skipped to the last few lines of Manav's poem.

"*We continue to live,*" he quoted softly. "*In undying separate illusions.* The everspace. That's what this means, doesn't it?"

He had excised Manav nearly six years ago now, but when a few months ago the man had twice come to his rescue during the fight with the falcon, Iravan had concluded Manav had multiple yaksha counterparts. He'd concluded that Manav had united with one before his excision, which had made it possible for him to retain some measure of his trajection.

Did that mean his capital desire had manifested in some form too? What kind of capital desire would make Manav and his other yaksha save Iravan, of all people? Did such consideration extend only to architects, or perhaps to Senior Architects? Senior Architects once were the most important people of an ashram, meant to inhabit all of an ashram's potential. Iravan knew how deeply those protocols were embedded into their culture. Thousands and thousands of years had cemented this legacy of the ashrams. It was not an unreasonable thought that Manav had inadvertently saved him because of a capital desire to serve the floating cities.

But the timing of it… If Manav had more than one yaksha, could it be that he had subsumed one already for his capital desire to manifest? Iravan's own desire to make amends had bled into him only after the falcon had become a part of him. It had formed during unity, then cemented in him after the falcon's subsummation. Before the subsummation, he had only wished to make reparations; but after that, the destruction of the Virohi had taken shape as his capital desire. He could hear the falcon's voice in his head, goading him into utter destruction.

If Manav had saved him because of his allegiance to the ashram structure, then Manav's capital desire was in direct opposition to Iravan's. Iravan had been flirting with a vague idea of finding the man's second yaksha and helping him unite with it—perhaps that would heal Manav now, and more importantly, give Iravan the support he needed in the Garden—but if this were true, then he could not take such a risk. What if Iravan helped heal Manav, only for him to defy him? His capital desire pulled him inexorably foward—and his past lives railed in him to fulfill it soon—Bhaskar,

Agni, Askavetra, Nidhirv—always Nidhirv, who had chosen their material bonds, but now wished him divorced from his own.

Images cycled from one life to another within the Etherium, and Iravan waited until one arrived from Nidhirv's life. In that life lay a secret he needed to decode, and idly, he projected the memory outward. Dust and earth churned in a soft breeze, creating the shape of the man. Bark moved like arms and legs, and leaves flickered like eyes. Nidhirv stood in front of them, a smile on his face.

Manav jerked up, his gaze widening and suddenly alert.

His mouth fell open, nearly childlike, and he watched as more earth rose to form Vishwam's burly shape. Vishwam put his arm around Nidhirv, who chuckled, his posture pleased but embarrassed—but before the memory could play out, Nidhirv froze. He wavered as if being wrenched away, then straightened, a strange smile glinting cold.

Iravan grunted in frustration. Still the same wavering, as if his past lives could not fully decide whether they wanted to love their material bonds or have him hate his.

Manav uttered a soft cry, hand to his mouth.

Like Darsh had been startled to see the projections before, the excised architect began shaking his head with a soft keening sound. His hand extended to touch the projection—and Nidhirv's cold smile disappeared, as he huddled into Vishwam again, before the smile flickered back into vengeance.

The Etherium cycled again, and Iravan allowed the projection to change into another past life—Askavetra, whose shape limned the grass and earth. He watched her pad toward the jungle, tracking a tiger-yaksha.

Askavetra's tall frame nuzzled the tiger-yaksha, her expression peaceful, before she flickered into standing ramrod straight, the chips in her eyes sharpening into silver. The projection flashed—changed into Mohini, embracing her spouses—*flicker*—it changed again into cold silvery eyes. What did this mean? What were these images trying to tell him? Why could they not decide? Or was this just an indication of his own undetermined mind?

Manav's keening grew louder. Iravan extended him a sidelong glance and sighed. These projections were eerie, though he'd gotten used to them. There was no use in punishing Manav and himself right now. He ended both their agony and stood up. It was clear his past lives were as torn as he was, speaking a message of vengeance before proclaiming the importance of material bonds. For three months after the Virohi were embedded within Irshar, Iravan had remained steadfast, unwavering. Something had occurred after that that was changing him. It had all started on the day of the Virohi's bombing, and if he tracked his thoughts, he could see this change had come about because of Ahilya.

Going there today had been a mistake; he should have listened to his intuition that had kept him alienated from the ashram for the last few months. He would not make this mistake again.

Iravan waved a hand and all the projections dissolved. Manav still shuddered, though his cries became quieter. With a last glance at the excised architect, Iravan left the chamber.

23

AHILYA

"It's a workable city," Eskayra said grudgingly. "We're still checking to see if the foundation is strong, but initial reports suggest we could move the citizens there as soon as tomorrow if we needed to."

"There is no need to rush," Airav said. "Conduct your assessments. Irshar can still hold us until you're ready. Isn't that right, Ahilya-ve?"

Ahilya nodded. "I don't feel anything from the Virohi, if that's what you're asking. They will no longer interfere."

Eskayra grunted, and made a small notation on the map in front of her.

The three of them were in the builders' chambers within the assembly hall—a narrow, wide room littered with books and rolls of parchment that functioned often as a makeshift library for the council's needs. A few doors down were the council chambers, and the solar lab, where much of the debris had been cleared. Here, in the builders' chambers, evidence of the ashram's upheaval still remained. Boulders the size of Ahilya's head stood as silent sentinels in one corner. Green stone chipped off the walls, flaking every now and then. Roots slithered everywhere, though several had been axed and tamed. The floor slanted, so Airav had to navigate carefully as he wheeled himself out of the chamber. No matter his words about patience, Ahilya could see that living in Irshar was a terrible adjustment for him.

Eskayra began to fold up the maps she had laid on the table, and Ahilya picked one up to help her. It was an accounting of the jungle that Eskayra had done using Dhruv's drones. The Garden had sent aid as promised, and its Senior Sungineer had spent the last few weeks in Irshar more than he had in his home.

Between the Garden's and Irshar's resources, all the streets had been cleared, and the roots of the core tree pushed back to create wider pathways more accessible to the general populace. Sungineering devices were given to all of Irshar, from streetlamps and glowglobes, to medprobes and heat shields. Even now, Dhruv was likely hunched over some diagram or another within the council chambers where Airav was headed. Kiana and Chaiyya already waited there to discuss the logistics of distribution.

Ahilya had not dared to join them. What could she contribute there? At least here she could help Eskayra with her knowledge of the jungle and archeology.

"For a council that was so intent on finding new cities only a few weeks ago, this lot does not want to move that quickly," Eskayra observed.

"Airav wants to prepare the citizens," Ahilya murmured. "Now that we've begun to take stock, we are finally returning to some sense of normalcy. To uproot everyone again without great need would be irresponsible. Who knows, only a few might wish to leave Irshar. Here and in the new city—we might rebuild civilization on more than site."

Eskayra grunted again, but did not disagree. The citizens of the landed ashrams were used to adaptation, with lulls and flights dictating the frequency and shape of their homes. Yet something had changed ever since Irshar had become the last ashram of humanity. The grounding in the jungle had created a desire for stillness, and even the damage to Irshar from Iravan's war could not contend with that.

For months, the citizens had begun taking ownership of their lives, finding different purposes and occupations than they'd been allowed in an airborne ashram. They'd found a chance to think of themselves as people with control, beyond architect measures, for the first time presented with a world where the architecture did not change, and architects were not superior.

In a strange way, Ahilya had achieved what she'd set out to do—and now with the vriksh holding the Virohi, the citizens had gained more freedom. They didn't need even Ahilya anymore to stabilize their structures. The council made gentle suggestions about the new city, but Ahilya had heard rumors of mistrust, and a part of her could not blame the citizens. These were people, many of them from Nakshar, who had lived during the Conclave in architecture that had denied them space, livelihood, occupation, and health. Of course, they did not trust the council.

Besides, the new city was built with an Ecstatic's power. Iravan's architects spoke each day to the citizens, spreading word of his benevolence and agenda, but skepticism regarding the Garden still lingered. People had refused the invitation to live in the Garden. They were not going to forgive Ecstasy so soon—not when Ecstatics had abandoned them and behaved like their enemy for months. The new city was as terrifying to them as Iravan, and gifts from the Garden were circumspect. It was why the council distributed sungineering equipment carefully, requesting Dhruv to build his inventions here in Irshar instead of transporting them from the Garden.

The thought made Ahilya sad. Once she and Iravan had campaigned for the right of Ecstatics to live as equals. They had thought to create a world where earthrages could be controlled, and airborne ashrams and newer ones in the jungle comprised of the Ecstatics could live in harmony—a vision of equity for all kinds of people, no matter where they lived. Now hostilities still ran rampant between the two nations, despite everything people knew. In some ways, moving to the new city, which had Iravan stamped all over it, would be just as bad as the Garden. Perhaps the citizens had the right measure of it.

"We need to make the city ours before we ask them to move," Ahilya said. "Some way to show them that it is not Iravan's, nor the council's. This close to the Garden, and under the thumb of the councilors..."

Eskayra's lips lifted in a small smile. "I'm trying my hardest, my dear. That man's design is sound, I will agree, but in true architect fashion he seems to have thought of total safety without providing any space for people to spend their days. The citizens here have learned to rely on themselves. We cannot take that away from them, and my builders are making accommodations for their way of life."

It would be a compelling argument for Eskayra to make, perhaps more than any other rationale of safety.

The citizens had always lived one earthrage away from danger. That was the nature of their lives in an airborne city. Lack of safety was a known variable. It was control they'd been denied, unable to choose their leaders or their professions when survival was at risk. Now, with the end of the earthrages, Umang was a citizen scientist, part of Eskayra's crew. Reniya and Vihanan maintained roads, a job which had once been the province of architects. Tariya had begun a nursery within the infirmary, caregiving for the children who had been orphaned in the Conclave's tumultuous crash. Laksiya, who had once been a Senior Sungineer of Nakshar, had evidently taken up chronicling the experiences of the survivors in a book she intended for history.

Changes were already occurring in ways of life, architects and non-architects reversing their roles. If Eskayra changed the structures of the city to account for this, the new city might be met with excitement not skepticism.

"If we migrate everyone to the new city," Eskayra said, "will that make it easier for you to do what you need to do?"

Ahilya's job was to extract the Virohi. What difference did it make if the citizens lived in this new city or in Irshar? She had set herself an impossible task. For days now, she had tried to commune with the Virohi, yet she had lost her chance by losing her nerve; she should have talked to them on that first night in the infirmary. Then, she had seen them as a dark, huddled mass that looked like herself. Now, no matter how she searched, she could not see them. They were still there in the vriksh, she knew. Every now and then, their weeping echoed in the Etherium. But they were hiding from her, their swarm flying to all corners, diffusing, as if they knew of her promise to commit genocide. She could not hide her intention from them. They were too closely intertwined. The heartpoison bracelet Iravan had made tightened around her wrist.

Eskayra touched her hand lightly, and Ahilya met her gaze. "He has been in the city, too," the Senior Builder said. "He has seen what I'm doing."

Ahilya looked at her sharply. "Did you speak with him?"

"Only to exchange notes. He has some thoughts about what could make things more useful for the citizens." Eskayra shrugged. "I would be a fool not to listen to his perspective. He did build the city, after all."

It was an unsettling thought—Iravan and Eskayra speaking with each other, without Ahilya. Did they ever acknowledge their history with her, or their present? What did they make of each other? Ahilya knew Eskayra's opinion of Iravan, but did Iravan know of Esk's proposition to Ahilya? She imagined it, the two of them speaking to each other in forced and polite tones, ensuring only to touch on relevant business at hand. She thought of Eskayra in her mud-stained clothes, and Iravan in his pristine black, silver tattoos running over his skin. The image was so bizarre—a mix of her past and future intertwined, that Ahilya shook her head to dispel it.

"You did not mention this to Airav," she said.

"There would hardly be anything to report," Eskayra said, making a face. "I do not see that man often, but there's a reason he made the city in that location. At first, I thought it was because he noticed our expedition equipment there, but he has been around the jungle surrounding the city. He's looking for something."

The yakshas, Ahilya thought.

Dhruv had already let slip that Iravan was away from the Garden for long days. It had made the Senior Sungineer irritable, the administration of the Garden and all communication with Irshar left up to him. He had done the best he could, but Ahilya had heard him complain to Pranav how much of it would be futile if Iravan came in and declared those decisions pointless, changing them on a whim. Ahilya knew how that must have irked Dhruv, but she had not said anything. The days they had confided in each other had long since passed, and she was not interested in playing political games of the council anymore, desiring to create a rift between the Garden's two leaders.

"My dear," Eskayra said softly. "Have you given anymore thought to what I said?"

Ahilya studied the woman, the brightness of her eyes, the steady, stable, secure gaze. Once, Iravan had looked like that.

She shook her head. "You don't really want to marry me, Esk. You know you don't."

"I wanted to before I left Nakshar all those years ago," Eskayra said quietly.

"But you left," Ahilya said before she could take it back. Eskayra's face fell, and she hurried to shrug a shoulder. "I don't blame you—that's not what I mean. Only that perhaps it was for the best."

She could not explain it, but despite everything that had happened, Ahilya could not bring herself to imagine a life where she had never met Iravan. Who she was now was tied so irrevocably to him. With Eskayra, Ahilya had been one person alone. With Iravan, she had become more—evolving herself as Iravan changed and evolved through his experiences. The Ahilya she was today—damaged, experienced, capable of compassion even to the Virohi—was because of him. Would she have outgrown her hostility of the architects, become a councilor, communed with creatures of the universe, all without him in her life? Iravan was tied to her, and he had shaped her as much as she had shaped him. They had grown around each other like two tree trunks, their roots so entangled, their canopy so enmeshed, that neither would ever really be able to separate from the other.

Her thoughts must have shown on her face. Eskayra tipped her chin up. "You are free of the Virohi now," she said. "You could be free of the past too. In the new city, we can build something new together."

Could they? After everything Ahilya had given to the Virohi and to the ashrams? After everything she had given to Iravan? What was left of her, now?

"I will never be free of my past," she said softly. A wan smile crept on her face. "I am an *archeologist*. The past is my home."

Eskayra did not return her smile. "You still want to save him, don't you? Save him from himself?"

"Is that so wrong?"

"No," Esk replied sadly. "It is not. You are still married, after all. But I wish you could see that you are already worthy. I think you wish to save the Virohi not because you see them as yourself, but because you see them as him. If that is true, you should think of the reasons behind what you want to do closely."

Her words were so surprising that Ahilya was rendered momentarily speechless. Deep down, she had always known that she and Iravan needed each other—that one without the other would collapse into the worst rendition of themselves. In those early days of Irshar's formation within the jungle, Ahilya had spoken to the Virohi because no one else could—but in so many ways, that was how it was with Iravan too. No one could get through to him the way she could. Eskayra had seen what no one else had; in trying to understand and save the Virohi, Ahilya was still seeking to understand him. In communicating with them, she was attempting to communicate with *him*. Was this a fool's errand? She and Iravan had balanced each other all their married lives, but look where that had brought everyone.

Iravan's seven-month absence back in Nakshar, the man he'd chosen to become, the convoluted reasoning behind his capital desire... Eskayra was saying *enough was enough*. That Ahilya deserved better. But what of Ahilya's responsibility in all this? She'd had a part to play in the man Iravan was now. That is what a marriage meant. In some ways, she would not have been *this* Ahilya and he would not be *this* Iravan if it weren't for the other. Eskayra would have her be finished with him, but was that possible at all?

If the Virohi were destroyed like everyone wished, and if Iravan's mind and conscience survived the annihilation, and even if Ahilya regained her former confidence, could matters simply return to the way they had been? Could she finish with him, this man who had owned her like she owned him? Neither of them had said goodbye, despite it all. And now when they could see each other with a thought, when they could communicate in a way they never had before within the Etherium… What would be the point of goodbye anymore? They could not escape each other. They were knotted, heart and rhythm, more than either of them understood.

Eskayra sensed her somber mood, and did not push. She simply sighed. "Did you find anything more?" she asked, gesturing to the maps in Ahilya's hand.

Ahilya shrugged a limp shoulder. Her mind was still full of everything Esk said, but she allowed the attempt to change the subject.

"The books don't tell us much," she said. "I have tried."

So much had been destroyed in the crash. The truth was that there hardly were any records remaining. Laksiya was not the only one chronicling the history of humanity. Whatever remained was guarded zealously—Basav kept all the architect records with him, and Ahilya had endured his revulsion of her while he told her in stilted stories anything that could be of use to her in order to extract the Virohi. She had collated her own information, and talked to the sungineers of Irshar and of the Garden. She had gone toward the tree trunk many times hoping for an epiphany, and simply touched it, searching in her mind, whispering for the Virohi. It was absurd that her situation was no different than it had been before—trying to describe a whole field of study with little help. She should have found it a path well traveled, but all Ahilya felt was exhaustion.

Eskayra took Ahilya's wrist in her hand, feeling the heartpoison bracelet there. "You should not have insisted on this. It will only hurt you."

Ahilya pulled away gently. "What hurts me, will hurt him too," she said softly. "That's what I need him to see. I think he does."

Eskayra's brow crinkled. She didn't understand—but Iravan had.

Ahilya had seen it on his face when she'd asked him to enforce the rules of their contract and make the bracelet. He was keeping his promise of sending resources to Irshar—he'd hardly needed such an enforcement. But she had asked for it because the both of them knew that he would rather destroy himself than hurt her.

Perhaps it meant that there was still a seed of affection for her inside him. He had told her explicitly after subsuming the falcon-yaksha that he wished to save her from the Virohi. Ahilya would have liked to believe that, but she knew Iravan could not have her harmed, not if he wanted his own Ecstatics to make amends.

They had played such a game all their lives, one of contesting wills. He would not give up his capital desire, but Ahilya had no urgent need to find the Virohi either.

She had vowed to share information with him *if* she found it, but she had not made any commitments as to *when* she would.

She would simply wait him out, wearing this heartpoison bracelet for her lifetime. Even her efforts now to find a way to destroy the cosmic creatures were simply to appease the council. Under the pretext of hunting for a way to end them, Ahilya secretly searched for a way to release the Virohi instead—that was the information she sought from Basav and her books. The longer it took for her to find a way to destroy them, the more compelled Iravan would become to release her of her vow—if for nothing, then because his own society would change.

By then, civilization would reform. She would erode him with her patience. His capital desire would remain unfulfilled—or, he would be forced to change it. Either way, Ahilya had already won.

She tucked the bracelet away out of sight. Eskayra watched her, then walked over to the far end of the chamber, rummaging among a few instruments. She returned with a small sungineering device the size of her palm, a thin glass wire jutting out from it.

"Do you know what this is?" she asked.

Ahilya shook her head.

"No," Eskayra said, frowning. "Why would they think to tell you when it was the sungineering devices you once used that brought about its invention?" She unspooled the wire from the device. "This is a seismometer. It checks the foundations and stability of the earth underneath. Maybe it can help you? If the Virohi are in the tree, and the tree is rooted into the planet, then studying the planet might teach you something of the creatures. The builders have been using it at the new city, but we don't need it anymore."

"Thank you," Ahilya said, surprised. She knew what it cost Eskayra, to give such a useful instrument away to her when she did not understand Ahilya's true purpose. Ahilya would not use it for the Virohi, but the vriksh? It was the only place she received any peace anymore, and physical knowledge of the tree could reveal information about the forest of her Etherium too.

Eskayra gave her a small smile. "I have to go to the new city again. I won't be back for days, but maybe next time you can come with me?" She leaned in and brushed her lips softly against Ahilya, and Ahilya froze, uncertain of whether to allow it, and what it would mean, now when her thoughts were still so full of her husband.

"Ahilya-ve?" a voice spoke from the door.

They turned to see Kamala standing there. Ahilya took a step back, her face heating, but it was already too late. Kamala had seen this intimacy.

The nurse shrugged as though it was not important to her what she saw, but she tapped at her wrist. "It's time for your medicines," she said.

Ahilya nodded. She could already feel the itch that would begin when they inserted the tubes into her veins.

"Think of a name," Eskayra said, as Ahilya followed Kamala out. "The new city will need it. And maybe thinking of the possibilities will show you that the past need not own you, Ahilya."

24

IRAVAN

He was kneeling on the floor, lacing his boots, when Dhruv's voice made him look up.

"You cannot be leaving again," the sungineer said with exasperation from the entrance. "There are things you need to attend to."

Dhruv stood ramrod straight, tension in every muscle of his lanky frame. Dark circles etched grooves underneath his eyes, visible beneath his glasses. His clothes were rumpled, evidence of the long nights he had been working both in Irshar and the Garden, and Iravan would have been sympathetic in another time, but he had spent such long nights all his life, and now the fate of the world rested on his shoulders. Dhruv was not alone in his exhaustion. Iravan felt it in every breath.

He rose from the ground and strode over to the chair where he'd draped his feather cloak. "My task is in the jungle," he replied.

He had been away for several days already, returning only to sleep and bathe. Part of it had been the urgency to find the yakshas, but another part was a desire to stay away from his chambers. Ever since the encounters with Ahilya, then Tariya, Iravan had been wary of his own home. Seeing Ahilya and the remains of a broken civilization was bad enough, but the conversation with Tariya had utterly shaken him, all of them a reminder of his material bonds.

There was a reason those bonds had trapped architects for centuries—they were seductive, even he could not resist their pull. The best he could do was distance himself from the ashram. What would happen to his vow to destroy the Virohi if he indulged this way? He would be no better than his past lives—and he could feel their insistence burgeoning within him, to redeem them and himself. He needed to keep his vision true. It was the only thing he could trust.

Iravan swept his cloak over his shoulders, feeling its familiar weight. He did not need the cloak for the jungle, not when he could manipulate the everpower, but there was no sense in using the power unnecessarily. The jungle was always cold, and this time he would not return for days.

He brushed past Dhruv into the hallway leading to the courtyard below. Dhruv kept pace, scowling.

"There's trouble in Irshar—"

"That I authorized you to deal with," Iravan interrupted. "Irshar is your affair, is it not?"

"Are the Ecstatics my affair too?" Dhruv snapped. "I don't remember you giving me authority over them."

Iravan turned to look at his Senior Sungineer. Dhruv returned his gaze levelly. There was a time when the sungineer had been polite to Iravan, then caustic, until finally they'd come to an understanding where they set their mutual dislike aside, knowing their successes depended on the other. Iravan was under no illusions that the man still despised him. Dhruv was only in the Garden because it gave him his best opportunity to advance his sungineering—something Dhruv cared deeply about, even if humanity had all but arrived at the end of its time. Iravan could understand such single-minded determination.

It was why he never interfered in Dhruv's work. Yet Dhruv's gaze was expectant, even belligerent.

Iravan sighed. "Perhaps you should tell me what has occurred."

"Yes. Perhaps I should," Dhruv said. He gestured with his head, and began to walk away, down the path that led to the training hall. Iravan followed slowly. "We sent a group of Ecstatics to Irshar to help with their rebuilding," Dhruv began. "They happened to meet their families. An incident occurred."

Darsh, Iravan thought, his heart suddenly racing.

"What happened?" he asked. It was all he could do to keep his voice calm, but his pace became faster so that it was Dhruv trying to match him suddenly.

The sungineer gave him a sidelong glance. "What you'd expect. Anger and outbursts. Yelling. It started with the Ecstatics trying to convince their families to come to the Garden with them, then quickly became an uncontrollable display of power. They're all reporting it differently, but some of our architects used Ecstasy on the citizens there. Trying to traject them, I believe. Pranav put an end to it, but not before the Ecstatics shattered some homes, and ruined precious belongings." Dhruv took a deep, unsettled breath. "They're going rogue."

This had always been the danger of uncontrolled Ecstatics—it was why they had been outlawed. Ecstatics by their very nature, were wild, keeping to few rules of harmony and accord, overcome by seeking their yaksha. Iravan had been in their place not too long ago. He and Dhruv strode in silence until they reached the training hall.

Constructed within the lowermost tier of the Garden, the training hall was a massive chamber with plants of every variety growing over walls and trellises, leading to the very center where Iravan had made a clearing. Ordinarily, Senior Ecstatics educated the newer recruits there, and on rare occasion Iravan held personal classes. Now, Pranav, Trisha, and Darsh surrounded three architects. Several others crowded around them, but as they noticed Iravan, they made way.

Naila was there too, and she studied him impassively, though there was a wealth of judgement in her expression. It irritated Iravan more than he could say. No matter his power, Naila had refused to accept a change in their relationship—seeing him as the mentor he'd once been. In her deadpan gaze now, he could see how short he was falling in her estimation. Is this why Irshar had sent her? She was as bad a reminder of everything as Tariya and Ahilya were. Material bonds were infiltrating his home.

Iravan stopped in front of the three Ecstatics, Dhruv halting next to him. He did not know their names, but he could see the guilt written all over their faces.

He pinched the bridge of his nose with a forefinger and thumb. "Tell me you did not go seeking trouble with the citizens of Irshar," he said quietly.

The three rogue Ecstatics exchanged uncomfortable glances. "They're standing in our way," one of them blurted out, an architect with mud all over their sleeves. "They could join us here, they *should* join us—we are architects, we saved them once—"

"You caused this once," Iravan said. "You created an earthrage by your very existence. You are supposed to be making amends to Irshar."

"Like you are?" another Ecstatic scoffed. "You have broken your material bonds. Why shouldn't we? We see how you behave with your wife. Is that how we are to make amends? If so, we're doing it the same way."

A silence rang through the people assembled. Dhruv stilled. Naila smiled a brittle smile, and a memory flashed in Iravan's head vividly, of a time when she had come to him in Nakshar's library, hoping to proposition him. After all this time, after everything that had occurred, this is what it always came down to. His treatment of Ahilya.

It doesn't change, he thought. *The way they judge me because of Ahilya. The way they see themselves despite knowing the truth of their origins.* He'd tried his hardest to sow reverence in their minds for complete beings. He hadn't been naïve enough to believe that simply sharing the truth would change their minds about their superiority, about their culpability in the destruction of lives—but somehow, he hadn't thought they'd go as far as to seek trouble. *This is why I have to control their capital desire,* he thought, growing cold. *This is why I must break their consent.* It was why he needed to find the yakshas, before one of them did.

The Ecstatic who'd spoken sneered at Iravan.

"What is your name?" Iravan asked softly.

"Rana," the man said, thrusting his chin out. "And making amends is your capital desire, not ours. I intend to—"

Iravan struck with the everpower.

It wasn't difficult, just a casual flick of his mind, and the air around the three architects warped for a brief second, squeezing just enough to make them all dizzy. Rana gurgled, clutching his throat. One by one, the three rogue Ecstatics collapsed, falling unconscious. The lingering silence was so loud that Iravan could hear leaves rustling in a swish of wind.

He gestured to Dhruv. "Keep them contained in one of your solarchambers until I decide what to do with them."

He began to turn away, toward the courtyard from where he would ascend to the jungle, but Dhruv seized his arm. "Aren't you going to address the rest?" the sungineer hissed. "You cannot just leave after doing this."

Iravan gazed at him coldly, and Dhruv let go, stepping back. He had spoken only for Iravan's ears, but it was obvious what he had said. Iravan saw the others staring at him, edging back. Within him, Bhaskar laughed hoarsely.

"You'd like me to address them?" Iravan said. "Very well." He turned to the Ecstatics, and raised his voice. "Listen well, Ecstatics," he said, barely keeping his fury. "Your only reason for existence is to make amends to complete beings. That is why you're here. Leave, if that does not suit you, but remember you won't get very far, not in this jungle that you cannot traject, not with me pursuing. I will find you in the Deepness, and I will find you in the first vision. Anyone else who makes trouble for Irshar will have to answer to me, and that—" He waved at the prone forms on the grass. "—is the least of what could befall you."

Iravan saw the mixed anger and exasperation on Dhruv's face. This was not what the sungineer had expected him to say, but Iravan was done being subtle. Humanity faced a very real danger if the Ecstatics got out of hand. He shouldered his way past the architects, striding away outside to the courtyard.

To his annoyance, Dhruv followed, heeled by Naila and Darsh. Iravan turned to face them.

"That was well handled," Naila drawled.

"You've only made it worse," Dhruv said.

"Are you going to excise them?" Darsh asked.

Iravan clutched his hair, dropped his hands, then inhaled deeply. "No, it wasn't. Maybe I did. Yes, I might—excision is the least they deserve after this stunt."

Naila, Dhruv and Darsh exchanged a glance. Darsh's face was a picture of fear and excitement at the idea of excising the rogue architects. It was the same expression he'd had when Iravan had killed Viana. In truth, Iravan did not know what he would do with those Ecstatics. He could not afford to start excising them—there was no easier way to alienate the rest than with that one action. But Darsh, of all people, needed boundaries. Darsh had not gone rogue, but he was headed that way. If a little fear tamed the boy, then so be it.

What he needed was a better society within the Garden, but except for the sungineers there were no complete beings in his city. In Irshar, they had schools, hospitals, a whole civilization. But in the Garden, each Ecstatic was trained to be a weapon toward the Virohi, and little else. Maybe that is what he ought to do, give them a higher purpose. But what higher purpose could an architect have other than self-destruction, when it was at an architect's hands that the world was destroyed repeatedly? If there was another role for them, Iravan could not see it—and worse, he could not afford to. Giving Ecstatics any identity beyond the one they had was a path to creating more rogue Ecstatics, each intent on their capital desire.

It did not mean that the Garden could not be improved. Darsh was only one architect Iravan had taken under his wing—he could not do that with everyone. He'd attempted to convince Darsh's parents again to build their home in his city. It should have been easy; the two were architects, once of Nakshar, no less. But Darsh's father had sent his apologies with one of the sungineers, saying it would not be possible, and Darsh's mother had said they would not be able to welcome Iravan in their home.

Their message was clear. They wanted nothing to do with him, or with their son. Short of dragging them to the Garden with the everpower, Iravan did not know what else he could attempt. If this is how they treated their only son, no wonder Darsh's loyalty to Iravan was unquestioned. He was starved for affection—and with

Iravan, he'd found a chance to be something other than what was dictated for him. Iravan had to create a Garden to allow that for Darsh. Find a way to keep the peace between these last two cities of humanity somehow. That was Dhruv's appointed task, but yet again, it had come to him. He ground his teeth, willing himself not to take it out on his lead sungineer who clearly had his hands full.

"How is Irshar?" he asked reluctantly, forcing himself to calm his voice.

"After this?" Dhruv made a face. "The council has demanded new architects from us. Someone whose amity to Irshar can be guaranteed. They've asked to vet the architects we send, and they wish for those architects to live *with* their families, and arrive for shift duty. Just like in an airborne ashram."

To tie them with material bonds, Iravan thought. Would this ridiculous fight with the Irshar and its history never end? He was attempting to free the Ecstatics, but freedom came at a cost. Nearly all the architects who had come to him had done so by leaving their children and spouses back in Irshar. His promises and power—and the truth of their origins—had prompted their arrival, but his hold over them was loosening. If he fulfilled this demand from the ashram, then whatever he was building in the Garden was forfeit. Ecstatics would return to Irshar, live with their families, rebuild civilization in the manner of an ashram, and forget all about destroying the Virohi. Irshar would find a way to bind them back into trajection—especially now that they had his sungineers working with them—and the Garden would diminish. Yet he could not deny Irshar's demand, not after what happened. The councilors would insist on it for their safety, and if he wanted to make amends, he would have to stand aside.

I need something else, he thought. *Something else to bind the Ecstatics to me so they do not wander away.* But what else was there beside the yakshas? He was already losing this delicate fight. He needed the Virohi *now* to end them, but he had given Ahilya a heartpoison bracelet. If she was not here, giving him information yet, it meant that she had nothing to give. His pressuring her would achieve nothing.

"Make it happen," he said harshly. Before Dhruv could embroil him in the details of how, Iravan took two steps away from them, then launched into flight, leaving behind a dust storm.

Frustration gave him speed. The jungle blurred underneath him. In the distance, he could see the vriksh's trunk, so massive that no matter how fast he flew, he still felt close to it. Iravan put on another burst of speed, scowling.

He was supposed to be building new systems, but he had never been adept at those—that part of Nakshar's councilwork had resided with Chaiyya and Airav, two architects Iravan had invited over and over again to the Garden, only to be met with polite refusal. Once upon a time he'd thought to collect Ecstatic Architects in Irshar to end the earthrages, but to make amends was the only reason for Ecstatics to endure now.

He had tried to condition the Ecstatics to desire it, with the culture he'd created in the Garden and the force of his personality, and no Ecstatic had yet united with their yaksha. How long would that remain the case? After all, corporeal yakshas were missing, but he still did not know what form the incorporeal ones took. For all he knew, they were invisible sources of desire like Kiana said, attuned toward each architect, already turning them. Perhaps that is why the three rogue Ecstatics had done what they had.

It was the reason he was here today again. He needed to find the yakshas before any of the Ecstatics did. Iravan descended, spotting a clearing, his feet light on the grass, the cloak closing in around him. Here in the jungle a dim light pierced the trees, and for a moment, he stood inhaling the scents, so alien yet so familiar.

The jungle was motionless, an anomaly he still found himself unused to, but if he focused, he could hear the small creatures hiding in the undergrowth—creatures that had once belonged to the airborne ashrams, the squirrels, the mice, the crackling and buzzing insects.

Iravan thought of Oam. The boy had known nothing about how life worked in the jungle and the ashrams; he'd thought these small creatures were present out here too, even during the time of the earthrages. If he'd been alive, would he find the return of life in the jungle as marvelous as Iravan did? The human species had kept to their dwellings, but other animals had spread, finding their paths on landing, though there was a hesitation to their life as if these creatures could not accept this new jungle fully.

Iravan desperately wished to see them now, as if the movement of a rabbit or a squirrel would make up for the stillness of the jungle. Seeing life here would be a confirmation that everything that had happened—despite the loss humanity had suffered—had been for the best.

Life in the skies was a lie. Here, amid the jungle, there was honesty.

Were the little ones scared? What would it take to sanctify the jungle for them? The Virohi were trapped within the core tree, but in some ways they were more a part of this planet than they had ever been. At least when they'd been part of Irshar they had simply been trapped within buildings—structures that could be destroyed. But within the core tree they were rooted to the planet. Is that why the small creatures did not trust the jungle? Perhaps in their own way, they knew how wrong the Virohi were. Perhaps the yakshas did too, continuing to elude him further because of it.

Iravan rolled his shoulders and began his hunt. The land gave way to him, trees and branches withdrawing from his path, responding to his everpower. Roots uncurled in front of him, and grass sank back, leaving a barren trail where he walked. Trees shifted, and he swept a hand, making the drooping leaves in front of him retreat.

Inside his mind, Agni laughed.

He could feel the other architect watching the jungle from behind his eyes. Never before had Iravan felt the presence of his past life so acutely—but he could do nothing to push the impressions away. Neither could he control that it was Agni now as he marched, striding with longer steps, his gait changing, his shoulders rolling the way Agni had once done.

He grew nervous that it was Agni behind his eyes. Any other life would have been manageable, but Agni had always been a little feral. They had lived in a time right before the war had occurred between all the Ecstatics, outlawing Ecstasy. Iravan could feel their presence as though they were stretching his own limbs, wondering at his body, his life. Could one of his past lives take over his body, if he let them? He grinned—then clacked his teeth together—for it was not he who had smiled, but Agni. It was imperative that he hold onto himself.

But he had felt something from Agni, a knowledge of the jungle he did not have, that would lead him to the yakshas. After all, Agni had known of the yakshas. Perhaps they had known of the falcon too. They might know how to track the others, and any secret knowledge to be gleaned from jungle plants. Iravan lifted a hand, and a tree crumpled, turning into ash. *So much power,* Agni whispered, and just for an instant, they lifted Iravan's other hand.

He yanked control back violently.

The falcon-yaksha laughed with morbid amusement.

Agni retreated, and Iravan came to a standstill within the jungle. A terrible fatigue took over his limbs, as though suddenly his body was unsure who it belonged to. He crouched, touching his fingers to the grass, hanging his head.

The Etherium had become a dangerous place. Each time he entered it, he was pulled into a memory of a past life, the sensation so vivid it took over his mind for long seconds. The only time he could hold on to himself in the Etherium was when Ahilya called to him, but that was no safer.

Could it be that this third vision was becoming an alien landscape altogether? Once he had feared that the Deepness would become so, his entry to that space restricted because of the threat of the falcon. If his past lives locked him out of the Etherium, how would he learn how to destroy the Virohi? How would he find the yakshas?

Slowly, his one hand came to grasp the stone blade of pure possibility he'd hung around his neck in a twine necklace. It was amazing how different this search for yakshas was compared to the one he had been on with Ahilya. That expedition had started it all for him—but hadn't he been on this path all along? A fight with Ahilya had led to that moment; they had fought about children, and Iravan had withdrawn to Nakshar's temple for seven months, before seeing his wife again. That time in the temple, trajecting non-stop—that had finally alerted the falcon-yaksha to his presence. The Resonance had appeared, and if Iravan had simply reconciled with Ahilya before, he would have been as unaware of the falcon as the others were of their own yakshas. He would never have been trapped in the pursuit of making amends endlessly if that had been his life.

His fingers still touched the slightly-damp soil, and a small bee alighted on them then flitted away. The jungle was reluctant to sustain life like it once had in the time of the ancient ashrams, but it must still have memory of it. Irshar had limited seeds and resources to grow food again; it was why they desired the Moment repaired. Their sungineering was already working. What if he could simply *give* them food? Could he grow things with the everpower? Would that be enough perhaps to make amends, and silence the demands of his past selves? Would it be enough that Irshar did not insist on finding inventive ways to take away his Ecstatics?

Agni was infiltrating his mind, but if he could find another way to fulfill his capital desire, he would never need to fear the Etherium. He wouldn't need to repair the Moment, his promise to Ahilya fulfilled. They could all find a way to destroy the Virohi together. Either way they could all be rid of this absurd game of power-play, needing to be the one in control.

Silver suffused his skin. Iravan trajected, and underneath him soil moved. He sensed the deep plates of the planet shift, sensed the seeds from the trees and plants lying dormant in the jungle. He could make them bear fruit. He could not operate outside of the realm of possibility, despite using the everpower, but this should be as easy as a Junior Architect's trajection. Irshar would not have to—

The soil underneath his hand burst, sharp spines rising from it, impaling his palm.

Iravan cried, wrenching his hand back, extracting himself.

His hand bled, but already it was healing, the skin knitting itself. He stared at the thorns protruding from the earth, and an image came to him through the evervision, of the smoky Virohi screaming. Of the falcon-yaksha thrumming its wings in panic. Of the rage of the planet in a silent echoing scream.

The ground he stood on caved in.

His feet slid, and Iravan folded the air with everpower, hovering as he saw the exact area he had been standing on turned into rubble. Somewhere deep beneath the planet, he heard a terrible roar.

He had one second of realization about what was going to occur.

Panicked, Iravan ascended, as trees came crashing down toward him.

25

AHILYA

They walked back to the infirmary in silence.

Ahilya had tried to make conversation, an observation here, a question there, but Kamala moved woodenly, speaking only in sparse words. The nurse had been from Nakshar, and though Ahilya only knew her from their association in Irshar, it was not hard to imagine what rumors Kamala had heard about her from her time in the airborne ashram. What did she make of the near-kiss she'd walked into, between Ahilya and Eskayra? The thought embarrassed Ahilya. How bizarre to think that once she and Iravan had tried to keep the problems of their marriage secret for the sanctity of material bonds. Now, their broken marriage was at the heart of the troubles for humanity, and any secret was meaningless. Kamala had caught Ahilya in a compromising position, and Ahilya felt intense dislike for her radiating from the nurse.

Each decision Ahilya made in her personal life now, whether to accept Eskayra's proposal of marriage, whether to finally divorce Iravan, whether to let herself feel innocent attraction, all of it had consequences for the citizens of Irshar. Iravan might not care about their marriage anymore, but he would not take kindly to her rejection. He would make Irshar pay in some way, consider it an insubordination. What kind of rationales would he make, trying to justify further violence, because of her actions?

Ahilya had never thought him a vindictive man, nor was jealousy his weakness, but she could not trust what she'd once known about him. He had changed, and several lives dictated him, each once tied with a material bond. She had no business kissing Esk, throwing the thin bond of her marriage in his face. She dropped her attempts at conversation, and kept steady pace with her nurse, trying not to give into fatigue.

Irshar spread out under their feet as they climbed a small hill that led away from the council chambers. Three months ago, when Ahilya and Chaiyya had made the city together, Irshar had been centered around the vriksh, the core tree rising from the center of a stone-paved plaza, the office chambers to one side, and homes and schools and other structures radiating miles in every direction. The constant assault of the cosmic creatures had eventually turned the flower-filled valleys into dangerous rubble, and far-flung residences into unmanageable zones. The council had ushered most citizens closer to the plaza, letting the outskirts remain unoccupied for a time for easier management—yet despite these changes, and the Virohi's interference, the ashram had remained largely the same.

Now, as Ahilya crested the hill, she saw how the vriksh's dominance had changed the landscape of not just the ashram but the surrounding jungle. The core tree was easily the largest tree around, rising high into the clouds, its canopy a layered structure that sheltered all of Irshar and much of the hills under it. The vriksh ascended from the plaza as it once had, but Irshar had changed into a dense, packed city within a bowl-like depression of the earth.

Instead of the luxurious sprawl of only a few months ago,

buildings clustered together now, held within jagged mountains that surrounded the city from all sides. Roots rambled from the core tree trapping buildings within them, and most buildings retained the strange, grotesque shapes of the Virohi escaping, an arm here, a frozen tentacle there, all evidence of the terrible battle. Though the ashram looked nothing like its airborne predecessors, Ahilya was reminded of all those times Nakshar had flown, a dense object too afraid of expanding.

There was the same fearful quality to the construction now, as though the ashram knew that its resources would be sorely depleted. As Ahilya walked, she had to wind her way past crowded roads and clustered citizens, past people pushing carts, wheeling barrows, and covering up holes in the road with shovels and spades. Repairs never stopped in the city, no matter the time of the day, night and day crews exchanging shifts. It was a restless way of survival, but the citizens had taken to it, finally in control of their lives to some degree. If Eskayra redesigned the new city to retain such control for them, perhaps she might convince them to move.

Ahilya slowed down as they passed a repair crew, chopping at the vriksh's roots to clear the path. Several citizens clustered there, speaking to each other, and she recognized a couple of familiar faces. Vihanan and Reniya had been citizens of Nakshar once. They'd been trapped in a pit with Ahilya outside the Architects' Academy when trajection had failed. Ahilya felt the urge to greet them, but then she glimpsed another person within the group.

Tariya's face was intense as she argued something with Reniya. Ahilya's embarrassment grew tenfold. Tariya was no part of the repair crews, unlike the other two, but she, Reniya, and Vihanan had always been friends, living a certain way of life in Nakshar as spouses of architects. It was amazing how some things remained the same no matter what else changed. Once Ahilya had felt unwelcome among them because of her inferior status as an archeologist. She felt no more welcome now, despite being a councilor of Irshar, perhaps because of it. Her marriage with Iravan had complicated things back then; it only exacerbated the ashram's problems now.

She turned away, but Tariya's gaze caught her and both the sisters froze. A thousand words crushed Ahilya's throat, but she could not speak them. The gulf between the two of them was too wide.

When Irshar had settled into a semblance of normal life after the Conclave's crash, the sisters had gone their separate ways. Ahilya continued to visit her nephews at the school and nursery every once in a while, but Tariya had become a stranger. At every turn, she'd opposed Ahilya, disdaining any attempt at reconciliation. She had been one of the most vociferous voices in the ashram, making her disapproval of the council clear, and even Ahilya's parents—who had survived the crash—no longer had her sister's consideration. It was as if in losing Bharavi, Tariya had finally understood the limits of what she loved. Ahilya had no place in her life anymore, except to be an object of disdain.

Tariya was not interested in leaving Irshar—and Ahilya suspected much of it had to do with her. In Tariya's mind, undoubtedly a new city was tied to both Ahilya and Iravan, one as its archeologist and the other as its architect. Eskayra was not the only one to think Ahilya might escape her past there. In the new city, both Ahilya and Iravan had a chance to remake themselves, to be free to pretend the errors of the past had not occurred—and Tariya was not about to allow that. Irshar was where Tariya was finally gaining influence. Irshar was where Ahilya and Iravan remained imprisoned and condemned, paying for their actions. Tariya had never been one to forgive easily. Though she worked at the same infirmary where Ahilya now lived, Ahilya hardly saw her. No matter her state, her sister's sympathies did not extend to her, and could she blame her?

Iravan had killed Bharavi, and Ahilya had witnessed the murder. What had she and her husband ever done except steal Tariya's happiness? They deserved Tariya's anger, and Tariya's gaze grew belligerent as if thinking the same thoughts.

Ahilya dropped her eyes in shame. She moved in a blur, away from the repair crew.

She had hardly taken two steps when a tremor shook the earth. Ahilya staggered and put her arm out to balance herself. People gasped, stopped in their tracks as they exchanged nervous glances. Parents grabbed hold of their children's hands, clutching them closer.

"It's all right," Ahilya called out, straightening. "It's just the ashram settling. The earthrages won't start again."

The tremors had been becoming more and more commonplace over the last few days, and the council had already issued advisories to the city, but still the citizens gave her skeptical glances. Over by Tariya, Reniya and Vihanan said something, seeming to nudge her toward Ahilya as if to ask for an explanation, but Tariya shook her head.

Ahilya wanted to tell them what she knew—that it was simply the everdust of the ashram learning its new shape now that the Virohi were no longer a part of it—but the explanation would not help these people. They did not trust her. They knew her as the Virohi's ally. In the past months, she had been to their homes to speak to the Virohi and settle them. Surely those from the expedition had told the others of her arguments to save the Virohi while Irshar trembled. Whether they once knew her personally or not, all of it became moot in light of her alliance with the cosmic creatures.

She could feel the stares piercing her skin. Every single one of the citizens knew of her relationship with Iravan. They knew of her status in the council. Did they know the bargain she made with the Garden too? Nothing was secret anymore. Strange to think that, when secrets had destroyed her marriage and opened chasms within their culture.

Another tremor shook the earth, and around her the path began to clear. Tariya, Vihanan and the rest turned their backs to Ahilya, while Reniya called out a command to pack up instruments and head back home. Ahilya walked away to where exposed green rock gave way to hard, cracked soil. The hole had been cordoned off, but she ducked under the rope, and knelt to the ground.

She removed the device Eskayra had given her from her pack, then plunged the glassy tube into the earth, pushing it as deep as it could go. The ashram around her was working on Ecstatic trajection, thanks to Iravan's architects, so the sungineering device buzzed to life as she switched it on. Its dial began vibrating. Ahilya felt a tremor run through her, as though emanating from the bowels of the earth.

Kamala leaned next to her in curiosity. "What are you doing?"

"The rages won't start again," Ahilya explained. "But not knowing when the next tremors will occur is disruptive. If this instrument can sense these tremors before they erupt, then perhaps the sungineers can enhance it to provide warnings. It's what the architects did with a plant called magnaroot once, to sense earthrages and send signals to the Architects' Disc to initiate flight protocol. A little warning could help the repairs."

The dial on the seismograph trembled. As Ahilya and Kamala watched, the dial pitched to the highest degree then shook there, as if wanting to swing further but unable to do so.

Kamala eyed the seismograph. "Why is it doing that?"

Ahilya frowned and turned the dial to adjust its frequency. Between her brows, she felt the vriksh calling to her in a wave of branches, though above her the canopy remained still. She could feel the Etherium yawning, pulling at her.

She paused in her attempts with the seismometer.

There was no point in denying the Etherium.

Ahilya closed her eyes and stepped into her third vision.

Immediately, the forest swallowed her. This time instead of the silence she had come to expect from the Etherium, a vibration rang through her. Shadows susurrated beyond the leaves, and stars spun above dizzyingly, a broken Moment blinking as though malfunctioning. The universe shone brightly, then burst apart in repeated flashes. Almost, she could hear voices, a dull roar like singing, like a raga, like herself. And through it, echoed the ever-present weeping of the Virohi, that grew louder, more deranged, more agitated. Ahilya felt the horror and pain of the cosmic creatures like a panic bubbling under her skin. Dark shapes buzzed in front of her, then disintegrated like bees. The Virohi were terrified of something.

Ahilya jerked away from the vision, breathing hard.

"Ahilya-ve?" Kamala asked, looking at her expression.

The Etherium slammed into her again, overtaking her vision.

Ahilya staggered, falling, and felt an eruption coming from deep within the earth. She saw the vriksh tightening its roots like a hand clutching the soil, trying to hold it together. She heard the cosmic creatures cry out. The tree loomed in her mind, rearing on itself, screaming in protest, a high-pitched whine that lasted for an instant, a hundred muddled voices echoing its scream. Ahilya blinked, unnerved, as the world righted, the vision disappearing.

She stumbled to her feet.

Kamala was opening her mouth, but Ahilya forestalled whatever concern the nurse would have. "Get inside," she said hoarsely to her. "Tell those people to get inside too, and stay there."

She waved a hand toward the repair crew, but there was no time to go warn them.

"Ahilya-ve—what—"

"Just go!"

Ahilya pushed a hesitating Kamala toward the repair crew, begged the vriksh to keep her sister safe, then turned and ran the way she'd come, back to the assembly chambers, nearly tripping and falling down the hill in her haste. Her feet pounded the broken stone pavement of the plaza, as leaves cascaded down from the vriksh, waving in the gentle breeze. She could hear the hysteria in her voice as she called out to startled citizens to get inside, as they stared at her in alarm. Ahilya rushed into the council chambers, slamming the door open to see Airav, Chaiyya, Kiana, and Basav look up at her, disconcerted. They had all been poring over another map, and Eskayra was among them, this time dressed in her expedition attire, sungineering devices strapped to her belt, evidently just about to leave for the new city.

"What happened?" Esk demanded, coming toward Ahilya immediately.

Ahilya opened her mouth to speak, but her vision *tilted,* and this time she saw the distortion blitzing through them too. She swayed on her feet, falling to the ground on all fours. Awareness burst through her in red-hot agony. Voices came to her through liquid sludge, *in the battery/rages unbound/your own brilliance*

She felt herself go underwater.

Ahilya kicked her legs, a vague memory of diving into a rock pool within Nakshar with Tariya when they were children. They had learned to swim together, splashing. How odd that she should remember this now.

Something was calling her.

No, she was calling *him*, a crooning sound.

They were calling him too, except they did it through her throat.

Ahilya grew winded. Root-like tentacles spread into her chest again. All of them were staring at each other, and then at her.

She staggered. Surfaced.

The architects responded first.

—*The Ecstatics*, Chaiyya asked, not a thought but a vague fear.

—*No, the Virohi,* Airav began—but saw himself thinking-not-thinking, speaking-not-speaking. His face drained of blood.

He approached the battery, and sat on the healbranch chair, knowing he was being watched by Ahilya and Dhruv. He did not say goodbye to Raghav. His husband would understand. Their love was stronger than this. He had barely formed the thought when pain—unlike any other shot through him. Blackness followed, one that he was infinitely aware of as though entering the Moment for the first time. His heart beat in terror as Ahilya asked, "How does this make me any better than Iravan?" *It doesn't,* he thought bitterly, *you two have destroyed us.* Chaiyya sobbed on his shoulders, and she—

She was pregnant, with twins, the healers said. What would become of Nakshar now? How would she ever manage newborns and the responsibility of being the lead councilor, during the time of the Conclave no less? Airav—but a hand clutched her heart as she thought of Airav and what he had been made to do for Nakshar's survival. She could not let that be for nothing. "Do you accept?" she asked, and the archeologist breathed out her anger, her acquiescence to her destruction in the acceptance of councillorship, and she/I

said, *You two deserve each other.* I watched her face fall, a punishment she deserved—but she is here, she is here, behind my eyes, rages, how, get out, *get OUT*

Ahilya pulled away. They were all staring at her. Dhruv's eyes were wide. Airav's mouth hung open. Kiana clutched at Chaiyya, eyes bugging out. Had they all seen these thoughts, these memories? Was this her thought at all?

Dhruv's voice was a whisper. "What is this?"

Ahilya swallowed. Her chest seized in the pain of being crushed by roots.

"A-Ahilya-ve," Airav stuttered. "D-Do you know?"

You two have destroyed us.

Eskayra turned to her, a question on her face. An image formed in Ahilya's mind, rising from her heart and flowering into her brain like a plant. The vriksh pulled at her, calling, calling.

She fled, responding to its summons.

26

IRAVAN

Iravan fought gravity. The air dragged him down, clawing at his limbs like a thousand hands. He breathed fitfully, as though inhaling mud. Was he ascending? The ground was still so close, chasing him. His eyes drew upward, to the slash of distorting trees, the snatch of blue skies, a streak of clouds. The everpower rushed through him, and he unleashed a burst of speed to try to break away, as rocks shot up toward him like arrows, slicing into his cloak.

The consciousness meld tried to suck him in. He could hear them, Ahilya, Dhruv, Airav, and the citizens of Irshar murmuring in his ears all together past sanity. Unable to pull up his shield, Iravan fell into his Etherium, his past lives cycling. He seized the first one he saw.

Isanya crept inside him like a set of bones. She flipped mid-air, and Iravan felt her curiosity and wonder bloom in his heart, just for an instant, before they were the same. He cried out as she brought up their arms in a straight line, shooting into the sky. Trees streaked past, rocks pelting them, scoring Iravan's limbs, and Isanya burst through the cover, into free air. Iravan didn't trust them to look back. He kept them pointed upward, Isanya rising them ever higher until it grew harder to breathe.

He spun around, facing the jungle again.

It astonished him how normal the terrain looked, the day bright and clear, the jungle as motionless as he'd left it.

Then the planet shook, filling his eyes. A massive orb that writhed restlessly in his vision, cracking into two, blowing into smithereens.

The vision lasted only for a second. When he blinked again, Iravan saw the jungle just as still as it had been. He clutched Isanya, not understanding, and the planet shook again, shrieking, a high-pitched whine in his ears.

Trees undulated in the wind. Through the stillness, Iravan saw giant tree trunks from the forest rise, then hurtle toward him like spears. The evervision shivered, the power of the three realms weakening. Isanya took over, turning them again, flying faster.

The planet followed.

27

AHILYA

She stumbled through the doorway, the voices of the Virohi filling her ears. Her vision swam, one step on the rubbly pathway of the courtyard—

The next on a gnarled root of the vriksh, her hand on its trunk.

She was here already. How?

The question was fleeting. She was here. It was all that mattered.

Ahilya put her forehead on the tree. *Let me in.*

The Etherium opened like a door between her brows.

A glimpse of the mirrored chambers—then she dropped within the forest.

Ridges and wrinkles in brown surrounded her, bark that was atrophying in front of her eyes, each sliver a window into a life. The scent of wood infiltrated her, but she could not place it. It reminded her of her childhood, a brief vision of laughter and regret. Leaves curled around her protectively, nestling her within her memory, and she heard the Virohi whisper, *We are here/Where is here?* Fear permeated her, but it was not hers, it was the suppressed fear of a thousand lives and memories, filtering through to her, because she was now in the vriksh, she *was* the vriksh.

In some part of her mind, Ahilya knew that she was not within the core tree of Irshar. That though she was touching it with her hands and head, she had fallen to her knees at its base, her eyes closed. But she was inside the tree too—and the world swirled around her in rings and loops, time cascading from one memory into another.

She lived and relived.

Waves came to her, drowning her before she resurfaced. Airav on the healbranch chair, Tariya's scream when they told her of Bharavi's death, Chaiyya's horror on learning of her Ecstasy. Ahilya trembled, one wave crashing as another receded, not knowing where she was.

When she breathed it was the breath of the tree, and she felt a compression, as Iravan turned her and all her siblings into a single creature—the assimilation of the core trees in the sky while the Conclave dropped into the earthrage. The trees had always shaped their citizens as much as they had been shaped. Their memory, their pain, sorrow and joy sparked within her body, burning to the tips of her fingers, to the space between her knuckles, to her lungs and her stomach, sifting, resolving, embedding in the same way the core trees had to the desires of airborne citizens for a thousand years. The pain of holding so much memory was excruciating, and the falling leaves of memories turned into thorns. Razor sharp, each of them with tiny, serrated edges, the thorns rained down on her, impaling her. The tree converted its memories into these vicious points, and plunged each thorn into her skin.

Ahilya screamed, horrified, as more thorns rained down on her, pinning her.

In a corner of her mind, she felt Iravan. The pain was excruciating, and she realized she was chanting his name. *Please,* she thought. *Please.* She—and the tree she was now—turned toward him, pleading.

28

IRAVAN

The planet grabbed at his limbs, the air warping around him in its attack. Iravan beat it back, attempting to breathe, but his skin was ripping and the air solidified in his throat.

It was strange that in this moment, with the planet killing him, Iravan finally understood the everpower.

Trajection worked on constellation lines, Ecstasy through raw power of desire. Yet there were layers to desire—a thought, an intent, and then finally the will to turn it into action, all within the realms of what was possible. It was never enough to simply want. One had to convert that want into something tangible, pushing the fleetest possibility into actualization.

But no want ever existed without resistance.

There was resistance from oneself and those around them. In airborne ashrams, all architects had once grappled with doubt about the reality of their second vision, and the weight of being saviors of civilization. Even Iravan had felt it as a Senior Architect—it was why he lived in Nakshar's temple alone for seven months, knowing Ahilya's questioning of him could seed doubt in his power. It was why architects were taught only to float in the Moment and do little else for the longest time, cementing themselves, believing in their vision, their purpose, their minds. The level of resistance one experienced from oneself and their loved ones was common to all architects; it was simply a way of life.

But there was another resistance, one not spoken of often.

Resistance from the subject of trajection.

In manipulating life, architects manipulated the existing desire of a life form to stay in its current shape, to follow the rules of nature in growing and decaying and dying. In essence, trajection was a competition of an architect's desire against the subject's desire. This was why plants had always been easiest. This was why trajecting higher beings could break an architect's mind. It was why Maze Architect Viana had died—her desire in competition with Iravan's own.

Iravan contended with it now—for the first time understanding that when he used the everpower he trajected not a being which was equal or lower to him, but one that was greater. A presence that could overpower his desire, without trying, simply by being.

Billions of years older than him and the yakshas, a mass of rock and metal almost as old as the universe—the planet vibrated, hard, on its axis. A living thing chasing him, intent on destroying him.

Iravan gasped, his body shuddering, blood turning cold. A million hands grabbed him, air currents cascading and intersecting, trying to trap him. He pulled through quicksand, but fire—*fire*—formed in tiny sparks at the edge of his vision, burning his skin. His cloak tangled in his legs, and he spun, trying to gain control. A roar filled his ears as a gale swept him off his intended flight path, flicking him sideways, making it nearly impossible to traject in the evervision. As a trajecting architect, he had learned to sweep aside the resistance from a subject—but none of his methods worked.

He felt the planet's awareness blaring, and memory flashed, of magnaroot during a fateful jungle expedition that had once reacted similarly, its opposing desire so strong he had been unable to make constellation lines. The skin around his eyes burned, and a deep horror of being blinded seized him.

But then Isanya broke through, her desire to be free melding with Iravan's, and they ascended high enough to feel the scorching afternoon sun on their backs, to see the curve of the horizon. Iravan's silver tattoos gleamed so strongly he could make their tracing out under the weave of the black kurta he wore. Control returned to him with a shock of sudden stability.

Iravan hovered, turning toward the earth again. From here, the jungle was simply a blur of green, like he were an airborne ashram. In the evervision, he felt the planet's desire echo to him in waves. Images rushed in his head, a stillness in motion, an unseen orbit around the sun. A glimpse of a battle, and the movement of tectonic plates—except unnatural.

It should have been simple. It had been simple. His desire against that of the planet, now that he had escaped its immediate clutches. But he was in the lower atmosphere still, and he felt the planet's power growing. The planet yawned open to swallow him, sucking him into a whirlpool.

He saw behind his brows Ahilya on her knees, suffering in the same way that he did. She hid behind the shapes of the Virohi, mutilated and assimilated with them. The corruption had gone so deep, it was impossible to tell if it really was her or the cosmic creatures that he saw. All of it looked the same, a shape that resembled her, yet decayed and weeping. They were calling. *She* was calling. In the end, what else was he supposed to do but listen to her?

His hands reached toward her. If this was to be their end, she was all he needed to save.

29

AHILYA

Help us, she echoed. Not her, but the Virohi, escaping erasure while their planet reacted in shock at what was occurring.

Help us, they echoed. Not the Virohi, but a memory of all of them, citizens chanting in sing-song, while unnamed versions of them sent out ineffectual desires to unknown entities in a fervent wish.

Help us, it echoed, not the memory, but this entity, condensed as a single woman carrying it all. Familiar trustworthy hands reached her, a scent of eucalyptus and firemint. She grabbed them, weakening.

30

IRAVAN

With his shields down, Iravan had no resistance when Ahilya pulled him into her mind in her frenzy. Within the strange forest, she lay on the ground, her eyes open, her skin impaled with glittering dark thorns that reached down from branches. Each thorn was a memory of the core tree, and each memory bloomed a dozen more, flooding her, assaulting her. Her eyes were unseeing. Ahilya screamed and screamed, and with her so did humanity.

The horrifying image jerked Iravan back into clarity. He found control, not of the place but of himself. He was an architect—he had been trained in holding onto multiple visions and keeping his sanity through it. He had been resisting the pull of her Etherium ever since she had sought him in Irshar's solar lab, but now he stood in her forest while he flew in the air, attempting to escape the planet.

The forest shook, and between each vibration Iravan saw a hundred more memories impale her—memories of the trees, of himself, of the Virohi and all the citizens. Iravan reached down to his wife, moving slowly through each wave of assault.

Her pain was his.

Don't, Mohini told him, and her eyes glinted like those of the falcon-yaksha.

Let it happen, Bhaskar said, and his laughter sounded like the falcon's roar.

If the tree dies, so do the Virohi, Agni growled, and behind them the yaksha beat its wings.

But Iravan held onto himself by sheer will.

Because it was him, *him,* listening to his wife scream—not their wife, but his, and that meant something, despite everything.

And his desire—*his*—flared in rebellion.

The tree shook, and he fell to his knees, wrapping her in his arms, forming a shield of his intent around them both. It happened in the Etherium borne of his connection with her, but it happened in reality too—he could see it, a shimmering of air around her body while she knelt at the vriksh.

Ahilya wept, trembling, holding on to the tree and him. Iravan screamed against the voices telling him to let go. The planet raged around the two of them—and only them, a whipping of their hair, wind like jagged pieces of glass, rain that thrummed drenching them, mud that filled their mouths, choking them.

Iravan locked onto his desire, trajecting each element separately, turning the mud into dust so when he coughed and breathed, Ahilya did too. He trajected, changing sharp rain into soft dew drops that melted onto their skins. The wind turned into smooth caresses, no longer scoring them, and he and Ahilya gasped, while the planet tried to assert its dominance.

He trajected with the everpower, dizzyingly fast—

And lost his balance, in the manner of forcefully pushing a door that was already ajar. Iravan flipped in midair, trying to stabilize. Isanya had left him, and for a second he felt horror, to be alone while the past lives of his Etherium retreated from the danger, while the planet attacked him, and the consciousness meld occurred.

Then it registered.

The planet had stilled. The attack of the memories had stopped.

This was a testing, a resting. The planet was spent for now, a brief lull occurring.

He could see Ahilya, holding onto the tree, her arms limp, slowly falling by her side. Her eyes were unseeing. In the Etherium, she was light as air, collapsing into him, the thorns receding.

He tightened his hold, brushing her hair back, leaning to check on her.

But she was spent, losing consciousness already.

Her Etherium winked out, banishing him once again.

31

AHILYA

When she became conscious, it rendered first in the forest like a dream.

She found herself lying on someone's lap, staring up at the canopy of the vriksh. She shifted, alarmed, but Iravan bent to her. She relaxed—because he looked like *her* Iravan. He was dressed in his white Senior Architect uniform, the sleeves rolled back, blue-green trajection tattoos on his skin. His near-black eyes were deep pools of concern. "I've been waiting," he said softly, relief breaking over his features. "Oh my love, I have been so worried."

He helped her sit up, and she stared around her. The vast forest of the vriksh was once again still—as still as it could be with leaves curling and uncurling everywhere as if in an airborne ashram. She could not sense the Virohi anymore, but a presence seemed wrapped around her heart. She looked down to her chest, expecting to see tight bands of roots holding her, but her fingers merely traced over her clothes.

"You are here? In my forest?" she croaked, her mouth dry.

"I've been waiting," he repeated sadly. "Waiting with my

Etherium open, hoping you would summon me, and you have." There were questions behind these words, she could tell, of how she had summoned him, of what had happened to her, but he did not ask them. How was it that he looked so much like the Iravan she had lost?

"It's because you have control here," he said, answering her as if he could hear the question. His smile was lopsided, wretched. "Oh my love," he whispered, leaning down, and she was surprised to see tears tracking down his cheeks. "I'm so sorry. I never wanted it to be this way."

His mouth met hers, and she opened her own, and felt him shudder against him. He tasted of salt, and terror, and regret, but before either of them could deepen the kiss, Ahilya felt the bands across her chest tighten. She pushed away from him, and this time she saw the roots wrapped around her, though Iravan did not seem to notice. She lifted her hands to her eyes and saw not fingers but branches protruding. She stifled her cry, closing her eyes tightly—

A fuzziness of existence where she was turning into the tree.

She screamed for Iravan, for Eskayra, for anyone to hear her—

And awoke with a jerk within the infirmary once more.

She knew instantly where she was. The familiar scents of herbs and ointments climbed up her nose the second she came to herself. She could hear the soft swishing of the pale-white curtains, and when she opened her eyes she saw the rock ceiling with the crisscross patterns, comforting in its familiarity.

She knew where she was, but for a confused instant she could not remember her name. The absurd realization came to her slowly, as if she could see it approaching but could not make sense of it.

From far away, she heard the sounds of people she had never met. It bothered her, but she could not immediately tell why. What did it matter that she didn't know those sounds? She couldn't know everybody, after all. That was not humanly possible.

Except I do know them, she thought. *I know them, because I* am *them.*

The events under the vriksh came rushing to her. The impaling, the pain, and Iravan's rescue of her.

She bolted upright, her body trembling, but someone reached out to steady her. "Slow down," the nurse said. "You need to slow down."

Her breath still came out too fast, her chest rising and falling too rapidly. She was wearing one of the infirmary's gowns. How long had she been here?

Wildly, she looked around at her private chamber. It was bare except for the cot she was on, and the nurse who had just spoken. The only light came from the window, and for some reason she knew the chamber had been kept dim because she had asked for it to be so. This is where she lived now. Not in Nakshar, not in an airborne ashram, but here in the jungle, within a medical ward. She pressed a hand to the base of her neck where the tightness had settled, but as she touched the knot it flared, so she dropped her hand and closed her eyes.

One, two, three breaths went by—until her vision adjusted. She opened her eyes again, and the image of the branches across her fingers receded. She saw her dark skin. She stared at the contours of her hand, at the moon-shaped nails.

I am... I am a person, she thought, and a hysterical sound escaped her at how foolish that thought was, yet how necessary.

She looked up at the nurse to see if she was laughing too, but other shapes caught her eyes, hovering behind the nurse. Three people stood waiting by the door. Not Dhruv. Not Naila. And certainly not Iravan, though she could remember the taste of his lips from the half-dream—no, these were councilors of Irshar. Of her ashram.

With those names, more information poured into her brain, like waking from a particularly consuming sleep. She adjusted her pillows carefully.

"What happened?" she asked, her voice hoarse.

"Do you know who you are?" the nurse replied quietly.

The light of clarity was pouring into her more rapidly. Ahilya raised her eyes to the nurse. Kamala, that was the healer's name. The urgency had passed; that's why Kamala was asking this question now.

"Yes," she answered. Her voice came as a croak. "I am Ahilya. I am a complete being. I am not alone."

The litany came naturally to her, an expected and learned response to this question.

For a long moment, Kamala watched her, not believing her reply. Ahilya barely believed her own words too.

An eerie sense came over her. She saw herself from behind Kamala's eyes, but she also saw a memory—Kamala with Oam. Oam wore a nurse's scrubs, but his braided curls were tied in a knot. They were chatting to each other in Nakshar's infirmary. Kamala smiled—*teasing Oam, asking him why he would go into the jungle on an expedition with this older woman. Jealousy streaks in my eyes, that he would choose her.*

Ahilya let the vision drop. Her heart raced as the other woman simply nodded and retreated, and Ahilya forced herself to take three deep breaths like she had been trained to. Slowly, gaining control over herself, she tracked the councilors as they watched the nurse leave and entered her personal ward.

Chaiyya and Basav drew closer to one side of her cot, pulling chairs alongside her. On the other side, Airav stopped his wheelchair, his gaze sad, the same expression he had each time he visited. Ahilya tried to school her expression, not wanting to answer inane questions about her health, but the effort was too much. It was all she could do to raise her eyebrows in the obvious question: *What happened?*

Chaiyya gave her a long look, sighed, then shook her head. "You've been unconscious for five days," she said quietly. "Your vitals were strong, yet you refused to wake. Do you remember anything?"

"Five days," she rasped, swallowing. "Where is Eskayra?"

"She left this morning," Chaiyya said. "She did not want to, but the new city site needed her. She will be back tonight."

Ahilya shook her head. "I—I don't understand. We were speaking to each other. We were in the council chambers..." Her eyes widened, and her hands shook. Events returned to her, of running through Irshar, of skidding to a stop in the council chambers, and then in her Etherium, being impaled by the thorns in the forest. Ahilya looked at her hands, expecting to find twigs instead of her fingers, sap instead of blood in her veins. "It was the vriksh, wasn't it? I remember its call to me. Wha-what happened? Did I—" Her voice came out cracked. "Did I hurt anybody? My sister—is she all right? I remember the ground shaking."

They had all clearly discussed the phenomenon in the last five days, and Ahilya saw Basav's repressed terror and anger in the pinch of his mouth. She wondered if he would say anything or let her question hang. Ahilya got the impression that he was trying hard to be civil.

"You didn't hurt anyone," he said, his voice clipped. "And the citizens, including your sister, are fine. Whatever happened did not impact them for now. But what you did... The vriksh..."

The others did not speak into his silence, and Ahilya shrank under their scrutiny.

"The vriksh was an anomaly to begin with," Basav said. "Even before you used it to anchor the cosmic creatures within the planet. It was the amalgamation of all the fifty core trees of the Conclave, created during a time of great upheaval. Core trees have always been sentient, this much has been apparent to us architects—but the vriksh is more powerful than any single core tree. It, as you said, called to you. It was behind what occurred."

"Why?" Ahilya asked. There was something chilling in the way Basav had spoken, like he was trying to hide something horrible behind his academic explanation.

"Tell me," Basav replied. "Do you see the cosmic creatures now?"

"No, not clearly, not since they escaped the ashram. You know this." But Ahilya cut herself off, frowning.

She had seen murmurs of citizens in there before, of Dhruv and Chaiyya, and she'd spoken to Iravan there. She'd seen the weeping, huddled shapes of the cosmic creatures too, though those had disappeared. Now past the leaves of her memories, she glimpsed something in the Etherium. A shadow and a whisper and a thousand tendrils of smoke bleeding into dark echoes. The Virohi were here, except instead of being a single mass of grieving shapes, they had diffused somehow to permeate the tree.

An image came to her in explanation—the cosmic creatures caught inside the vriksh like little seedlings, traveling through osmosis into her mind.

But not just her mind.

All of the citizens' too.

Her eyes grew wide and she stared at Basav. He saw her comprehension.

"You understand then?" he said softly.

"I— I—"

Basav's voice grew cold. "When you allowed the cosmic creatures into the tree, you gave them access to all of us, architect and non-architect alike. To our knowledge, our memories, everything. To the codes of trajection. They have more knowledge about us than we do, they know what we have forgotten about ourselves. You already know this, don't you?"

Ahilya remembered that time in Nakshar when she had seen the desires of people spark within the rudra-tree. When she had understood how archival memory was created, and how it was maintained within a core tree. The vriksh's sentience, its life... these were the lives of people, a living history that had formed within its trunk, and that dictated everyone's reality within the ashram. All the lives of every citizen on Irshar were inextricably tied to the vriksh. And with the Virohi within the tree, the vriksh was tied to the Virohi too. A choking sound emerged from her throat.

Chaiyya reached forward, concern on her face, but Ahilya pushed her aside. She couldn't bear to be touched, not when she had been violated so deeply already, not when she had violated others in return. She felt sick.

"We're calling it overwriting," Airav said quietly. "The Virohi have access to the tree, and they have always seen you as one of them. Now that they have access to us through the tree, through *you*, they are attempting to take over our consciousnesses. Should they succeed, we will lose ourselves—to be human no longer, but this corrupted version—whatever they wish us to be. Our perception of reality will begin to warp. I'm afraid, Ahilya-ve, that humanity might simply become their vessels."

"Like me," she whispered.

All three councilors nodded. Ahilya shivered. She had been resentful of the others for never knowing how she suffered with the cosmic creatures, but she never wanted this. She could imagine it clearly—each thorn of memory filling her with the citizens' secrets until she was a nothing but a vessel that held all of them. Then with her at the helm, the Virohi would reach for each of these people in turn, connecting to them through the vriksh. A true hive mind, until each of the citizens became mere marionettes, sheaths of skin and meat holding nothing but the Virohi. The Virohi had split into architects, holding them as a vessel alongside yakshas, but this would be every single person. All of humanity lost to its mind, brief flashes of memory reminding them of who they had once been. It was like the old joke she and Dhruv used to tell each other when discussing their place in Nakshar. What was worse than erasure? An everlasting memory of it. Ahilya thought that she might vomit.

"What triggered this?" she asked, past the stone in her throat. "After all these days and weeks, why did the Virohi attempt to overwrite us now?"

"Does it matter?" Basav said.

"If we know it, perhaps we can prevent it from occurring again."

"We cannot know it," Basav replied, nearly spitting. "It is likely a natural consequence of things occurring. And it is already too late to prevent it. Now that they are in the tree, the process of overwriting has begun. Perhaps the Virohi needed those last few weeks to evolve and understand their new position before attacking us. Perhaps this was always going to occur right from the time Iravan-ve created Irshar and manipulated all the other core trees, making them *open* to the Virohi's infection. We can never know. All we know is the effects that rendered when we all momentarily became you. We became your playthings. For a brief time, we lost ourselves completely, our consciousnesses tossing around inside your own."

Ahilya's hands tightened on her covers again. She stared at the fabric, the coarse weave of cotton, the tiny patterns on the cloth. Scattered images came to her, of the vriksh weeping, and Iravan reaching his hands for her. She tried to build a complete picture, but it was as though she was performing archeology on herself. The feeling was so bizarre that the tightness in her neck increased, itching.

Overwriting, she thought—and Basav called it them becoming her, but no, this was about Ahilya becoming the rest of these people. Not the other way around. Did it make any difference?

Pieces of the puzzle appeared and vanished in her head. Iravan, the mirrored chambers, the manner they had spoken in and communicated before—and then what had happened with the vriksh. She had started down this path to be recognized. She had once wanted to be important. Everything she had done had been motivated by it, once upon a time. Archeology, the study of earthrages, her every action, all of it had contained the seed of her pride. She had become entangled in the architects and their lives, in the politics of survival, but who was she really? Just a simple archeologist, with little training for anything else.

Ahilya closed her eyes, and just for an instant she saw not the nightmare she lived in, but a shining moment of the past. Iravan and her lying on their backs, looking up at the sky from one of Nakshar's terraces, discussing and theorizing arbitrary matters, which neither of them ever could imagine would become real. Very carefully, she smoothed her hands over the covers, knowing that the others were watching her every move.

"All is not lost," Airav said softly. "This incident has given us a warning of what can occur, but while the Virohi are contaminating the tree—and you—like an infection, as long as you keep control over yourself, you will slow their corruption. You will be the necessary barrier between them and us. But if you don't, if you give in or give up, it is likely that the Virohi will convert us to what they wish. Suffice to say, if they did so we would be erased."

Ahilya could still feel the thorns under her skin. What Airav said was tantamount to allowing herself to live with such an attack, while holding onto her reality and self. How could he ask her this so callously? Did he not know she was weak?

"I have failed you once already," she said softly. "I have failed you many times."

"We know," Basav said shortly. "Which is why we have thought of a solution."

"This is an opportunity," Chaiyya said gently. "Ahilya, you would never have been able to extract the Virohi from the tree. All your attempts so far have failed, and none of us know enough about the Virohi to help you, not with all our records so lost. But if they're contaminating the core tree and are visible to you there, you can use your control of the vriksh. You can help Iravan destroy them."

Ahilya recoiled, staring from one to another. "I wouldn't know where to begin," she said, swallowing. "I don't have true control of the tree, and I only see the Virohi in shadows. I don't know where they are, and if I did, I wouldn't know how to destroy them."

"That," Basav said, "is why I am here."

From his satchel, he removed a thick book. Ahilya had once owned a similar satchel. She had carried it everywhere, but now Basav had taken over that affectation, carrying his most precious possessions with him at all times. No place was safe, after all, not since architecture could change on a whim even for Senior Architects.

She glimpsed other items in the satchel, more books, a few faded pictures of Basav with a woman and children, some documents that looked official. She did not know what they meant, but suddenly she received a glimpse from behind his eyes, as he was presented with honors for the work he did in his ashram. Basav's younger face shone with pride before withering away into memory. Ahilya shivered as if she had done something wrong by glimpsing this.

In the infirmary, the Senior Architect opened the tome. Upside-down though it was, Ahilya could tell that it was an ancient architect record. The paper was yellow with age, and Basav lifted each page carefully like it was the most delicate child. It was shocking that he had recovered this from the Conclave's crash. How much other literature had they lost? Ahilya still did not have access to all of the remaining records, though with her corruption, this rejection finally made a perverse kind of sense.

Basav did not offer the book to her. From the way his fingers clutched the pages, Ahilya knew that it pained him to share whatever knowledge it contained with her, with a non-architect.

But Ahilya was no stranger to such architect records. She had seen others of this kind before—books with no words but only beautifully drawn pictures, in colors made out of plant dye and paper of the thinnest bark. Iravan had once brought her something similar as a gift. He had seduced her with the promise of more. She leaned forward and studied the image, though Basav held the book away from her. A tree covered the open page, broad-trunked and healthy. Yet cracks bled on the tree, leaking not sap but blood. Though the tree stood erect, there was pain in the posture, reverberating from its branches in the tightening of the leaves and the clenching of the branches.

"I have been arming myself with knowledge of the trees ever since the creation of the vriksh," Basav said slowly, still staring at the book.

Basav led the charge for communing with survivors of the fallen ashrams, attempting to record architect history, trying to hold onto the version of the past he was familiar with. Ahilya had known the tragedy of such an endeavor, but his pain disconcerted her now. The lines on his face, the way his fingers shook. He was barely holding on to sanity, and she wanted to reach out a hand, comfort him despite his abhorrence of her, but Basav looked up to meet Ahilya's eyes, and she flinched.

She wanted to tell him she wasn't infiltrating him, not willingly at least, but the words stuck in her throat. She looked back to her covers.

"What I tell you now has been a great secret, even in architect circles," Basav said, his voice gravelly, holding onto his fury. "Understand that I would not share this if there was any other way."

She nodded once, but Basav did not acknowledge it. Instead, he traced a finger over the image. "You already know that we excised architects who showed Ecstasy. In your ashram, the councilors used an Examination of Ecstasy, but within the Seven Northern Sisters, suspicion was enough. We did not seek proof that would only be ambiguous, at best."

Ahilya stared at him. In her mind's eye, she saw Iravan in a deathcage, his sleeves rolled back, as he faced the Conclave of all the sister-ashrams in a sham trial that was meant to unhinge him. Basav had never wanted Iravan to live. He'd stepped into the deathmaze, opening himself to being trajected into madness, all to prove a point. She had called him a bastard for it, she had railed against him. Even now, she could not help her distaste. Ahilya stirred, wanting to put some distance between them.

Basav's flat gaze swept across her as if he could hear her judgment. "We were not so frivolous, gambling with survival," he said coldly, his eyes taking in the other two councilors too.

Ahilya watched her own shame and confusion spark across Chaiyya and Airav's faces. All three of them had once been councilors of Nakshar. She had fought for Ecstasy to become legal, but before her time the other two had been part of the laws to uphold the Examination of Ecstasy. Basav's unspoken disgust and recrimination was clear—had Nakshar followed instant-excision, humanity would not be in the jungle, facing extinction.

Was that the path she had not taken, then? Would that have prevented all this? His ashram had destroyed lives. His ashram had excised children. *We are all wrong in some measure,* she thought. *What can we do, except work with what we have been given?* It should have been a comforting thought, but all Ahilya felt was misery. Was this to be the destiny for their species then? To make mistakes over and over again, to destroy themselves because of hate and arrogance and superfluous power grabs? *The Virohi truly are foolish,* she thought in morbid irony. *To wish to become like* us*—they have to be mad.*

"The codes for excising an Ecstatic Architect were wrought within the core trees of the Seven Northern Sisters," Basav continued. "Your ashram might have drifted from tradition in terrible directions, but even Nakshar kept to this as did every sister ashram. Only Senior Architects of a city knew how to trigger these excision codes. In some ways, it is a similar trajection they orchestrated with the Architects' Disc when subsuming an offending ashram—excising its core tree into tiny parts, then absorbing the remainder of the ashram into itself. Every ashram had this knowledge."

Ahilya had a horrifying image of an airborne city sending a thousand tentacle-like roots into another airborne structure, splitting it into fragments and sucking its pieces into itself, while the core tree burst into powder. Even imagined, the violence of it shook her.

It was the danger Nakshar had faced in opposing the Conclave and supporting the claim for Ecstatics to be free. The Conclave's crash into the jungle had ended the need for such political maneuvering, but once Nakshar's total erasure had held the city's councilors at chokepoint. It was the reason Chaiyya had sacrificed Iravan and the other Ecstatics, opening them to excision and paving the path to illegal experimentation on them for powering an Ecstatic battery. How different things would have been had they all simply treated one another as human beings, worthy of respect and care. *But we have shown time and again that we are not capable of compassion,* Ahilya thought. *We do not care for the other. We* create *the other.*

She had been such an outsider once. Now it was the Virohi.

Silent laughter built in her head. "How is this to help me?" she asked.

Basav looked at her, frowning at her tone. "If you had found a way to extract the Virohi, we would be having a different conversation," he said. "Iravan-ve knows the codes of excision, and I would simply have had you contain the infection within a single part of the vriksh, and hand it over to him to excise. But he cannot control the Etherium like you can, so you are our only option. You will have to perform the excision."

He turned to another page. Then, reluctance in every inch of his movements, Basav handed Ahilya the book.

The second sketch was beautiful and horrifying. Two architects of indeterminate gender faced each other under the boughs of a massive, leafy core tree. Circles of radiance emanated from each of their bodies, but one was on their knees—clearly an Ecstatic—whereas the other stood glowing blue-green, clearly a Senior Architect. Stars wheeled overhead connected through constellation lines—a representation of the Moment, Ahilya knew. Jagged shards of lightning flung down from the stars, powered by the looming Senior Architect's trajection.

Ahilya flipped a page, her heart racing. The Ecstatic Architect's face was thrown back in a scream. The circles of radiance around their body diminished, as she continued to flip the pages, becoming smaller and smaller, until the architect was no longer within the boughs of the tree. The last image showed the Ecstatic Architect prone on the floor. Discarded. Alone. Excised.

She raised her eyes to the other councilors. Each one of them had once committed such an act.

"Excision," she breathed. "When you excised an architect, you did not simply cut them from their yakshas. No—you didn't know of the yakshas. You cut them away from their ashram's core tree. From the codes of trajection. Am I right?"

Basav's silence was answer enough.

Ahilya felt nauseated.

Iravan had always been tight-lipped about excision. He'd told her excision cut an architect away from their power, but how could architects do so without trajecting each other? Architects were forbidden from trajecting people or their core trees—each of those actions was a sign of sure Ecstasy. So they trajected the ashram instead, withdrawing permissions until the Ecstatic was unrecognizable by the city as a citizen. The tree was coded to protect architects over non-architects, but if they took away the tree's ability to recognize the Ecstatic as a citizen, as a person or a human being, the core tree would become compliant. And instead of a Senior Architect conducting excision, the core tree would attack the Ecstatic.

Ahilya imagined it—a core tree, with all its power, sloughing away at an Ecstatic's consciousness, seeing their life as a contaminant to the ashram, much like a forbidden jungle plant. Once, Nakshar had chosen not to recognize ordinary citizens as part of the ashram during the Conclave. Ahilya had taken Chaiyya's borrowed rudra bead and changed the permissions, protecting her sister and the rest of the non-architects, unwilling to sacrifice them for the council's politics.

But the council had always done such calculations, even unto their own. Each time they'd sent an architect to be excised, they had stripped away that architect's humanity.

Perhaps the Ecstatic had withered away, their power leaking with their consciousness, until nothing else remained. Perhaps their loss of self came not from their inability to traject, but because they had been cut off from their society. That is what had happened to Manav. To Maiya, who Iravan had shown her in Nakshar's sanctum, and to all those who had been found guilty of the power for thousands of years. They lost their ability to traject *because* of the loss of their mind. Hadn't Iravan told her often that in order to traject, one had to hold onto their own consciousness, their own will. Tied in a thousand ways to a core tree, with memory and consciousness fed to it through every act, the separation from a tree would be devastating to an Ecstatic Architect. Ahilya stared at the picture in the book and imagined the total obliteration of a person, performed in concerted cruelty, all because they were different.

No wonder there was such hate and fear of excision in architect circles. When Iravan had told her long ago that Ecstatics would not be recognized as humans by other councils in the Conclave, he had not spoken out of simple fear. He'd understood the mechanics of it, of the fate that awaited each Ecstatic. This is why he and Bharavi had made a pact. Why the ashrams had preserved their excised architects within a secret sanctum, away from the rest of their society. Why they kept the truth about what happened to an excised architect such a mystery, even going as far as to make architects have children before revealing its secret to their spouses. All citizens revered their core tree, architects more than others. These were actions borne of guilt—each lie piling atop the other until all of it crashed to the jungle.

Did the others really expect her to do this to the Virohi?

The heartpoison bracelet around her wrist prickled in premonition. Ahilya pushed the book back into Basav's hands. "I am not an architect," she said, her throat thick. "I cannot excise using constellation lines."

"The constellation lines are secondary," Basav replied, scowling. "You do not need them. You are connected to the vriksh. It is a matter of will, and a simple technique of visualization—an act of severance. Call the Virohi to you. Convince them to stay with you, close enough to feel them. Then sever them from the vriksh, cutting them away from everything. Then, we can finally be rid of the cosmic creatures."

"No," Ahilya said. "Please, don't do this. You know how cruel it is. You've seen what happens to excised architects."

Basav frowned at her. "Are you refusing the council? Are you placing these creatures above humanity itself, even after what I told you about overwriting?"

Ahilya shook her head, backpedaling. "No," she said hurriedly. "No, I just meant I—I won't be able to do this—you expect too much of me—I can't—I don't have that kind of control—"

"Try it," Chaiyya urged. "Try to call them, right now. You already know how. Let's find out here and now."

She could not say no. Even as Chaiyya commanded her, the fuzzy darkness of the Virohi hummed in Ahilya's mind, and she imagined the cosmic creatures like the singular entity she had seen before. Particles flaked to her, forming a body in her own shape. The Virohi swarmed in front of her, huddling again, their fuzzed dark head buried into their hands, sobbing. She imagined an axe. It appeared in her hands, a sharp thing made of wood and mistakes.

Ahilya knew this was not real, that this was a visualization—but the Etherium was a realm of personal perceptions. Compelled by the looks of the councilors, she approached the shadow-figure, and caught by her will, or perhaps simply trusting her, the Virohi did not move. Their body jerked in silent shudders, their cries silent yet echoing in the Etherium, as she placed the blade by their neck.

Ahilya felt its cold glint on her skin.

The axe dropped from her hands, disappearing. Her mind blanked in terror. She backed away, and the fuzzy form of the Virohi disappeared, back into a buzzing hive that flitted away into the forest.

In the infirmary, she clutched her head in a posture eerily reminiscent of the Virohi themselves, breathing hard. The others stared at her.

Genocide, again. Was she going mad? How was it possible that only she could think such a thing abominable? Were they right after all—was it always a question of *us* or *them*? Perhaps it was the natural law of life, predator or prey, the only way to survive. But she had lived with the consequences of that thinking all her life. Architects had chosen to erase non-architects in similar calculations. They'd chosen to other their own. When you considered a sentient race as disposable prey, where did that leave you?

"Would that not hurt us too?" she asked. "If the Virohi have already become a part of us, destroying them would destroy parts of us all."

"What choice do we have?" Basav said. "We cannot let the entire plant die for want of saving a branch. We will have to prune. That is what it means to be a councilor. Architects have always known this."

"Perhaps such pruning will take parts of ourselves away," Airav said. "But it will be worth it. You know what we are up against."

"This is the same thing the Virohi thought," Ahilya said. "When they split in the first place, they thought they would be all right, despite losing parts of themselves. Now you would do that too—lose what you have by destroying the Virohi."

"We must strike first, before the Virohi evolve and strike us," Basav retorted. "You think we came to this decision easily? We understand that we might experience some loss. Perhaps in cutting them away, you will take away crucial memories of our lives." His hands tightened over the books, and she thought of the loss he had already experienced. "We have no choice," Basav said again. "This is the only way."

Ahilya shook her head, trying to deny him. Basav had described excision as similar to subsummation, but the architects understood subsummation as erasure—that was how they had attacked and overtaken offending ashrams.

Ahilya had *seen* subsummation occur. She had seen what absorbing the falcon-yaksha had done to Iravan. It had not erased the falcon; the yaksha had merely become a part of Iravan, indistinguishable from her husband, bleeding its rage and memory into him. What if that occurred with the Virohi too? Humanity would still look and feel human-like, but echoes of the Virohi would remain within them. None of them would be as they were, and the Virohi would be destroyed fruitlessly. Even if she excised the cosmic creatures, what remained of humanity's survivors would be human no longer. Such an act, in and of itself, would be human no longer.

The council of Irshar would not see it this way, but such a thing would be a kind of overwriting too. There would be no return from such violence, and it would hurt the citizens as well, a corruption worse than the one she endured for it would be more subtle. She had once thought to strike in violence at architects too. Look where she was now, operating just like them.

If she did this, which of her memories would die? Ahilya saw herself separated from the knowledge of Tariya or Bharavi or Iravan, even the pain she had felt at their hands and through their actions. Would she trade it? If bad memories were all she had of them, those was still hers to keep. She was an archeologist, yet here they were asking her to cut away—erase—part of their history. Who would they become?

But perhaps this is what we need, she thought. *To become something else. Someone else.* It was a dangerous thought, and she shook her head, unable to articulate all this to the councilors.

"I don't think the Virohi were overwriting us simply because they could," she said desperately. "I think they were attempting to flee something."

The three of them studied her with mixed expressions of pity and disbelief.

"It doesn't matter—" Basav began.

"It does," she said. "It really does. Iravan's war on them—the bomb he exploded—hurt them, and they've changed since then. They've evolved in ways we are not acknowledging while they became part of the tree. I saw them grieving, weeping, and I think it is worthwhile to examine why."

Without waiting for them to reply, Ahilya threw the covers off her, and staggered to her feet. For a second, she swayed, unsteady, but before any of the others could reach her, she took a few wobbly steps forward, reaching for her clothes, shedding the gown she had been given.

Airav and Basav averted their gazes, but Chaiyya stared at Ahilya, eyebrows raised.

Ahilya's mind raced, a sick feeling spreading through her, making her want to vomit. She had vowed to Iravan she would tell him everything she learned of the Virohi, including any means to destroy them. That she had been looking for ways to save them was secondary; with what the council had told her now, she was duty bound to share this. Already she could feel the heartpoison bracelet tightening around her wrist. It could tell that some part of her wanted to hide this news, and it was warning her of the consequences of doing so.

But even if the council did not see subsummation this way, Iravan would. Surely he would? The memory of him waiting for her within the Etherium sparked in her mind. He'd said she'd summoned him there as always, but if so it had been unconsciously done. Even if she had, he had stayed—not shielding himself. He had attempted to save her from the overwriting, perhaps against the wishes of his capital desire.

He was once a reasonable man, and he had experienced subsummation. He had accused her of corruption, but his corruption by the falcon-yaksha's hate had undone him. She had kept faith in his return to her, despite Eskayra's proposition, despite the way things had been between her and him for the last many months. That kiss in the Etherium had shown her she'd been right to do so. She still had a chance to convince him of her point of view. She had to do it now. Before any of the others could speak to him.

Ahilya finished dressing, and moved toward the door. If she could get to him, to *him*, past the falcon and his past lives and his capital desire, there was still a chance to prevent genocide. Speed made her movements clumsy, and she banged into the edge of her cot.

She stopped as Basav rose to block her way, a scowl on his face, his hands shaking with emotion. "You have already done enough damage with your sympathies for these creatures," he snarled softly. "You are to obey the council's wishes in this. Do you understand me?"

Iravan had demurred to his capital desire in the Etherium, when she had been attacked. He had saved the cosmic creatures because it meant saving her. She had to believe that meant something. Ahilya stared at Basav, her pulse racing.

"Let me pass, please," she said quietly.

Basav stepped out of her way. Ahilya walked past him, but his soft words came to her nonetheless. "Do the right thing, Ahilya-ve," he said, the suffix an invective in his mouth. "Enough lives have been lost because of you and your husband."

32

IRAVAN

"How are constellation lines created?" Iravan asked.

Around him, the Ecstatics of the Garden shuffled. They were back in the main assembly chamber, though this time none of the sungineers were present. Dhruv had taken nearly all of them to Irshar to keep Iravan's promises. Only a few remained here to maintain the technology for the Garden, and they kept to their solar lab, away from the Ecstatics. Iravan did not bother them. He'd never claimed authority over them.

He stood in the center with the only people he commanded. The Ecstatics collected in a circle around him, deathly still, watching him intently. No one was trajecting, and hardly anyone glowed, away from the Deepness as they were. Not wanting to involve sungineers here, or waste any energy, Iravan had eschewed the use of glowglobes in this chamber. His skin provided the only light, ricochetting off blue-green phosphorescence, gleaming on his blade pendant, reflecting off the pools of water.

It was enough light to see the expressions of all the other Ecstatics. Hostility dripped from the gathering, in the cold stances, the suppressed murmurs, the raised eyebrows. Iravan had still not released the rogue Ecstatics from their makeshift prisons, but already his architects who were in Irshar were living with their families. This hostility was to be expected—both for bowing down to Irshar, and for his refusal to let architects out of the Garden when they requested to do the same.

He had called this class to gain control, but only his closest contingent looked truly curious. Darsh studied the gathering, his arms crossed over his chest, as though unable to believe none of them knew the answer. Reyla frowned, moving closer to Naila, a questioning look in her face.

Naila sighed. In a sea of black uniforms, her white kurta shone with Iravan's light. He did not expect her to participate, but perhaps the habit was too ingrained in her not to answer his questions.

"It's a matter of will," she said, reluctantly. Her voice, though quiet, echoed around the chamber. "One has to visualize them in one's head, and it is actioned desire that manifests as constellation lines. Each line becomes stronger the more we impose our will on it, yet each line must be different and subtle, and an architect must be careful to choose the stars to create a particular effect. You can create a wall of jasmines by imposing your will on a blooming jasmine star and combining it with the possibility of a single jasmine growing on a wall. Or you can do so by stringing a bud with a different vine that already climbs the wall, performing a grafting. But the lines themselves are a persuasion, a seduction. Our wills cannot be forceful. We can damage a star, so we must be careful to give the star, the plant, the life and possibility, only as much as it needs and no more."

"As much as it needs and no more," Iravan echoed, nodding. Naila had repeated almost word for word what he had taught in Nakshar's Academy once. It was amazing she remembered it so clearly. He turned to Darsh. "How is this different from Ecstasy?" he asked.

"It's pure power," the boy replied. "We don't create constellation lines, but we force our will and we change the plant in some way."

He relapsed into silence. More and more, Darsh concerned Iravan—with his moody silences and frequent frowns. Was it merely an effect of adolescence? Or was it Ecstasy, and everything their survival had become?

Iravan did not push. He simply nodded and did not correct Darsh's answer.

In truth, there was more to it. Changing the nature of the plants did involve some measure of constellation lines. The force of desire during Ecstasy might present as a simple ray of light from the Deepness while performing Ecstatic trajection, but that force split within the Moment to become constellation lines. It was the difference between constructing the lines and having them be constructed for you, and Iravan had ridden the wave of pure power into constellation lines multiple times.

The Moment, the Deepness, even the Etherium were all intricately connected. But for most of these people, it was an academic question. What they knew of Ecstasy was taught by him. And today, he was holding this class for one reason.

"This," he said quietly, "is the everpower."

He flexed his fingers, and around him a maelstrom arose, one of dust, earth and wind. The air warped to create a rhythmic chiming, reminiscent of the bells within Nakshar's temple—a sound he had not heard in months, but which was imprinted in his memory. The current lifted him up, his feather cloak billowing. He spun in a small circle, arms outstretched, and radiance burst from his skin, throwing shimmers of light across the dim chamber.

The Ecstatics had seen him do these feats before while he

prepared for the war with the Virohi, but it seemed to finally hit them that he intended to teach them this, when he had been so guarded with his secrets before. Eyebrows shot up, and the muttering took on a new, excited flavor. Those who had been slouching suddenly straightened, their eyes bright as they tracked him. Iravan felt a surge of satisfaction.

He gently descended and let the everpower go. The audience settled, though eager eyes still watched him.

"Attempt to amalgamate your visions," he said to them. "Your first vision, the Deepness, your Etherium. Try to imagine them as the same."

The architects muttered, throwing each other confused glances. "Like combining the Two Visions?" someone asked in a loud whisper. "Isn't that dangerous?"

"It is dangerous, but safety has never been an architect's lot," Iravan replied coolly. "Acknowledge they are the same and you have control. Desire it. I will intervene should anything go wrong."

Around him, one by one Ecstatics started to glow as they entered the Deepness. Some of them frowned, others closed their eyes. Naila, of course, did not attempt anything. He could see the question in her eyes, of what he thought he was doing, but it was imperative they learned this skill. Everything that had happened—their entire future—hinged on this one thing.

In truth, holding this class at all infuriated him. He never wanted to teach anyone the everpower, and he had been counting on fulfilling his capital desire without needing to.

Yet the events in the jungle had taught him a brutal humbling lesson. There were forces that even he could not contend with. He could not shake it, the battle within himself, that somehow he should have let Ahilya die when the planet attacked—and that was what scared him more than anything else. That he could not trust his past lives and what they were telling him. That he could not trust who he had become, who Ahilya had become, not when both of them were so corrupted in their own way. How ironic that after all this time his problems had remained the same.

Once he had been unable to tell right from wrong even as a Senior Architect, pressed by his promises to the council and his vows to his wife. Then he'd had Bharavi to counsel him. Now?

Iravan gazed at the students.

Now, he supposed, he had these untrained Ecstatics. If the temptation of everpower did not seduce them enough to stay with him, he did not know what would.

He began to stride through the gathering, noticing the stuttering blue-green tattoos on dark skin, as the others entered and left the Deepness in their attempt to combine their visions. Eyes opened and closed in frustration, and people were muttering on the impossibility of his ask.

Iravan opened his mouth to call out another instruction, when movement at the doorway caught his eye.

Ahilya entered, her gaze finding him instantly with the light coming off him. She did not speak, nor attempt to break into his mind, but he sealed his shield tight over his Etherium. He could not bear it, he knew, seeing into her turmoil and memories.

Would it even be her? Or would he see some version of *them*? After the events five days ago, he had paced within his chamber, willing Ahilya to wake up and summon him to her Etherium. He could still remember their phantom kiss—he'd indulged in a moment of weakness, knowing that she was corrupted by the Virohi—but if his goal was to separate her from the cosmic creatures, he could not allow her to infiltrate his mind again. The more she resembled them, the more his capital desire would weaken, infected by her closeness to the Virohi. It was enough that she was fine physically.

That was all he needed to know. After that encounter in the vriksh, he had asked Dhruv to confirm that for him and shut his own Etherium down.

Yet looking at her now, Iravan was uncertain if the Senior Sungineer had been accurate in his report. Dhruv's assessment must have been hearsay, for Ahilya looked dead on her feet, her tired gaze sweeping over the gathering before she made her slow way to the platform.

A chair began growing there in anticipation of her, and this time she took it, nearly collapsing onto it. Her skin looked ashy, and Iravan could tell even from here that she was having trouble breathing. Heartache so strong seized him that his hands curled into fists. He watched her close her eyes. He tried to calm himself.

It was disconcerting how much he wanted to comfort her. Was that a manipulation of the Virohi? Who would he be comforting, and would she allow him to? The fury climbed in him. This is what he had done to her. Him and the Virohi. A thousand deaths would not be enough to atone. Erasing them was only the beginning. If he could, he would choose to do this again and again, not for any other crime, but the crime of what they had done to *her*.

He tried to still the anger coursing through him. How would he go about purging the Virohi from her? For all he knew, the infection ran too deep, and there was so much he did not understand. Her Etherium that she'd dragged him into, unlocking their ability to speak to each other in their minds. The way the vriksh and the Virohi were connected. That mysterious energy in Irshar's solar lab that he was certain had to do with Ahilya in some capacity. How strange that the only one capable of untangling these mysteries was at the center of it all. He was an architect—he built. But Ahilya was an archeologist, trained to see disparate pieces and make a cohesive narrative out of them. If there was anyone that could provide an explanation, even the beginnings of one, it was her. It was, after all, one of the things that had brought them together in their days of courting. Would she be able to decode herself, while changes were occurring to her? The very thought of it spun his mind, like looking into an infinite mirror.

Others had noticed Ahilya. Ecstatics began to shift on their feet, perhaps expecting another confrontation.

Iravan gestured to Reyla and Darsh to continue the class. They were among the youngest here, but they were still the most experienced, now that both Pranav and Trisha were working with Dhruv. Reyla was a natural Ecstatic. She was the only one of them who had found the Deepness before finding the Moment. She had taught him how to braid his power in the Deepness in different ways, a move essential to the first assault on the Virohi with the bomb. He had already discussed the everpower with her, and how it could be similar to Ecstasy in some ways. The two were equipped to carry on this class, breaking down the steps to achieve everpower, even if they themselves had not mastered the evervision yet.

Leaving the children, Iravan strode over to Ahilya on the platform. Naila followed him, while someone brought them a bowl filled with ripe pears and apples, placing it on the table that had begun growing.

Ahilya acknowledged him with a nod. She looked sorely like she needed to eat, but though the words were in his mouth, to ask her to partake, to feed her if he must, Iravan resisted the urge. He sat across from her while Naila took the last chair. On his wife's face, Iravan read his own tiredness, and for an instant, he allowed them both to rest. To stay with each other silently, just because they could.

Naila looked from him to Ahilya, then smiled. "Well, this is cozy," she said, before helping herself to an apple. The sound of her crunching into it grated on Iravan, but Ahilya threw the Maze Architect a small, wan smile.

"How can I help you, councilor?" he asked finally.

Ahilya's eyes drifted back to the class where Reyla was speaking in her soft voice. She took in the Ecstatics, then focused on the roof. She seemed to be tracking the dust that swirled there constantly.

"What happened?" she asked. "Five days ago. That attack."

"What do you think, Ahilya-ve?" he answered carefully.

Ahilya's gaze cut to Iravan. "It's the planet, isn't it?"

Of course, she had worked it out. Why was he surprised? He nodded, once.

She leaned forward. "Is that why you're teaching them this everpower? Do you think they can help?"

The truth was that he didn't know. He didn't even know whether these Ecstatics could learn the everpower. That skill had come to him after trajecting all the core trees of the sister ashrams into submission while still in the skies. The act of simply thinking about his chair in the Garden while talking to Nakshar's Ecstatics when they'd named Irshar, the way the Conclave had formed, the bridges he had constructed during the crash, the shape Irshar had settled into when it landed, all these things had occurred simply because he'd desired them—nay, barely imagined them. He had begun understanding the limitations and possibilities of the power after his subsummation of the falcon-yaksha, but it had begun with the core trees.

Or perhaps it began with his unity with the falcon. If so, he still had to decode the method. Everything he'd learned, he'd learned on his own. His first Ecstatic experiences had occurred before he'd known the falcon existed. His first attempts with the everpower had happened without clarity. All of those had been chaotic, out of his control, and he had learned true control only on uniting, then finally subsuming the yaksha. But if everything was really a slow slope of understanding, could he not accelerate it for these architects? He'd had to discover all this on his own, but he was here now, and he could give them shortcuts. What else was the point of so much knowledge and power? It all began with them first finding a way to amalgamate and view their three visions as one thing, even if they did so briefly.

Ahilya was gazing at him, her brow crinkled. Iravan could feel her attempt to break past his shield, to look into his mind to unravel all this.

"They can help," he said, an answer to her question.

"Why?" she persisted. "Because all your consciousnesses are connected? Or because you Ecstatics are connected in some special way?"

"Both," he muttered. "In varying degrees."

All Ecstatics had an affinity for each other, he had learned this much. Back in Nakshar, when the falcon had once tried to take him over, he had summoned a few Ecstatics to him without his knowledge. Consciousnesses were connected after all, this was the truth of their world—and if the Moment connected all architects in a way, then it stood to reason that the Deepness did the same for Ecstatics. If some Ecstatics had found the Deepness due to his desperation, then did it not make sense that he could bring them to the everpower in the same fashion? He was as desperate now as he had been during his fight with the falcon-yaksha, except this time he had control over his desperation. This class was an attempt to train them with restraint. He would much prefer to do it this way than have them find the power at a time when he could do little to direct it.

Ahilya watched him, waiting to see if he'd say more. Naila stopped eating, to look at him askance.

"For the love of survival," the Maze Architect murmured, "would it kill you to give her a straight and full answer for once, sir?"

It was Ahilya who answered. "He does not trust me. He does not trust how much of me is still me, and how much the Virohi."

Naila quietened at that, and Ahilya looked away too, but Iravan could see in the trembling of her lips how much it had cost her to admit that. She did not blame him for his distrust, not this time. She was suffering the consequences of the Virohi too. Perhaps she had already lost herself. He alone knew the pain of that.

He did not realize what he was doing until she jerked back. His hand covered hers, squeezing it in comfort. "I'm sorry," Iravan said quietly. "I am not trying to be oblique. If I can answer something fully, I will. Please ask."

Ahilya nodded and slipped her hand out of his grip. His palm curled ever so slightly as if to trap her touch in his.

"You wanted to know everything we discovered," she said. "The Virohi are overwriting citizens and I have been told to destroy them for you."

Iravan raised an eyebrow. He had predicted the contamination of Irshar's society long ago. The overwriting did not surprise him, but Ahilya being here did.

"Then you finally see reason?" he asked. An excited edge entered his voice. He leaned forward. "Do you know *how* to destroy them?"

Her fingers circled the heartpoison bracelet around her wrist. Ahilya studied it for a long time, then looked up to meet his gaze.

"Do you have footage from Dhruv's drones?" she asked. "From when the Virohi emerged out of Irshar?"

His excitement still skulked under his skin, but he tapped at his bead bracelets and entered the sequence to access those sungineering records. Holograms hovered over his wrist, showing the three of them the events from a few weeks ago. Irshar crumbling. The Virohi coming alive in strange shapes, pulling out of the architecture. The jungle motionless, then lurching with imminent storms. Ahilya made him pause the recording several times—to watch the Virohi lurking near the vriksh before they attacked Iravan, and then again to study the jungle which was quiescent for so long even though the cosmic creatures had emerged from Irshar.

Finally, she leaned back. She seemed relieved.

"What did you see, councilor?" Iravan asked quietly.

Ahilya opened her eyes. "We all saw the same thing," she said. "The jungle was not under attack from the Virohi after they came alive. The cosmic creatures were just hovering by the core tree. They were confused."

"But the jungle changed even if the drones didn't record it," Naila said. "Your expedition experienced it, didn't it? Massive mountains forming, hills and trees levelled."

"Yes. But all that occurred only after the Moment shattered. It was not an effect of the Virohi's extraction. Not even the Virohi's intent. The landscape changed because of what happened to the Moment."

"And is that important?" Iravan asked, raising an eyebrow.

"Yes. It is." Ahilya met his gaze. "I think there is a reason the Virohi began overwriting us. They were scared."

"Of what?"

"The same thing you were. The immensity of our planet. I've never seen them like that. Desperate, angry, selfish, yes—but never terrified in this manner. There is more here, something that is forcing them to overwrite us, some kind of defense mechanism."

Iravan studied her. She *would* say something like this, words of a corrupted mind, intent on saving the Virohi. But she was also simply Ahilya. Could he afford not to listen to her?

"Indulge me," she said softly, reading him, and Iravan cracked a smile. He gestured for her to proceed.

Ahilya took a deep breath. "Through all the time that I have known them, the Virohi have wanted form," she said. "They have wanted to be bound by physical law, in order to experience life in a way they have not done before. They escaped their home planet, which was on the brink of destruction, to evade erasure. I have come to know the cosmic creatures closely, and all along they have wished to find immortality and eternity, while needing to be bound physically. It is a contradiction, don't you think? The cycle of birth and rebirth in our world gave them an opportunity to manifest such a contradictory desire when they found a kind of immortality in the architects and yakshas. Reincarnation allowed them to live forever. They found a way to endure, even if the act unleashed earthrages."

"You paint a sympathetic picture of these creatures," Iravan said, frowning. "But you cannot simply dismiss the earthrages as a side-effect. They might not have unleashed the rages immediately after their release from Irshar, but it was only a matter of time. They've already attempted to destroy our world, driven by their mad desire to seek form. We found sanctuary in the skies, but I have seen the manner in which they plundered other worlds. They destroyed everything there, and they would destroy us too."

"Yes, but once they found our planet, they never again sought to go to those other planets," Ahilya said. "Here, on our world, they found beings such as us who were complex consciousnesses. After all, humans existed long before trajection did. You and I saw that in the caves in the habitat long ago. Our planet perhaps was the only one they visited where life had evolved to host complex beings such as us—beings that could give them what they sought."

Within Iravan's Etherium, Nidhirv flashed for an instant. In that man's time, the cosmic creatures had been invited to split. Nidhirv had been initiated as an architect in a ceremony where he had helped bring the Virohi into birth, creating the split of an architect and a yaksha. Earthrages in that time had been smaller things, more contained, and Ecstasy had been encouraged—as had been the unification with an architect's yaksha. Vishwam had indicated that their world, their culture, was special—the final eventual home of the cosmic creatures. Everything Ahilya hypothesized corroborated Iravan's knowledge. It made him uncomfortable, as if she were secretly trying to manipulate him.

"What is your point?" he asked.

"When you shattered the Moment, the cosmic creatures grew mad. I remember the way they screeched, and in the Etherium I saw them, weeping, grieving, always grieving. They attacked you in the skies not because you were trying to eliminate them, but because you shattered the Moment."

"You're saying they care about the Moment?" Iravan asked skeptically. "They have *destroyed* the Moment—they ripped it apart each time they attempted to take birth in our world. They infiltrated it to infect the architects."

"If you choose to look at it that way, yes, they did destroy the Moment. But in another way, the Moment has always been their home, their plane of existence. Earthrages occurred from the very beginning because the Virohi—this alien species—tried to embed themselves into the planet through the Moment. The cosmic creatures are formless beings, but in the Moment they found a kind of form. Trajection came to our species because of their activity in the Moment, and you and I could only trap the Virohi in the Moment. It all revolves around that dimension. Of course, they care."

Iravan said nothing, but he could not deny the sense in her words. He himself had seen the form of the Virohi in the Moment, not just when he and Ahilya had trapped one creature, but afterward, when he had wrenched the entire hive through the Conduit to explode them with his sungineering bomb. Outside the Moment, the Virohi had looked like snaky, sinuous smoke, but within the Moment, he had seen their stars.

Shaped like rocks that melted into moisture, or like orbs that shifted with a thousand fires, the Virohi's stars had looked like no other possibility Iravan had ever encountered. It was as if even the Moment with its infinity could not truly contain their shape. Architects presented as dust motes, but true creatures of infinity like the Virohi... of course, they had found some kind of a home in the Moment. This is how they must have always existed. Iravan had been unable to see them that way before the eversion, but once Nidhirv had seen the Virohi in such a form, bringing their consciousness into life as an architect during a birthing ceremony.

Naila's brows arched in understanding. "If they care about the Moment... Then you think the overwriting was triggered because the Moment was destroyed?"

Ahilya turned to her. "I think the destruction of the Moment is connected to the overwriting, yes. And I think if we neglect to address this larger reason—whatever it may be—then we will be inviting a bigger problem."

Still, Iravan said nothing. Everything Ahilya said indicated a corrupted mind, hell bent on defending the pestilence of the cosmic creatures, but he had visited the core tree in the dead of the night several times in an attempt to understand how to extract the Virohi. He had felt the Virohi's grief, seeping through the tree. Ahilya's council did not understand it—and Iravan was not about to explain it to them—but had she not embedded the Virohi in the tree, the cosmic creatures would have destroyed him and the planet in their madness, before being destroyed themselves. Without the Moment, they would never be able to find any kind of form. The planet would have ruptured slowly but surely, and the Virohi would have diminished too, decaying until they were no more—unable to escape to another dimension, unable to rebirth, trapped on this plane.

Ahilya had saved them all. She would not take credit for it, he knew; he had seen the way her own council constrained her, and how she seemed to allow it. But even if what she said about the Virohi's intentions was true, it still did not change the threat.

"I am grateful for what you did for me," he said. "But none of this changes the corruption we face due to the Virohi's actions. Now that the Virohi are in the tree, they cannot escape it. Your council is not wrong—no matter what they are escaping, the cosmic creatures will defile us. This is the prime opportunity to destroy them and be done with them. You should listen to your council."

"I think they're mistaken," Ahilya said flatly. "Iravan, think of what happened immediately after the Moment shattered. It wasn't simply another earthrage beginning. This was a total reconstruction of the planet in a way, a distortion. Hills appearing out of nowhere, chasms opening, trees growing against nature's laws. This was not just something occurring on the surface of the earth, or in the skies like a skyrage. This was overarching, comprehensive. A level of storm we have not seen before, occurring from deep within the planet's bowels. A reckoning, seeping into the very elements of air and water, metal and soil, changing all rules and coming at us from the very core What would you even call something like that?"

"Planetrage," Naila said quietly. Her eyes were wide.

"Yes," Ahilya said, turning to her, relief on her face that someone had understood her. "That's exactly right."

Planetrage, Iravan repeated in his mind.

It was a good term for it, for what else could describe the way the earth had rioted. The way in which air had become vacuum, and dust had turned into icicles, and boulders and rocks had tried to harm him. Ahilya was speaking of the time when the Moment had shattered and the planetrage had first roared, but the planetrage five days ago had been triggered by him. He had manipulated the jungle with his everpower, attempting to grow food for the ashram, find the yakshas, create a home for the small creatures. All those things were accumulations, one thing piled on top of the other, his every use of the everpower a distortion of the planet. The will of the planet was to remain a certain way, but with the everpower he trajected it to become something else.

The consequences of his fight with the planet were the same as an earthrage created by a Virohi's split. Perhaps the Virohi had seen it coming. Perhaps they knew this would be a consequence. What the cosmic creatures had done to the planet by splitting themselves was trajection too, perhaps with an ancient and inscrutable form of the everpower. The earthrages weren't caused by the split. They were caused by the Virohi's forced investiture into the planet, while the planet defended itself.

Trajection, Ecstasy, and everpower—each of those destroyed the planet in a similar way, all of them a disease. Iravan had been hoping to teach his Ecstatics the everpower, but if Ahilya was right—and she was—then any use of it would simply magnify another planetrage. Within trajection, after all, lay the seed of its demise. No matter what he did, he was doomed to fail.

I cannot escape it, he thought numbly, his head spinning. *I will forever be my own enemy. Doomed to destroy, never to build.* How ironic he had once been an architect.

He had always meant to annihilate the Virohi, but what he needed to do was destroy *himself*. Every trace of this awful power, sooner or later, removed. Every part of him reduced into nothing.

"I think the planetrage is the greater threat, Iravan," Ahilya said, into his silence. "We need to focus on ending that. When the Moment shattered, the planetrage started, and we experienced it again five days ago. But all of these were just the first tremors—which flattened the land already, killed hundreds of people. Next time it could be worse. Whether or not you destroy the Virohi, the planetrage will continue until you reconstruct the Moment. We will all be gone." Her voice grew quiet, insistent, and she reached forward to take his hand, her fingers fluttering over his heartpoison bracelet. "You are the only one who can repair the Moment," she said softly. "If you found a way to stop this greater threat, would that not be making greater amends?"

There it was, always the thing that separated them. Her desire to save those creatures. Not the planet, not humanity, but for some reason, the cosmic creatures.

Iravan snapped back into himself as if he had been struck.

He stood up, wrenching his hand back.

"You are trying to manipulate me," he said coldly.

Ahilya stood up too, slowly. "Iravan, no," she said. "I'm really not."

"No?" he sneered. "What am I to conclude from this? You want me to spare the Virohi, against your own council's wish. You want me distracted, repairing the Moment now when you don't need to hold me to this anymore." His fingers circled the dark bracelet, and he snapped it into two. It had been useless to contain him anyway, when he was above those ailments. He had been wearing it as a courtesy, a promise given, but he had already fulfilled his promise.

"I have given aid to you," he said. "Medicines, food, technology, that is why you needed the Moment repaired. You know that you have no more hold over me, and this is why you come, making arguments about newer threats. You have the means to destroy the Virohi but you don't want to use it. You think you can sway me with your arguments, but I can see how well you've thought them out, wanting me to follow along. Do you take me for a fool, Ahilya?"

"In many ways, yes," she replied evenly, but there was no heat in her voice. "But you have acted with reason before, Iravan, though I could not agree with you. Listen to me now. I am not lying about any of this."

"You are trying to change my capital desire," he said. "This is what you have been attempting to do from the very start. That's why you had me make the heartpoison bracelets in the first place. Deny it and be a liar."

"Am I changing it?" she challenged. "Or am I clarifying it? Iravan, do you want to destroy the Virohi, or make amends? You are conflating the two, and therein is the root of your problem. That is the only thing I am trying to affect—the only thing I have from the start."

The words were so close to the disturbing thoughts Iravan had about his conflict with material bonds that his suspicion grew tenfold. "My capital desire is for me to decide," he spat. "If the planetrage is so dangerous, then destroy the Virohi like your council desires you to. Give them to me, and let *me* destroy them, if the thought makes you so queasy. I will help you with this planetrage after we've done this. And *that* will be my making of amends."

"It will be too late then," she said. "You saw how the planetrage affected you, and if you are injured in your ridiculous battle with the Virohi, then it will be all for nothing. You almost died already when the Virohi attacked you after you bombed them, and—"

Sudden sounds of commotion rose, drowning out the rest of what she was saying. The three of them whipped around to face the class they had all but forgotten. Somewhere, Reyla was shouting, and Naila wore the same grim expression from the fight between Darsh and Kush, as though preparing to break up another altercation.

Then Reyla's words grew clearer.

"No," the little girl was shrieking. "No— that's not— you shouldn't— What are you doing?"

Iravan saw his confusion and alarm on his wife's face, and then they were both running behind Naila, pushing through the crowd. Iravan stopped, blinded momentarily. Light flooded his vision. He could barely discern the shape, but it appeared like a slim, spiraling vortex. Ahilya clutched his arm; only she touched him this way.

The both of them recognized what it meant. They'd seen it before, the only two here who had ever seen something like this before.

This was a vortex of unification.

Someone was uniting with their yaksha.

33

AHILYA

The nightmare of the last vortex flashed in her head. Iravan walking into the column of silver as though hypnotized. The way she had run after him, the both of them tumbling into it together. Lights everywhere, and being suspended mid-air, the falcon's gigantic wings surrounding them.

The unity with the falcon had saved Iravan, but it had ended him too. It had changed him beyond recognition, the falcon's intent poisoning the man she had loved. Neither of them had known it back then. Hard to believe it had occurred in this same habitat, when it looked so different now.

Iravan's capital event had manifested in a terrible justification of genocide. It had brought the fifty sister ashrams crashing down from the skies, erasing a thousand-year-old history, condemning the sister ashrams to become the last survivors of the human species. What would the merging of another Ecstatic and yaksha do? How would anyone survive this? Ahilya's arm still clutched Iravan's. She didn't know if it was because she wanted him to do something, or so she wouldn't simply fall.

Iravan released her grip gently then cleaved through the press. Ahilya tried to follow, but other bodies had closed the gap. She remained standing where she was, able to see the radiant vortex only through flashes between moving people.

Someone nudged her, and she turned to see Naila standing on her tiptoes beside her to see past the others. "It's Darsh," the architect reported grimly. "I don't think there is an actual yaksha—not like you said Iravan-ve had with the falcon. And it doesn't look like a full vortex that you described, either."

Ahilya swallowed a few times to clear the dryness in her throat. "An incorporeal yaksha, then," she croaked out. "The others haven't been seen for a while. Not even by Iravan. We don't know where they are."

"Does it matter if the yaksha is incorporeal?"

"I don't know. I haven't learned anything more about them for months." How could she? She'd forgotten she was an archeologist. She had become a councilor, and then… whatever this was.

Naila gripped Ahilya's hand, and together they moved through the crowd, weaving their way to the front. "Last time you said the Virohi attacked you when Iravan-ve united with his falcon," Naila said.

The memory still terrified Ahilya. She had stood as a shield when the cosmic creature had begun unravelling Iravan. She had protected him with her consciousness, wrapping him in a cocoon that the Virohi had been unable to pierce. But she had not returned from it unscathed. Her body had shed her unborn child because of her time in the vortex. Her mind had opened her Etherium to Iravan's. And she had made the Virohi aware of her presence. It was one reason all the Virohi had gravitated toward her after the Conclave had landed, attacking *her*, sensing *her* as a threat. It was the reason she had become such an active player in this cosmic game. Iravan had been right—she should never have been involved to this extent, but the choice had been made for her by her actions.

Ahilya could feel the cosmic creatures spreading through her chest and neck, a connection that resembled the core tree, an entangled root ball extending its branches, a growing amalgamation of the two entities forming within her, seeping into her brain and consciousness. The creatures were quiescent now, as though sleeping after being drained, and it startled her, to think of them in such a way. Did Virohi sleep? Iravan had accused her of humanizing them, but that seemed to be occurring on its own.

"They won't interfere this time," she replied to Naila. "They have no reason to."

Only one Virohi had attacked her and Iravan back then, but that was because they had tried to stop that creature from splitting. This time, all the cosmic creatures were trapped in the vriksh. What would be the point of them doing anything? They were already where they wanted to be. In the tree, and in her mind. The conversation with Basav and the others about overwriting returned to Ahilya, but she did not fear the Virohi in the way the others did. No, what she feared were the yakshas and the Ecstatics. She feared this vortex.

Naila's hand squeezed hers sensing her terror. "Steady, Ahilya-ve," she said. "I'm right here. You're not alone."

The words were reminiscent of her healing litany, but unlike with Chaiyya, Ahilya did not question it from Naila. She squeezed back and didn't let go.

"So what do we do?" Naila asked.

"I'm not sure we need to do anything," Ahilya replied. "Except..."

She trailed off. The unification of a broken cosmic creature was a merging of an architect and a yaksha—two halves that built. It was a unification of construction, but one of destruction too. Iravan had found himself after the unity, but he'd lost parts of himself too. After he had united with the falcon, the rest of the corporeal yakshas that had once lived in the habitat had disappeared, never to be seen again. The entire habitat had reshaped itself. She had woken up to incredible change. Would such a thing happen again? She could not account for Darsh, who was going through the unity now, but the Garden? Ahilya glanced around at the swirling foliage so like an airborne ashram, and the slim trunks of trees, waving slightly in the breeze. It was calm. Too calm. The hairs on her neck rose. This place would not remain the same. She knew it.

"I don't think this will be as smooth as it was for Iravan," she said quietly. "Maybe we should clear the chamber of these Ecstatics so they don't interfere or wreak any damage?"

"Clear the chamber," Naila repeated. "You and me. Clear this chamber of Ecstatics."

Ahilya heard her own incredulity in the other woman's voice. What authority did the two of them have? Naila was disdained for not having joined the Garden to become an Ecstatic. And Ahilya… well, she did not think the Ecstatics would hold her in high regard, not after her demands of Iravan, and certainly not when she viewed the Garden with so much contempt. The two of them were interlopers, their authority only as much as Iravan gave them. And he had given them none.

Still, Naila rolled up her sleeves. "It's always something easy, isn't it?" she muttered.

Shaking her head, she strode forward, and Ahilya followed.

34

IRAVAN

Iravan shouldered through the thrum until he was right where he'd left Darsh and Reyla. He already knew it was the boy attempting to unite with his yaksha. He could see the boy's two presences in the Deepness next to the shattering supernova of the Moment, both Darsh's dust mote and his incorporeal yaksha, circling each other warily.

Reyla stood trembling in the Garden, watching Darsh apprehensively. Iravan could see her shape in the Deepness too, a small bright frisson of light among all the others of the curious Ecstatics who had begun glowing blue-green, jostling their way in both the visions to get a clearer view. He made to approach Darsh, but Reyla caught his arm.

"Wait, he's—" Reyla's voice was a whisper. Small tears of fright pooled in her eyes. "Iravan-ve, right before… He did something to the Deepness. When we were trying to teach the others to find the evervision, the Deepness changed."

Iravan nodded, then gently disengaged. "Leave the Deepness," he called out. "All of you."

One by one, light trickled out of the assembled Ecstatics. The chamber dimmed, the only radiance coming from Iravan's silver, and Darsh and Reyla's skins from inhabiting the Deepness.

"You too, Reyla," Iravan said to the girl.

She looked for a second like she was going to argue, but then she winked out of the velvety blackness too. Reyla joined the others in the crowd, leaving Iravan and Darsh alone in the center.

He approached Darsh slowly, careful to not startle him. The boy was glowing as expected, being in the Deepness, but there were no tattoos on his skin for now, which was a welcome sign. He had not begun trajecting toward his unity, and from the Deepness Iravan could tell that the yaksha had not begun either. Darsh and his yaksha were simply circling each other endlessly in recognition.

Perhaps that is why the vortex of light in front of Darsh was but a slim pillar, more a simple thin rod than the kind of spiral Iravan had unleashed with his own falcon-yaksha. Iravan and the falcon had created their vortex through their Ecstatic trajection of each other, but if Darsh and his yaksha were not trajecting one another yet, it made sense why the vortex was still misshapen. Though the pillar shot straight into the sky, the light from it was bent with black, leaching darkness in vapors. Iravan could not recall anything like that from his unification, but of course there was no reason Darsh's would be the same. Too much had changed since then within the realms, and Darsh's power was not identical to Iravan's own.

He stepped closer to Darsh, then dropped to his knees. This close, Iravan could see blue-green flickering deep in the boy's eyes like a flame, in and out, in and out. Darsh was frozen, his body so still it might have been a statue. Roots circled under his feet, curling around his ankles.

In the second vision, Iravan watched Darsh and the incorporeal yaksha from a distance. The yaksha sparkled, an amorphous watery form hovering in the darkness. A tug formed on Iravan's heart, something akin to familiarity, but he did not have time to discern it now. Neither the yaksha nor Darsh were supertrajecting, but what if they began suddenly? Would they be able to find each other's stars in the Moment, when splintered pieces from other possibilities were floating everywhere, instead of being frozen like they once were? What if they hurt something or someone else in the process? What if they broke the Moment further?

He had thought about this after the Moment's destruction. He had been prepared for it, and he'd told everyone in the Garden how they were to proceed if their yakshas beckoned to them. That it had happened to Darsh instead of another Ecstatic was good; Darsh's loyalty to him at least was unquestioned. There would not be resistance. Still, Iravan was careful. This here, now—it was an event of purity, witnessed by no one else before. It was the closest thing to sacrosanct, to truth, an architect could experience in their condemned lives. He would not lead Darsh through it with confusion.

"Darsh," he asked in a low voice. "Can you hear me?'

The roots around the boy's ankles tightened. His chest rose and fell in a steady beat, and his eyes were pools of blue-green light.

Then, slowly, as though being forced, his face turned toward Iravan. He nodded, and flames of blue flickered and died again in his eyes.

"Let me guide you," Iravan said.

The yaksha shot out a slim ray of light from the Deepness into the broken Moment. In front of him, Darsh began to tremble. The boy's dust mote in the Deepness burgeoned with light, and he aimed it toward the Moment, presumably toward the stars of his yaksha. To traject each other was a basic step of unity. That is how it had occurred with Iravan and the falcon too, but an unexpected wave of blackness rippled through the assembled Ecstatics like a searing cord, connecting a few of them.

Cries of shock echoed as Kriya, Somdev, and Lana tipped their heads back, spasming where they stood. They dropped back into earth, crumpling.

Panic seized Iravan.

He saw instantly what was occurring. Darsh was not trajecting his yaksha as he was supposed to. He was taking power from these other Ecstatics to power himself, trajecting them in a dangerous, terrible shortcut. Trajecting a higher being was always dangerous, even for someone like Iravan. Viana flashed behind his eyes. When he had trajected that architect in Nakshar, he had killed her. In his ignorance, Darsh would do the same thing.

The architects in the Garden writhed, groaning on the floor. Iravan flapped his wings in the Deepness, hesitating, even as Darsh made to traject the architects again. Had the boy been using the linked trajection that Iravan had used in the battle with the Virohi, Iravan could have severed the lines of power. But in the midst of unity, anything Iravan attempted could harm Darsh.

"Listen to me," he said urgently. "I'm going to help you, do you understand? Whatever you are doing, let me lead you through this. You have to trust me."

As he said the words, Iravan trajected a beam of light in the Deepness to encircle Darsh's form within a lasso. Instead of feeling Darsh's power inside himself, Iravan simply became aware of it. He closed in on Darsh in the second vision, as the boy and his yaksha trajected haphazardly into the Moment.

Darsh's rogue trajection manifested once again. More Ecstatic bodies connected to each other with a dark cord, before crumpling. Vaguely, Iravan forced his attention to remain on Darsh. Slowly, very slowly, he brought the boy closer to him in the Deepness as Ecstatics started to fall in the Garden.

35

AHILYA

Ecstatics fell.

Ahilya saw Iravan notice the architects, then disregard them. He was too preoccupied. He would not help.

Naila was ushering architects to the doorway, encouraging them to leave the assembly hall. The youngest of them listened. Naila had the innate authority of a Maze Architect, and she'd learned her tricks at Iravan's knee. But most others paid no attention. Several Ecstatics were lit with the light of trajection, though many simply watched wide-eyed as a dark, smoky band connected to their compatriots, before crumpling them.

A wave of helplessness immobilized Ahilya. Did she have a role here? For all she knew, this had happened before and was normal. She and Naila were likely overstepping. Iravan certainly wasn't alarmed. She could see him next to Darsh. A look of intense concentration covered his handsome face, and though she sensed his worry, she also sensed his purpose. He felt in control.

The others seemed to be more curious than terrified. The courtyard still looked the same, but the whispers of the leaves were growing louder, filling her ears in a rush. The ground was moving ever so slightly, and she glanced down to see grass withering, caving into dirt, and deep cracks forming across the floor. Nobody else seemed to be noticing the phenomenon. Was this expected?

Trees shook as a gale blew through the chamber.

Some serious-looking Ecstatics approached Naila and surrounded her. Soon they were nodding, listening to Naila's caution. Some began to lead the younger architects away while two of them picked up the fallen Ecstatics and led them toward a quiet corner.

Naila gestured with her head at Ahilya, her instruction clear. *Follow the healers.* Ahilya nodded and left the Maze Architect to usher recalcitrant Ecstatics toward the doorways. She crouched next to the two healers who were examining one of the fallen architects. One of the healers, a woman—Shayla, Ahilya thought her name was—pulled the unconscious architect closer, examining their face. The other healer—Bipesh?—pulled open an eyelid. Thin strands of black swam across the fallen architect's cornea. The two Ecstatics crouched back and exchanged a look.

"Him?" Bipesh asked softly. "Or the lackey?"

Shayla shrugged. "Darsh is a child. Even if it is him, isn't it ultimately *him*? Can we really trust him?"

"No choice, is there?" the other muttered. "Who else do we have?"

Iravan. That's who they were talking about.

In the Etherium, Ahilya could feel Iravan's love and concern for Darsh, and how he wanted to make this as painless for the boy as he could. She took the fallen Ecstatic's hand in hers, as other architects brought more bodies to lay around them, fast converting the space into a makeshift infirmary.

"Has this happened before?" she asked.

"No," Bipesh replied. "But Ecstatics recover. That's why you see the rest just watching."

It seemed a brutal way to live, but Ahilya did not comment on it. "What's their name?" she asked instead, nudging her head toward the person lying in front of her.

Shayla gave her an assessing glance. "Ravi, I think. Not sure."

Ahilya nodded. "Do you not have a place you can take these people to heal?"

"*Can* they heal?" Bipesh replied, shrugging his shoulders. "We don't know what this is."

Ahilya said nothing. Healing aside, something horrible was clearly happening to one of their own, to so many of their own if the sounds behind and the arriving bodies were any indication, but neither Bipesh nor Shayla seemed to care. Even in Irshar people had hope for a better future. The ashram had its share of problems, but it was still an ashram, a community, built together by so many people.

This Garden was not. Was it possible to create a community of Ecstatics? Ecstatics were individuals in the greatest sense of the word. Iravan had tried to unify them, but without a set of laws, without any codification, all they had was a legacy and a future of death. Regret was the only thing Iravan had given them in certainty.

The chamber shook, leaves raining down on them. Ahilya saw dust swirling in a whirlpool. Darsh's unity with his yaksha was changing the Garden, just like Iravan's unity with the falcon had changed the habitat. Last time she had fallen unconscious, unable to witness the change of the habitat. Now she could follow the movement of dirt, whooshing around them in slow, rising streams. Small chunks of soil mixed with root shards and debris flaked off the ground. The pillars and walls around the edge of the chamber rearranged themselves in a design she could not foresee. If she stared at the flowers, she could discern slivers crinkling away from them, joining this strange whirlpool. All across the chamber, streams of dust were rising, intersecting, and now more people were noticing this, pointing at the change silently cascading around them in swirling patterns. Murmurs grew, the architects torn between watching this and keeping their eyes on Iravan and Darsh.

The Garden would look very different from what it had once been, but perhaps none of them were in danger. After all, the habitat had reformed after Iravan's unity without harming either him or her. Ahilya could only hope the same thing happened here.

"Can they heal?" Shayla asked her, repeating the question, obviously expecting an answer. "Do you know anything about it?"

Ahilya entwined Ravi's limp fingers in hers and closed her eyes. In the forest of her Etherium, memories flashed between leaves. Foliage rained down, and each leaf was a page out of Ravi's life. Ravi, smiling at another architect. Ravi, focused as they trajected. Ravi, with their eyes glinting, mouth open in a rictus of pain—a memory made in real time—though in front of her the architect lay nearly comatose.

She jerked away, dropping their hand.

"What?" Shayla asked. "What did you see?"

Ahilya did not reply. She touched another fallen Ecstatic, the one nearest to her. Similar images pounded her, vapors of joy, whispers of sadness in her Etherium, each memory ending with the architect clearly in pain though the architect themselves remained unmoving.

What did this mean? What could she do? What was the vriksh showing her? Whatever Iravan was combating with Darsh, she was certain her husband was not aware of this. Shayla and Bipesh followed her as she crouched next to another Ecstatic, images forming within her Etherium. She heard Shayla's questions, but finally abandoned her examination.

Iravan needed to know this. That the affected architects were in pain, that Darsh was changing them in some way. But could she afford to distract him now? His focus was too intense. What if she disrupted whatever he needed to do? She considered pulling him into the forest of her Etherium like she had done before. There, they could talk.

But it would take too long.

She couldn't risk such a move, not right now.

Nervously, Ahilya watched Iravan crouch next to Darsh, speaking soft words.

36

IRAVAN

In a corner of his mind, Iravan could sense Ahilya and her attention. His shields formed around his Etherium, not enough to cut her out, but enough to not be distracted, not when he was operating on such a delicate level.

Ignoring the events in the Garden, Iravan kept his focus on the Deepness.

There was a real danger to creating new fully realized Ecstatics. He had seen that first-hand when Rana and the rogue Ecstatics had attacked citizens of Irshar, fighting Iravan's command. He knew he could not raise an army of Ecstatics, each of them intent on their capital desires, challenging his, but Iravan knew too that unity with a yaksha was inevitable. He had not seen the corporeal yakshas for some time, but incorporeal ones could have been fluttering among them, unseen and invisible since they'd all crash-landed. After all, this had once been the yakshas' habitat.

He had tried to prepare the Garden, but now a powerful wave of sadness and compassion filled Iravan. He wanted to take Darsh in his arms and comfort him.

He had designed a protocol, one that everyone knew. Any time an Ecstatic was summoned by their yaksha counterpart, he would guide them through the unity. But the events with the rogue Ecstatics had showed him that influencing the Ecstatics through the sheer power of his personality, through custom and law and repetition, was not enough. He had needed to think of a way by which any Ecstatic that united with their yaksha would choose *his* capital desire over their own. There was only one way to guarantee that. Only one way to ensure the Ecstatic merging with their yaksha did not result in death and calamity for the human species. That secret he had shared with no one, not even Dhruv.

I'm so sorry, Iravan thought. Grief gripped him, melded with shame.

Slowly, inch by inch, he tightened the lasso around Darsh in the second vision. He drew Darsh closer in the Deepness until his falcon enveloped the boy's form. Close as Darsh's yaksha was to him, it followed too, held within Iravan's wings—though Iravan did not attempt to touch it with his lasso. Darsh's Ecstatic ray of light still pierced the lasso, aimed into the Moment, but this close Iravan could discern the jet of light Darsh trajected was an intricate collection of dots, weaving between the strands of Iravan's lasso without touching them, so Iravan remained unaffected in the Deepness as he'd hoped.

The boy's form struggled, a dust mote that vibrated enough to make a keening sound in the silence of the Deepness. In the first vision, Darsh remained immobile, but the light in his eyes grew bluer.

Iravan imposed his will, and the lasso he had trajected began to leach hair-thin fibers. The fibers converted into a dome, closing Darsh and the yaksha within the Deepness. He flicked his wings, and a slim filament of light extended from the dome, capturing the supertrajection of both Darsh and his incorporeal yaksha in a sheath.

Awareness flooded Iravan. A sense of the yaksha's emotion, confused, patient, watchful. Darsh's emotions too, grief and fear and clarity. By sheathing Darsh's trajection in his own light, Iravan could see the trajection the boy and his yaksha were doing in the Moment through Darsh's eyes. He could see the manner in which the yaksha had found Darsh's brittle stars in the shattering universe, how Darsh's light ricocheted from star to broken star, attempting to reach the yaksha in a pattern of unity but instead finding those of the Ecstatics and trajecting them.

It really does come to this, Iravan thought. Darsh was already harming the Ecstatics, trajecting them without their consent. What Iravan was going to do to him now was a flagrant violation of consent too, abominable and similar in every way. What other choice was there?

Iravan superimposed his will on Darsh and the yaksha. An intricate web of light emerged from his dome to intersect with the trajection they did into the Moment. Iravan navigated, and slowly, stealthily, he curved the boy's intention, seeping it with his. He changed Darsh's capital desire, reaching far back into Darsh's consciousness, so that the boy's capital desire transformed into one of making amends. He bled his intention into the boy in a careful manipulation of Darsh's past lives. This was not just a trajection. This was Darsh's ruin. Iravan could only hope that after all this, the boy still remained himself in some capacity. He could only hope that he was not changing Darsh beyond his capital desire, that he was not making the boy his servant, his pawn.

In the Garden, Darsh's head snapped back, staring at the ceiling.

His body began to shake.

Iravan saw the cord around the Ecstatics drop as Darsh's trajection in the broken Moment wavered.

But that lasted just for an instant.

Darsh's memory spiked, and all of Iravan's visions filled with the boy. He blinked—but he was Iravan no longer, he was the boy, and images flooded the both of them. Of being younger, being held by his architect parents proudly when he was discovered as being capable of trajection in Nakshar. Begging them to help him, when Maze Architects dragged him away to be trapped in a deathcage. His mother in Irshar after the Conclave's crash, and the way she had walked away from him when he'd asked her to join the Garden.

Tears trickled down Darsh's eyes, blue-green, shimmering blood-like. Iravan heard his thoughts in his own mind. This was the ashram he was to make amends to? His scream built in Iravan's throat.

"NO!" the both of them cried out, and Iravan realized with horror that Darsh had leached his emotion back into him while he'd attempted his maneuvering.

The dome and the sheath shattered in the Deepness.

Darsh's form exploded in a blaze of light.

Darsh and his yaksha zipped away from Iravan, turning to face him as though only just seeing him. In the Garden, the boy spun, his hands balled into fists. Light leached from him, thrusting into the Moment, and the dark cord that had only just fallen away from the Ecstatics thickened, a hundred times more powerful, whipping around each and every Ecstatic this time, spearing them, sparing no one. Cries echoed everywhere, followed by an ominous gurgling silence.

Iravan's eyes widened, in late recognition that his plan had failed. All he saw were thick black cords intertwining between the

Ecstatics as Darsh trajected them to gain more and more power. Blue-green light blasted out of the boy like the rays of a sun, and Iravan shielded his eyes, momentarily blinded.

Rocks fell, dust entering his throat, choking him, and he fell to his knees. Around them the Garden fell apart.

37

AHILYA

A graveyard surrounded her.

Ahilya stood immobilized, staring at the thick black cords weaving between all the Ecstatics. Whatever was happening was taking them all over, one by one. The nurses, Shayla and Bipesh, hovered a few inches in the air, their heads thrown back, their eyes glassy. Their bodies were limp like everyone else's. Some Ecstatics fell, writhing on the floor, others spasmed where they stood. Some tried to run, but the intricate black cords caught them, and all of them led to Darsh.

The boy was little more than a ball of blue light, facing Iravan as her husband fell to his knees. The ground shook, rocks cascading from the walls in a thunderous rumble. Water gushed somewhere, and the slim trees in the assembly hall whiplashed. She tried to move, but her feet were locked in place. She saw earth climbing up her shins, hardening into rock. Whatever change was occurring in the Garden, it was keeping her from interfering, perhaps for her own safety. Horror seized her as she saw more black-clad Ecstatics rise and fall with bone-crunching sounds, some crumpling inwards as though the blood and flesh were being sucked out of them.

Naila was locked to her knees too. The Maze Architect had returned to her when more and more Ecstatics had begun falling. She whimpered now, her eyes widening. Her hand seized Ahilya's. They stood there, helpless and immobile, watching the horrible destruction of the Garden.

Through the black weaving of Darsh's trajection, Ahilya's gaze caught on Iravan. The ground he and Darsh stood on was beginning to rise like a pillar. Reyla darted forward as the platform became a giant tower, rising with the three of them atop it, and leaving the rest of the Ecstatics behind. The girl had lit up with the light of trajection. Soon, the three architects were lost to view behind ricochetting light. Still, the other Ecstatics writhed, crumpling on the floor, their bodies popping in bone-crunching sounds, their skin becoming liquid and oozing over the ground.

Naila closed her eyes tightly, retching. Ahilya simply watched this happen from behind her own horror. She felt numb. She felt frozen. How long until whatever was happening to the Ecstatics reached the architects of Irshar? Ahilya could not tell. Naila was not an Ecstatic, but all architects were connected—all of humanity was, especially now when there was only one core tree. Whatever was happening to these Ecstatics could occur to Irshar's architects. To all of them, whether complete beings or not.

Within the forest of her Etherium, Ahilya saw memories flash with a leaf-fall. A fleeting glimpse of a mother screaming while she held her child. A pale, sparkling face, shining with embarrassed pride. A stuttering young woman as she shyly proposed. The leaves rained down in a cascade, a hundred memories, then a thousand, each memory leaching from the Ecstatics who were writhing in front of her.

She tried to breathe. She tried to think.

She was meant to do something.

There was a reason the vriksh was showing her this.

But was it the vriksh at all? Perhaps it was the Virohi overwriting the tree. How deep had the bonds formed between the cosmic creatures and the core tree—and where did her influence end? Who was really making a decision, and for what purpose? For all she knew, anything she did now would result in further catastrophe, overwriting all of them.

Perhaps she should simply remain still. Wait for this to pass. But one way or another, she was party to this, witnessing this, forced to feel the pain of the Ecstatics bleed into her. *Call the Virohi to you,* Basav said from before. *Convince them to stay with you, close enough to feel them. Then sever them from the vriksh.* Basav had meant for her to collect the cosmic creatures. But what if she could use something similar on these Ecstatics?

Ahilya forced herself to see these people lying around her. Their faces morphed, but she tried to remember all the names she knew. Shayla, Bipesh, Ravi, Jyaishna, and so many others who she had come to know through their work in Irshar in the last few weeks. In the forest of her Etherium, shapes grew behind the leaves. Other Etheriums connected to the vriksh. She had never been able to influence anyone else's Etherium except for Iravan's—but that had been before the Virohi were embedded within the tree. What if, through the overwriting, something else had become possible? What if more doors had opened to her in the Etherium, each one leading to the consciousness of a different person?

The third vision was mutable. Iravan had seen his as several things. And the vriksh had always responded to her emotion. She had been confused when the thorns impaled her before, terrified, unknowing of what was happening or why. Her fear and the

Virohi's had turned the vriksh's memories into pain. But that had occured when the Virohi had been escaping the planetrage.

There was no planetrage now.

The Virohi were quiescent.

What if she embraced those memories instead of fighting them?

Heart thudding, Ahilya touched one of the leaves, folding it within her hand. Images overtook her vision, of one of the architects laughing within their airborne ashram—but before the memory could impale her Ahilya forced her will on the leaf and turned it into a soft grass. As if that were signal, the forest of fallen leaves changed, and she was submerged in a pool of soft grass, swimming within the architects' memories.

Triumph surged in Ahilya. Her hand riffled over the grass, and more memories of the core tree flashed through her. She had changed the image successfully, but how much control did she have here? These memories were but lives of the people, each blade of grass connected to a consciousness. Could she influence their consciousness? Could she protect them?

Ahilya stood in the center of a vast grassland surrounded by Ecstatics. She stood in the assembly chamber, black-clad architects warping around her.

A risky plan formed in her head.

38
IRAVAN

A paroxysm of coughing overtook him. *Slow down,* he tried to say, but the dust was too thick. His chest hurt with the effort of breathing. Darsh stood in front of him, staring down at him. Had he seen? Had he understood what Iravan was attempting to do? Dark cords banded themselves around Darsh's chest, connecting to the Ecstatics in the assembly hall. Darsh clenched his fist, and Ecstatics collapsed. Their limbs broke. Their skins sloughed off. They did not heal.

Waves of blackness enveloped Darsh like mist. The boy was barely visible to Iravan, though still only a few feet away from him, feeding off the power of the others. A few minutes ago, he had stopped shooting his ray of light in the Deepness. He simply stood there, surrounded by vapor, a glint of coldness in his eyes.

Shock hurtled through Iravan to note that Darsh had stopped trajecting. He had never seen Ecstasy like this. True, he had destroyed Viana accidentally, but he had actually trajected into the Moment. He had not simply desired her death. Trajection worked in extradimensional realms, and one had to manipulate the Moment from the Deepness to affect change in reality. Darsh had somehow bypassed this basic tenet. Almost as if…

As if he were using the everpower, Iravan realized, his heart hammering in terror.

Screams rent the air, and Iravan panicked. The ground he and Darsh were standing on was rising. More bodies were spasming, other Ecstatics somehow being blocked from entering the Deepness. How was Darsh doing this? What would it achieve? Iravan stared, not understanding, as Galan, Divena, and Vivek shot up in the air, their bodies impaled by thick curling smoke-like vines, before crashing back into the earth. Were they alive?

A soft breathy voice spoke behind him. Reyla stood there, trembling, her hand touching Iravan's kurta lightly. She had left the protective circle of the other Ecstatics. For some reason, the cords had not affected her, and now the both of them rose on the platform along with Darsh. Iravan reached out a steadying hand to the girl as the ground shook again and she stumbled.

"Iravan-ve," she breathed. "I tried to tell you. He did this before. I don't know how, but we were both trying to attempt our evervision, and then he warped the Deepness. Let me show you how."

Her skin lit up with the light of trajection, and suddenly she was there in the Deepness right next to Iravan's falcon, her tiny burst of lights glimmering.

Reyla trajected before he could speak, a pattern of astonishing complexity, half-network half-vine, and in the evervision Iravan noticed it was not just the shattered Moment she was trajecting, but she was twisting the velvety Deepness itself, folding the space around Darsh. How was this possible? The realms were separate, and though he asked for his architects to view them the same way, what Reyla was doing was removing the barrier of separation altogether. Iravan had asked for a shift of *perspective*. This was rendering that shift in reality.

Reyla's trajection took form. Some of the cords connecting to Darsh stripped away from him in both the visions, reacting to Reyla's folding of space.

Darsh turned his blue-green gaze toward her. He raised his arm, and brought it down in a slashing motion. Iravan had no time to react.

Reyla's soft sigh turned into a cry. The little girl fell, her light winking out.

Iravan roared then in grief, and inside him the falcon responded. His ray of light in the Deepness grew sharp like a blade, and he swung toward Darsh's dust mote without thinking, like he once had in a fight with the falcon-yaksha.

Darsh parried just as easily as the falcon. He trajected his own beam, and split Iravan's light into two. Iravan hammered with another ray, then another, a barrage of them shooting from him like missiles, but Darsh dodged them easily, him and his yaksha dancing between Iravan's beam, returning a volley with their own shards of light.

The Deepness transformed, contracting around Iravan like he was in a deathmaze. Wonder and awe bloomed in Iravan as he realized that whatever was happening was mimicking that sungineering technology. Reyla had said that Darsh was doing this, but how? Iravan had no time to dwell on it.

The boy and the incorporeal yaksha spun next to each other, dizzyingly, their shapes becoming impossible to distinguish. A powerful ray of light emerged from them, its edges sharp and thorny, resembling a serrated brittlevine.

The vine enveloped Iravan, crushing him.

In the Deepness, the falcon's wings grew trapped as Darsh

unleashed a massive web of power, each thread sharpened like a blade.

He was attempting to cut Iravan off from the Deepness, but in Iravan's heightened sense of the evervision, it would not only cut him off from the one realm, it would do so in all the realms. This was not mere trajection. This was a kind of excision.

The boy's ray of light hurtled toward Iravan, too fast to stop.

39

AHILYA

Perhaps it was because she had already given so much of herself to the Virohi. Perhaps it was simply a natural function of overwriting.

In the end, it was not so hard.

Ahilya stood in a vast grassland and imagined a shield. The grass of memories—the lives of the Ecstatics—rose in a wall. *Build,* she thought, and an ethereal barrier grew around her, grass hardening into bark, keeping the force of what Darsh was doing back.

The Ecstatics' memories solidified into recollections of strength. Images came to Ahilya of different people. Of a time when they had been Maze Architects and Junior Architects, keeping their ashrams afloat. Of a time when they had believed in themselves, and the sanctity of their purpose. Ahilya held onto this strength, building the barrier, keeping Darsh out. She pulled open the doors to her house, one after another, and allowed the consciousness of all these people to filter through to her like air, pulling them the same way she would pull Iravan into her forest.

Shadows flickered in the Etherium, then came rushing to stand next to her. Their silhouettes were recognizable, though they were wisps of smoke. Bipesh, Shayla, Ravi, Jyaishna, and all the others who lay fallen in the Garden—their minds opened to her in the Etherium, and they waited for her command.

Like an architect, Ahilya trajected, turning will and desire into actuality.

Resist, she thought. *Wake.*

Around her, black-clad Ecstatics started to stir. She gripped Naila's hand, nudging her to open her eyes. The two of them stared as the Ecstatics blinked in the Garden, their eyes widening. An awe grew inside Ahilya, the recognition of the Ecstatics' emotion. Black leached out of the Ecstatic's eyes, and their skins returned to normal. Their bones healed, and one by one the dark cords connecting them to Darsh faded, glimmering away, so that soon Ahilya could see nothing but the broken assembly hall, and the staggering Ecstatics around her reviving themselves. The construction of the Garden continued to change, but instead of the destruction wrought by the duel, the same soft flow of dust churned in whirlpools.

Whatever Darsh had done, she was reversing it. The *Ecstatics* were reversing it, pulling themselves back together, even unto repairing their own bodies in an awe-inspiring, grotesque remaking.

Ahilya turned away from them. She silenced the sounds of bones clicking together, or cries and screams, as the Ecstatics reformed themselves. She could just glimpse Iravan, the terrified look in his eyes. She had done all she could to help him—taken the Ecstatics out of the equation. She would deal with the horrible implications of her power later.

For now, she willed Iravan to survive his fight.

40

IRAVAN

Iravan battled for his life.

Not even with the falcon-yaksha had he experienced this trajection. He had not known that excision could be done from the Deepness. The falcon had tried to subsume him—but this combined assault of the pocket-Deepness and the ray of severance shook him, making an escape impossible.

He attempted to summon the Conduit, but that would mean leaving Darsh alone here, to wreak his damage. So he darted within its small chamber, trying to escape Darsh's attack. His intention formed to trap Darsh again, to put a stop to this somehow, but he did not have enough time to understand how to carry it. The falcon of his form crashed into one wall then another, attempting to evade the relentless pursuit of Darsh's arrow-like rays, intent on immobilizing him. The bird thrashed, still caught in the web of Darsh's making, leading him on as it tried to escape.

Darsh hunted, unyielding, with his yaksha.

Iravan saw the boy's form chasing him in the Deepness, light appearing like a drawn bow, sending thousands of excision rays toward him. The falcon spun, wings wrapped around itself, trapped yet fleeing.

A ray grazed his wing. Deep pain lanced through Iravan, and in the first vision he stumbled on shaky ground, a rupture opening in his side where a wing might be, blood gushing down. Furious memory awoke in the falcon's form—

Without his volition, the falcon screamed, a horrible echoing sound that nearly deafened Iravan.

The bird unwound and faced Darsh in the Deepness, trails of web falling down its wings. Iravan could only watch, horrified, as the falcon inside him took over, sending out a trajection of such fast linking toward the incorporeal yaksha that Iravan almost thought he'd imagined it.

Darsh's yaksha detached from the boy, flying toward the falcon in the Deepness, flooding Iravan with immense power. The contracted Deepness forgotten, Iravan entered the evervision, and saw it occur in all the three visions—

The same lancing of excision that Darsh had been attempting to perform on him, but done with the entire force of reality behind Iravan this time.

The falcon swung a wing down in a massive obliterating weave.

The Moment, the Deepness, the Etherium, all shivered.

The jet of silvery light from the evervision cleaved Darsh's form in the Deepness, splitting it into jagged shards.

For an eternity, everything seemed to freeze, reality holding its breath. Sparks lingered, shining.

Then Darsh winked out of the Deepness.

Iravan moved slowly toward the boy who still stood on the platform within the first vision. In a hopeless part of his mind, Iravan thought that he'd been mistaken, that he had won but had not harmed, that it was all going to be fine.

Then light seeped out of Darsh, like water draining.

His body grew dark and pitched forward into Iravan's arms, cold as ice. There was no heartbeat, no bloodflow, no life.

Across the distance, Ahilya was on her feet while others around her knelt in pain, still recovering from Darsh's onslaught. Iravan's horror and pain and shock were etched on the lines of her face, in the way her mouth hung open, in her eyes that were finally seeing him for the monster he was.

Within him, the falcon laughed, sinking its talons into Iravan's skin.

A cry of despair filled Iravan's throat.

He howled then, an unearthly sound of madness. The Garden shook, reacting to him, the plates beneath everyone shifting and breaking, mud sinking, roots whipping, thorns and brambles rising from every plant while icicles pierced the earth. Behind Iravan, the rock face split open, a tunnel rapidly forming to lead into utter blackness.

Iravan cradled Darsh's dead body, and embraced the dark.

41

AHILYA

Ahilya kept her eyes trained on the ceiling of the assembly hall. Despite the thrashing it had taken from Iravan and Darsh's combined powers, it was reknitting, though not in any manner she had seen before. This was the same cascading whirlpool of silvery dust that had begun before Iravan and Darsh had started to duel, and it was evolving. It was like neither the weaving of plants or roots, nor the layered construction of stone or rock. It wasn't the manner in which the Virohi had changed Irshar's architecture, nor the undulating effect of everdust which made one's eyes hurt. This resembled the slowest, most hesitant kind of construction. At the edges of it, Ahilya could see simply light, like dancing spots across her irises. The spots flickered and disappeared, coming together only to come apart again.

It reminded her eerily of how the everdust had been so long ago, when she had first entered this habitat in pursuit of Iravan after his abduction by the falcon-yaksha. Back then, the dust had been sentient, waiting for her to think something, responding to her like an affectionate pet. Even now the shimmering was cautious, as if this dust was weighing the lives it was surrounded with, changing itself and the architecture, yet doing so without startling anyone. Ahilya had been watching it for longer than an hour, ever since Iravan had disappeared. Perhaps she was the only one watching; if so, she could see clearly, the silvery light intersecting and crisscrossing, air made solid, as it rebuilt the roof without ceremony.

Vaguely, she was aware that the assembly hall had become even more chaotic after Iravan's departure. The army of Ecstatics had left, the architects leaning on each other as they retreated, presumably to get more healing. Someone had alerted the sungineers, and orange-clad people hummed everywhere, talking to each other, rushing around carrying medprobes, seeking counsel from each other and Irshar's own sungineers. Ahilya had caught a glimpse of a harried-looking Dhruv bursting into the hall, calling out orders, before he'd been swept away from her view. There were other citizens of Irshar here too, normal citizens who milled about, staring at the hall having never visited the Garden before. Several Ecstatic children who had been cleared away by Naila had returned. They were crying, leaning on their families arrived from the ashram. Ahilya caught a few adults quietly weeping too.

Kamala had come to see her only a few minutes ago. The nurse had led her away from the activity to a quiet corner, and checked Ahilya's vitals. She'd given her a curious look, then left without comment. Ahilya supposed that was a good thing. What more could be happening to her, anyway? She had suffered the Virohi, suffered the vriksh, even suffered the Etherium. She answered Kamala's cursory questions, then lapsed into silence.

Naila sat with her, making quiet sounds of frustration, her fingers entwined with beads, old ones of an airborne ashram. They did not look like rudra beads, so perhaps they belonged to another city. If Ahilya wanted to know, all she'd have to do was focus on

Naila and the woman's memory would come to her, but she was damned if she denied her that consent. Here in this moment, the Maze Architect was her only ally.

Naila hadn't moved from her spot, keeping close to Ahilya ever since they'd claimed this corner of the Garden for themselves. Each time someone came to speak to Ahilya, she'd fended them off. Ahilya saw past Naila to the weeping people. An urge took her to rise and comfort them, to speak with them and allay any fear. For reasons she could not fathom, she felt responsible for this situation—and their grief and confusion bloomed in her mind as if the emotions were her own. She thought again of what Basav had told her, and the manner in which she'd seen into Irshar's councilors' minds. *It's beginning,* she thought in a kind of distant horror. *The Virohi are overwriting the others, and that's why I can sense them so keenly.* Her body shivered and a soft whimper escaped her.

"Try and rest, Ahilya-ve," Naila murmured without looking up, still unentangling the knots on her beads. "There is only so much quiet they will allow you. Try to silence your worries."

Her advice sounded similar to Chaiyya's usual instruction before talking to the Virohi, but of course, Naila would know those basic practices. Perhaps she'd taught them once at Nakshar's Academy.

Ahilya looked away, back to the shimmering ceiling, trying to obey.

In the forest of her Etherium, she hunted for Iravan. The vriksh had settled again, once more curling softly around her as she strode through the forest. Between her brows, she could sense her husband, but he felt fuzzy, as though he were a great distance away. His shields were back up, but in her mind's eye she could still see his haunted face. She could hear his wretched sounds of despair. Darsh's body fell over and over again, an image caught on loop. Try as she might, she could not rid herself of the image.

All of them knew the horror of what Iravan had done. Did they know what *she* had done? The afternoon was already blurry, shapes and shadows twisting and losing themselves in the caverns of her mind, but Ahilya knew one thing with certainty. She had found the Ecstatics of the Garden within the Etherium. She had pulled them to her as if she were a powerful magnet. Then she had controlled them—forced them to create a shield against Darsh, then commanded them to resist, to fight. She had imposed her desire onto them.

She had overwritten them.

She felt cold, and blindly she reached for the blanket Kamala had left for her. The ceiling. That was where she needed to focus. *Look at it,* she thought, trembling. *Isn't it fascinating. It is so fascinating.*

It was no use. A horrible understanding was pouring into her. Airav had told her that she was the necessary obstacle between the Virohi and the rest of humanity. *If you give in or give up, the Virohi will convert us to what they wish.* But what did the Virohi wish except for form? And whose form were they most familiar with? Ahilya reached and gripped Naila's hand without seeing. In the process of overwriting, the Virohi were blending the barrier of consciousness, giving Ahilya unfettered access to the others. They saw Ahilya as one of them. Perhaps she was the gateway they needed, to infiltrate the others. In controlling the Ecstatics during Iravan's battle with Darsh, she'd simply given the cosmic creatures more access, accelerating the process of overwriting.

Basav's voice mocked her in her memory, *Do the right thing, Ahilya-ve.* She had been trying to, but she had committed as gross a violation as Iravan had. What he had done with Darsh was visible, but her manipulation? She felt ashamed of its secrecy, as if she had done something dirty in saving the Ecstatics. Had Iravan felt similarly? Had he struggled with these feelings too, in trying to do something he felt was right? In a strange way, Ahilya finally understood her husband, now when she did not know where he was.

Naila squeezed her fingers and gave her a gentle nudge. Ahilya glanced to where the architect gestured. The Senior Sungineer of the Garden marched toward them, a grim look in his eyes.

Dhruv stopped a few feet away and glared at Ahilya. "We need to ask you something. Come with me."

He was looming. He knew how much Ahilya hated that. She turned back to study the ceiling instead of meeting his gaze. "You don't need me for everything," she muttered.

"It turns out we do for—"

"For fuck's sake," Ahilya said quietly. "Do something yourselves, the lot of you."

From the corner of her eyes, she saw Dhruv raise his brows. A spasm of guilt rushed through Ahilya. She was not fending him off just to be difficult. She was afraid she couldn't trust herself right now. What if she inadvertently tried to overwrite them again? Yet she knew they couldn't do several things without her. To refuse their summons was another aggression, throwing their helplessness in their faces. She stood up, sighing. Naila rose beside her, and Dhruv glanced between the two of them, then shrugged. He began to walk away, expecting them to follow.

Naila grinned. "You've become a bit too patient lately," she said softly. "I like seeing you angry, again. It feels like you."

The statement was meant to reassure Ahilya, a reminder that Naila was still here, that she'd been there at the start of this calamity and chosen to see Ahilya through all her different evolutions. But it was Ahilya's anger that had set them all on this path. Her rage and Iravan's arrogance. Silently, she followed Dhruv down a leafy pathway, and around a corner within the courtyard of the assembly chamber.

She staggered to a stop, her jaw falling open.

The main courtyard still resembled the one Iravan had created so long ago, with meandering narrow roads bordered with flower-lined bushes and hidden alcoves. This was where Iravan had created his throne room, the same place where she had come to make her demands and where he had conducted his class of Ecstatics before the battle with Darsh. The cave mouth leading to Irshar had been an opening in the rock—but now—now— Ahilya clutched at Naila to keep her balance.

It was not the hills of no man's land she saw in front of her, separating the Garden from Irshar.

She saw Irshar.

The cave mouth simply opened into what looked like a wall of the infirmary, where a few feet from her the nurses of the city bustled about going in and out of patient rooms as always. Was she imagining it? But no, Dhruv was striding straight into the cave mouth, entering Irshar, and as she followed, she saw dust swirling everywhere reshaping the architecture.

Ahilya wanted to ask Dhruv what had occurred, but there was hostility in every line of his posture. She knew he had come to her against his wont. She, Dhruv and Naila passed chamber upon chamber in silence, stepping over the roots of the vriksh that had expanded into the Garden—if this place could be called the Garden anymore. Ahilya tried to make sense of it—this merging that was occurring so silently, but she couldn't fathom it. Was this because of the battle with Darsh? She had noticed this dust before Darsh had exploded with light.

They came upon a chamber full of black-clad Ecstatics. Several lay on the floor, while others watched over them, the nurses of Irshar administering medicines. The Ecstatics all seemed comatose, and Ahilya saw their glassy eyes, their mouths hanging open. A shiver went through her. Dhruv made an impatient sound in his throat, and Naila tugged her gently. Ahilya followed them around a corner and outside the infirmary.

The rest of Irshar had not escaped this strange transformation. Ordinarily, the infirmary would lead into the main quadrangle with the vriksh. Now, though the vriksh remained, the plaza was heavy with blooms of jasmine from Iravan's assembly hall. More pieces of the Garden were scattered everywhere—the dense solar lab caught between two residences of Irshar, and Iravan's massive tower sprouting out of a nameless courtyard, surrounded by low lying buildings of the ashram.

Dhruv disappeared behind a large ixora bush, and Ahilya and Naila followed. Naila uttered a low, awed whistle through her teeth as they entered a chamber made almost entirely of bio-nodes, those massive sungineering devices which resembled solarnotes. The outside of these bio-nodes resembled pale frosted glass, but as Ahilya took a vacant seat, she saw images flicker all around her on the true screens of the devices. This was not a solar lab. It was something else—a solarchamber.

The others stopped murmuring when she entered. A small rectangular wooden table had been brought into this solarchamber, and Dhruv sat at one of the heads of it, leaving space for Ahilya at the other. Chaiyya, Airav, Basav and Kiana were all present as main councilors from Irshar, sitting on one side of Ahilya, where Naila took the only remaining seat. On the other side were representatives from the Garden. Two Ecstatics, Pranav and Trisha, and one other woman, her smile not quite reaching her eyes, who introduced herself as Dhruv's lead sungineer, Purva. Ahilya studied them all.

"I don't know where he is," she said before they could ask. "I can't sense him."

Dhruv scowled at her from the other side. "Iravan, what he

has done—what has happened to the Ecstatics, and now what is occurring all over—" He cut off, visibly trying to keep himself under control.

Ahilya was surprised at this subtle castigation of her husband, but it made sense. With Iravan gone, Dhruv was in command of the Garden, and she read his nervousness. His hands shook as he removed his glasses and polished them on the edge of his kurta. He was as ill-equipped to be the lead councilor as she had been. How far the both of them had come from their days of secret machinations to gain a council seat.

"What *has* happened to the Ecstatics?" she asked. "I saw them in there…"

"We don't know," Pranav replied. "But we can guess. None of us are able to traject anymore."

Ahilya had never spoken to Pranav before, but she knew he was one of Iravan's top Ecstatics, once a Maze Architect of Nakshar, and a man who had both been imprisoned by the council she had been on, yet someone who had escaped excision because of everything she had done to protect him. He knew who she was, of course. Yet in his guarded gaze, she saw nothing but indifference, and it was almost comforting to feel as if she did not matter to him, that she was just another citizen. For a fleeting second Ahilya was grateful.

"Only the Ecstatics?" she asked. "The rest of you can traject?"

Naila shook her head. "No, Ahilya-ve, we can't either. But the rest of us haven't been able to traject since the Moment broke."

Chaiyya nodded, and Ahilya paused. Of course. She'd known that. In everything she'd learned since the Moment breaking, she had forgotten that the primary purpose of the universe was so architects could traject.

Pranav waved a hand toward the infirmary. "Either way, now the

Ecstatics have joined those ranks, because the Deepness is damaged too. And it's hitting us worse than it did ordinary architects. Reyla says this is why Darsh lost control. He was trying to work in a realm that was changing as he trajected."

Ahilya thought of the glassy-eyed stare of the Ecstatics. Maya flashed in her eyes—the Ecstatic Architect she'd seen ages ago in Nakshar's sanctum, when Iravan had told her about the truth of Ecstasy. The ones she'd seen in Irshar's infirmary resembled Maya so fully. She shivered, remembering her control of them in her Etherium.

"You seem fine," she ventured, staring at Pranav.

"For now. But I don't think I, or any of the other in the Garden, will be exempt from this too long."

"You think this is Iravan's doing?"

Pranav studied her. "Maybe? But I think not. The Deepness isn't the Deepness anymore. It seems to be folding around itself much like in a deathmaze. And your architects cannot fully sense the shattered Moment either, though that is to be expected."

"The three visions are collapsing," Chaiyya said. "We think it is an effect of the Moment breaking. If Iravan is right, and all the realms are the same in some way, then the breaking of one was sure to have a massive consequence on the others. It is a wonder it has taken this long."

Ahilya felt nauseated. Another calamity to add to her and Iravan's list of transgressions. She did not need to ask why the collapse of the three visions was occurring now, she already knew it. Darsh had begun to unite with his yaksha, and unity by her experience brought about great change, both physical and metaphysical. Darsh's unity with his yaksha had triggered the collapse, perhaps tipping an already wobbly rock off balance straight into the chasm of confusion.

Naila's skin lit up as if to test it, but she quickly darkened. When she spoke, she was breathless as if she'd run a mile, and her eyes were wide. "This… this collapse of the three visions," she breathed. "Is this the evervision?"

Pranav shook his head. "No. The evervision is a matter of perspective. Iravan-ve could always see the Moment, the Deepness, and his Etherium as separate things but he could also see them as the same, a switch that only he could do. The evervision is afforded to him, and only to him, because of his power. But this—" He waved his hand. "This is really happening. We have been calling it allvision." Pranav shrugged. "There is a difference, even if it is a philosophical one."

"It is more than a philosophical one," Naila said, her voice troubled. "Because *is* it actually real?" Her glance flicked to Ahilya, mildly apologetic, before turning to the others. "Maybe it is a corruption of the Virohi. Maybe we *think* this allvision exists because the Virohi are corrupting us."

"The corruption is not helping," Airav said. "But Iravan shattered the Moment. The Moment affects consciousness, so it breaking changes our experience of reality. Yet what happens in the Moment renders outside of it too. Destroying it essentially unmoored reality. Subjective perception and objective reality are both broken now. We are headed toward a collapse of everything, matter, language, meaning, even thought."

"We're fucked, in short," Dhruv said. "From every side."

A silence echoed after those words. Ahilya studied her hands on her lap. They were trembling, but she watched it happen from afar, Dhruv's words rippling through her.

"We cannot lose hope," Airav said, breaking the quiet. "This decay of reality—this dissolution—is occurring fast, but we are still here. We can still hold meaningful conversation, we can still experience a shared reality, such as it is. Things are returning to their source, but both Irshar and the Garden were created of the original habitat. Our societies split into two, but the building blocks of these two places were the same. They were both made of everdust, though of course Irshar eventually encompassed the Virohi and the vriksh too. Now…" Airav spun a finger to indicate the pictures on the bio-nodes. "It appears that it is all coming back to what it once was—the original habitat. The city is trying to balance itself, which means we have hope of balancing ourselves too. Eskayra has already begun the migration to the new city for those citizens who are willing."

"What?" Ahilya asked, her head snapping up. "When nightfall approaches?"

"Time is not a luxury we have," Dhruv said. "Dissolution is already occurring, and it is likely to become faster. Sungineering is compromised with the loss of the Deepness. We are working this on the new energy from Irshar."

He gestured toward the chamber, and Kiana nodded and placed a torch on the table. Purple sungineering light bounced off the bio-nodes, until Kiana turned it off.

If sungineering was unreliable and Ecstasy was dead, then humanity had reached the end of the line. Food, medicine, light, all of it was now on its last rations, reality itself forfeit. To send survivors out to the new city, scattering them when everyone needed to stay together, was so preposterous that Ahilya's voice shook with emotion.

"If this is true," she said, "then all the more reason to stay here in Irshar, or the Garden, or whatever this habitat is now. How do we even know if the new city is safe? We could be sending the citizens to more doom. You could be sending Eskayra to her death."

"We are all dead sooner or later," Dhruv said flatly. He stood up, and everyone turned their eyes on him. "We are all living with risk now. Reality's first laws are already changing."

He approached the closest bio-nodes, swiped on the glassy screen a few times, pressing buttons, then stepped back.

The images all over the solarchamber changed. Ahilya could still see the dome of the shimmering dust, this time more clearly than before, but she also saw the jungle beyond. The trees that had until recently been stationary were now quaking as though an earthrage were imminent. The landscape shrunk, and Ahilya realized it wasn't merely the trees quaking. Dhruv was somehow capturing the skies too, and a distortion cracked the blue sky, a splitting in the middle of the air like lightning, but black, tiny cracks over and over again. Images flickered again, of mountains and valleys that had formed indiscriminately after the battle with the Virohi, and a roaring, painful sound reverberated through Ahilya's bones. Irshar and the Garden stood in the middle of this, but the images shuddered, several bio-nodes blanking out as undoubtedly drones fell from the air before newer ones replaced them.

Naila exchanged a startled glance with Ahilya. They were both thinking of the same thing. Planetrage.

"Dhruv's drones have reported strange events," Chaiyya said. "Fire breathing within water vapor. Dust translating into leaves then phasing back. Weather morphing in seconds, and gravity failing with rocks floating on their own. The city Iravan built is holding, much like the habitat here, for whatever reason. We are hedging our bets for survival—which is why only volunteers are allowed to go to the new city."

She left the rest unsaid. If humanity had a chance, they could not all be caught in Irshar. This way, there could be some survivors. If they survived the planetrage and the subsequent dissolution, they could save the species.

Ahilya looked away from the bio-nodes, her head splitting. She was so tired now. How much devastation could the human mind take? She thought of her sister, and Arth and Kush, and the children of the ashram. She could not fathom it. The end of everything. *Maybe this is what it was like,* she thought. *Back when they were debating whether to fly away or to stay down here. Maybe that's why some of them chose to fly, and the others to build habitats. Not a disagreement like we thought, but a desperate hedging of bets.*

"Did you know about this?" Basav asked her quietly.

She could not look up. "Yes," she whispered. "I—I suspected it. Iravan and I talked about it." In halting words, she told the others of what she'd been discussing with Iravan before Darsh had begun his unity with the yaksha. "If the Moment breaking has caused this, then only the repair of the Moment can fix it. But—"

But Iravan had wanted the Virohi first, driven in his hate and rage. She had the means to destroy them, and she and her husband were still standing on opposite ends, holding their entire species hostage, arguing the fulfillment of his capital desire against what she thought was right.

In the Etherium, she felt the Virohi's terror. The wrongness of sacrificing them, when they had grieved the Moment in a way none of them had, filled her with a queasiness. Who were they, really? What was their true form? What would finally release them—save them in the manner they needed to be saved?

She wanted to tell the others what she was thinking. She wanted them to help her.

But Ahilya couldn't form the words.

These people hated the Virohi; they hated her. They would not listen. They would think her corrupted if she argued the Virohi's case now—when the answer was so obvious to them that the cosmic creatures' destruction could end their own misery. She did not know the wisdom of defending the Virohi anymore. The Virohi were already giving her more power and access than the others could know. Perhaps this new ability she'd found in her Etherium was simply an unconscious function of overwriting. Yet Ahilya could sense that the Virohi in their advanced, evolved state were trying to tell her something. The knot of roots in her chest tightened over her. The overwriting, the repair of the Moment, their fear, this was all connected in some way. She felt the puzzle pieces circling her, but they were too hazy, too senseless. She could not share these arbitrary notions with the others.

"We need Iravan," she said, her voice small. "Here with us, helping us. But I—I still don't know where he is."

"Fortunately, I might have an idea." Dhruv beckoned to her, and waited until she had arisen and joined him. He tapped at one of the panes of the solarchamber, and the whole thing turned black then whisked up. Watched by the other councilors, he led her to a rocky wall, pointed at it, then stepped back.

It took Ahilya a moment to understand. This was the same wall where Iravan had disappeared. She stared at it, then back at Dhruv.

"Desire it," he said softly.

Ahilya touched the wall with trembling fingers. She closed her eyes, picturing Iravan in her mind, and between her brows, she thought she caught a glimpse of him. Just a shadow and silver light, glinting from between the leaves.

She focused her desire, like she had done so many times. The tree within her mind bloomed. Images seared her mind, Iravan on a staircase, rock and earth pouring upward around him, an underground labyrinth, a cavity in the rock.

Then the rock face in front of her split open and the images subsided.

Dust and earth rained down on her face, and she stepped back as a long crack separated the blank wall, only big enough for her to squeeze through. Two sungineering drones zipped past her at once, entering the darkness first.

Dhruv nodded, unsurprised. "As always," he said, "he will speak with you, and you alone." He stared at Ahilya, and in his gaze she felt the weight of every other person's fear and judgement. "You can get through to him. Will you go?"

42

IRAVAN

Iravan gave himself to darkness.

He fled the Garden, everpower carving a path for him, and he blindly followed, carrying Darsh's body. Rock, earth, root, all of it exploded, leaving a maze behind—but he continued to flee, far from them all. The plates of the planet shifted as Iravan hurtled deeper into unknown mountains. Once a creature of the skies, now he folded the earth around him, escaping, but he didn't care where he was going. He only knew he needed to leave before he hurt someone else. He needed to lock himself away, even if it meant he would never see daylight again. A treacherous, rough path opened in front of him, and he placed one foot in front of the other, long legs moving fast, scrabbling, climbing, sharp, jagged rocks tearing at his clothes and skin, leaving bloodied marks behind. He moved until he could move no more. Until Darsh's weight in his arms grew heavy, and his entire body trembled.

Iravan sank to his knees, surrounded by cold rock. Light gleamed in this pit, radiating from his skin. The cave he'd trajected was only wide enough to hold him and the body but no more. Loose rocks rained down on his hair, and he heard the furious crash of rock in the earth.

Here, all was silent.

He brushed Darsh's limp hair aside. He touched his cold body with his fingers, cupping the boy's cheek. Darsh's eyes reflected no light. He looked so much younger than fifteen, just a child who had trusted the wrong man. Who had worshipped a monster. Tears cascaded down Iravan's face, and his chest hurt. Holding the boy close to him, Iravan wept, careening into disbelief then horror.

Half-descended into madness, he tried to traject into the body. He had all this everpower. He could use it. Air eddied in front of him, and he forced some of it into the boy's lungs. *Breathe*, he commanded. *Breathe, and live, and forgive me.*

The body spasmed, unnaturally so, and he knew that though he could do many miraculous things, this one he could not. Consciousness had already left Darsh, and even everpower could not achieve the impossible.

He clutched Darsh's body and howled. Images chased each other in his broken mind—of Oam who had been so frightened, and Viana whose skin had erupted with bones, and Bharavi who had screamed his name. *Death has become such an easy answer for you*, Ahilya had said, and he grieved because she was right. He had loved this boy, and thought of him as his own, but fatherhood had always been denied to him. This was inevitable. Perhaps in giving Darsh his affection, he had brought about the boy's demise.

The questions seeped out of Iravan. A horrible clarity grew in him. Still clutching Darsh, he pushed the everpower into the rock around him, shrinking the space, enclosing himself in a silent tomb. Roots grew from the rock, wrapping around him so he couldn't breathe. Slowly, methodically, Iravan sought to destroy himself, because now he could see how he had brought all this about. He turned the everpower into his body—

Something knocked him away, and he looked up blearily. The three visions were not three anymore, they were amalgamated, and in his deranged mind he saw the falcon-yaksha fly to him like a creature of legend.

It was small enough to perch onto his shoulder, a thing made of light, and though he could feel its weight, Iravan knew the falcon was not really there—but what was real anymore? The falcon's crooning was like a song of seduction, and in that moment, Iravan saw how everything he had done had been at the falcon's bidding. He had never wanted war with the Virohi. He had never wanted to destroy. Ahilya had asked him what his capital desire was really worth, whether making amends really was the same as destroying the Virohi, and he thought, *You have corrupted me*, as the falcon chirruped on his shoulder.

Iravan's hand shot out to clasp the bird's neck, but the falcon only laughed, dissipating to reform around him—mirrored a thousand times, a million times. The creature became massive within Iravan's eyes, and he felt its rage and corrosive hate bleed into him. In the folded space of the amalgamated three visions, the falcon's wings wrapped around him. His Etherium blinked in and out—a sludge of reality—and his past lives surrounded them, their eyes glinting silver. Each of those past lives had a tiny bird perched on their shoulders.

Help me, Iravan thought desperately—but Nidhirv, Mohini, Askavetra, Bhaskar, and behind them a thousand other lives, all crowded him. His vision condensed to a single chamber of darkness, silvery lights surrounding him as the past lives stalked him. He discerned the coldness in their gazes. He retreated blindly, stumbling and tripping, rock cutting him. Too late, he understood. He had let the falcon in too deep—allowed it to infiltrate and infect his past. His past lives were its minions now, their desires corrupted as he once had been.

They loomed in his vision, their skins glowing iridescent blue, then silvery, as if they were fighting the falcon's control too. Iravan saw the moment when the falcon took over. Nidhirv's face twisted into a cold smile. Askavetra's mouth went slack, while Agni howled in feral laughter. Their bodies grew bigger, and they reached down, their hands overlaid atop each other, resembling silvery wingtips as they strangled Iravan.

He struggled, weeping, as the falcon's intent poured into him. He saw Ahilya within his Etherium, a shadowy haze, and knew that she was coming for him. *No,* he thought frantically. *No. Stay away.*

He couldn't breathe. The falcon gleamed, and—he didn't even see it coming—he couldn't tell how—

His visions vibrated like a dewdrop in the wind, then a great distance opened up between him and his thoughts. He viewed his body moving from afar. The way it trajected the everpower, earth and mud swirling in front of him, the immense constructions being made with purpose. His body half-flew, half-strode through a labyrinth as above him rock shot up thousands of feet. Stairs grew, and beyond it a familiar city full of spires and towers appeared, a gift he had once thought to make.

He recognized the trap. He fought to free himself.

The falcon tightened its talons—Nidhirv, Bhaskar, and all the others, pressed down, their knees over his chest and arms, pinning him while he struggled—

Iravan shrank.

43

AHILYA

Dhruv equipped her with sungineering devices.

They stood together facing the blank wall of rock. A few minutes ago, Dhruv's assistant, Purva, had collapsed the solarchamber to shrink it further, in order to conserve sungineering power. Ahilya glanced behind her, and saw the other councilors retake their seats, their voices hushed as they pointed toward the images still pouring from the Garden's drones. All of them were still in relative privacy, the solarchamber now a semi-circle closed by the rock wall.

Ahilya caught Naila's eyes and smiled slightly, but Naila simply watched, worry in her eyes. She did not like the idea of Ahilya going alone in search of Iravan, but in the last few minutes, each of the councilors had tried to open the rock wall like Ahilya had. They had tried it with her, then alone, but none of it had worked. They had even tried to enter it after Ahilya opened it. Even that had been futile. The rock had simply closed, nearly taking their limbs with it.

No one was surprised. Iravan had coded this gate for one person alone, just as he had all that time ago when he'd first made Irshar in the skies. It had always been about the two of them. Dhruv had sent his probes forward but they'd returned nothing but fitful images of rock. Ahilya had no idea what she'd be met with, but all she felt was a giddy excitement, bordering on vertiginous. She was going to fall over a terrible precipice, and it would be a relief.

Dhruv tapped her shoulder, and asked her to turn. Ahilya tugged on the harness, trying not to disturb the delicate devices Dhruv had placed around it.

She tried to contain the sense of unreality breathing inside her skin. What was she doing? Was she really going to go to Iravan and turn over the Virohi? He would not fight the planetrage without that assurance, not now when she had the method to destroy the cosmic creatures. What would happen to her, and the rest of humanity when she excised the Virohi? The cosmic creatures were irrevocably tied to them all now. The other didn't see it—they wouldn't—but Ahilya could sense it in the Etherium. She wouldn't have to snap a branch of the Virohi as much as set fire to the forest, burning each person and memory to satiate Iravan. Would he make her do it while he watched? Would he comfort her while she wept? The thought was such madness that Ahilya began hyperventilating.

She looked to the ceiling, which was still reshaping itself. She tried to anchor herself, but instead of seeing the Garden as it had become now, she saw a memory of thin trees waving in and out of her vision. She saw the trees of Nakshar, that had once grown in the outer maze of the ashram, during landing. Dhruv was placing sungineering devices—not just normal devices, but experimental ones—on her harness. She was leaving for a dangerous expedition. She could almost hear Oam flirting with her. She could hear Naila's arrogant replies from the past. And Iravan—she could sense him too, a pull on her heart and behind her brows.

Her feelings for her husband now were no different from those during that fateful expedition. Then her turmoil had been caused by his seven months of absence. This time, it was because of something worse, but in her mind, had she not already said goodbye to him, both times? What was left for them? Now when she went to him, would they finally see each other? Would they finally reconcile? Is this what it would take for their marriage—an evolution of the species, and its erasure?

A soft sound of hysteria built in her throat. "Just like old times," she muttered.

"Just like," Dhruv replied.

Ahilya jumped, turning her gaze to him. She had not expected him to speak. She had been talking to herself, a coping mechanism she had adopted ever since the formation of Irshar, though for the most part she'd done this in the conflicted privacy of her head. She stared at the sungineer, and he looked up from her harness. The words hung between them, of apology and explanation, but Dhruv cleared his throat, and Ahilya swallowed, and the both of them looked away, unable to say it.

Still, Ahilya felt a lessening of the weight on her shoulders.

Perhaps after all this time, and everything that had occurred, they did not need to say anything. Perhaps that had always been the substance of their friendship.

Dhruv stepped back, asked her curtly to spin again, then adjusted some of the devices on her harness, pulling a few strings taut. He had not explained what these devices would do, and she had not asked. She recognized the basic instruments of an expedition, a wrist compass, a headlamp, snap-shovels and machetes. The rest were clearly meant for the Garden's solar lab to measure whatever it needed to.

"Almost done," Dhruv said. He crouched, and tightened a rope around her waist with nimble fingers.

"Oh good," she replied. "I can't wait."

They were silent for a time again, until Ahilya spoke again, her throat thick. "I don't think I can do this," she choked.

"It's not supposed to be easy," Dhruv replied, remorseless. "You are corrupted by the Virohi—of course you don't want to kill them."

"That doesn't trouble you?"

"What would that achieve? One way or another, this is our only choice. Whether you like it or not, you have to do it."

"I meant my corruption. You are taking it well."

Dhruv uttered a soft, humorless laugh. "Should I walk small around you too, little sister?" he said, using an endearment he'd only ever used when they were young children. "You look like Ahilya. You speak like Ahilya. From everything that I have ever known of you, you think like Ahilya." He glanced up at her. "As far as I am concerned, you are Ahilya. For now, for me, it is enough."

Unexpectedly, she felt tears in her eyes, and her cheeks tightened in trying to hold them back. Dhruv fell silent, continuing in his work.

"The councilors of Irshar told you about overwriting," she said at last. "This corruption could happen to you too. Do you not fear that?"

Dhruv continued to tie knots, attaching and testing various instruments, but she saw the furrow on his forehead. Finally, he sat back on his haunches and stared up at her.

"When that happened," he said, "when I became you temporarily, I thought I had lost myself. I couldn't sense where I began, and where I ended, like my body was porous and my thoughts were covered with cotton." He lifted a hand and Ahilya saw it tremble. "I am questioning everything now. Are all my actions my own? What about my thoughts, my judgements, my feelings? Who do those belong to? Who is pulling my strings?"

Dhruv shuddered and Ahilya's heart sank. What had she

expected? Dhruv feared his erasure. The complete breakdown of self. Is that not what she feared too—what she had with the Virohi before? Her kind had been completely left out of architect histories, and how was overwriting different from that? Something in her posture must have changed, for Dhruv's head snapped up, as though he could hear the whispers of a thought she was too terrified to acknowledge.

"Is there something you're not telling us?" he asked quietly.

Almost, she spoke it aloud. Sooner or later they would all know. Her hand circled her wrist, fingering the heartpoison bracelet, feeling the miniscule thorns growing from it.

If she voiced the thought, it would become true. She would be poisoned. She could not risk it yet.

"It's a hypothesis," she murmured. "With the three visions, the habitat, everything returning to source, I wondered if this is where overwriting is headed."

Dhruv frowned, standing up. He placed one more instrument on her armband, silent for so long that Ahilya thought he wouldn't speak.

"You are not the only one to think this," he said at last. "Sungineering supports this theory."

"What do you mean?"

"Sungineering is not working on constellation lines, nor is it working on Ecstatic power. This technology from Nakshar has somehow tapped into something more fundamental, bypassing the need for the Moment or the Deepness. We discussed it in Irshar's solar lab, you remember? Trying to find the substrate of trajection. Well, I think I've found it. I understand Irshar's devices better."

Despite everything, Ahilya's mouth fell open. "You mean the foundation of an architect's desire, don't you? Are you serious? Our devices are responding to pure architect will?"

"It is hardly surprising. Trajection and Ecstasy are manipulated forms of desire. You said so yourself back then."

She had. Still Ahilya couldn't believe that Dhruv had managed to find such an energy. It felt like sorcery. "Is this the everpower then?" she said, trying to understand.

"No. I don't think so. Everpower is still an advanced manifestation of trajection. This is simpler." Dhruv scowled. "In sungineering terms, we are returning to an understanding of an architect emitting a field of desire. We always thought our devices worked on either a trajection field or constellation lines, but this new energy proves that things are simpler than that. We are working on a combined will. Desire, in itself, captured and used, while each architect struggles with their survival bound to the rest of this community. Something like this energy would probably never manifest if allvision wasn't occurring and overwriting didn't happen. But it only started making itself as apparent after you embedded the Virohi in the tree. If we knew what it was back then, perhaps we'd have understood the dangers of overwriting instantly. It is becoming stronger every second, which means overwriting is becoming stronger. We are all headed to a convoluted mess of being. Even as we use sungineering, each device now is a warning. Much like what trajection has been."

Ahilya watched his pinched mouth, the focus of his gaze. "You haven't told any of the others about this, have you?" she asked.

Dhruv shook his head. "Once you destroy the Virohi and overwriting ends, this power will come to an end as well. There is no point in agitating the others."

"You are all right with that? Letting this incredibly useful energy die out?"

"Not all energy that can be used should be used," Dhruv replied darkly.

And Ahilya remembered how it was Dhruv who had first

designed instruments to use Ecstasy. He had created the battery that had incapacitated Airav and weakened the Moment. He had evolved the battery into a bomb to finally shatter the Moment.

She and Iravan had always blamed themselves for using the technology, but Dhruv must surely have felt some level of responsibility. Suddenly, it became clear—his aversion of her, the breakdown of their relationship, the choices that she'd made that had led to his own. He blamed her for so much, but he blamed himself as well. She was the reminder of everything they'd planned together, that had led them both here. He had once encouraged her, and so she was his mistake. No wonder he couldn't bear to look at her.

Whatever warmth she had felt earlier disappeared. Dhruv worked for a few more minutes, doing his final checks, then cinched an armband tighter, and stepped back in finality.

"You're ready," he said, his voice carrying.

The murmurs of the other councilors behind them stopped. Chairs shifted, then people rose, flanking them, patting Ahilya's shoulders, wishing her good luck. Naila gave her a swift hug. "Are you sure you want to do this?" she asked. Ahilya gave her a half-shrug, and for an instant, it appeared that Naila wanted to say something more, but when Dhruv came forward again she reluctantly stepped back.

Ahilya turned to the sungineer. "Any last advice for me?"

"Yes," he said gruffly. "Remember he is your husband."

The instruction took her aback. For Dhruv to say this, when he had opposed her marriage, when he'd never liked Iravan… She understood what he meant, of course. Iravan was still a man, still just a person. She could not forget that. Ahilya nodded curtly, then turned to face the blank wall. The others retreated, though Ahilya still sensed them hovering behind her. Eyes closed, she probed the confused tangle of roots in her mind. The rock face separated, opening up again in response to her desire. She held her breath and squeezed inside.

At first, the darkness was absolute, the little drones Dhruv had sent earlier too dim and far to reveal anything.

Then her vision adjusted.

She was in a small cave. No, not a cave. The beginnings of a tunnel. Behind her, the rock had already closed again in gnashing creaks. She was alone with the drones inside the earth, unable to see anything except the slight sprays of mud and glistening rock. Water ran somewhere, tinkling in her ears, and through the shifting light of her headlamp, Ahilya glimpsed hair-thin roots clinging to the wall face.

Her breath came out loud, echoing in her ears. "Still with me?" she asked aloud.

Static stuttered from the devices Dhruv had asked her to embed in her ears. A few garbled sounds, but then the drones hovered closer, perching on her shoulders, and—

"—hear you," Dhruv's voice said, clearly. "How does it look?"

Ahilya inhaled deeply. "One step at a time," she said.

She meant it both literally and otherwise. She only could see one step ahead by the light of the drones, but the path opened with each step she took too, in creaks and shifts of the earth. In a way, it was no different from her last jungle expedition, a nudge of a root in her mind here, a brush of a branch against her arm there. She was still the buffer between the complete overwriting of others and the Virohi. The sooner she found Iravan, the easier all of this would become. Provided, of course, he listened.

Garbled sounds came to Ahilya as someone else spoke. "—safer—jungle—over—?"

"Yes, it is safer," Dhruv snapped. "Perhaps you did not see the images of the planetrage?" A pause, then exasperatedly, "Of course, there can be a cave-in. I thought you understood that nothing and nowhere is safe anymore, but, look, she's fine. Just talk to her yourself." His voice grew clearer. "Ahilya, tell her you're fine."

Ahilya walked on in the darkness. Instinct told her to turn to the right, and as she did another crack opened in the rock with a soft shower of dust. She squeezed through again, continuing her blind trek, until Naila's voice spoke in her ear.

"Ahilya-ve?" the woman asked. "Are you all right?"

"I'm fine," she said, trying not to cough as musty air crept up her nose and throat. "It's opening a path for me. I can breathe, though it's stale."

"See?" Dhruv's voice again, further away, and then, "Oh rages, not you too. I thought you were in the new city."

More static and crackling, then Naila's voice was replaced by another familiar one. "We keep missing each other," Eskayra said softly, clearly having taken the communication device from Naila.

"You're back," Ahilya said, relieved. "Are you safe?"

"Are *you*?" Esk replied. "No, don't answer that—I know why you are doing this, and I know you are not safe. Ahilya, I—" The amusement left Esk's voice, and Ahilya imagined her trying to calm herself, and bite back any words that would make it worse now. "The migration is happening swiftly," Eskayra said, deliberately changing the subject. "I thought you'd want to know. The Ecstatics that he sent to the ashram have helped with convincing citizens of Irshar. Given that this lot actually cares for the citizens unlike the rogue ones he sent before, I suppose I should thank him for making my job easier. Maybe you can pass that onto him when you see him."

Ahilya smiled in the darkness. "You never say his name," she observed.

"It is not his name that matters to me," Esk replied. "It is yours."

The smile froze on her face. Ahilya paused, and her hand drifted to her earpiece. She imagined Esk's features pinched in pain. The dewdrop face. The rosebud mouth. The kindness in her eyes. "Eskayra," she whispered. "Please. Not right now."

"I know," Esk returned. "I'm not asking for anything. Just be careful." A soft rustling sound like the device was exchanging hands, then Eskayra's voice again, this time further away, speaking to someone else. "—suppose you did think this through—"

"—people—no faith—" Dhruv replied irritably, his voice soft then louder. He'd finally taken back the sungineering device from Eskayra, "As if I would send her to her death."

Ahilya began walking again in the darkness. "Wouldn't you?" she asked.

"No," he replied to her shortly. "Not even my worst enemy. And certainly not you."

It was more sentimental than he'd ever been, but Ahilya couldn't help remembering the cave-in they'd survived when they'd been children, caught in Nakshar's architecture before her Maze Architect parents could rescue them. If Dhruv was being so vocal about his feelings, then the thought of the planetrage scared him more than he had let on. Or maybe this was the overwriting already occurring, and Dhruv had taken a tiny step toward joining the hive mind. If so, did it mean that overwriting could mend broken things? Like her and Dhruv? Like her marriage with Iravan—or Iravan himself? It was a dangerous, seductive thought. She couldn't follow it, especially after Eskayra's near declaration.

The drones went suddenly dark, then dropped on her shoulders, attaching themselves to her harness. A dim light glowed everywhere, the same shimmery substance that had created a dome over Irshar. Not everdust, but a substance of the planet, morphed somehow through the everpower. Ahilya waved her hand through it, but it did not dissipate. It was like passing her hand through light, as the substance merely reformed around her moving fingers.

She emerged on top of a vast roughly-hewn ramp of rock, staring down into a chamber. Phosphorescence gleamed here and there, reminding her of Nakshar, and her heart skipped a beat. This was no natural cavern. This was Iravan's doing.

She glanced behind, but the path had already closed. "How far am I from you?" she said.

"Not very. In fact..." Dhruv trailed off, and Ahilya imagined him checking something on the bio-nodes. She trod carefully, noticing the ground becoming firmer. "In fact," Dhruv said, again, surprise in his voice, "you're approaching—new city. Eskayra—miles above you, before—headed."

Ahilya frowned. "Already? It took us a long time to get there from Irshar."

"The planet—changing, and paths are different—" More static burst but she could still understand. "Eskayra—evacuating faster—see?"

Ahilya began to climb down the ramp, her body growing cold. She was reminded of the time she had descended into a similar cavern in the habitat, Iravan's hand clutched in hers. Then the two of them had found carvings on rock, recalling the true story of Ecstasy. And now...

She reached the bottom of the ramp, and stared. Carvings were hewn everywhere again, this time on freestanding slabs of wall so she felt like she were walking through a rocky life-size maze. The drones kept her company, but enough light was pouring from the pictures embedded in these walls. Images of people blinked at her, a young woman petting a tiger-yaksha, then another man, laughing with his friends while planting seeds into soil. More and more on every rock wall, images of men and women and children, living their lives, singing, playing, dancing, each of them an architect trajecting either in an airborne ashram or one that had been in the jungle. Ahilya felt chilled, watching this eerie deja-vu. Not a museum, but a mausoleum, rippling with an alien familiarity, full of regrets and shame.

"What—this?" Dhruv whispered in her ear.

"Iravan's lives," she replied, swallowing. "His past selves, all of them shaped by the everpower."

The further in she walked, the clearer the carvings became. Perhaps Dhruv understood that she was too overcome to speak. He did not ask her anymore questions, though she could hear the sound of his breath in her ear.

She recognized Mohini with her two spouses, watching the children of the ashram play. She recognized Agni, out in the jungle, carrying a bow on their back. Scenes upon scenes of love that she'd never heard Iravan speak of when describing his past lives to her. Why had he made this now? Had he finally seen the error of his capital desire?

Ahilya stopped in front of a wall where the phosphorescence gleamed brightest. These carvings depicted one man's story. Short, dark-skinned, his features rounded but his body sunken in…

"Nidhirv," she said. "This is from his time."

Nidhirv stood next to a man who could only be his husband, Vishwam. This past life had haunted Iravan most of all, and she could see his reverence in this sculpture. Vishwam's face was carved with love, each plane of his cheek smoothened. Nidhirv stood with him, his head on his husband's shoulder. The two men tended their house. They hunted in the jungle. They made love.

"You need—moving," Dhruv said, more static interfering with his words. "—planetrage—help—"

He was not wrong, but it took effort to peel away from the wall dedicated to this one life. Ahilya reached the end of the mural, no wiser as to why Iravan had chosen to mark this life alone. Her fingers flickered over Nidhirv's face. *Who are you*? she thought. Nidhirv looked nothing like Iravan, but in those expressions of love and domesticity, she discerned a deep longing that felt like her husband.

Dhruv cleared his throat meaningfully, and she turned away from the mural, hurrying along the chamber again. Other walls flashed by, each displaying more lives, but none had the same depth to them as Nidhirv's. The archeologist part of her itched to examine them more closely, to find answers to questions she didn't know, but she had been sent here for another reason.

She found him finally at the very center of this vast cave, seated on a short staircase that led to nowhere. The thing could have belonged to the Garden's assembly hall, if it were not in this strange city of murals and ghosts.

Iravan did not move when she approached, but he had seen her come, of course. His Etherium was still too shadowy for her to tell, but he knew her tread.

He did not acknowledge her.

His head remained bent.

In his arms, he held what could only be a body, sheathed in plain jute cloth. Where had he acquired the cloth? Ahilya did not truly care. She knew her mind was asking inane questions to distract from his face.

She sat down next to him, slowly. His stillness scared her. His expression was too calm. Iravan's silvery light bathed them in its radiance, but the invisible darkness leaching from him provided its counterpoint, as though he were made of marble too. This was the man who was going to help them? He seemed so lost.

The rock floor in front of Iravan began to rise. Roots grew from it, curling around the sheathed body on his lap. Rock opened to reveal mud, and tendrils of roots carried the body toward the earth in a final, gentle embrace. A choked sound escaped Ahilya. She watched as slowly Darsh sank into the ground.

When the ground was smooth again, she turned to Iravan.

He had been watching her.

"Ahilya," he said, too quietly. "Why is it always the children who die?"

44

AHILYA

She did not know how to reply, or whether an answer was expected. Iravan's Etherium opened to her for the briefest of instants, and his memory took her over in a forest of falling leaves.

The falcon lifting a wing, slashing Darsh down.

Iravan trying to yoke Darsh's capital desire.

Viana shattering into a million bones.

His grief at their lost pregnancy.

Ahilya flinched, shirking back. The ground in front of them churned, and the slabs of rock cracked in loud rumbles of earth. All the murals shattered, the casual violence of it chilling her. The ground absorbed the debris instantaneously, and everything glimmered for one instant before the entire chamber was lost to shadow with the loss of the phosphorescence. The only light came from Iravan now, and ashes flew in front of Ahilya, tasting like her husband.

Here in this new place, away from everyone else, Iravan flooded her mind. Different though this cavern was, it reminded Ahilya all too much of the habitat when the both of them had discovered everything that had led them down this path. His body was unmoving next to hers, and she stared at him, meeting his silvery gaze. Her Etherium opened wider, and she called out to her husband in a whisper. He appeared, parting the leaves to kneel next to her on the forest floor, though this man's eyes were a familiar dark.

Her visions wobbled, and the Iravan in the forest and the one in the cave merged, so that it was suddenly impossible to tell one from the other. The cracks in the cave floor resembled the roots of the vriksh. The light leaching from Iravan in front of her intertwined with the shadowy dusk of the Etherium. She blinked, trying to separate the two Iravans, but it was as if she had drunk the most potent rasa. In this great influx of information, Ahilya felt everything from her husband, his confusion, his rage, his grief and terror—and his alien stillness too, as though something terrible that he could not control lurked within his body. What had happened to him? Who had he become?

Ahilya slipped her hand inside his, feeling his cold skin, trying to anchor in his physicality. How long had he been sitting there? Did his feather cloak not warm him anymore?

"Iravan," she said, and her voice was small. "Come home."

In the Etherium, she heard his soft sob.

"Darsh's parents," he asked. "Do they know?"

"Yes." Ahilya had seen them briefly in Irshar's infirmary, being tended to by the nurses. She'd seen their stricken faces, heard the awful shrieking of Darsh's mother. The sound echoed in the forest, manifesting in Ahilya's memories, and Iravan closed his eyes, his face crumpling.

"No parent should have to endure that," he whispered.

His grief pounded at her, leaves falling around her within the Etherium as the two sat in stillness in the cave. In each leaf she saw him from a lifetime ago. The two of them on their wedding day exchanging garlands of promise. Lying on a rooftop within

Nakshar, their legs entwined as they theorized survival. Preparing his research before he became a Senior Architect. On and on the onslaught came, surrounding Ahilya with his emotion. He caressed her face in one. He walked away from her in another. They stood against each other, bodies shaking after a fight. He held her in his arms, as she bled from their lost pregnancy.

Iravan's hand shook convulsively in hers as he watched the same images, and his loss felt as real as if it had occurred yesterday. He had always wanted children—but the Virohi had erased his possibility of fatherhood. She could feel the cosmic creatures inside her, watching this, grieving with her—and Iravan sensed them too.

You should not have come, he whispered in the forest. *Leave, Ahilya. Please, I'm begging you.*

She stared at him, confused, unsure if he had spoken or if she'd imagined this. What he was showing her, what he was saying—why were these things important now? She tried to coalesce her vision into one, attempting to bring herself back to the cave, the only reality she was certain of, but it was like trying to keep her balance on a narrow beam that shook the more she tried to grip it.

"Those carvings you made," she said, her voice hoarse. "What—what were they?"

"Did you like them?" he whispered. "I made them for you. Lives lived and forgotten, and at their heart always the material bonds. I did not make one showing our life together, I didn't think you would like to see it after everything we've endured, but you already know—you were the best of them all. I have been so fortunate."

Ahilya recoiled, taken aback. His words were soft, and in another time, they would have sounded loving, but she discerned a strange turmoil in him. There was a reason he had made the murals for her. Not as a gift, but as… a test? A reminder? Was he trying to tell her that she had won? That her material bond to him was honored, honoring all the others too? He said she was the best of them, but he did not trust her anymore. A dozen questions flooded her mouth, but she spoke the most important one.

"Why are you here, Iravan?" she asked.

"I found them," he answered.

He stood up slowly, pulling her with him. Where Darsh's body had disappeared, the earth began to move, opening into a crevasse. Pinpricks of silver light covered his skin, and the staircase they had been sitting on rippled forward into the chasm. Iravan tucked her arm inside his and they began descending. Ahilya kept her eyes on the steps, blinking in the deeper darkness. At the bottom, the air smelled surprisingly fresh, but there was something else here, a strange presence.

"Iravan?" Ahilya asked.

Light poured out of him, shooting across the chasm. Shapes materialized out of the darkness. Huge shapes. Massive eyes. Tusks that curved. Paws the size of her head.

"Yakshas," she breathed, and heard Dhruv's soft gasp in her ears. She had almost forgotten the sungineer was privy to this conversation. "They've been here all along," Ahilya whispered.

Just for an instant, the Etherium receded and her vision cleared. She disengaged from Iravan, approaching the closest yaksha, a gargantuan bear-like creature that slumbered on its front paws, its breath heavy. Faint light was trickling away from it in sparkles, curving around Iravan who still stood on the last step. Further ahead was the tiger-yaksha, so large that it towered over her though it was asleep, its head resting on its forelegs. As with the bear-yaksha, light seeped away from it in sharp glimmers.

There were more too, one gigantic creature after another, each the size of a small mountain. Ahilya saw a massive raven, its wings wrapped around itself as it perched on a rock, then a gargantuan lizard, its tail so long and thick, she had to climb over it like it were a fallen tree trunk. Countless more lurked behind, in shapes too abstract to make sense, creatures she had no names for yet, with humps and tusks and feathers. All had once been simply jungle creatures. How many of these corporeal yakshas existed? How many architects had survived the crash from the skies, those who would come to claim them? Or could it be that these yakshas simply were waiting for their architects to be reborn? If so, time was running out, and there was no guarantee of their unity.

Ahilya made a whole circuit, studying as many creatures as she could, without wandering too far from Iravan's light. In her archeological mind, she was already making records. She had seen many of these animals before. The bear-yaksha was one of the beings she had tracked, a lifetime ago. How big had it grown? Who did it belong to? Had it been Ecstatically trajecting when she'd tracked it? She couldn't remember. Giddiness overtook her, and a small laugh escaped her. How differently she viewed these creatures now, from all the misfired hypotheses of before. Shaken, her palms sweaty, Ahilya returned to Iravan's side. The two of them watched as silver dust motes rose from the slumbering beasts, all of them coalescing around him. The Etherium rushed her, and she inhaled sharply, trying to hold onto the brief clarity she had experienced.

"You were always right," Iravan said quietly. "The yakshas were hidden in some part of the planet, building in the way that only they could for thousands of years. After I united with the falcon, all of the others left the habitat to come here. I think this area was once another habitat. Maybe the yakshas were the reason this was the most viable place for your new city, the earth here stabilized by them through the ages."

Now that her eyes had adjusted, Ahilya could tell that the cavern extended for miles beyond the first creatures she'd circuited. She could distinguish deep inroads and tunnels, catacombs that one could lose themselves in for the rest of their lives. Light floated in lazy spirals back toward Iravan, circling him.

"You believe they built this?" she asked.

"They are Ecstatics, after all. They can supertraject. They must have done so when the Moment and the Deepness were functioning normally. Perhaps after you and I appropriated our habitat, and took it from them."

Ahilya's mind buzzed with possibilities, a dozen questions, one after another. Why had the yakshas built this? Had they known about the planetrage before it occurred? Or was it simply their desire to merge with their architects that had helped them create this? An attempt to help civilization find a new city? She asked none of these questions. These were academic concerns. It was not why she was here.

The light around Iravan grew brighter. It almost seemed as though the bear-yaksha was becoming darker the brighter Iravan became. Silvery particles of light still flowed toward her husband, rising from the shapes of the sleeping yakshas all around her. Was he doing something to them? She had no way to know. She did not understand the everpower. Within the vriksh, Iravan grew stronger, his eyes glowing silver like the man in the cave. It meant something, this merging of the two Iravans, but Ahilya could not focus.

"Incorporeal yakshas too?" she said at last. "Are those here?"

In answer, Iravan simply grew brighter.

Light was pouring into him not just from the yaksha animals but from all over the expansive catacombs. From corners that twinkled, and amorphous-cloud-shaped vapors that blinked before dissipating. A horrified sense of calamity grew in Ahilya.

"What are you doing?" she said, her hand over her mouth. "Iravan. These yakshas..."

He did not reply, but his form in the Etherium shivered. She could see it happening like an architect, both in front of her and in her mind—the image of Iravan surrounded by light, his feather cloak fluttering lightly around his shins as if the movement of light created a wind.

And Ahilya understood.

This was no ordinary radiance that moved around him. This was the power of the yakshas themselves, both corporeal and non-corporeal. It swirled toward him, and with each swirl the yakshas became smaller. It was like watching time reverse, the bear-yaksha shrinking every second, the tiger-yaksha diminishing. All around them, the giant creatures shrank, unable to fight what Iravan was doing to them.

Ahilya turned to him. Her voice came out in a horrified whisper. "Why?" she asked.

The light was so bright on him now that she could barely discern his features.

"I suspected this," he said softly. "But it never truly registered, though there were so many hints. When Bharavi came to my rescue during the spiralweed attack in Nakshar's library, the kind of kinship I felt with her yaksha… I felt something similar in a past life with another architect's tiger-yaksha. I'd hoped such familiarity with the falcon would teach the others to enter the Deepness, but I did not ever have the time to test such a thing." Iravan shook his head, spilling shafts of silver light. "The yakshas have always had a way of communicating with each other. I had been denying the falcon inside me, but now…" His voice grew softer, barely a whisper. "It speaks to me now. Telling me to take all of these over too, the way I took it. One last time in finality. Taking their desire to strengthen it."

"Subsummation," she whispered.

The bear-yaksha uttered a growl. Light burst out of it, enveloping it, and Ahilya cried out, shielding her eyes. She saw the light race toward Iravan, who spread out his arms in welcome. The radiance seeped into him through his very pores. His eyes were almost entirely silver, not just the pupil and irises but the sclera too.

When next Ahilya looked, the bear-yaksha was gone. Nothing left of it, no evidence of its existence, not even the weight of its body on the slightly muddy floor. Who had this creature belonged to? Had its architect felt it disappear? What had Iravan done? This was an immortal creature, one of the most ancient ones of their world, that had lived for thousands of years, and Iravan had destroyed it with a thought.

Ahilya remembered the Ecstatics in Irshar's infirmary. She had thought that they'd been damaged because of her control of them, but they had stopped trajecting because of Iravan. Because he was taking their power into himself by subsuming their counterparts. Ahilya's shaking hands went to the sungineering device in her ear. She tapped at it, comforted to still hear Dhruv's slight breathing, listening to this conversation. Perhaps wondering what she was seeing.

"Dhruv," she whispered. "The Ecstatics—"

"Yes—" His soft, panicked voice reverberated in her earpiece. "Something happening—screaming—Pranav fainted—" The words cut out, back into static.

Iravan stared at her, his eyes utterly silver. Perhaps she imagined it, but for a second it appeared that silver wings of light sprouted out of his shoulders. The effect was magnificent, and terrifying. Ahilya couldn't hold his gaze.

"You're killing them," she whispered.

"I am freeing them," Iravan replied, as tiny teardrops formed in the corners of his eyes like the smallest jewels. "If I hadn't stopped

Darsh, he would have killed the others in the Garden. I am taking away the danger of such a thing."

"You don't know that, Iravan! I saw what happened to the Ecstatics—this is like excision to them—"

"It is completion," he snapped. "The yakshas allowed the architects to traject—it is this connection with their creatures that gave them their power. Alone, without the presence of their other half in the world, neither architects nor yakshas will be able to traject. By subsuming them, I am giving the architects hope of becoming complete beings. And if it harms them…" His voice grew icy. "They are architects, protectors of humanity. They will thank me for my service in keeping humanity safe from themselves."

Ahilya thought of all the architects she knew—not just the Ecstatics, but others like Naila, Chaiyya, her nephew Arth who had shown capabilities. She had to stop him, but she didn't know how.

Her eyes darted around, watching one yaksha after another shatter in sparks of silver. A part of her wondered why the yakshas were allowing this, but she already knew the answer. For centuries, the yakshas had been passive creatures, leaving humanity alone, though with each trajection they had called to their architect. Yet sentience occurred through spontaneous will. Even the falcon-yaksha had forgotten itself, and had only found who it was the closer it had come to uniting with Iravan. These other yakshas would not have that autonomy. The falcon had evolved itself, seeking—and now it sought to take over the others.

"You're not doing this for them," she said, turning back to Iravan. "You're doing this for yourself. You want this power—the falcon wants their power. Why?"

Iravan smiled. "You want my help with the planetrage, do you not?" When she nodded, his smile grew cold. "Have you come to give the Virohi to me then?"

His tone sent a chill through Ahilya's spine. She took a step back.

"Fighting the planetrage will kill me," Iravan said, walking toward her, as she continued to back away. "But I have already embraced death. What do I have to fear from it? I have sieved and sifted through my memories to find what will occur to me after my death, and the truth is that I will return to becoming a Virohi after this final life. If I never fulfil my capital desire, then I am lost forever, but even if I complete it, I am condemned to become them. So you see, I am not afraid to die, Ahilya. Only to turn into these creatures."

"You did not try to understand them," Ahilya replied. "You feared them too much. You still do."

"And you don't?" he asked, raising an eyebrow. "That is telling."

"They—they've evolved, Iravan. After being a part of Irshar. Especially after being a part of me, and now in the core tree—"

"Ah, the core tree." He stopped, and earth rippled in the cave, mud shaping into tangles of roots. Ahilya, still backing away, tripped, but Iravan did not seem to notice. He was staring at the earth-made roots as if seeing the vriksh in Irshar. Within her Etherium, where she had invited him, he looked around them at the fall of memories that cascaded over his face. His features were growing cold, dispassionate.

"Your Etherium is a forest now," he said wonderingly. "For me, the third vision was always so confused, but you found stability and solidity there. You owned your third vision in a way I never could."

It had taken Ahilya a long time to understand her Etherium, since she and Iravan had stopped that first earthrage together in the habitat. She had only been able to view Iravan within it, both their third visions connected in a unique way, but after the vriksh had absorbed the cosmic creatures, after she herself had opened the door to the vriksh in her mind, possibilities had tied her to the rest of humanity.

"The core tree gives me the stability to hold the image of my third vision," she said. "I've always controlled the vriksh's permissions—"

"And so you found control of your Etherium too, in amazing ways." Iravan nodded. "But your control of the third vision did not start with the vriksh. Only cemented with it. Regardless," he said, shrugging. "I did not thank you for protecting the Ecstatics from Darsh, for protecting them from the collapse of the three visions."

Ahilya jerked. "You know about the collapse?"

Iravan waved a hand, and she saw it waving both in the Etherium and within the cave, a dual vision that made her eyes hurt. She blinked, trying to hold onto the reality in the cave.

"It was imminent," he said. "After what happened to the Moment, such a collapse was inevitable. I did not understand it when I was battling Darsh, but I've had time to think about it all now. The visions are all melting into each other, and one would think it would give me greater power—I, who am a creature of all the three visions. I, who have mastered them more than anyone else. Yet all my everpower, all my knowledge, all my wisdom, and control of this space still eludes me. For so long I wondered why is it that you could control it in a way that even I could not? Why has the Etherium been always beyond me?"

"You said it was a place of guidance," Ahilya said.

"A window to the world outside of you, but a mirror into oneself too. In some ways the same as the Moment and the Deepness, but the Moment has always been an architect's reality, and the Deepness an Ecstatic's. Yet everyone has access to their personal Etherium, architect or non-architect. It is a mirror to consciousness, doing what it does best. Reflecting."

That's why she had seen the Virohi as herself, giving both her and the cosmic creatures an identity they had needed for their communion. Her Etherium manifested as mirrors too, except she had converted that into a forest, so her mind could freely walk within the consciousness of the tree. She had controlled it, to find peace, to find herself.

"I—I see," she said.

"Do you?" Iravan replied, shaking his head. "Do you really see how special you are? Because that's the thing about mirrors. Only a sufficiently strong being can look into one to see and accept who they are. I was never that strong. My fury and desire for control got in the way, and all I ever received was guidance. But you? You have always been stronger, and so you were given control, not just to see who you were but to evolve yourself, to choose to become what you could. You—you have always been amazing." Iravan laughed, and the sound echoed in the cavern and the forest. "How far you have come, my love, from an unknown archeologist."

There was admiration in his voice, but it was laced with poison. "What are you getting at?" Ahilya asked.

Iravan tilted his head. "You have been keeping secrets, haven't you?"

Ahilya's eyes grew wide. How could he know? She hadn't dared to think about it, keeping it a secret from herself. Her fingers came up to clutch her heartpoison bracelet. He tracked the movement, his mouth thinning.

"Iravan," she said. "Please. Listen—"

He uttered a *tsk*ing sound, so unlike him that she couldn't understand it. This was her husband, but his mannerisms were changing from second to second. The lift of his lips, the tilt of his chin, the way he crinkled his eyes and smiled. They were movements of his body, fluid and familiar, but they were not-him too. She had seen something like this before—back when the Virohi had looked like her in the mirrored chambers. Who was he? Where was he?

Iravan chuckled, and the sound shook her, echoing in the cavern, filtering into the Etherium so the man in there laughed too. "You could not keep secrets from me even if you wanted to," he said softly. "I am a part of the vriksh too, my memories a part of it just like any other citizen's. I sense your purpose inside it. If the others had some familiarity with the Etherium, they would be able to see it too. I might not be as strong as you in that place, but I understand it more than most."

Ahilya continued to retreat, hands open in front of her, her mind racing. She thought that she should run, but how far would she get with everpower at his disposal? He could simply churn the rock to trap her. He could encase her in a wall if he wished. He had not allowed her to come to him out of sentiment. Suddenly she knew why she was the only one who had been let in here. Why Iravan had summoned her far from everyone.

"For so long I have wondered why you would stand in my way," he said. "Why you would not let me kill the cosmic creatures."

"Because it's wrong," Ahilya said. "Because it is genocide."

"That's why you started, yes. But that is not the only reason anymore, is it?"

He was almost upon her, though his pace was unhurried. She could see him despite the radiance coming off him, the unearthly eyes, the tattoos bursting on his skin. The silver silhouetted by black, and within it this creature wearing Iravan's body, speaking to her in her husband's voice. Iravan moved in a blur of speed, inches away from her, and his voice grew softer, a blade within a sheath. In the vriksh, he straightened, coming closer as she stumbled away.

"You have been thinking of an alternative to genocide from the very beginning. And now you've found something. You, who looked into your Etherium, and saw others in the mirror. You who have given of yourself so completely to those who are so alien from you." Iravan studied her. "Tell me, Ahilya. Did you tell your council how you *want* the Virohi to overwrite everyone? How you want to save the cosmic creatures at the cost of humanity?"

A sharp inhale of breath echoed in her ears. "Ahilya—what the fuck—" Dhruv said, stunned. "—is—true?"

She didn't need to reply. Iravan reached a hand and plucked the sound piece from her ear as if he had heard the whisper. It was the two of them alone again, and Ahilya had never been more terrified.

Her head spun. The idea had been in her mind ever since the beginning when she'd lamented that she had to be the one to deal with the Virohi. Then, she had been exhausted with her responsibility, resentful of the freedom of others. But ever since the first overwriting, the idea had grown into an opportunity. It had started building after what she'd done to the Ecstatics during the fight with Darsh. She had asked Dhruv about his experience of overwriting for a reason. She'd worried about it, felt sick about it. But no matter how she tried, this was the only solution she could see. None of the others suspected it, not even Eskayra—but Iravan. He'd always known her heart.

"Would it be so bad?" she replied. "Iravan, architects have always believed that consciousnesses are connected. Can you not imagine that in reality?"

He just laughed, a cruel sound. "You always did want to save everyone. I didn't think you would go to such lengths."

She took another step back, but her body hit a wall. She was out of moves. There was no place to run.

"Overwriting has already begun," she returned. "I didn't intend it when I sent the Virohi to the vriksh, but there is no reversing it. Whether we like it or not, the Virohi are here, and—"

"They have corrupted you. That was the problem all along. But now they are attempting to corrupt me, and this I cannot allow." Iravan's hand brushed a strand of her hair away from her face, and his voice grew deathly quiet. "They have been scraping away at my desire to destroy them. My past lives grow confused, one instant rejoicing in their material bonds, the other instant reminding me of my purpose. The falcon is the only thing remaining steadfast. It projects what I must see, but there are so many of the Virohi and there has been only one of me." Iravan's silvery gaze filled her eyes. "So you tell me, Ahilya," he murmured. "Why do I need this power from the other yakshas?"

His fingers settled on her cheeks like soft petals. She saw his purpose clearly. The falcon had always been the greatest, most aware of all the yakshas, maturing and evolving through centuries, seeking its lost half. It had hated the Virohi, the creatures who had put it through insentience and a total loss of itself. In subsuming the falcon, Iravan hadn't simply cut it away, he had absorbed it fully, all its rage and purpose.

And now Iravan was more that creature than anything else.

And she—

She was the Virohi embodied, the one thing that stood in his way.

Tears filled Ahilya's eyes and her hands came up to clutch Iravan's wrists.

"Iravan," she said. "I chose this."

"We've always saved each other, haven't we?" he whispered.

Across his mind, through the window of the Etherium, she saw images cascading. Iravan staying behind during the earthrage that had killed Oam, sacrificing his own safety for hers as they ascended to Nakshar. Ahilya flying away from the ashram to an unknown habitat and to certain death on the slimmest chance to find him. Iravan rising to fight the skyrage, then falling in the sky. Ahilya rushing through the Conclave, bleeding, attempting to save him from excision.

All of it culminating into now, where he wished to make amends to complete beings because he wished to make amends to her. His silvery eyes sparkled with terrible intention and tears. Ahilya felt the grip of his fingers tightening.

"Please," she said. "I love you."

"I have failed you," he whispered back. "So deeply."

Iravan wrapped his hands around her neck, and squeezed.

45

AHILYA

Her reality condensed to shards of horror.

Iravan's hands pressing her throat. Pain rippling through every inch of her body as if she were being flayed. A nightmarish realization that her husband was trajecting her.

Her visions collapsed, breaking into meaninglessness. She fought for breath, and though he was not crushing her throat yet, it was only a matter of seconds. She could tell by the trembling of his fingers.

Yet the danger was not in what his body was doing. The danger was his mind, which was dismantling her piece by piece.

Her bones crackled. Her skin was on fire. In the crashing depths of her consciousness, Ahilya saw Tariya shatter into ribbons, she watched Viana explode into thorns, and—

Blankness.

Everything s l o w e d for a dangerous, horrifying instant. She knew she would soon be no more.

In desperation, Ahilya fled completely to the vriksh. The forest shook at her scrambling arrival. Iravan followed her, for in her panic she had left the door to his mind open. Ahilya tried to banish him, but it was too late. She couldn't drop the Etherium—this was the only place she could fight back. Iravan glowed with the everpower, stalking her as she ran. Her fear gave her speed and purchase, and the vriksh read her intention, attacking Iravan with branches slashing at his silvery face.

A whiplashing root curled around his waist, holding him back for several seconds. Ahilya exerted her will, and the root tightened, wrapping him head to toe so only the silver blaze of his eyes was visible. A stutter of hope escaped her mouth. His fingers loosened on her throat. She had control here, and she had learned the ways of the architects—

Iravan obliterated the roots, destroying the memories easily with the power of the yakshas blazing in him. He had never been able to control the Etherium, but with the visions collapsing and reality wobbling, the playing field was level. Within the Etherium now, neither of them had the upper hand.

Still, Ahilya fought.

She ducked under a branch, hurling will and intent at him haphazardly. More roots curled, and she saw leaves obscuring Iravan's vision for long seconds before he conjured a whirlwind to sweep them away. The ground rose to stop him, trapping his feet, but he converted it into flowers and marched forward, his aloof expression never changing. She fled, wishing to hide, and a whole copse appeared out of nowhere between them, branches and thorns impaling him, but Iravan sliced through them in another soundless explosion. Ahilya heard humanity scream, and within them the Virohi. Panic seized her. She could not win. He was too practiced. He was an architect—more than an architect. He anticipated every move, every deflection.

Tattoos blazed on his skin, and Iravan curled his right hand into a fist. Ahilya cried out, pain gutting her, spreading through her limbs. She fell to the floor, but flipped immediately to her back, crawling away. He was almost there. Tears ran down her face. He looked nothing like her husband, with silver suffusing him, and in the dimness of the forest, he was a startling light, silver wings flowing from his shoulders in the form of massive falcon.

Iravan, she thought, desperately. *Stop! This isn't you. This isn't you.*

He reached for her, as she willed the tree to break him.

46

IRAVAN

Iravan fought to destroy himself.

The falcon was using the everpower—and he attempted to seize control, obliterate his own existence—but it was too powerful. It had created an army.

He saw himself from afar, trapped behind his eyes, watching as he desecrated Ahilya's forest, chasing her, attacking her. In the underground caves beneath the new city, his hands trembled, all his willpower spent on ensuring his fingers did not crush Ahilya's throat completely. When his fingers loosened, he felt a brief flash of victory. Ahilya raked in a breath—but it was all either of them could manage, frozen in this eternal moment of horror as they were, his body overpowering hers.

For hours, imprisoned in his thoughts, Iravan had tried to wrest control back from the falcon. He had tried to step away from Ahilya, he'd tried to slow his approach. He had begged her to leave, but each time he managed a sliver of control, the falcon took over. It used his mouth to speak, inflicting its will through his past lives. It sounded like him, so much that even Iravan did not know who he was anymore. He had tried to reclaim his past selves, and shown Ahilya with the sculptures he had created in brief moments of lucidity that he loved her. It was the shoddiest of clues, but he had given in to the yaksha's hate, and he could not attempt any more. He had subsumed the falcon, but it had won. He had chosen to fall into the falcon's trap—not Nidhirv or any of his past lives, but *him*. Now it was too late.

Ahilya whimpered in front of him.

He wept.

It had astonished him at first that the falcon's plan was to traject Ahilya, a complex, complete being. Architect consciousnesses were broken, but complete beings stood against cosmic creatures, shielding the world from an earthrage.

Then Iravan had remembered. He'd used Ahilya's consciousness to reform his, a blueprint to knit himself back with the falcon in that first act of unity. The falcon *knew* Ahilya because of it. Now with Ahilya a vessel for the cosmic creatures, the falcon knew exactly how to destroy her.

When she threw a branch at him he rejoiced, but the falcon swept it aside with the everpower. When she used roots to trap him, the falcon crushed them, even though Iravan wanted her to escape. He attempted to slow his feet, to gain enough control to be clumsy as he followed her, but the falcon hastened him. *I've always been too weak,* he thought. *The Resonance always knew it.*

Ahilya fell, scrambling back, and Iravan uttered a cry of horror. The falcon was upon her, landing lightly with his body.

His finger twitched, tightening around her throat. *Destroy,* the falcon whispered. *The cosmic creatures. Destroy.*

Reality distorted, the vriksh in the Etherium shrinking, behind it the mirrored chambers tilting, and the echoes of his grief and horror splintering around them.

In a final act of will Iravan snatched at the everpower, trying to seize it back from the falcon. He could tell from the brief flicker in her eyes that she saw him, *him,* not this mad creature who was killing her, but him. *Please,* he begged, asking her to save her and himself somehow. *Please.*

47

AHILYA

As his hands relaxed for an instant, Ahilya finally saw her husband.

He was on his back, only his eyes visible, as fingers and limbs held him down, each of his past lives crowding him, suffocating him. She saw the terrified whites of his eyes, the whimper as he tried to inhale, the pathetic scrabble of his fingers as men and women pummeled him, trying to take control over his body. Each of these people looked familiar, and Ahilya realized they were the very ones she'd seen in the carvings he'd created. Finally, she understood his message. Those carvings had been for her, to warn her, to beg her for help.

She screamed, his name echoing around them, and the men and women turned back at the sound, their gazes silvery and emotionless. Ahilya knew that they were infected. The falcon was controlling them, warping their desires to its own, and in turn they were holding Iravan down, choking him with the same infection.

Iravan's fingers on her throat twitched, pressing harder. She could see the will it took him to fight them in his silvery eyes. Tears streamed down his cheeks, and in that instant, he looked like he had always been, before he'd found the Resonance, before he'd become aware of the falcon-yaksha. She knew he held onto his lucidity by a fingernail. Any second these past lives would subsume him again, pushing their desire down his throat, choking him until all that he exhaled would be their command.

She trembled in both visions, watching this utter loss of himself when his journey was supposed to purify him. She knew she was seconds away from death.

It was too much. It was too horrifying. She and Iravan saw each other, and she tried to show him that she still loved him. That she understood. That she did not blame him.

Leaves rained down in her Etherium like a downpour of grief. Each one a memory, each one a thorn that had once impaled her.

A strong memory was essential to hold onto a sense of self.

For the architects, as for herself.

Ahilya jerked, seeking a strong memory of the both of them, and the vriksh responded. A single leaf fluttered toward her open palms, and within it she saw herself and Iravan embracing. Ahilya crushed the leaf and the flakes trembled in her hands. With all of her will, she released those flakes into the air again—and they soared toward Iravan, still held down by the ghosts of his past lives. Fragments drifted to him, and he inhaled them, ingested them. She saw his throat move in a swallow. His fingers loosened around her throat, but Ahilya gripped him, and inhaled the leaf-fragments too. Lights sparked behind her eyes, carrying her, and—

48

AHILYA

She came to herself suddenly.

She had been elsewhere, right? Something had happened to her, bright and inevitable and terrible. Ahilya looked into the mirror she was staring at, trying to remember what she'd seen, what she'd experienced. But it dissipated like a dream, and she blinked to the reality of her present.

She was in her home in Nakshar, the one she had grown up in. Tariya had married Bharavi and moved away to the architects' quarters, and this place was Ahilya's, now that their parents had left Nakshar. She stared at the rustling leaves of the walls, the soft sunlight streaming in through the windows. In her memory, she could hear the veiled disappointment from her parents that she and her sister had not been born with the power. Were they here, would they have been proud that both sisters were marrying architects? How strange to think that this house, with all its memories and grief and laughter, would be dissolved into the ashram when she left it today to go live with her new husband.

Ahilya smiled, thinking of the frantic days of the past, Iravan's nervous proposal in the library alcove, and how his head had been bowed, his hand held out in humble offering. She could see her giddy acceptance, while she slipped her fingers into his, pulling him up, stuttering her yes. He had caught her unaware with the proposal. She had been light-headed since then, moving in a trance of happiness.

"Ahilya?" his voice came, and she turned, still smiling. "Are you ready?"

She saw herself through his gaze, beautiful beyond anything she'd ever been. She was dressed in a stunning, embroidered sari, the color of a rosy glinting dawn, the thread glinting gold and tracing animals in a jungle, as though pulled out of one of her archeological books. Ahilya had gotten this sari specially made, an indulgence she would never have thought to put the weavers of Nakshar through—but if one couldn't be sentimental about one's wedding, what was the point of anything? She giggled at Iravan's hungry gaze, barely recognizing the sound coming from her lips.

Iravan had never looked more handsome. He wore white, a shin-length kurta and narrow pajamas, reminiscent of a Senior Architect though he was still only a Maze Architect. It was a reminder of the bonds of marriage and their importance for the ashrams and all architects. When an architect married—any architect—they were allowed to wear the white of Senior Architects. Ahilya's heart leapt in delighted premonition. This uniform… He wore it well.

Iravan glanced down at the himself, and gave a rueful shrug. "It feels unearned. But Airav-ve insisted."

"He knows that you are bound to take a seat on the council next to him," she said. "They can't deny you that." Ahilya reached forward, and ran her fingers over the brown rudra-beads hanging from his wrists. More hung around his neck, each of them earned, an indication of his responsibilities. The both of them knew that

she was right. Airav had indicated it to Iravan in measured words, and Bharavi had confirmed it without ceremony. With Junain's passing, the council needed another member, and Iravan's study of consciousness was by far the most promising of all the candidates in serving the ashram.

"If it happens—" he began.

"When it happens," she corrected.

"—I'll want you by my side. The Senior Architect's induction ceremony is only for architects, but I intend to change things. I won't have you missing it."

"I'll be there," she said. "Always."

She tipped her head back, trying to freeze this moment in her mind. She wanted to remember him this way forever. His too-long jet-black hair curled around his ears. The darkness of his skin, healthy and glowing. The tilted smile on his lips, part-lazy, part-excited.

Iravan reached for her and sighed. "I would kiss you," he said, "but I might ruin this lip paint."

"Before today is over, we will have ruined each other in many ways," she replied, grinning.

He threw his head back and laughed at that. "Is that a promise?" His fingers tucked an errant strand of hair behind her ear, and in the mirror she saw his desire had formed a jasmine on the nearby wall. He plucked it to place it over her ear—a fitting ornament. Then he was grasping her hand, and they strode side by side to the waiting attendees, coming together for their wedding day.

Faces of friends and well-wishers blinked at Ahilya. She could not focus on anything except this wonderful, wonderful man holding her hand. Bharavi grinned, Tariya wiped away her tears, and there were others too, architects Ahilya did not know the names of but who Iravan had invited.

And then they were facing each other by the small fire of purity. Iravan was so very handsome that she could cry.

"No second thoughts?" he murmured. "Now would be the time."

Instead of replying, she began her vow, their hands intertwined, and they said it together, promising to traverse a path together or not at all. His hands skimmed her waist, pulling her closer as they ended on the same note, and she raised hers to his shoulders, feeling both their bodies meld as their lips touched.

Ahilya felt the breath rising in his chest, the warmth of his lips, the sensation of his skin. All of it felt like home—and it was important, it was so important that she remember this, that she never forget. He strengthened beneath her, sighing, and sunlight and laughter took her over, and everything else faded into shadows. Ahilya closed her eyes, and—

49

AHILYA

Iravan's sobs filled her ears.

With all three visions merging, Ahilya watched as he scrambled away from her in the cave. He looked like himself for the first time, wearing not the black uniform of the Ecstatics but his Senior Architect clothes, a white shin-length kurta with his sleeves rolled back accompanied by narrow white trousers. On his wrists and around his neck hung rudra-beads, but they were no longer the complete set. Cracked sungineering wiring peeked from within them, an indication of something broken, though the beads still buzzed with energy. Reality rippled—distorting—and he vibrated for an instant, his clothes turning black, his hands still trying to crush her throat, as if reality wished to hold him hostage to that awful moment. It was as if different realities were cascading one into another, and for an instant, Ahilya saw both the images together, overlaid atop each other. Iravan scrambling away from her, dressed in his Senior Architect uniform, and Iravan in his Ecstatic black, fingers still pressed to her throat. Which one was true? What did she trust? By sheer force of will, not believing anything else was possible, Ahilya stabilized the image, and Iravan—her Iravan—remained in the cave, staring up at her, while the one who had been trying to kill her vanished.

"You came for me," he wept. "You came for me. Why?"

She threw her arms around him protectively. "In this life and the next," she whispered, repeating the words of their wedding vow. "In this world and every other."

He cupped her cheek, but shook his head. "You cannot hold this reality forever," he said. "I suspected it after I united with the falcon, after I subsumed it." In this space where they could see into each other's minds, explanations poured out of him, and Ahilya saw them in all their urgency.

It had begun when he'd united with the falcon-yaksha in the habitat. The falcon had built like silence in his head, slowly yet steadily forming a voice in his mind. At first, he had not questioned it—it was a part of unity.

But the rage had cemented, tearing away everything else in its loathing. The falcon had stripped him of himself, piece by piece, until all that remained was this creature of shame and shadows. He had given too much to the yaksha in an attempt to find himself, and the creature had infected not just Iravan's life but his memories, his past lives. Systematically, it had replaced the love the past lives had for their families with fury, breaking the tethers that had kept them anchored to life.

"Do you understand?" he whispered. "You want me to help you, but the falcon will never allow it. It has the everpower now, and it is going to destroy everything through me. It is not just the planetrage that is the threat, it is me. The falcon is going to kill you, and then it will kill the rest of them, all in its desire to kill the Virohi." His hands shook in hers, panic seizing him. "It cannot see beyond its anger. It cannot see anything but the Virohi within you. I have to end myself. I have to end this."

Ahilya pressed her will and the past lives retreated, though their intention—commanded and warped by the falcon—pushed back against her. She knew she could not hold them back forever. That this fragment where she and Iravan could talk was already diminishing. She was holding reality at bay. Could she change it completely?

Iravan saw the questions on her face. His voice grew frantic. "Please," he sobbed. "Please, Ahilya. There is no time for anything else. Only you can end this. Here, with the power of the vriksh, only you can end me. They are a part of me. Please, Ahilya, please—"

She knew what he was asking her. Now, when she had caught him in an instant of vulnerability, she could turn the tree against him. For brief seconds while she held this shard of reality, she could obliterate his memories—and then him. All it would take was calling the leaves of his memories. She could crush them under her feet. The way Iravan had once crushed her rudra-bead between her fingers.

It would not be an end to this nightmare.

It would be an end to him.

Shadows grew in Iravan's eyes as the past lives crowded into him. His voice was changing, as was his face. His clothes were darkening to the Ecstatic black. Silver was creeping into his eyes, reflecting her. "Let me go," he whispered.

"No."

"Ahilya—" His voice was growing colder. A glint of sharp smile. "Please—"

"No!" She gathered all her love for Iravan, all her frustration, their fights, their anger, their pain, their memories, their *life* together. She called a maelstrom of leaves to swirl around them both, whipping her hair in a gale. The leaves rushed, becoming a tree, tall and slender, forced by her mind—but before they could root deeper into the Etherium, Ahilya raised her arm and an axe appeared, the same way when Basav had charged her to destroy the Virohi.

She brought the axe down in a brutal gesture.

The tree that was filled with her husband's consciousness split down the middle, turning immediately into ash.

Iravan disappeared from the Etherium.

50

IRAVAN

Blankness.

Emptiness that lasted for a long, interminable instant.

He did not know where he was, or if he was.

There was a cut deep within his consciousness, and Iravan pressed down upon his heart as if to cauterize the wound. He saw sap pour out of it, but it was black and star-studded. Slowly, he understood. He was not really bleeding. The core tree was leaving him.

Ahilya's Etherium receded in flashes. *Blink.* The forest shivered. *Blink.* She turned to mist. *Blink.* Her hand dropped the axe.

It must have only been seconds, but to his eyes everything was slow. He had enough time to notice the shock on her face. Enough time to watch the glinting axe be absorbed by the ground. Enough time to see her mouth open in a cry.

Memories lurched, and he saw above him a blue sky. He was flying, flying, flying—

And then he was falling for an eternity.

A mote drifting out into the sky, alone in the black void.

His visions skewed horribly—and he saw himself tumble in shades of blue, yellow, and red—as if different versions of him were falling over and over again, back into his body. A vast disconnectedness echoed in his ears like the discordant hum of sungineering gone wrong. The edges of his sight blackened, a tunnel vision. Behind, he saw his past lives chase him, on the wings of the falcon-yaksha. Ahead, and at the end of the tunnel—death in an endless void.

Iravan lurched blindly onward, and leapt into the void, away from his past lives.

He heard the falcon's roar as it reached him. The shadows still lurked within him, and he saw Nidhirv's silvery gaze, along with Mohini's and Askavetra's. Each of his past lives surrounded him as he fell through this tunnel, circling him as if he were prey and they were a flock of hungry birds. Their hands extended, making to grasp him; they reached into the tunnel to clutch at his miniscule, disappearing body.

Then he slipped past their reach.

Floating in a neverspace, he stared back into the tunnel. A moat of nothing surrounded him and the past-lives, and they were unable to breach the thin wounded wall around him, but he knew it was only a matter of time before they figured out a method. Tattoos still covered his skin, and though he was trajecting the everpower, the tattoos were no longer silvery-gray. They were blue-green, as if he were trajecting the Moment or the Deepness. Between him and his lives an ocean opened, and the ocean was his ability to traject, leaking from him like blood.

He spun away from the past lives, moving in panicky circles.

He no longer fell within the forest of Ahilya's Etherium. He could not sense the Virohi, or the rest of the citizens.

He could not sense her.

He felt the divorce like a slicing of his limbs, and tears gushed down his face, uncontrolled. To be forsaken now, when he had finally learned to see. It was poetic.

"I—I'm alone," he stuttered.

His physical reality slammed into him, and Iravan choked, a fist covering his mouth as if to keep from retching.

Ahilya fell to her knees next to him. "I'm sorry—I'm so sorry—"

His visions were melding one into another, and with her in front of him within this cave, his fall came to a standstill. He knew he was tethered in the cave because of her. Iravan took a deep shaky breath. "You excised me," he said wonderingly.

"I—I had to," she said. "Iravan, they were killing you, they were killing you."

He raised a hand, and the movement felt alien, mechanical. Who was he now? To be excised not just from the core tree but from everything, all of humanity? What did that make him? His hand touched her hair, and he felt himself shudder.

"It was the right thing," he said, and his voice sounded strange. In some part of his mind, he wondered where she had learned such a thing as excision. She had behaved like an architect. How did she know it would work? He didn't know what to make of it, or of her now.

Ahilya closed her eyes and swallowed "I—I just meant to stop their influence on you, to stop them from destroying you. How do you feel?"

I'm excised, he thought, and the very words were terrifying. Hadn't he feared this right from the beginning, from the Exam of Ecstasy that he'd undergone in Nakshar? Hadn't Bharavi once threatened him with it when he'd first detected the Resonance in Nakshar's temple?

He could still feel his trajection power, a hairsbreadth away, like a limb that he could still use but which was atrophying fast. The fear of excision had hung over him for years as an architect in Nakshar, the obedience to the ashram's rules, the secrets he'd kept from Ahilya. It all flashed in his head, his wretchedness of being trapped in a deathcage during the Conclave, waiting for this inevitable moment.

In the end, it was Ahilya who'd done it.

It was only fitting.

He felt the falcon's frustration and its rage as it clawed for the remains of the everpower through the tunnel he'd escaped from, but Iravan dismissed it. The falcon could not hurt him, not for a while yet. Ahilya had done the unthinkable. All he could feel was relief.

"Thank you," he whispered. He wanted to weep—but it was as if all his emotion was being held at a distance. *I'm in shock,* he thought. Everything seemed so slow. There was so much time. Why had he ever hurried? He wanted to sit down and never stand up. He wanted to sleep and never stop.

"Do you—do you still have use of the everpower?" she asked.

Iravan nodded slowly. "For a time," he whispered. "Only for a bit."

He flexed his fingers, and earth rose in the cave as he trajected, but his power bled away from him as if his body had been split in half. He tried staunching the flow, tried to retain his power, but it was continued to dribble away, gushing. He knew it would be futile. Hadn't he seen others excised in the same way? Hadn't he excised Manav?

In the airborne ashrams, Senior Architects would maneuver the Ecstatic Architect into a deathcage. They would change the orientation of the ashram so that the core tree would begin thinking of that member of the ashram as a dangerous creature, becoming intent on destroying the Ecstatic. The trajection triggered the tree to attack the Ecstatic, and cut away their consciousness from itself, but every excised architect still retained trajection for a few minutes, until it withered away within the deathcage. That was why the shields over the deathcage were maintained. That was why the protocol of excision was so carefully guarded.

It would all occur to him now.

Everpower was within his reach, but only briefly. Only for minutes. In the next hour, it would all be over. Knowing what he did now—how the use of such power destroyed the planet, unleashing a version of planetrage—Iravan could only feel freedom and a profound loss, for everything that the others would endure. He? Well, he had already suffered the worst.

Gently, Ahilya sat him up. He leaned on her, his whole body grown cold, unable to move. The bleeding of the power felt like a physical wound, pain rebounding with every slight movement. His heart spasmed, and he thought he might be having a cardiac arrest. The pain in his shoulder was so acute, each inhale felt like burn wound.

Iravan swallowed hard, willing himself to hold on. Would his body heal now like it once had with Ecstasy, now that he'd been excised? He doubted it—trajection manifested the ability to heal, but excision likely took it away. The pain he felt, in his chest and his shoulders and limbs, was an indication. His body was failing. He was aging, finally caught up to everything he'd put himself through for the past few years. He had behaved like a man much younger. He had cheated death many times. To finally let go would not be so bad. At least he had his mind. He had become so used to his loss of self that he rejoiced for this kindness.

Ahilya studied him, her eyes full of guilt and concern. Iravan gave her a tight, grim smile, the best he could manage.

"The falcon-yaksha," she asked softly. "The other lives that were killing you. What has become of them?"

"Gone," he said, wheezing. He could see them in the back of his mind, and the falcon would always be a part of him now after he'd subsumed it. Yet Ahilya's action had pushed the creature far enough away that he could finally see it as a separate entity again. He would never be rid of it. He could feel it still, its rage at being small and useless again, trying to resurrect his past lives to use once more as minions. "They can't hurt me anymore," he said. "I am not bound by them, or their capital desire."

The thought was heady. Freedom from them finally? What would he do with it? Who would he become? He no longer had any need to destroy the Virohi, nor to change the world. He wanted to live—for as long as he could, for the fleeting time before the planet razed away.

Iravan tried to push himself up. The yaksha's desire still echoed in him, to destroy the Virohi, but now it was simply the memory of a temptation he knew not to succumb to. How much had he already done in thrall to the falcon? He would never be able to make amends, but it had never been about that. It was about doing better. He could not atone for the past, but in whatever way he could, he could help repair the future. If only he had thought like this before.

Ahilya had been watching the passage of emotions on his face—perhaps she had felt echoes of it, connected as she was to his Etherium. Her eyes gleamed with tears. "Dissolution still comes," she whispered. "We need you."

Finally to make amends, he thought. But his hands trembled.

"I don't know if I can do it," he said. "I have never known how to rebuild the Moment. I don't think it is possible. The Moment is an extradimensional reality, and it was already weakening. You are asking me to rebuild a universe of consciousness, and now when I have only minutes left of the everpower—" Iravan shook his head.

The task was mammoth. It was why he hadn't done it, not even at the peak of his power. He had not wanted to deplete himself, so he'd gone about fixing the problems the shattering had caused. He'd given Irshar resources, food, technology. But if repairing the Moment was the only way to combat dissolution, he'd have to look through this sludgy, messy, soup of allvision. He'd have to pull out shards of the Moment, fragments of stars which retained consciousness. And then, somehow, he'd have to weave it together to rebuild this massive architecture. How was such a thing possible? He did not have the expertise. He did not have the time. Everpower was trickling away from him in a torrent of his wounded consciousness.

"If you don't find a way," Ahilya whispered, "humanity is lost."

Her fingers were entwined with his. He felt her skin, the coolness and familiarity of her touch. Slowly, he lifted her hands to his lips. His kiss was paper rough, a mere whisper, but he felt her tremble. Her eyes full of grief and curiosity, the contours of her cheeks, and her hair falling around her face—all of it filled him with love. Ahilya looked older, but she had never been as beautiful, as real, as alive, as she was now. *Humanity is lost,* she'd said, but what was humanity if not her? She who held their fate in her hands.

He had wanted to save her. All along, that was what he'd wanted to do.

He freed one hand, and touched the stone blade hanging around his neck. A half-dreamed and unacknowledged possibility flickered to him, one that he'd nurtured in that shadow space between dreaming and waking. The home he'd built for her in the jungle flashed in front of his eyes, the relaxed seating, a single large bed, a playground. Iravan had been saving the last of the everdust—the last of possibility—for his marriage, despite everything that had happened with her. He'd never thought himself a romantic. He was learning so much now, at the end of all things.

A soft sound escaped him, half horror, half laughter. "I may have a way," he said slowly. He fingered the stone blade. "Pure possibility might help me repair the Moment. I'm not sure how, and the everdust contained within this is limited." He raised his eyes to her. "All I can do is try."

She nodded. Perhaps she had seen what he'd intended the everdust for through her Etherium, but he was grateful that she did not question him.

"The subsummation of the yakshas is a problem," Iravan continued softly. "It has made the falcon stronger, and the falcon will try to seize the last of the everpower from me. When I am repairing the Moment, I will be vulnerable. I will have to find a way to release those yakshas from the falcon—if such a thing is possible. It is so much more powerful than it has been before."

Again, Ahilya nodded. He saw from her memories the state of the Ecstatics he'd sworn to protect. Glassy-eyed, uncomprehending faces, images from the infirmary of Irshar, right before she left to find him. He'd begun subsuming the yakshas before she'd arrived, and she'd told him that his subsummation of the yakshas was akin to excision. Could he reverse it, take the power away from the falcon, and unleash it back to the architects somehow? The yakshas were gone in the shape they had existed in once, but would the architects survive if he returned this power to them somehow? What could he do in a few minutes? He could barely stand. *All I can do is try*, he thought, misery washing over him.

"What about you?" he asked. "The overwriting... What will become of you?"

Ahilya shook her head, not answering, but explanations tumbled in his mind from hers, too fast to catch. He gathered the gist of it, brief images of a hive mind, of the vriksh spreading, and a thousand voices speaking from her mouth. He pulled her to him then. Her arms came to wrap around his body. They held each other for a long instant, and Iravan thought of the last time they had been this way, before he'd gone to fight the falcon-yaksha only to subsume it. How long ago was that? Three months? Four? When time was about to melt into the sludge of allvision, when his own time was so limited, what did it matter? This moment was all that mattered.

They didn't say goodbye.

They didn't speak or try to reassure each other.

It took a long time, for Iravan's legs were shaking too hard to stand, but finally he rose, gathering his will to him. The rock they stood on arose in a soft column, carrying the two of them upward, responding to his everpower as if nothing had happened. Ahilya supported his weight in the silence. Her eyes were on him, watching his chest rise and fall as if afraid he would forget how to breathe, now that he was so alienated. Iravan pressed her hand with his, and his touch was limp.

The column erupted from the ground. They stood on a small hill, and beyond them rippled the city he had made for her. It extended for miles around, but through the prism of his bleeding power, they could make out details.

Pillars that were engraved with carvings of airborne ashrams. Gleaming marble walls etched with yakshas, painted in careful colors. Stained windows made of ice, but that were warm to the touch somehow, radiating with sunlight. Tapestries of moving foliage where glorious, fragrant flowers changed shape constantly to show pictures of the crashed Conclave, then the Garden, then a solar lab from some forgotten ashram. Above this magnificence—this temple of humanity and all that it had once been—the sky glimmered with incandescent light. In the distance, shapes appeared, citizens of Irshar arrived here as part of their migration. Ahilya stared at the city, speechless.

Humility unlike anything before filled Iravan.

"Ahilya," he whispered, and she turned to him. "Ahilya-ve," he amended.

She who had control of the core tree now. She who embodied both the alien and the familiar, the other and the intimate. She who was humanity in all its shapes.

Iravan took a step back and knelt at her feet, his head bowed. Tears filled his eyes.

He felt her surprise, and her hand hovered over him, and he cocked his head to see the shock on her face. The blade of pure possibility pulsed against his skin, and he thought in wretched clarity, *Too late. I have seen you too late.*

Her mouth opened, but no sound came out.

Iravan stood up abruptly, and stepped back. Wind whirled around him, and he launched into the sky to finally do better.

51

AHILYA

She stood immobile for long seconds, staring after Iravan, until something nudged her feet. Ahilya looked down to see a tree root jutting out of the soil. She was certain it had not been there before, but she felt its pressure against her again as if it were telling her to move.

Still, she hesitated. Here, on this patch of ground, she had excised Iravan. Here, he had ascended to the skies again, in a final task that she had set him. Ahilya-ve, he had called her, and for once the suffix did not embarrass her. No, she felt a strange sense pour into her, something akin to honor.

She blinked, knowing she had no time to think this through. Iravan had already left to do what they all needed him to do, and she had to prepare the others.

Ahilya climbed down the hill in a daze, tree roots breaking through the earth, nudging her on until she could see the migration from Irshar clearly. The citizens poured in thick crowds, a wave of humanity appearing out of the jungle. So many, so fast? How had all of them come here so quickly? She could not distinguish the faces of the refugees, but she could see them traveling down roads, coming from many different directions. She could see the towering trees of the jungle waving all around the city, and it did not make sense.

Why so many roads, why so many inlets? She knew her mind was trying to distract her from the horror of what had happened, and Ahilya clutched at these inane questions like a branch within a flood, keeping her from sinking into grief. She could not fathom it yet, everything she and her husband had undergone.

There would be time later, if they survived this. She was not alone in her suffering. Whatever was happening here in the jungle and the new city was clearly an effect of everything that had transpired between her and her husband. She and Iravan had used the memories of humanity as weapons against each other. Ahilya could imagine memories ripped away from individuals, a pain that was physical and deep like a cut, yet buried deep. Humanity would feel the loss, if not immediately then gravely, and for the tree, it would manifest as a wild recoiling of branches, a closing to protect itself while it felt the loss of all those memories. Perhaps it had already happened, confusing and alarming all the citizens. There was worse yet to come.

Here and there, Ahilya saw black-clad Ecstatics trudging with the others. As a part of Iravan's Garden, most had been aloof and arrogant, feeding on his resentment—but the merging with Irshar seemed to have wrought a change. Reunited with their citizen kin, they moved through the gathering stopping often to assist those who fell, those who lingered. No one seemed to be in charge of them anymore, but they had fallen back into known roles as architects, meant to protect humanity.

Did they have any power left with Iravan gone? Were they no longer seeking their yakshas? The council had claimed no

Ecstatic could traject, and Ahilya did not think her battle with Iravan had changed the Deepness to allow for it again, though the extradimensional realms were merging. Yet Iravan had subsumed all the yakshas. From what Dhruv had said, Pranav had evidently fainted. Surely the Ecstatics must have felt a loss within themselves—and perhaps it was this loss that was motivating them to seek the familiarity of their friends and family that they'd disdained not too long ago. The architects Iravan had sent to Irshar to make amends had opened that gate, and recent events had swept the others back into the embrace of their material bonds.

It was a startling thought, to consider material bonds still a factor in their civilization when so much had changed, when she'd seen the corruption of a capital desire, and the redemption her bond to Iravan had offered the both of them. But what were material bonds if not compassion and care? What were they if not love? Ahilya herself had tied her life to her sister, to Iravan, and ultimately to the Virohi, in a strange bond no one could have conceived. If all that a material bond was meant to be was humanity at its most human self, then perhaps there was still a chance the future she intended could be balanced. She needed all of them now—architects, non-architects, Ecstatics, citizens of Irshar and those of the new city. No one could be left out of this war now.

A shape detached from one of the waves entering the city, approaching her—Eskayra perhaps, or Chaiyya, or Naila. Ahilya's earpiece was lost in the rubble below, but her sungineering had started working again, so Dhruv would have known of her arrival. She braced herself to hold strong to her decision, no matter what her friends said, yet as the shape became clearer, Ahilya paused. Of all the people to approach her, she had not expected her sister.

Her long hair tied behind her in a messy tail, Tariya climbed the hill slowly. Ahilya's sister had never been one to exert herself physically, her body prone to severe tiredness, her limbs shivery. After Bharavi's execution, she had only grown more fragile. Still, Ahilya knew better than to ask about her welfare now—her sister would only disdain her questions. She hurried to catch up to Tariya, then the both of them began to climb down to the center of the city wordlessly.

There was a lightness to Tariya's steps at odds with the grief that still breathed under her skin. Some of her sister's beauty had returned, as if she had come to accept her grief, letting it shape her instead of fighting it.

Ahilya did not know what to make of her presence. She could feel her like a tug in her mind. If she tried, she would be able to hear her sister's memories—but Ahilya held the current at a distance. It was only a matter of time it swept her away. She was prepared, but the others were not. She would not go into it without warning them.

Tariya stumbled, and Ahilya went to help instinctively, but before she could Tariya straightened. Her sister arched an eyebrow.

"You left Irshar?" Ahilya asked, to cover up her move. "I thought you hated the idea."

"I still do," Tariya replied dryly. "But this is Irshar."

Surprised, Ahilya paused to study the city. In the distance she could see the vriksh, but what she had considered a trick of the light was occurring in real time. The vriksh was growing again, ever larger, its canopy blooming high, its boughs stretching to shelter the new city. As she watched, spires and towers came under its deep shade, entering an artificial nightfall. The same strange dust that had hovered around the Garden and Irshar before trickling into the new city.

We didn't get to decide a name, Ahilya thought in slow wonder. After today, they might not need to. *They* might not be. It was a sobering thought.

Ahilya had deliberately not been paying attention to her Etherium, but watching the tree expand to cover the new city was too big to ignore. She sensed the leaves fluttering over her face in the third vision, and it was all she could do not to sink into their embrace. Perhaps the tree recognized this city as part of its own self. A sibling territory. A sister-ashram. Wrought as part of another habitat, one long lost.

"What is going on down there with the citizens?" Ahilya asked. "What do people make of all this?"

"Why, are you going to provide us an explanation?" Tariya said. "Are you going to save us, Ahilya?"

The words were caustic, but Ahilya did not rise to the bait like she might have once. She simply studied her sister, and though color bloomed in Tariya's cheeks, her sister smiled, her expression satisfied. Tariya's eyes glowed as if she had won something. She might as well have been skipping.

"You're in a good mood," Ahilya observed.

"You are in so much trouble," Tariya replied, shaking her head. "They are livid."

Ahilya didn't need to ask who she meant. She could well imagine Dhruv rushing to the other councilors to discuss what he'd overheard, the rest of them panicking and helpless, fearing an attack on their consciousness.

"They tried to cut down the vriksh," Tariya told her, the mirth leaving her.

An act of desperation, Ahilya knew. She could not blame them. "What happened?"

"Nothing happened. They *tried.* People were complaining of terrible symptoms of illness—dizziness, forgetting their names, unsure of what life was like in the airborne ashrams, sometimes unable to recall even what they did hours ago. The infirmary was full until the council decided to axe the tree, but the tree didn't let them—or perhaps their minds fought it. Everyone knows we are all tied to it." Tariya fell silent, and Ahilya chewed her lip.

So Tariya knew enough about the vriksh to know how everyone's minds were connected to it. Was it simply knowledge she'd picked up as Bharavi's wife, or had she felt something of Ahilya's battle with Iravan? Or—most likely—the council had been forced to share the danger of overwriting, especially with those who worked in the infirmary, so as to better help the patients.

There were no real secrets between the council and the citizens anymore. Tariya was influential in her own way, and she would have objected to the assault on the tree, simply as a matter of principle, to oppose the council. Ahilya could well imagine it—her sister standing in front of the vriksh demanding an explanation. The council would not have found it easy to push her aside. Either way, if the citizens already knew of their connection to the vriksh, it made Ahilya's job easier.

"They sent you to speak to me?" she asked.

"I am the least threatening, according to them," Tariya replied scoffing. "They don't know better, do they?"

Fierce pride radiated from Tariya, warming Ahilya's skin as if a soft warm fire lived within her. Pride for herself or for Ahilya? With Tariya, it could be either, but Ahilya didn't probe, and nor did she ask for an explanation of her words. Tariya was not threatening to her. She was Ahilya's vulnerability, and Ahilya would not change that for the world. The two continued on in silence until they reached the city.

Tree roots splayed out everywhere, widening to become as thick as a limb. The ground was uneven, shifting constantly, if slowly, so that Ahilya finally took Tariya's hand in hers, despite her sister's squawk of protest. She could see gaps in the floor closing, knitted over by roots that plunged below, while the canopy of the vriksh waved far above the spires of the buildings. In the time it had taken for the two of them to come here, the tree had already wrapped this new city into whatever had remained of Irshar and the Garden, returning all that was separated to the same source. Soon, the canopy would enclose them in a dome too; Ahilya could feel the tree's intention.

She hastened the two of them, weaving past the people milling about, exclaiming at the tree. Tariya pointed them to a low building with a stone courtyard, outside which Umang stood sentry. He waved Ahilya and Tariya in hurriedly. Green had erupted over the stone slabs of the courtyard, and right in the center, a solarchamber blinked—perhaps the same one Ahilya had left from.

The two sisters entered to see the councilors seated around a table. Several architects stood about too, as Chaiyya and Eskayra delivered instructions to them. Hands full of parchments and solarnotes, the architects pushed past Ahilya, until only the councilors remained, intent on their discussion.

"Well," Tariya announced. "I brought her."

The others jumped, then stared, shocked that she had actually managed to lead Ahilya there. Their gazes swept to Ahilya, shock giving way to fear and alarm.

Basav stood up, his whole body trembling. "What have you done?" he shrieked. "What have you done, you foolish girl?"

Dhruv looked at her like he'd never seen her before. Chaiyya and Kiana drew back, their mouths trembling. Eskayra's face was unreadable. Pranav was ashen faced, huddled within a shawl. Only Naila gave her a slight nod, while Airav simply appeared as though he had known they would come to this instant all along.

Ahilya took a chair. She studied all of them, her gaze lingering on Pranav who had fainted after Iravan's subsummation of his yaksha. Then she turned to Dhruv.

"So you told them?" she asked.

"That you mean to kill our species? That you mean to overwrite us all." Dhruv uttered a snort of disbelief. "Yes, Ahilya. I told them."

"Overwriting cannot be stopped," she said. "It's not possible."

"You did not even attempt it," Basav began. "You wanted this all along."

"You are corrupted beyond recognition," Weira cried, pointing a finger at her.

The others began to murmur too, and Chaiyya clutched Airav's hand, her eyes shining with silent tears. In the solarchamber, the buzz compounded, as if sounds were bouncing off the glass screens, multiplying. Ahilya felt her mind tighten as though pinched—their fear cascaded into her, rippling—and she saw the vriksh balk, its roots weakening and shrinking, reacting to their desire. Her eyes met Eskayra's over the din, and Eskayra put two fingers to her mouth and released a shrill whistle.

Everyone silenced, gaping at her, then back to Ahilya.

Ahilya did not wait for them to begin murmuring again. She spoke, her voice sharp. "I won't lie to you. Overwriting is not going to be easy, and it's not preferable. But this is the only way to survive dissolution."

"Iravan-ve," Airav began, but she cut him off, raising a hand.

"He has refused to destroy the Virohi."

A stunned silence greeted her words. Basav's eyes bugged out, and he was the one to break the quiet. "Are you saying that you changed an Ecstatic Architect's capital desire? *The* Ecstatic's capital desire?"

"He changed it himself," Ahilya answered. "He has freed himself of the falcon-yaksha's hold and of the past lives. But his everpower is waning."

She could see their curiosity regarding what had happened, but there was no time nor purpose to filling them in. If overwriting was going to occur the way she imagined, they would soon all be privy to her memories anyway. Right now, to tell them that she'd excised Iravan would only raise their hackles.

"Iravan has promised to try to repair the Moment," she said instead. "But there is a reason he refused to destroy the Virohi. He could see finally that there is only one way for us to endure. We can avoid extinction and erasure, but we have to do it together."

"Together how, exactly?" Dhruv asked, suspiciously.

She swept her gaze over them, the mutinous and scared faces, the trembling bodies. She knew she was not asking them an easy thing, and Ahilya's voice softened. Her encounters with the Virohi had already had a brutal effect on her, and she could not deny the loss of herself she'd experienced. What she was about to suggest to the others would be to unleash such a loss on themselves, and everyone. They deserved to know why. She tried to explain.

"Ever since the Moment broke, the Virohi have been terrified. They were badly injured by Iravan's attack on them with the sungineering bomb. I have seen them weep, and I believe they started the overwriting as a way to strengthen their consciousness against dissolution—something they saw occurring. The Moment has always been an anchor of our reality, but it was a manifestation of consciousness too. Without consciousness, there is no perception of reality. You all know this already."

No one spoke to object, but Ahilya saw a few of the council frowning, Dhruv among them.

"With the Moment gone, our reality became forfeit," she continued on. "The only reason dissolution has taken this long is because the Virohi began overwriting us. Reality needed a new anchor, and the vriksh was that anchor. Without the Virohi, the core tree was the sum total of all our remembered consciousness, but *with* the Virohi, it became something greater, a mini universe.

Reality and consciousness intertwined in the vriksh the same way they once did in the Moment, and only the Virohi could do such a thing—they are creatures bound by physical laws yet not caught by them."

Ahilya felt a strange exhilaration. The explanation had come to her when Iravan had nearly strangled her. It was as if in that moment when she'd lost it all, pieces had clicked together in her mind. She'd felt sorrow, and grief, and terror, because she'd assumed she'd die before she could share this with the others. But she was here now, and the others were listening.

"The Virohi are overwriting us, but it has all been for a reason," Ahilya said. "We have felt the effects of dissolution because the overwriting is incomplete. The core tree is connected to us, and because we do not desire to be merged with the Virohi, we are fighting this assimilation. It makes us weak. We are ready prey for the planetrage and dissolution, and we are at threat of extinction—Virohi and human alike. But if we stop fighting this assimilation, if we encourage it, then it is possible we could stand together against what is to come. With us no longer resisting the tree's desires, the tree could root into the earth deeper. It could anchor. Iravan could repair the Moment and fix our reality, and we—"

"We would be erased," Dhruv said. "We would no longer truly be human beings."

"We would evolve," she replied. "Into something else. Yes."

She knew the impossibility of her ask. The ability to make an enduring change for the survival of their species, yet do so with a deep loss of themselves… She had contended with this question as had Iravan. In a way, that question had defined both of them, and their marriage. It had set them on this course, long before either had known they were destined for it. No one person could answer this question.

But perhaps a people could.

Finally, it was all their choice. Not her burden alone, nor Iravan's. But all of theirs.

"This is drastic," Chaiyya said in a small voice. "There are other methods apart from overwriting. The vriksh has codes embedded within it to preserve architects and citizens, and I could show you methods to heal the Virohi. If you entreated—"

"Are any of us capable of healing the Virohi?" Ahilya asked. "I know I am not—you are asking me to heal *cosmic* creatures, and any knowledge of trajection will not be enough to heal a massive consciousness like that."

"You don't know that," Chaiyya argued. "Architects perform healing on consciousness all the time."

"For small injuries and with the Moment intact," Ahilya said gently. "With time, and with patience. But you could not heal Airav fully, Chaiyya. You could not heal Manav, or any of the other excised architects. What the Virohi suffered with the destruction of the Moment is akin to that, but greater, so much greater."

Chaiyya opened her mouth, then closed it, frowning.

Basav spoke into her silence. "Even if healing won't work," he said scowling, "this is still too drastic. Nothing like this has ever been attempted in our histories—even when Ecstasy was legal. The Moment is broken, but the Deepness is intact. Maybe the Ecstatics of the Garden can help all of us become Ecstatics. We could unify in the Deepness—perform some kind of supertrajection. If he cannot help us"—Basav pointed at Pranav who huddled down—"that little girl—Reyla—she seems to know enough about the Deepness; she could guide us along with the others."

Ahilya's brows rose, surprised. Pranav hunched lower in his seat, not meeting her gaze as she glanced at him. It was a measure of how shaken Basav was with her proposal that he was suggesting this. Not just to become an Ecstatic, but to be guided by Reyla—a girl so young he would not give her a second glace if she were in his Academy.

"Has Reyla escaped the effects of Iravan's subsummation?" she asked gently.

Pranav shook his head silently.

"I thought not." Ahilya sighed. "You're welcome to try," she said to Basav, "but the Deepness is not working as it once was, remember? It is already melding into the allvision. Besides, do you think the collective will of the Ecstatics is capable of doing this? They are exhausted, as we all are. I will not browbeat you into this, but I do not see any other way except this."

Basav's body shook and he buried his head in his hands. The others fell silent too, and on their faces she saw their revulsion, desperation, and panic. They were clutching at straws, seeking another solution when there was nowhere else to turn anymore. Perhaps it was their panic making them forget things that had occurred; or perhaps, like Tariya had mentioned, they were simply experiencing a loss of memory. Either way, Ahilya felt their grief and it was her own. There was nothing she could say to comfort them. All she could do was give them a few precious moments to come to terms with the enormity of her request.

"It is not possible," Purva said, speaking for the first time. Ahilya had almost forgotten the sungineer's presence, but now Purva leaned forward, her face drawn into a skeptical frown.

"You realize what you're suggesting, don't you?" she said to Ahilya. "You are saying that all of us need to align our desires toward one thing. We can sit here in this council wanting and hoping for that, but how are we to make this possible for every survivor?"

"We've done this before," Eskayra pointed out. "When we faced the Virohi after the crash of the Conclave, the non-architects aligned their desires toward a singular purpose to create a defense for Irshar. Architects are used to this kind of thing too, in the Moment, working together."

"But the time with the non-architects did not truly work," Purva said. "When the Conclave crash-landed and we faced the Virohi, you had to take control, Ahilya-ve."

"Is that what you want, Ahilya?" Dhruv asked quietly. "Complete control of humanity?"

"No," she said at once. "I am suggesting the opposite. Last time I had to be in control, because the core trees and the habitat were conditioned to obey me first. The Virohi bent to me because they recognized me from the time I stopped the first earthrage. But what if the reason everything has been so hard, even for me, is *because* I took that control? What if I took myself out of the equation altogether?"

"Are you suggesting suicide?" Dhruv asked dryly.

"No, of course not. But right now, my consciousness stands as a buffer between the rest of the humanity and the overwriting. I have stood in control of myself, letting the Virohi only find form as me. But if I stepped away, letting overwriting occur, control would not be with any one of us."

"A true hive-mind," Basav said, his face revolted. "Like the Virohi."

"Like the Moment," Ahilya countered. "A network of consciousnesses. A Moment as if it were alive."

Basav's furrowed his brows in confusion. Ahilya felt a jolt of victory. He was listening.

It was Chaiyya who spoke, her voice shaking: "The last time overwriting happened, all of our consciousnesses merged. It was chaos, it was terrifying, and we became you. That could be our permanent state. We wouldn't know who we are, let alone be able to fight the planetrage or dissolution."

"We wouldn't need to fight. The vriksh would do it, and we would lend it our strength, our purpose. As long as all of us willed with our deepest minds to survive and endure—as we have done before—the vriksh will follow our command." Ahilya leaned back, exhausted. "I cannot think of another solution. Is it not worth the attempt?"

"Is it?" Dhruv asked. "What you are suggesting is that all of us allow you to do this so none of us have a sense of self. So there is no I, *ever*, for our species. It would be a kind of dissolution too, all of our minds become one entity, our closest secrets open to the others, our shame and pain and all the indignities we've ever suffered, memories and feelings and ideas we would take to our graves, all of it privy to be seen and judged. Our powerlessness exhibited to everyone, in our smallest, pettiest ways. Is that a good thing? To be seen in your nakedness, in your vulnerability?"

"But not just in those," Airav chimed in quietly. "We would become one, in our greatest ways too. In our compassion and beauty and kindness and love. We would not be persons. We would become… a people. With all the good and the bad. And once the neural bridge is complete between the Virohi and the vriksh, once the overwriting has taken place, then we will truly be able to fight our extinction."

"Without a choice," Dhruv retorted. "With no knowledge of what such overwriting is going to do to us, and no knowledge of what we are doing either. With no sentience, for all we know."

"But with agency," Airav replied softly. "Together."

There was a silence as the rest of them absorbed this.

Ahilya looked from one face to another. Trisha, Pranav, and other architects from Irshar were nodding slowly, as though this was something inevitable. Airav gave her a small smile; architects had been trained for this, they were used to consciousness-based communication in the Moment. There was precedent for personal truths being bared to one another. That is what the Examination of Ecstasy was, the encounter with veristem, and in so many ways the architects already shared one mind in the shared reality of the Moment and Deepness.

Yet the non-architects…

Dhruv, Purva, and Eskayra shifted in their seats, frowning. She could read her doubt in them… to lose all power the instant they had received a small measure of it. Had Ahilya not feared such an erasure once? How could she suggest this, when her kind had been on the receiving end of erasure through history? Perhaps back in the early days of flight, when the non-architects and architects had to decide what to do for the survival of their species, they had been presented with such a choice too. Maybe erasure-evolution like this was the only way forward then. But Ahilya had suffered too much to think it permissible. She didn't say anything. To this point, she had no defense.

In the silence, Tariya cleared her throat, standing up straighter as Ahilya and the rest of them turned to her. "If anyone's asking," she said, her voice trembling. "Then I am with Ahilya."

This was surprising. Ahilya tried to catch her sister's eye, but Tariya steadfastly refused to meet her gaze. Instead, she spoke to the air. "We have been denied control all our lives. Citizens have suffered because of architects, and we've lost people we loved—some of whom were also architects. My wife—Bharavi—" Here she choked, but rallied before anyone could speak. "We have lacked control, but this overwriting would provide us with something equal to the rest of you. I don't think the citizens will object. It will be a form of shared control."

"It will be a form of no control," Dhruv said. "No one entity would have control. That's the entire point. Whatever we become will be greater than we are as individuals. This is the opposite of what you and your citizens have been demanding."

"It's still better than what we've had so far," Tariya shot back. "All along we've had to work according to what the council has allowed us to do. Even here, even in Irshar. But this way, we'd be no more nor less than the rest of you. You sit here making judgements and decisions for everyone. Well, this way we would have a seat at the table too. All of us, every one of us. Are you going to deny us that if we wish it among us?"

Ahilya tried to hide her humorless grin. Tariya was her sister through and through. They had never seen eye to eye on things, and Tariya's reasons were different from Ahilya's own, but perhaps everyone could see now how they were related. The citizens had long desired control of their lives, and many had chosen not to leave Irshar because of it. Perhaps this would not be such a difficult thing to ask of them.

Dhruv seemed to be coming to the same conclusion. He removed his glasses, and rubbed his eyes. "You all are making a lot of assumptions," he said. "A hive mind—a network and circuitry like this—we have nothing to protect our consciousness. No breaker."

"We would simply implode," Kiana said grimly, agreeing. "That much informational flow, for any of us to see and experience that without any preventative nodes. It could be very bad. It could be the chaos of before, a thousand times worse. Perhaps the only reason that is not occurring right now is because Ahilya provides a buffer." The sungineer's keen eyes studied Ahilya. "What if you continued to be the buffer? What if you guided this overwriting slowly instead of simply standing aside? Is it possible we could network like a hive, but still somehow remain ourselves? That we could enter this with more control?"

Ahilya thought this over. "Maybe," she said slowly.

She had not suggested it, or dared to consider it, dictated to by her desire to not become a tyrant. But if she did guide the overwriting—if she controlled the onset of the flood—perhaps they could find their way back to their selves. An image formed in her head—all of them nestled within the vriksh, sleeping, their minds caught in a dream-state while the vriksh reacted to their unspoken desire to survive, its roots sinking into the earth.

The image had come too soon, too clearly, an answer from the vriksh for her unspoken question of forcing this decision. "It's possible, I think," she said. "It wouldn't be overwriting, if we could still remember a part of ourselves. It would be…"

"Cohesion," Airav replied, and Ahilya nodded. The two of them were already doing it, connected in a strange way. This Cohesion was already occurring for those who were aligned.

Chaiyya looked disturbed, her gaze moving between the two. "If we agree to this, there would have to be rules," she said. "Only volunteers, only adults. We cannot ask every single person, especially children—"

"No," Ahilya replied sharply. "It has to be everyone. The tree is coded to all the citizens, architects, non-architects, Ecstatics, adults, children, every single one of us alike. And we need to desire a single thing from it, survival, the same way we would when desiring a safe landing in the jungle in days past." Chaiyya opened her mouth to object, but Ahilya shook her head. "We cannot afford anything else," she said, finality in her voice. "If we are going to do this, then we *all* have to do this. No negotiation, no exceptions. Anything else would be too much of a risk. We have no idea how the core tree will respond if we sever ourselves before we even start."

Perhaps Chaiyya was thinking of her infant daughters—and for an instant, a deep misgiving entered Ahilya. What was she thinking, asking for such a massive change? What if the children got hurt doing this? Shock and terror gibbered in her, but she tamped them down. There was no other way forward. They were all facing *extinction.* This was the only way to protect the children.

Finally, one by one, they all nodded. Basav looked horrified but resigned. Chaiyya simply appeared tired, her face a scowl. Airav looked pleased, and the non-architects upset. None of them really liked this solution, but they didn't have to. They were discussing the end of their species as they knew it. How could any of them come to it willingly? Still, they had agreed—and it was enough.

Ahilya slumped in her chair, suddenly tired. "It will happen soon," she said quietly. "I can feel the vriksh in my mind, calling to me. I can barely hold this Cohesion back as it is. With overwriting occurring so quickly, Cohesion will occur soon too, and I have to prepare on how to guide it. So go to your loved ones. Stay with them, and tell them what is occurring. Comfort them if you can. We will all reckon with ourselves soon enough."

The others arose, leaving hastily. Tariya stared at Ahilya, as if about to say something, but she simply shrugged a shoulder and left with the others. Soon the chamber was empty, save for Naila, Eskayra, and Dhruv. Ahilya did not ask Eskayra to leave—she knew it would be futile. Sure enough, Esk came and sat down next to her, and took her hand.

"Did he hurt you?" Eskayra asked quietly.

"Yes," Ahilya replied.

"And was it worth it?"

The other woman's gaze was soft, free of judgement. Ahilya looked at her, at the bow-shaped lips, and the short hair, and the strength within her. For a small instant, she allowed herself to detach her mind from Iravan's. It was like shrugging off a particularly heavy, all-consuming, cloak. She felt naked, like she did not know herself. Not even with the Virohi—her identity churned and spit out—had she felt such an alienation, simultaneously strange, and terrible, and lonely, and exhilarating.

Ahilya leaned forward and pressed her lips to Eskayra's.

Eskayra's mouth opened under hers, willing and eager, and for the first time in a long time, Ahilya felt a stirring of desire. Esk's arms circled her closer, her lips brushing over Ahilya's neck on the soft bruises Iravan had left, fluttering over her face to hum over the tear tracks, then back to the mouth where she willed Ahilya to heal herself. She tasted of earth and hope and resignation, and it was too complex an emotion lurking within the softness of the kiss. Ahilya knew there were others around perhaps watching them, but she couldn't care. She was so desperately lonely, and it had been so long. With Cohesion occurring, what was the point of privacy? Everything was ending, then why deny herself? At least with Esk's touch, she remembered that she was still alive, if only for a few more hours.

Eskayra broke the kiss, pulling away with a sigh. "I have waited," she said. "And I'll wait longer. We have to work our way toward this."

Despite herself, Ahilya blushed. "I didn't think the kiss was that bad."

Esk gave her a slight grin. "Not the kiss. *Us.* You have so much to sort, don't you?"

From another person, Ahilya would have felt rejection—but Esk's hand was still intertwined with hers, and she leaned forward to kiss her forehead. Ahilya understood. *Later,* Esk was saying. If there was a later.

Ahilya turned away to study Naila, who had remained seated. Neither she nor Dhruv had looked up to her and Esk, both of them lost in their thoughts. Naila was studying the same beads she'd had before, twining them around her hands. What did she see in them? What significance did they hold for her? Ahilya felt a passing curiosity but brushed it away.

"Are you all right?" she asked. "Iravan subsumed all the yakshas. Yours included. I don't know how the Ecstatics are still walking."

"They fainted, as did I," Naila said, shrugging. "But you saw Pranav revived. None of us feel any different to what we have before."

"And those who were in the infirmary? The rogue Ecstatics?"

"Revived as well, and released. To be with their families and loved ones when the migration began."

"Is there an explanation for their revival?" Ahilya asked.

"None that we know," the Maze Architect replied, her mind clearly preoccupied.

Iravan had said that subsuming the other yakshas would be like completion to the architects. Is that what these people felt? Or perhaps the effects were not visible yet. The shock had presented itself, but not the whole consequence. What did it matter now, anyway? The yakshas were gone, but the architects were still here. Human, and soon to become part of Cohesion.

"Naila," Ahilya said softly. "You should go. To your friends, your lovers…"

"I am here, Ahilya-ve," Naila replied, her voice quiet. She gave Ahilya a swift, roguish wink, but the expression was pained, as if she couldn't quite hide her fear.

Ahilya did not press her. Such fleeting choices were all that was left to them. Naila would leave if she told her to, but whatever her reasons, Ahilya was grateful for her company.

She turned to Dhruv instead, who had begun dismantling the solarchamber. The stone courtyard appeared beyond it, grass and tree roots writhing, so that soon they sat around a round table under a sky wreathed by the vriksh's canopy. One by one the bio-nodes came down, all except a single one. Dhruv pulled up a chair and sat in front of it. Though the images of the approaching planetrage were clear, his eyes were unseeing, staring as if into his mind.

"Dhruv?" Ahilya asked gently.

"I am where I belong," he said, a soft scowl on his face. He turned back to the bio-node, swiping at a few images. Ahilya did not know what to make of it, but he was allowed his secrets and thoughts too, for as long as he could call them his own. She tipped her head back, staring at the strange swirling shield above the city. She felt the vriksh in her mind, preparing itself. Slowly, second by second, Ahilya watched the leaves rain down in the Etherium. When the last leaf fell, Cohesion would begin, but if she were to guide it, she'd have to be purposeful about taking control.

"You agreed to this," she said to Dhruv softly, tipping her chin down to glance at him. "You know something, don't you? It is not like you to agree to something like this so quickly."

Dhruv's scowl became bigger. She had not asked a question, and he owed her nothing.

When he spoke, it was a surprise. "Cohesion was inevitable from the start," Dhruv said. "This new sungineering has been working because of overwriting, but it was never simply the power of desire of the architects. It has been the desire of every human being. We bypassed trajection and constellation lines, and have gone to the substrate of what trajection means." Dhruv took in a shivery breath. "You want to know why the architects revived? It's because they are tethering themselves in the overwriting, into this Cohesion instead of their yakshas. This is where we were headed all along. Cohesion is inevitable."

"Does that mean we will succeed?" Naila asked.

Does it mean you think this is not my fault? Ahilya thought passively. Dhruv simply shrugged his shoulders. It was enough. Ahilya understood. *They had a chance.*

She turned back to the sky. The last leaf fell in the Etherium. A startling burst of terror overwhelmed her, *what am I doing, what am I doing.*

Ahilya dropped into the void, and it embraced her.

52

IRAVAN

He ascended far above the planet, where the air grew thin.

He could still fly with the everpower, and traject the elements enough to breathe, but with every movement, the power leaked out of him, the wound of separation from the core tree making him wheeze. He'd ascended so he wouldn't be distracted by the planetrage, but he had only minutes until the everpower totally left him. Then, he would tumble to the earth and the planetrage would take him. Shocking to think that everything hinged on only a few minutes. The chance to repair reality itself. He laughed, but tears ran down his cheeks. What could one man do? Ahilya was pushing her faith in him to a point of insanity.

She was there down below, along with the survivors who would soon become her. Iravan stared at the curve of the horizon, the orange-golden hues of the planet and the cascading, brilliant storm. He stared beyond the planet at his first real glimpse of the universe, a billion stars filling his vision. Ahilya prepared humanity, but they would not win this if he did not find a way. And so, Iravan tried.

Embedded in the evervision, he studied reality. Once, the Moment had appeared as its own entity alongside the Deepness and Etherium—three interdimensional realities that ran parallel to each other. The Moment had resembled a globule of twinkling stars, the Deepness a cavern of darkness, and, superimposed through them, the Etherium had changed constantly, finally becoming a realm where his past lives had blinked at him.

With the collapse of reality, and dissolution imminent, the three universes blended into each other in what Ahilya had thought of as the allvision. He saw the collapse as a sludge of wavy light, shards of the Moment floating in pinpoints, colliding with a curving, melting darkness that was undoubtedly the Deepness. Isolated edges of torn-off stars floated everywhere. Frayed constellation lines hung loose in a mockery of some architect's will. Lights blinked and darkened, and rubble-filled dust swam from the erosion of reality. Iravan looked into the allvision and saw space debris—light bending in unusual ways, tripping his mind, and lava that echoed into amazing fractals. Shadows lurked everywhere, warping into cadences of wispy brightness. In the blending of the Etherium, he saw the councilors of Irshar, and Ahilya, talking around a table, as if they were right next to him. He wondered if they would hear him if he spoke.

Focusing, Iravan tried to interpret only the Moment.

Architects always understood the Moment as a plane of consciousness. Dissolution had proven without doubt that it was an anchor of reality. Yet the Moment was so much more than either of those things.

He stared at the broken universe, and willed it to make sense to his eyes. For him—and him alone—the Moment flickered.

It became a tapestry of broken shards, reminiscent of bio-nodes. In one pane, Iravan saw Nidhirv laughing with Vishwam. Bhaskar smiled in another, mending a basket. Agni read a scroll lazily in yet another. On and on, a million images of his other lives. And there—as himself too, in Nakshar's solar lab talking to Dhruv as they exchanged sungineering trackers. As he screamed within a nest of magnaroot, while Oam shuddered in fear. As he and Ahilya lay in each other's arms, so much younger.

Iravan saw himself, but he saw other people too. Ahilya saying goodbye to Eskayra in one frozen pane. Weeping silently in Nakshar's library, anxious because of his long punishing silence. Running through the ashram with her sister Tariya, the both of them laughing little girls.

He had summoned the Moment from the allvision, but this—this still seemed too reminiscent of the Etherium. Did that then mean that he could not repair the Moment at all? That it was too late, that the messy sludge of reality was too far gone to correct? The Moment should have shown him possibilities of consciousness—a frozen state of being—but this was a dissection of events that had occurred, or were about to.

He focused on a group of images showing the assimilation of humanity with the Virohi-vriksh happening now. If *now* was a word that could be used when time appeared as discrete pearls. When any narrative was meaningless. When the past, present, and future were just moments.

Not just moments, he corrected. *This is* the *Moment.*

Seen in a way he had never before.

He was overtaken by awe.

Responding to his will, the Moment was showing him what it was, finally. A reality with a relationship to time. Had the early architects known this? It was called the *Moment*; of course, it was related to time. Of course, it resembled the Etherium. Consciousnesses were merging in a way they never had because of dissolution. Architects had always connected one possibility to another within the Moment using constellation lines, and in doing so, had impacted reality, changing a plant's state of being. But now, during dissolution, the remains of the Moment were merging different star-shards. Consciousness was already climbing to its next state of being. Nothing he did now would return things to the way they were.

A deep sadness filled Iravan. In his hubris, he had destroyed reality, yet perhaps there was no other way this could have gone. The Moment had weakened since the very first investiture of the Virohi into an architect, and each subsequent earthrage had continued to weaken it. This dissolution was more than a thousand years in the making.

He gathered the everpower to him like a cloak. To repair the Moment—in whatever way he could—would mean interfering with what the universe was trying to balance. He was about to put his fingers into this messy sludge and pry pieces of reality apart, hoping the puzzle pieces would lock into their earlier form on their own, as an aspect of retained memory. Doing so could prove disastrous.

But he had made a promise to Ahilya, and it was no longer his decision alone. Whether he acted or not, humanity was forever changed. They were already at the end of the line—all they had were bad choices. He would let the rest of them make the decision of what they wanted to be. He would let them find their place in the world in the way they saw fit, not the way he did, with his desire to make amends. After all, wasn't that what Ahilya had asked of him all those days ago, when she'd marched into the Garden to bind him with a heartpoison bracelet?

The allvision beckoned to him, reality translating into blinks.

Iravan's past lives circled him, but this time at a distance. Their eyes were silver, and he knew the falcon had contaminated them fully, corrupting them with its hate. It was waiting for him to make his move, so it could make its own.

You weren't always like this, Iravan thought to his past. *You made choices of love before.* He watched Nidhirv, Askavetra, Bhaskar and the others in his third vision, but the third vision was slipping with the collapse of reality. His past lives crowded him, reading his intent.

Iravan took a deep breath. If he was to fix the Moment, he would have to begin with himself.

As an architect, that was essential—his will needed to be pure and unshakeable. His past lives still lived within him, driven by the falcon-yaksha. If he did not combat their resistance first, whatever he wished to do could be undone by his own self. A slip while he tried to pry one consciousness apart from another, a small flicker of his fingers while he teased apart the fragments… These mistakes could ruin everything. What he intended needed the precision of a surgeon, and he had one chance, and one alone. Iravan could not afford to give control to any of his past lives in those instants of reckoning.

Besides, he'd already told Ahilya he needed to neutralize the falcon. It was too powerful with the subsumed power of all the other yakshas. It battled inside him, roaring to take control, attempting to grip the everpower with steely talons as he clutched it with his crumbling fingernails.

Wrapped in the everpower, Iravan began projecting his past outward like he'd done before. Dust rippled around him in the atmosphere, space debris and vapor misting and coalescing. Figures appeared in front of him, the faded forms of Mohini, Askavetra, Bhaskar, Agni, and then Nidhirv. If he could only break the falcon's control of them then he could ensure the falcon would not interfere.

The yaksha anticipated him snatching at the projections. Though Iravan knew it would occur, a grunt escaped him.

Stars in front of him blinked, rearranging themselves into a gateway, and beyond it a massive, labyrinthine maze that extended above and below him as if it were a sungineering hologram. Awe filled Iravan because he knew this maze was his consciousness. It glittered like glass, walls rising in front of him, rippling with memory. Standing within the Moment, he stared at a million collected panes, iridescent and colorful images rushing across the glass surfaces, each image showing him a version of himself.

A smile twisted his lips. He had seen his consciousness as a maze before. This was an invitation, an acceptance of the falcon to finally find the victor between them. Only one of them would emerge; only one would hold the reins of this consciousness they both shared. *We come to it again*, he thought. How many times had he done this? First with the Resonance, then with the falcon-proper, and now this. Of course, he had not won by subsuming the falcon-yaksha, he could see that now. This time, he had arrived at their last battle.

He sensed the falcon's laughter, and for a brief instant Iravan felt a deep affection for the creature. For thousands of years they had circled each other. This was a battle so long coming. What would the yaksha unleash on him that he had not already endured?

There was no way forward but one.

Iravan entered the maze.

53

AHILYA

The noise swept over her, horrifying her and making her scream, until she realized it came from her. Even so, she could not stop—she was the noise, and the cacophony filled her mind, the worst memories unmooring her. A collective vision of the Conclave falling to the jungle. Bodies tumbling everywhere, ripped away—and within the mass of combined consciousness, an absence like a tearing of her limbs. Panic filled her throat, and the screaming stopped just for an instant because *she could not get the sounds out—*

Silence.

Then a ringing sound, shrill and continuous.

Her movements were slow… wooden. She couldn't remember where she was. Who she was.

She stood in a forest. Her bare toes grazed the soil. Wet earth squelched under her feet. The shrill sound echoed from all directions. Something was rushing through the forest with the force of a storm. A dark mass blinked in the distance, hurtling toward her. She squinted, trying to understand it. Leaves cascaded from the trees, scraping off branches, and roots withered into dust, so that suddenly she stood on an empty plain. All around her, the forest was depleting, leaves that had fallen only seconds ago now rising higher and higher. They became a wall, a wave, rearing upon itself, and suddenly she realized—this was what that black mass was. A hurricane of leaves that had been rushing toward her, that was now upon her—but no, not leaves.

Faces. The leaf-wave contained a thousand faces, all twisted in agony, *pain, pain, pain.*

She backed away, stumbling, horrified. The screams from those faces came to her, and she recognized their voices—her sister, her friends, her family.

Ahilya turned and ran, but there was no escape from this. The wave rose higher, leaves swirling within it, its crash over her imminent. The wave rushed her, but she snatched at herself desperately—

Splashing water.

She was in a small, deep pool.

She was in Nakshar. In some corner of her mind, she knew this was a memory. That her mind was constructing sense in a slipping landscape of meaning. She blinked again, wiping her nose with her wet hands, and saw her legs underwater.

Next to her, Tariya appeared, spitting water, her eyes terrified. Tariya looked no older than ten, her hair sticking to her face and neck, her big eyes wide. "What do we do?" she gasped. "What do we do?"

This was a mistake. We should not have attempted this. The two sisters had gone swimming in one of Nakshar's pools, but they'd been warned by their parents not to do so because the architecture of the ashram was changing. The girls were non-architects, they would not be seen in the council chambers through the sungineering devices. *I've killed us,* Ahilya thought, because it had been her idea. Of course, it had been her idea. But it was not the pool she feared. It was a rising wave, with strange sounds of horror rising from it.

She kicked her legs, relentlessly, her arms reaching toward her sister as the water whirled around them. Tariya's breath gasped in Ahilya's ears—

And it was the gasp of all of them, the sum total of humanity.

Time stood still.

She was back in the forest.

She *was* the forest, for the forest was that wave of leaves, hurtling mindlessly through the landscape of the Etherium, and she was now within the wave. Sensation grew confused, strange details popping out of oblivion. The grain of wood visible on parchment, blooming into a tree. A cracked mirror, radiating endless light. A string of pink yarn unravelling on a sari. A field of stars, littered with constellation lines. And through it all, screaming, endless weeping.

It was too much. Too much information. Too many emotions.

She lost track of herself, falling into one memory then another, again and again—but something tugged her up back, a glimpse of what she had been, sungineering equipment hanging off her, an archaeologist heading for an expedition.

<*Ahilya?*> the Virohi asked, a question to remind her. To confirm who they were.

Ahilya, she thought. She remembered.

She wrenched her eyes open, and the courtyard chamber that she and the others were in melded, as if she were viewing it through liquid glass. Next to her, Eskayra's gaze was glassy, her mouth open in an *O*. Dhruv and Naila were frozen too—but as her visions tilted, Dhruv, Naila, and Eskayra turned to her, their eyes shining.

She felt their fingers touch hers.

In a blink, they were next to her in the mindless wave of memories, their silhouettes misty and shadowy but *there*. Roots grew around the courtyard, wrapping around the three of them, climbing over their limbs, anchoring around their waists, holding. Another startling memory rushed through Ahilya, of Nakshar landing within the jungle during a false lull, all of them breathing together, desiring the very same thing. Survival. Safety. Led by her, they all saw the same memory, the will of the city attuning within them, their consciousness aligning.

Synchronicity unraveled from her, blending into her friends and beyond. She felt her movements mimicked, her thoughts mirrored, a dance of neurons firing from a thousand brains, all singing the same song, all echoing the same raga of oneness.

Across the new city, tree roots rushed, wrapping the citizens within them. The canopy of the vriksh elongated and thickened, breathing, and roots hurtled with more speed and ferocity. She—they—this Cohesion—saw people huddling together within buildings, arms wrapped around each other, and the roots of Cohesion surged up through cracking floors, binding them to it. Some fought the cocooning, but most of them closed their eyes, letting the tree take them.

Were we right? Ahilya wondered. *Surely, everyone must feel the peace of oneness.*

Protection, the tree whispered, and all these thoughts were the sound of the humanity, and the Virohi, and a thousand consciousnesses combined.

Arms grasped and anchored, leaves growing over the roots, nests growing to secure men, women, and children within them. With each anchoring, shadows appeared in the Etherium with her as the vriksh's roots raced over every living creature within the city.

With the eyes of a thousand people, and the vision of the roots clenching the earth, Ahilya saw everything.

The ashram—this amalgamation of the new city, Irshar, and the Garden—resembled an orb. From top to bottom, the vriksh contained it. The shield of dust had hardened into bark, crisscrossed with veins of branches, becoming stronger than its parts. In Ahilya's mind, this new ashram looked like Nakshar—a design that Iravan had once created. Diamond-like, heart-strong, embedded with the consciousness of every living thing this planet contained—all standing together as one entity. She heard the planet's shriek at this audacity.

Understanding cascaded into Ahilya. There had always been two parts of it, memories entangling with consciousness. As more and more architects appeared within the Cohesion, their knowledge poured into her—and she saw. Just as the Moment could show possibilities of human consciousnesses as stars, and the existence of architects as dust-motes, this Etherium showed the shadows as controllers, and the leaves of memories as something that could be controlled. The image tilted almost into a star-filled universe of the Moment, forced by the combined consciousness of the architects, before she righted it back into the forest.

Ahilya held her awareness tightly. She could not let the architects take charge of it. It had to be her, lest this Cohesion take them irrevocably. It had to be her, or there would be no coming back from this.

I have to guide this, she thought, trying not to fear it.

You already have, the construct whispered, reassuring her.

Ahilya's eyes widened. She knew it was true. Still, she wavered. If she gave in now, there would be no return. What if this Cohesion left them all mindless? What if they imploded?

Cohesion is inevitable, Dhruv whispered to her.

She heard the planetrage come, watched the rumbles of earth, the tsunami of storm head toward the last orb of survival in the planet.

Surrender, Cohesion whispered, and Ahilya saw the intention of the planet to annihilate this pestilence.

Surrender, Cohesion whispered, nudging her, for if she did not give in now, they would not endure.

Surrender, Cohesion whispered, urgency across its surface.

Ahilya surrendered.

54

IRAVAN

At first, the maze was silent, innocuous, almost eerily so.

Iravan floated through it cautiously, watching images from his lives blink on the glass walls. It was like being inside the Etherium—he saw Mohini washing her hair. Himself poring over a book. Askavetra chatting to someone. Bhaskar shaving. All scenes of unremarkable instants within unremarkable lives. It was meant to lull him into safety, but surely the falcon must know he would see through it. He didn't know the shape of the battle, but his guard was up.

Pathways opened at the end of the corridor, and Iravan took a turn at random, knowing instinctively that his task was not to find his way out of the maze. He had to get to the center, where he would finally face the worst the falcon would throw at him. Then the maze would unravel on its own, with one of them at the helm of his consciousness. Everything until then would be a distraction, a way to weaken him, soften him, to make easy pickings for the creature. This was always the falcon's method.

Clutching the everpower, he turned a corner—

And saw himself standing there, his body riddled with silver tattoos, his eyes shining like moons.

This was a projection he'd made only a few seconds ago, before the falcon had seized it, but he could see the creature reflected in the false-Iravan's eyes. Instantly, he understood. The falcon was going to unleash one projection after another at him for him to battle. That's why it had taken control of them now. But to start with his own image? Did the falcon expect he would find it hard to face himself, now, after everything he'd endured? He had tried to kill Ahilya, and he still stood here. What could be worse than that?

Iravan raised his hands and said, "I don't want to fight you," both to the projection and the falcon-yaksha.

Controlled by the creature, the projection grinned. Its tattoos grew brilliant, blinding him. The projection moved forward, lightning-fast. Dust twisted around Iravan, and he felt the everpower slipping from him. The projection attacked with its mind, and Iravan felt it like a punch to the stomach. As his eyes closed, and he grunted in pain, he fell into the memory of—

Irshar.

Iravan opened his eyes and blinked. A strange sense came to him that he was not really in Irshar, that something had happened to the ashram and he existed on a different plane. But the sense was fleeting. He inhaled deeply, and the air smelt fresher than it had in days. He was in Irshar, and it was a magnificent terrifying monstrosity he had created in the skies. From his open balcony, he could see the ashrams of the Conclave peeking out of the mist. He had attached them to his construction by manipulating their core trees. It was a construction unlike any the world had seen before, a mutilation of the ashrams, but the pain of what he'd endured rushed through him. Only a few hours had passed since he'd rescued himself and the other Ecstatics of Nakshar from brutal experimentation. So many things had been experienced for the first time.

Next to him, Ahilya lay on the bed they had been resting on. Her body was curled in on itself. Her cheeks were marked by tears, and her breathing was erratic. She was whimpering in her sleep. Her arms wrapped her belly, and she shook her head. Dark blood pooled around her trousers.

Their child. They had lost it. Iravan felt his grief catch in his throat like a sob. He approached the basin and dampened the bandages that he'd trajected, then approached Ahilya, and undressed her carefully, making sure not to wake her. Slowly, carefully, he began to clean her.

His fingers paused—for behind his eyes, he could detect another presence, a life he had lived once—but it disappeared as soon as he tried to capture it. He shook his head to clear it, to give Ahilya the attention she had always deserved. What she had endured—what she still did—he could not imagine such horror and pain. His possibilities for fatherhood had disappeared long ago; had he been to blame for her pain then? *Traject me,* he heard her say. *Heal me. Make it so it never happens again.*

He'd refused her, not knowing the effect of such a thing—but perhaps that had been premature. Iravan raised his hand to his eyes and studied the blue-green tattoos. It was as if he was seeing himself from afar, and he shook his head again, trying to dispel that feeling.

Traject me, she'd said.

Why had he denied her this? He had lost his possibilities for fatherhood, but she was to blame for this miscarriage as much as he was, surely. She had never wanted children—not the way he had—and she had held him hostage to it. She had jumped into the vortex when she shouldn't have. She had told him nothing of her pregnancy when she should have.

He had her permission to change her.

He could do this. It would be easy.

The Deepness glittered, and he aimed a wire-thin jet of light toward the stars where Ahilya's consciousness shone. Her body shifted. *Traject me,* she'd said.

So he did—

Iravan wrenched out of the memory—

He was back in the maze, and on his knees. The false-Iravan loomed over him, the smile on its face deranged, the eyes shining silver. Iravan stared up at this twisted version of himself, and saw the creature's tattoos blink in preparation of drowning him in another such memory.

No, he thought, gasping. *No, that is not how it was.* The memory he was being shown was perverse. He had never thought in such a way about his wife. He had never believed it was her fault, never trajected her back then, not even on her asking. This was the falcon's doing. Ahilya had shown him the truth. She had delved into her memories, reminded him of who he had been. Reminded him of the possibility of the man she had married. The falcon had eschewed all other lives, instead choosing to show him a version of himself—but whatever else he had forgotten, Iravan knew he had never hurt Ahilya in such a wretched way.

This is not me, he gasped, as he remembered the vision of changing her body to suit his needs. *This is not me.*

The false-Iravan smiled, its lips rising in mockery. Tattoos curled on its skin, and he read the intent of cruelty on its face.

Desperately, Iravan clutched the stone blade dangling from

his neck. The everpower responded to him, and a massive branch conjured itself from the debris and dust floating around. It hardened into an axe, and Iravan swung it at the projection. The false-Iravan disintegrated into powder, the ghost of a smile still lingering in the air.

Do your worst, he thought. *I will destroy each of your minions.*

The falcon merely laughed, a cackle that seemed to reverberate around the strange maze.

Breath heaving, Iravan moved forward through the labyrinth of his consciousness.

55

COHESION

Awaking.

A curious stillness, like vibrations emanating from rock.

Stability that washed over it like a wave—dampening its chaos and reviving its peace at the same time.

Hands, fingers, tongues, roots, seeds, fruit, it was everywhere, it was everything. With the last consciousness returned to it, Cohesion ballooned far above its bodies caught in the tree. It saw with a thousand eyes, it breathed with a million mouths. Neither humans, nor cosmic creatures, nor tree, nor animals—it was nothing at once, and all of it, a sum greater than its parts. Joy, exhilaration, acceptance, grief, hunger, curiosity, despair, it saw everything in all their little minds, and it wept because all it felt was a vast and drowning love, *love, LOVE.*

Sentience was enormous, beyond anything that could be captured in thought. It could only be felt, through every pore of skin, through every leaf that whispered, and every scent that washed over it.

Being alive—existing—This had always been the purpose of life.

Life meant experiencing, witnessing, participating. The sip of nectar from its bee-mouth. The inhale that was deep enough to burst a lung. Rain against its bark-skin. Wind raking the serrated edges of an elm leaf. The laughter of children chasing each other through sun-baked streets. Vapor rolling off its bird wings. And within it, the quiet of mind watched in wonder. Each instant precious, each instant filled with awareness. So deep that it was impossible to distinguish between Cohesion that watched, and Cohesion that was being watched. To finally do this—it was so deeply reassuring that its little bodies hurt with how much they were releasing.

I know myself, it thought to their little minds. *Because I know you.*

Cohesion danced, reveling in its existence. Looking inward and outward and seeing everything. *We are one*, it thought. *We are I, and I am one.* Its hive-like body buzzed with glorious perception, and a melody emerged uniting all of its pieces into a singular purpose. It knew the melody—the raga of harmony, but it was also the raga of indivisibility, of accord, recognition and identity. Not a single melody but a symphony of voices and thoughts, of little waves moving together like schools of fish, making a singular ocean. It was aware of every flutter, every whisper, and all of those were its own.

I am the whole world, it thought—but then the world rumbled.

It felt it in their feet, in its roots. In each striation of muscle and each spasm of heart.

Cohesion looked away from its wonder. It saw the approaching storm, trying to annihilate its remarkable existence. Now when it had finally found itself, a great sense of tragedy filled it to be destroyed.

A vast denial erupted from it, the raga of harmony growing sharp like a blade, emerging like a shout. *NO!*

The planetrage came.

56

IRAVAN

He realized his mistake only several minutes after leaving the projection behind. Iravan hefted the everdust axe in one hand, while the other came to fumble around his neck to feel the blade of pure possibility. Had he used all of the everdust within his pendant to create a weapon against the false-Iravan? He knew he could not infinitely convert possibility from one thing into another. Now that the axe was made, it would remain so. The only reason his stone blade could be used as everdust was because he had always wished for it to be the strongest, most malleable substance possible. Yet in using it now, had he depleted all of it?

His fingers clutched the blade, and Iravan shivered. The blade was smaller, and though some everdust remained, he could not waste it. This was the last everdust on the planet. He would need it to repair the Moment. He had acted desperately—and maybe that was the falcon's plan all along—to force him to use pure possibility in this fight. It would not be the first time the falcon had tried to make him lose what was important in his distraction. It had done so before when Ahilya had needed him to help fight the Virohi. Iravan could not let it win this way.

The mirror panes around him changed, blinking, but Iravan tried not to look at them. He would find no clue to the falcon's intent there; he had to imagine the falcon was showing him this deliberately as a way to disorient him. No hidden messages in the windowpanes. Only more of the falcon's assault. He clutched the axe in both his hands tightly, and floated forward, ignoring the images on the glass walls.

Around another corner, a different projection awaited him.

The light from the blinking bio-node reflected around him, making any shape difficult to see. The figure looked familiar—was it another Iravan, sent by the falcon to unmoor him? He knew himself. The falcon would not be able to seduce him with lies.

The projection was not him.

Askavetra stood there, leaning casually against a mirror pane, watching him come. Iravan slowed down. He tried to remember everything he knew of this life of his. Born during a time when yakshas were considered dangerous, yet Ecstasy was not yet outlawed, Askavetra had always been curious about the jungle creatures.

He approached, and she spun to him swiftly, her arms shining in silver—but this time Iravan was prepared. Instead of waiting for her attack, he swung the blade at her neck. He threw all his weight behind the swing, but she moved quick as lightning. Her hands came up to seize the axe from him, but Iravan resisted—and the pull between them sent out spikes of silver, illuminating the maze. They both tumbled into her memory.

She was in the jungle.

Inches away from her stood a massive tiger-yaksha, its striped tail swinging behind it cautiously. She knew she should leave, return to her ashram, that this creature was dangerous. But hadn't she come seeking just such a creature? *They will destroy your material bonds,* she thought. That was the risk of yakshas, and why any interaction with them was forbidden.

Yet Askavetra had heard stories from other ashrams where people still communed with these creatures. She'd heard whispers of a time when architects from her own ashram had disappeared into the jungle to live with the yakshas, attaining great powers in doing so. Her mother had told her those men and women had been abducted by the creatures, but Sariya had whispered they'd gone willingly. Why?

Askavetra approached the tiger-yaksha slowly. It was so tall she had to look up at it, but keeping her terror at bay, noticing its sharp teeth, she continued forward, attempting to still her shivering. The yaksha bent low, and she stopped moving.

Its maw touched her briefly, and then a purring sound emerged. The yaksha nuzzled her neck, and despite her fear Askavetra laughed. She reached a hand to brush its fur—

Images cascaded through her mind—

Through *Iravan's* mind—

Of another young woman the tiger-yaksha had belonged to, a woman he had known, *Naila,* who he had felt amity with. He remembered silver light leaching from the tiger-yaksha toward him; watched as he subsumed the tiger-yaksha, and Naila crumpled, the memory of her past lives ripped away from her. The image exploded and expanded into a cloud. He saw architects of the Garden and a landed Irshar collapsing in deep pain as he broke consent and all promises of ethics by taking from them what was never his.

Iravan tore away from the vision, breathing hard. He returned to the maze, his mind spinning. He was still locked in ludicrous combat with Askavetra, who smiled a twisted smile, and he thought, *I let this happen.*

It was a shock to learn that the tiger-yaksha had belonged to Naila, though he could see clearly now the linking of it, and the forces that had pulled her life into his orbit. In some ways, they had always been connected, had always known each other—but he had ripped all knowledge of her past from her, bonds of friendship be damned. That was the effect of his subsummation of the other yakshas. He had done so because of the falcon's madness and influence on him, but the weight of responsibility still crushed his shoulders. *It was still my body that did the action, even if my mind was the yaksha's,* he thought.

Askavetra's eyes shone in satisfaction, and he knew he was giving into the falcon by thinking this way. He was making himself weaker. Iravan snarled, and tried to push the axe toward her neck, to end her and the falcon that controlled this version of her.

Askavetra dropped her grip on the axe.

It happened in the same instant. The axe connected to her neck, and her hand locked around Iravan's throat, clutching the stone blade hung around a vine.

Iravan felt deep terror. *No.* He willed it, and his necklace remained around him, resisting Askavetra's pull. But her hand tightened, and particles drifted from the pendant, diminishing everdust. The pendant grew smaller.

The axe decapitated her.

Askavetra vanished in a swirl of air, extinguishing shards of precious possibility.

57

COHESION

Drawing on memories of everything it was made of, Cohesion stood against the planetrage.

It bent their heads, protecting against the rising gale of the planet, as its branches swished around the nest. Wind shrieked, gusting across the cocoons of its people, and a storm razed over the jungle, withering everything in its ravenous path.

It felt the planet's fury in every inch of them. Rocks rose in the air, hurled at its canopy, but it braced its head and hardened into its strongest form. The sounds were terrifying, akin to a monstrous gnashing of teeth. Water rose from the bowels of the planet, into tides over a thousand feet tall, slamming against the nest of its existence. Within, the people shook in their cocoons, and Cohesion screamed as some of them drowned, winked away from its power. Heat climbed over its skin, burning away the roots, scorching the leaves of protection. Holes appeared within the canopy, and it scrambled, attempting to fill itself with new growth, leaves and shoots bursting hastily to cover the holes. It felt the pain of burning deep in their marrow, and saw the planet fling more fire at them in the form of molten rocks that melted its sap.

Terror and sadness overtook it. Flashes of memory—the pain of separation, the rise to the skies, the final and late acceptance that it had always ever been one people, united at its source as sentient beings. They who had once been called Virohi—the other—they who had been not so different from the complete ones. Something rose in its memory, a glimmer of acceptance, and an echo of blue-green tattoos. *We were architects once,* it said, and knowledge whispered from within it.

And as the planet hurled its elements at them, large balls of debris smashing against the nest, Cohesion twisted the tree of its body—no longer simply protecting, but attacking, *trajecting*, in return.

Roots writhed, hurtling outwards from the ashram, smashing into boulders before they could reach the nest. A massive tsunami loomed over them, but the tree sent out an intention and a wall formed to break the wave. Below, more roots anchored into the soil, creating plates of bark, layers upon layers of them strengthening the earth, preventing an erosion. Rocks dashed everywhere, but spears of branches erupted from the tree, impaling the rocks before they could reach the cocoons. The canopy grew thicker, absorbing the worst of the dust, filtering fresher air down to its people while above smoke and dust obscured visibility. Energized by the power of such enormous desire, sungineering drones that had been lying in wait zipped through the air, hurtling like missiles into gigantic debris, disintegrating them into dust.

A hundred ashrams, no a thousand—those from sister cities, and those that once had been subsumed—arose in a crescendo of memory, feeding years of survival back into themselves. Cohesion reared, fighting for its survival, while the planet churned trying to annihilate it. Cohesion lost parts of itself, but it stood too, rooting further. There was terror but there was an exhilarated sense of victory woven through it. The planet was throwing everything it had at it, but Cohesion was holding. It was surviving.

58

IRAVAN

He hobbled through the maze faster, panic chasing him. The mirror walls were growing darker, and behind every corner lurked a shadow, a threat. He knew he could not win the fight with the other projections. His hold on the everpower was too shaky, gripping it with icy fingers that slipped and bled. Each time he'd pulled himself away from a memory, he'd used precious energy, and he was unable to fight on so many fronts—submerged in the memory they drowned him in, unable to prevent their physical attack, incapable of holding onto everpower while they tried to steal possibility. Precious minutes had already ticked by—an estimation of time his body made in this space where time itself had no meaning.

He turned into another corridor, and saw Agni.

Terror rose through him.

Agni's eyes blazed, and Iravan turned and fled, knowing that of all his projections and past lives, this one was the most powerful, this one scared him the most. Behind him, he heard Agni's feral laughter as they set chase, and Iravan half-floated, half-ran, losing his orientation, only to careen into a silvery-eyed Bhaskar who appeared out of smoke and gripped his arms tight.

Iravan cried out in panic, attempting to swing the axe, but Bhaskar's grip was too strong and the axe fell and vanished into nothing. A shimmer of light—Iravan tumbled into Bhaskar's memory—but before it could hold him prisoner, he wrenched his body away and shot out of the man's grasp to flee to another corridor of the maze.

He heard their voices, not just Agni and Bhaskar who were chasing him, but others too, Mohini and Isanya and Jeevan and countless others all the way back to the little girl who had been the first of them, whose name he didn't even know. Their cackles filled the air, and he fled in the forest of mirrors, stopping short only to retreat when he heard one of them breathe in amusement, hiding behind a corner.

He did not know where in the maze he was, or what the projections would do to him, all of them together. All he knew was he would not survive their combined onslaught.

Iravan crept away, turning again then stopped.

Everything was silent here. The walls gleamed at him, no longer panes of mirror, but mere shards of blackness, curving endlessly. The corridor in front of him was tight, dense. He understood the architecture suddenly; the maze was radial. By sheer luck, he'd found himself closer to its center. Did that mean he was closer now to the falcon? Is that why the projections had disappeared?

He could no longer hear them. Perhaps they would appear when he least expected it. Each step was a trap, each glance of light a terror. But at least the falcon was a known entity. His past scared him more than that creature.

He moved forward, but his movements were stilted. He floated, but it was discordant, like a leaf that was being pulled this way and that by a terrible wind. Iravan followed the curve of the maze and in the distance saw a circular chamber, so like the chamber in the Etherium that Ahilya spoke of that he paused. All the mirror shards changed to reflect the falcon-yaksha. The bird gliding in the sky, searching for him. The falcon colliding into Nakshar, right before it abducted him. Wrapping its wings around him to keep him safe while he and the bird plummeted from the sky after the first skyrage. On and on, from the time of separation when the falcon-yaksha had formed, becoming a gigantic creature, lost and alone—until the point of subsummation, when Iravan had shrunk it with his power.

What did it mean that it was only the falcon he had to face now? Had he evaded the projections once and for all? He was too panicked to feel relief at the thought.

Blinking hard, Iravan stumbled forward toward the mirrored chamber and his destiny.

59

COHESION

It was hurling massive branches at the planetrage, breaking the onslaught into chunks, when the world flashed, blinding Cohesion's every sense.

Air shivered.

Sound ceased.

It happened for the merest instant, so tiny that if Cohesion were not *Cohesion*, aware of every minuscule part of itself, it would have missed the flash. It continued to beat back the planetrage, creating a massive wall of branches nearly a thousand feet high against the tsunami attempting to sweep it away—but within its mind, a panic spread. The parts of it which had once been architects understood it first, and Cohesion watched understanding bloom in all of its other parts like light beaming. The flash was a lull. The battle was too easy. Cohesion had been winning, but it was never meant to be this simple. Earthrages had occurred before, and each time a lull had happened, it had only paved the way for something terribly ferocious to come on its heels.

It slung sharpened trunks like missiles into fiery rocks, disintegrating them, when the flash occurred again.

Fragments of the planetrage broke apart, then another flash, blinding Cohesion's eyes. Within it, voices rose and fell, churning out their memories, Virohi, human, animal, tree, all delving within themselves for an explanation.

And a word appeared in Cohesion's mind like the softest whisper.

Dissolution.

The planetrage flashed again, and in blind overwhelming panic, Cohesion pushed its intention to survive, but—

60

IRAVAN

He did not find the falcon within the circular chamber.

Surrounded by blinking mirror-shards stood a familiar man. Nidhirv looked like a wraith, short and dark-skinned, his body bent slightly. His eyes glittered silver like all the other projections, and an echo of wings sprung from his shoulders in a mirage. Still, Iravan paused, surprised.

This is who you send? he thought. Of all the lives he'd lived, he'd become most familiar with Nidhirv, but Iravan had left his capital desire behind and with it any need to learn any secrets from the man. Why would the falcon think this man would affect him the most, delivering the killing blow?

Iravan held the miniscule blade of everpower tight in his hand. The blade was so small now, it was a mere sliver, and he knew he would not be able to use it against whatever Nidhirv unleashed on him, not if he wished to repair the Moment with it afterward.

He'd lost his axe somewhere in the manic run within the maze, escaping from the feral projections, but now, with Nidhirv's familiarity, a morbid curiosity froze him. Half-horrified, half-fascinated, unable to do anything but endure what was coming, Iravan watched as the projection blazed forward, carried on silver wings—

Nidhirv blinked.

Next to him, Vishwam was still talking to the council chair, a formidable wrinkled-face woman called Oma who always made Nidhirv feel like a child, no matter that he was nearly fifty now. Nidhirv tried to pay attention. To school his features into supporting Vishwam, knowing what Vishwam was asking. After all, his husband had practiced this very speech with him before. Yet Nidhirv couldn't help the feeling of disassociation creeping through him. He was here, but had something happened in the last few minutes that he'd missed? These episodes of disconnection had grown more frequent, along with the pain in his chest. It was why he and Vishwam were here, petitioning Oma to change the rules surrounding the birthing ceremony.

"—is indeed sacred," Vishwam was saying. He sat on the grass next to Nidhirv, his hand stroking Nidhirv's knee, though his attention was on the council chair. Above, a lush banyan whispered in the wind, giving them shade. "Think about it, Oma. The Virohi are The Ones Who Are Ourselves. They exist in an unknown place, and we call them our precursors, but what do we truly know about them? We bring them into birth—"

Oma frowned, holding up a hand. "It is not our business to know who they are," she said. "It is enough that they give us the power, and that we seek our yakshas to complete the circle of death and life."

"It is this circle of death and life I want to preserve," Vishwam said earnestly, his eyes glittering. "Would you not want to find Aditi in another life yourself? Would you not want to marry her again, and protect her? I know your love is strong."

"Aditi is my life," Oma replied. "But that is not how the cycle of rebirth works." She cast a glance at Nidhirv, who stared back at her, trying not to blush. "Is this what this is about? Nidhirv, your sickness? And your grief, Vishwam, at losing him?"

"That is not what we're discussing," Vishwam said, but Oma's eyes were full of sadness, directed at Nidhirv. She had seen through their subterfuge so easily. What was the point of denying it?

"How bad is it, my friend?" she asked softly.

"It is bad," he whispered. "Every day it is worse. More painful. I do not have many days left."

"Do not say that," Vishwam said angrily, but Oma only shook her head in sorrow.

"I am sorry," she said, sighing. "I truly am. You have had too little time with each other, but the other ashrams and elders would not agree. You are asking to change the very fabric of the ashrams, to have a choice regarding uniting with your yakshas. But this is not a choice an architect can have."

"We—"

"No, Vishwam. Denying yourself completion will set the ashrams on an irrevocable path. You do not know what you are seeking."

"We are seeking time with each other. Not just in this life, but every other." Vishwam's hand tightened on Nidhirv's. "We will find each other, in every life—"

"You think you will be lovers in every life?" Oma said. "Even if you are reborn in the same era, there is no guarantee. Your life—the future life—will make its choices. You could be born years apart. You could be born in different ashrams. You could be unknown to each other, or perhaps parent and child, perhaps colleagues. What will you do then? Break every bond of society?"

"Of course not," Vishwam replied. "Love comes in different forms, and we know better than to expect we will be lovers always. But if we had guarantee of finding something as sacred as we have now, wouldn't that be its own adherence to our culture?"

"No," Oma said. "It would not."

She stood up, fury in her movements. Her piercing gaze ran over them.

"What you are contemplating is beyond horrific," she said, her voice tight "Unity, balance, and return, *these* are things that dictate our society. Not this evil idea you have of reaching beyond your life. Not this desire to set yourself above everything we know. Your love for each other cannot supersede the greater path of a consciousness returning to itself. It must not—otherwise everything we have done to bring the precursors into this world will be a crime against them, meant for our own selfish need for power. It would be a crime against *us* and our halves that await us in the jungle. Abandon this path, Vishwam, and enjoy the time you and Nidhirv have with each other in this life. I will expect you to retire to the jungle when your time comes to seek your yaksha."

The two watched her leave. Vishwam's hand was clasped around Nidhirv's so tight that it hurt, but Nidhirv did not say anything. He had known this would be the outcome. He had warned his husband.

Vishwam turned to him, scowling, as though hearing this thought. "Don't you start that again."

Nidhirv smiled tiredly. "I did not say anything."

"You did not need to." Vishwam brought Nidhirv's hand to his mouth, in half-prayer half-promise. "There has to be a way. There has to."

Nidhirv pulled his husband into an embrace, smelling his skin, and told himself this was enough. That Oma was right, and this one life was a gift. But as Vishwam leaned forward to capture his mouth, terror flew through him, for his inevitable end, to be separated from his husband, to never find him again.

And within the glittering maze, Iravan recoiled in shock.

The implications tumbled in his mind like debris in an earthrage. He could almost taste his husband from a lifetime ago.

It began with them, he thought in disbelief. Unity with a yaksha had been built into Nidhirv's culture, but Vishwam had suggested a deviation—one that had ultimately led to the outlawing of Ecstasy and the repression of yakshas in the generations to come. One that had led to the oppression of the non-architects, the rise of earthrages, the total destruction of the planet, and eventually the rise of airborne ashrams. Nidhirv had neglected the falcon, creating Iravan's life. All because he had been sick, and Vishwam had wanted more time with him.

You did this, the falcon said, and Iravan saw Nidhirv's silver eyes pouring with tears. *You brought death, because of your love.* Disgust poured into his mind, gushing from the falcon, and though Iravan knew the falcon was guilting him now deliberately, he found that he had no defense.

We didn't know, he thought desperately. *We didn't know.*

But he could not deny the truth. The path that Nidhirv had taken—that *he* had taken—had led their whole society into devastation. Bharavi's death, all the excisions, all the earthrages, the utter annihilation of the planet, all of it laid at his feet.

The falcon sensed his despair. It fed on his vulnerability. *Look at what you did,* it whispered.

Nidhirv disappeared, and in his place, the false-Iravan appeared again, looming over him.

See, the falcon mocked, using his voice. *As I see.*

The projection put a foot on Iravan's chest, and pushed. He was swept away, again—

Back in Nakshar. He saw himself, a Senior Architect, and next to him sat another architect. Manav, at a time when they had both been councilors. They had never been close, but Iravan had always felt respect and kinship with his colleague. They had worked together as equals. He laughed with Manav as Airav made a dry comment—but then the vision changed, and days passed, and Iravan watched himself marching into Vishwam's—no, Manav's home. He watched as he excised Manav within the deathcage. Each life was distinct and unique, even if tethered to its past lives or those yet to be born—he knew this—but all he could see was Manav—Manav who had once been *Vishwam*—while the man shook and quivered, reduced to nothing with his alienation from Nakshar's core tree.

No, Iravan thought horrified, in some corner of his brain.

Yet the vision moved forward inexorably, uncaring of his shock. Iravan saw the focus on his own face as he let down the glass of Manav's deathcage to perform the complex trajection of excision. Manav tried to fight, his body blazing blue-green, but Iravan—assisted by the rudra-tree—was too powerful. The ashram divorced from Manav, recognizing him as an outsider, a danger, an other. Grass grew around Manav, directed by the rudra-tree, and Manav screamed as the foliage attacked him. In Iravan's eyes, the man merged with Bharavi, and he saw himself killing the both of them within a deathcage.

Do you see? the falcon whispered. *This is what you did. To the man who loved you.*

No, no, no, Iravan thought, backing away into the darkness, but the image of Manav's excision played repeatedly in front of his eyes. He was trapped in this nightmare, unable to deny the truth.

The other vision the falcon had shown him was punishing, but he knew in his heart that it was the falcon's corruption.

But this—

This had been *him.*

He had destroyed Manav.

His capital desire had been to seek vengeance against the cosmic creatures. But Manav—united with one of his yakshas—had sought to protect Iravan. That is why he had not fought his excision. If Manav had once been Vishwam, and if Vishwam's greatest desire had once been to love Nidhirv, then Manav and his yaksha had no choice in rescuing Iravan from the falcon. He could see now why he had felt such affinity for Manav's incorporeal yaksha. What were yakshas if not manifestations of deep desire? Without Vishwam, Iravan would have been erased.

And Iravan had excised him.

Each decision had been catastrophic. To deny his yaksha as Nidhirv, in order to stay with Vishwam… And then, to excise Vishwam-as-Manav once Nidhirv had become Iravan…

Iravan's shoulders shuddered with a heavy weight. He screamed in denial and grief and fury.

The vision vanished, and he was back in the glittering maze of the Moment within the central chamber. All around him, the panes reflected Manav's excision, but in the time he had been trapped here with his nightmares, other projections had arrived.

Nidhirv pulled away from Iravan, Bhaskar stood next to him. Agni, and Askavetra, and Mohini, and Jeevan—all of them surrounding him.

Iravan cowered between them as they loomed. They looked like his past lives, but superimposed behind them was the falcon-yaksha, its wings spread wide. There was no escape.

Give up, the falcon said. *I am the better, the stronger, the wiser of the both of us.*

Give up, the projections echoed.

Iravan shook his head. He tried to stand, to flee.

The projections rushed him.

61

COHESION

The pause was eternal.

Cohesion was frozen, aware of itself in a terrifying moment of stillness.

Everything else was frozen too, each boulder of the planetrage that suddenly seemed motionless mid-shot. The sky caught in a ripple like a picture of a rumpled blanket. Water droplets that remained unmoving in a rain that did not fall.

The silence was deafening.

Cracks appeared from the heart of everything frozen, like a cave-in, sucking matter and rain and earth and soil and the whole planet into a yawning blackness.

So fast, so long, yet instantaneous. Cohesion had no time to respond.

Everything ripped—edifices crumbling, the vriksh snapping through the middle, the great blackness eating all physicality up. Dissolution chewed through the planetrage, coming for Cohesion from all directions.

Cohesion balked, an animal in a trap. Stunned, frozen, helpless.

Prey.

62

IRAVAN

His past lives choked him, their projected hands throttling his throat. Iravan gasped, his eyes bulging—he felt their touch inside his body, creeping inside his muscles, curling through him. He felt them pounding in his heart, and lurking beneath his skin.

The projections disappeared one by one from the maze, but Iravan knew they had only retreated inside him. He could see the gaping crumble of reality and meaning rush toward him—and the projections had crept within him now as if he would provide a final sanctuary. The thought of having them take him over again like they had when he'd tried to kill Ahilya choked him. He scrabbled at his skin, scratching it, leaving bloody marks. He tried to claw them out of him, but it was already too late. His hands froze, midway to his throat, and his mind clouded. Mohini chuckled with his mouth, before the laugh swept into the deep-throated cackle of Bhaskar. Feral, hysterical, insane, the past lives pushed and probed his body, and spun around, a thousand visions of reality bending.

Through their attack of him, Iravan realized one thing.

Dissolution had come.

He had not even begun to repair the Moment, and it was already too late.

The blade of pure possibility swung around his neck, and he clutched it desperately, willing reality to stabilize. Out of options to traject or fight, he simply hurled his will at the blade, hoping for the remaining everdust to respond.

Before his intention could complete, one of his lives used his hand to snatch the blade away. He willed his mind to use it, tried to believe those were his fingers clutching it, that his mind that was superior to theirs, but everything he did was futile. There were too many of them. Light cascaded around him in rainbow hues, and he trembled, trying to reach the blade.

No, he thought aghast, as Nidhirv inhabited his body. He read the man's thought. How easy it would be to bring back Vishwam with the everdust.

No, Iravan thought again, but some other life knocked away Nidhirv's to grab at the everdust and fulfill its own want.

The falcon screamed, trying to get at the blade as well, its mad intention to kill the cosmic creatures, destroy Cohesion, still ringing through matter and time.

Iravan could do nothing to stop them. He was a marionette, obeying their bidding.

Overpowered, he diminished.

They infiltrated him.

63

COHESION

It ruptured.

Lost its mind.

Careened into madness.

Its sentience crashed, caving in as dissolution smashed into it, chewing away parts of it, taking away meaning and sense. Each loss was painful, each piece of information lost like an amputation. Its mind broke, trying to connect disparate pieces of itself, attempting to hold its own form with narrative.

Fire tore at its roots, ice freezing its people who rested within its boughs. Light shifted, and the tree yawned and caved, stretching far beyond reckoning, crushing parts of itself into balls, killing its citizens.

Dissolution destroyed them all, dissolving, distorting, demeaning. A great warping occurred, and everything bent, keeling over, a twisting within circles. An elongation and slowness of sensation—huge shrill sounds, except no sound could scream in such a terrifying way. Nausea and insanity, and Cohesion could no longer fill the gaps with memory. It could not hold form. It could not assemble meaning.

The hive disintegrated in order to save itself, like a tree flinging out seeds in a storm in order to ensure its survival. Tearing and burning, the little minds popped out of the singular existence, floating free from Cohesion, bodies falling limp, minds hurtling through space, meant to be alone, alone, alone.

She was one of the abandoned.

She opened her eyes and screamed.

64

PAST LIVES

They took control.

Like a rabid pack of beasts, the past lives rushed into the man's familiar body, jostling each other to take over in a feeding frenzy. Nidhirv ascended, only for Isanya to creep into the back, arching it, before Askavetra ruffled her shoulders, striding forward. Bhaskar grabbed her hand with his, and the body shuddered as both Agni and Mohini tried to inhabit it. Agni won, and the force of the victory tossed the body through the atmosphere before it steadied. A feral smile grew on their face, the expression cold, then the falcon smashed into Agni, taking over control. The heart still beat, but life in the body was waning, and before the others could do anything, the falcon used the everpower to shave a sliver of possibility from the blade around the body's neck. Silvery particles rose, and strength returned to the body—Bhaskar crept in while the falcon rejoiced. A blink, and muscles tore as Bhaskar laughed manically, straightening, *he had this body now, it was his*—

But Askavetra returned, this time with Mohini next to her in a terrible alliance. The two of them snatched at pure possibility—

wishing to be alive for one glorious instant, and more possibility diminished.

Deep within his mind, Iravan watched this horror occurring to what had once been *his* body. On and on they came, wearing him like a cloak, discarding him before the next attacked, all to steal the last slivers of possibility.

Their arrogance to be in control, their self-hate, consumed the blade of everdust. None of them could win, and in the end they all lost, while Iravan remained trapped, his body violated.

They continued on one after another, one being replaced by the other.

He closed his eyes, waiting for it to end, praying for the collapse of reality.

65

AHILYA

She was a tendril, caught in the wind.

She drifted for eons, swirling away from the heat of the battle. *Becoming.*

She had a body, she knew, but she could not feel it. She was everywhere and nowhere, but then she separated. A deep, terrifying sorrow filled her. A sense of smallness.

Though her eyes were closed, she could see the rupturing of Cohesion like tiny burns in the fabric of a great consciousness, scorching the lives within. Still, she reached for its sentience, despite knowing that to be a part of it now meant pain. She did not care. She did not want to be alone. There had been belonging within Cohesion, a freedom she had craved all her life, a possibility of becoming more than the one person, the one, small, non-architect she had been. Cohesion had shown her *everything* that she could be. She did not want to be away from it. Terror filled her to be so lonely.

<*Ahilya*>, Cohesion whispered, giving her a name, an identity.

She shook her head. *No. No, no, no.* She did not want to be Ahilya. She wanted to be *it.* To be named was to become the other. *Please no,* she wept.

But with the name came meaning, a brief notion like a dream remembered.

Cohesion was breaking apart, but it still recognized her. The combined consciousness returned memory to her, and she saw herself in Nakshar, with a man she had once loved, a man she had once belonged with.

It was a message. She was not alone. Despite Cohesion's rupturing, she had always had someone else alongside her on this journey, for better or for worse. Someone else witnessing her life. Someone else who knew her, in all her shame and glory.

Like a child seeking comfort, Ahilya searched for him.

Weeping, alone, terrified, she turned, seeking him.

Reality shattered.

66

IRAVAN

He existed in a place beyond the body, for his body was not his own. It was an object, being controlled by other versions of himself.

Still, he heard her through ears that were now someone else's. He saw her through eyes that were no longer his own. Beyond the collapse of stars, and the breaking of language, he recognized her.

It was not his body anymore, but he reached forward with an intention, a will, that was still his.

He did not have arms to call his own, but he reached for her, because she was calling him, and she was a memory of trust and home. He might be nobody anymore, but like always, he was nothing without her.

67

TOGETHER

They raced toward each other across time and space. She staggered through the debris of the city, and he left the moorings of his body to tumble into her arms.

Something chased the both of them, a gaping black hole that ate away at everything. Light bounced in all directions, faces distorted, shapes meaningless. Still, they constructed meaning with the failing bindings of their minds, holding each other, though neither of them had bodies to do this with.

Layers of reality tumbled around them, the entire edifice of meaning crumbling. They found each other, but they couldn't remember. They seemed to be in the mirrored chambers, and

He looked within and saw

the falcon
Nidhirv
Bhaskar

She looked inside and felt

the vriksh
the Virohi
architects

Agni	*non-architects*
Iravan	*Cohesion*

He saw nothing.	She saw everything.

Time and reality froze.

They stared at each other, and into each other.

The broken shards of the Moment echoed, needing to knit together, seeking to know.

Who are you? they thought, a question to each other and themselves.

He blinked.	She breathed.
I am not	*I am*

the falcon	*the vriksh*
Nidhirv	*the Virohi*
Bhaskar	*architects*
Agni	*non-architects*
Iravan	*Cohesion*

A great consuming power shifted, and their two consciousnesses connected within the Moment. Separate and part of their selves, yet belonging to something greater.

Who are you? the Moment echoed, with their wonder.

The mirrors cleared.

Nothing, he wept.
Neither this. Nor that.

Everything, she sobbed.
This too. That too

They saw themselves within each other.
And the universe reflected back.

68

TOGETHER

A gargantuan AWARENESS slammed into the both of them.

Spearing through their bodies and minds, stilling *everything*.

Ahilya felt Cohesion extracted, consciousnesses tumbling into individual bodies.

Iravan saw the everpower disintegrate, and all the yakshas he'd absorbed pulled away from the falcon, their power bounding back into his body.

The last drop of everdust blossomed between the two of them, growing higher, and higher, and higher like a balloon encompassing them.

The creatures of the universe—those cosmic creatures the both of them had once been—keened in joy and exuberance, and darted everywhere within the balloon as if they were bees. They reflected everything, the planet, trees, clouds, stones, weather, a splinter of smile, a fury of grief, human faces, and yaksha shards. Cohesion had broken, and they had been released from it like everyone else. Now for the first time, they had found their form. Bound by everything, yet creatures free from everything too.

His hand found hers.

Her fingers tightened in his.

The balloon ruptured, and the buzzing of the cosmic creatures escaped into the universe beyond, but their sensation—their memory—remained, absorbed by a terrifying, ancient, overarching consciousness.

I AM, the universe whispered/blared/reflected.

Their bodies crushed together.

They wept.

Caught by each other, Iravan and Ahilya felt a cascade of overpowering, familiar emotion that they'd once named love, vibrating between them like a tangible, physical, terrifying energy.

They closed their eyes

and submitted

into nothing, and everything all at once.

Stillness shook them, overwhelming and peaceful.

The world filtered back like a song, and they floated on a river, entwined with each other, their eyes unseeing and remembering and full of stars.

69

AHILYA

She knew her eyes were closed, but somehow she could still see. She knew she had eyes. That was a good sign.

Ahilya floated within her body, but her body was everywhere. She felt the hard ground under her back, grass tickling her ears, a soft breeze lifting her hair up from her forehead. She felt other things too—the tread of her foot over a broken stone. The sensation of her roots planted deep into the soil. The movements of plates underneath the earth, and the striations of water somewhere. The boundaries of her mind extended to the whole planet, and the effect was calming and disorienting. It was as if she were one of Dhruv's drones, capable of seeing it all yet focusing and magnifying on one thing at a time, to see it in completion. She knew if she opened her eyes this sensation would come to a standstill. This was the last time she would feel this—the certainty permeated her. She savored her existence in this haze fully. *The moment before birth*, she thought. *This is what it must feel like.*

When she was ready, she finally opened her eyes.

At first, she was confused. She was staring into the sky, but all she saw was a floating miasma of orange, gray, and blue. This was another shard of broken reality. The nightmare had not ended. She felt a great fear rake over her

Then, the miasma shifted and she glimpsed a rising dawn. She realized she was looking at clouds. Gray clouds, not stormy but cleansing. A soft rain began to pour and she inhaled the scent of petrichor, breathing deeply with *her* lungs, feeling *her* chest rise and fall. She had been everything and everyone, but there was a personal, sacred pleasure in acknowledging her body now, the one she had lived within all her life.

Slowly, she pushed herself up to her elbows. She was on a hill near a plain of grass, but not too far from her the earth had been ripped by massive craters. Streams of water trickled into the holes, making deep wells that cascaded into clear ponds. Humongous rocks the size of mountains lay everywhere, veined with tree roots. As she watched, grass covered them rapidly. The rocks grew smaller, until they were reabsorbed by the earth, making the landscape level. She felt the lilting, cascading flow of movement underneath her, the rock still settling into the soil.

The jungle had completely retreated from where she sat. She watched it retreat further, far from her plain of grass—finally becoming a separate entity. She thought she could hear an ocean somewhere. *An ocean,* she thought wonderingly. As an archeologist, she'd always assumed oceans existed well below the surface of the planet, for how else would a jungle thrive without water. Yet it was astonishing to think that they could now see those oceans. That they were likely surrounded by them, the whole planet turned inside out and self-correcting into something more inhabitable. Reality was mending, the principle of physical laws reasserting. She had woken to a new world, and much of the landscape was different. She would have to begin anew, trying to understand its climate.

Flowers erupted around her, and Ahilya touched a wild daffodil in a wondrous haze. There were no bees here yet, but she knew it was only a matter of time. Life had survived; it was obvious because she was here, living. Life they'd brought back from the skies on landing, and one that would free itself in this new world. Around her hill more buds poked out of the ground, so that soon she was surrounded by a field of white flowers. Ahilya inhaled, breathing in the rain and the unseen ocean. Her eyes burned with tears of catharsis.

Beyond this startling beauty, the last city of humanity arose.

Irshar, the Garden, whatever they chose to call this dwelling, was far from where she sat, but Ahilya could still see massive spires rising, and pieces of rubble strewn across the city. People moved along the streets, looking like small dots, but Ahilya sharpened her perception so they loomed in front of her, crying with sorrow and joy, a woman hugging another, others already beginning rescue efforts for those trapped by the wreckage. The city was a broken mess of roots and branches, and a group of citizens were ripping apart a tree-cage, helping others out from the boughs. Several citizens appeared unhurt, though dust and earth caked everyone's faces. A massive tree rose from the city still in remembrance of the vriksh and Cohesion. Its trunk was marred down the middle, as if lightning had struck it. As Ahilya watched, the tree started to wither. The edges of it grew blurry. Slowly, slowly, dust cascaded from it. This last core tree had done all it could. Now it rested, and Ahilya felt its relief and joy inside her as if it were her own.

She dropped her sharpened perception. It made her breathless to hold it too long. She stared at the city, a hunger in her. There was a synchronicity of movement within it, which seemed so familiar. As if all the people within were working in tandem, with no need to speak. As if they could read each other's thoughts and knew their intents as well as they knew themselves. Instinctively she knew it was a lingering effect of Cohesion. If she wanted, perhaps she could reach their awareness, and join it. But she remained apart for now, merely watching.

She wondered how she had come to be here, all alone on this plain. She had been a part of the tree, hadn't she? Reality had melted. Who or what had righted it?

She couldn't remember, and she let the questions die. She simply sat there, feeling at peace, feeling the drizzle. The rain was light, just enough to melt into her clothes and skin, refreshing her, and she reveled in the silence. Whatever was occurring with the synchronicity felt natural. Her third vision seemed to have faded away. For that too, Ahilya was grateful.

Eventually she became aware that she was not alone. Ahilya turned her head and saw, not a few feet away, another body lying spreadeagled on his back.

Iravan stared up at the sky, tears leaking from the sides of his face. His breathing was slow and he didn't make a move toward her, though one hand was outstretched in her direction, as if only minutes ago they had been touching each other. His other palm lay loosely curled. Something shone inside it, like the tiniest, most precious pearl. He did not seem to notice her, and she took her time, not seeking his attention, but merely content to study him.

He looked… changed. Pieces of him were familiar, taken from different times in his life, as if reality had been unable to decide which one was really Iravan. He was just as handsome as ever, his dark skin the same almost-black. His hair was no longer silvery though—instead, his salt-and-pepper locks had returned, except a shock of bright gray fell across his forehead as if to declare to everyone that he was not the man from Nakshar, but someone else, someone evolved. His clothes were the black of an Ecstatic, but they were riddled with the slashes of the brightest white. Reality had solidified him into this image, his choices and coercion coexisting. Ahilya did not know what it meant for his future.

He turned slowly toward her, and she saw then that his eyes were black again. The silver was gone, but when she looked deeper, she thought she could see sparks of gray still lurking inside. His fingers twitched toward her, and slowly he sat up. Ahilya extended her hand. She touched him, and loosely he stroked her palm.

"Are you all right?" she asked softly

"No," he said. Then after a long time, after a deep, shaky breath. "Yes. Yes. Are you?"

She could not form the words, but he seemed to understand. Iravan nodded, and his eyes returned to the sky. Tears still fell down his face, but either he did not notice them or he did not care to wipe them.

Neither of them spoke for a long time.

"Is it over?" he finally whispered.

"It's over," she confirmed.

"Then we survived."

She looked back to the city, where more people released others from the remains of the battle. "Many of us, yes. Did reality?"

It was a foolish question perhaps, but Ahilya had experienced too much to not ask it.

"I—I think so," he said. "Do you remember much?"

Wisps of memories floated across her mind. The ferocity of the planetrage. The unity of Cohesion. The utter reality-shattering presence of dissolution that made her chest heave with wrongness. And then, beyond it, a terrifying, massive, utterly inhuman sentience.

"That awareness," Ahilya said, choking. "What was it?"

Iravan turned to her, and there was fresh awe and shock in his eyes. "I—I don't know. Did it feel like... What did it feel like to you?"

She tried to remember. The unspeakable, gargantuan awareness, so full of power that power itself was a small word for it, crushing her, surrounding her, then mirroring her.

"It felt like a great eye," she whispered. "Indifferent, immense, terrifying and benevolent, all at once. I felt every inch of myself, every pore, but more than that." It was hard to explain, even to him. The definition of who she was had expanded, beyond Cohesion into the whole universe. She felt it inside her, an unbearable emptiness that felt so very full too.

"I was everything," she said, at last.

"Yes," he said.

"Did you feel it too?"

"Yes," he said again. "Yes."

They fell into silence, each of them lost to their thoughts. Iravan's fingers skated over hers, and she gripped them tightly. Perhaps he was feeling the same thing she was. How was one to recover from such an experience? She stared into the sky, mirroring him, rain falling on her, and for an instant she saw beyond the reaches of the planet into a kaleidoscope of stars, the rhythms of the universe moving to the cadence of a personal, echoing, everlasting song. Ahilya wanted to speak, to shift the mood, but she felt caught in the moment. She wanted to tear apart from it, but she was too absorbed. A profound sense of immensity enveloped her, cushioning her, and she knew that she would never be the same again.

When Iravan spoke, it was a comfort.

His voice was husky, as if it was only supreme will that wrenched the words from him. "What happened to the Virohi?" he rasped. "I saw them, and…"

"They're free," she said, knowing it only when she spoke it. The words came easier now that she'd begun. The immense presence drifted away, though she knew she could be absorbed by it if she only allowed herself to.

"I don't understand how," she continued, "but the Virohi became one with that awareness. They saw their true form."

"And with them, so did we," he murmured. "So did we."

She nodded. "I—I did not know that we could become something like that."

She felt for the awareness, and it was a comfort to know that she could wrap herself in it. *We are so much more than we've ever known*, she thought. *Why did we forget this? Why did we never seek to know this?* Tears gushed down her face, and she wiped them away, her breath catching. She had always sought an expansion of her identity in hoping to become like the architects. She'd seen the familiarity of the Virohi, found them to resonate with her. She had never imagined this.

"That immensity…" she said. "We saw—we became—the universe."

"Yes."

"And the Virohi allowed me to see the universe in this way?" Ahilya asked, grasping for understanding.

Iravan nodded slowly. "In a way, you allowed each other. It couldn't have happened without you. You were right about the Virohi. You said they were attracted to the Moment, and the Moment has ever been a universe. The Virohi were cosmic creatures, their consciousness as large as a universe too, and it was no coincidence they found form in the Moment, to split within it to become architects and yakshas. They have been seeking that form, a thing that is not truly a form at all, so massive and all-consuming that it is everywhere and everything. They destroyed each Moment of other planets, always seeking, never finding. When they finally found it, they showed it to you. For you have been a part of them ever since you gave them your identity."

"Then this vision of the universe was their gift to me in return?"

"No more or less than your understanding of them was your gift to them," Iravan said, smiling a little. "The Virohi evolved because of you, because you saw them as one of you. You gave them your form, your memories, and you saw them as worthy of protection from the very beginning. You alone could have done something like this, because of the kind of person you are. On their own, the Virohi were on a doomed mission. Sooner or later, they would have destroyed the whole universe, thousands of planets, all because they would have been unable to find their universal form. Sooner or later, they would have devolved into their worst versions. But with you... You stopped them and freed them by embracing them."

Iravan's voice was quiet, but still the immensity of what he was saying terrified her. Ahilya's thoughts buzzed. He was not speaking of the Virohi alone. He was speaking of himself, and the redemption she had given both him and the cosmic creatures. She had helped the Virohi when no one would—helped *Iravan* when no one would—but Cohesion had helped *her.* Without the others, she would have been able to do nothing—she could see that now, for all of the journey she had taken to get here. How close they had all come to disintegrating.

So many steps and missteps, she thought. She was grateful she did not know the immensity of her responsibility in the beginning. Her fingers curled around the heartpoison bracelet still on her wrist, and it came apart in her hands, crumbling into ash. Her mission fulfilled, her vow complete. To release the Virohi, and to give them to Iravan, share them with him in a way.

"If the Virohi gave me this access to the universe," she said haltingly, "then how did you experience it too? You were disconnected from the Virohi. You were never part of Cohesion. But I felt you too."

"I came to it from a different path," he said softly. "I think a part of me always wanted erasure. I just did not understand the kind of erasure I sought. I thought erasure meant a meaninglessness of life, no significance and value to anything we did. As an architect, I wished freedom from the hold everything had over me, my past, my future, all the expectations I've lived with, my own and those of others. But that was never the erasure I truly sought. I sought this—the ability to be nothing, while being everything all at once."

He fell into silence. Ahilya had promised the council of Irshar she would bring Iravan erasure, but she hadn't known the truth of that promise. She recalled what Basav had told her about Ecstatics and their capital desire. *It is about fulfilling a need. Until it is fulfilled, the Ecstatic Architect can never be free.*

And that freedom—in the end, that is the only thing an Ecstatic needs.

They knew, she thought. *The architects of the old knew.* Perhaps Basav had forgotten what that freedom meant, or maybe he hadn't known, but the early architects did.

Iravan seemed to be following the same thought.

"I remember vestiges," he said, his fingertips flickering on his cheeks as if he could recapture the images. "Memories of memories, too shaded to make any sense. I questioned what happened to Ecstatics in their last life, those who united and subsumed their yakshas, but I think I understand now. In Nidhirv's time, they reunited with their yakshas freely, and society was in balance. It was bred into their philosophy to attain that universal form, and I think their capital desires had been one thing and one thing alone, wrought by their culture. Their capital desire *was* for unity, nothing beyond that, a fulfillment that occurred when they found their yakshas, instantaneously. I don't know for sure, I am disconnected from my past lives now, but I think for them unity and subsummation with their yakshas happened together. Their combined desire was reborn back into the universe, the same way they would bring the Virohi into birth, and the body of both yakshas and architects would nourish the soil in a voluntary act of death. The true meaning and purpose of an ashram. To return to the fold, to the universe's embrace."

Ahilya imagined it, as if she were seeing all this in one of those ancient architect records like a picture. An architect looking up at the sky. A universe wheeling above, stars and light brightening, but behind it the energy of that immense consciousness, breathing the same breath as the architects.

"To do such a thing," she breathed. "We have experienced it now too, but to think such a thing commonplace..." It brought tears to her eyes. How much had been lost and forgotten.

"They had tremendous power back then," Iravan said. "You know the kinds of trajection they could do, things we could never do in our airborne ashrams—do you remember we saw amazing trajection back in those first carvings within the habitat? I never understood how much power they had then, but trajection is a matter of will, and their will, their consciousness, their culture, was more unified than ours. Nidhirv was a being of great power, all architects back then had been. We were not, so when all of you became Cohesion, your mind unified by it, a single strengthened thing, you—Ahilya—mimicked what the early architects always did. Though you separated from Cohesion, you found the strength to fold your consciousness into the universe, all in the pursuit of knowing yourself, evolving and freeing yourself. The Virohi used this event to finally achieve that which they were meant to do from the very start."

"The early architects did it unto death, though," she murmured. "We didn't die."

"You almost did," Iravan said, reminding her quietly. "And

some parts of you did. Something must always die for there to be a new birth."

Ahilya looked to the city, and the remnants of the vriksh. The tree was gone now, ruptured from the outside, still slowly withering into ash. The vriksh had protected her. It had completed her. Containing all of humanity, it had cushioned her from everything that had threatened to take her under, reminding her that people and their memories were fleeting, but this shared tradition—this immense, beautiful, shared experience—was still hers to tap into.

She and Iravan had changed their culture and their species irrevocably. Birth and death had always been central to their lives, but how far they had taken it. From their arguments for a child, to the one they had almost borne, to this—a step taken for all of them.

She still felt the cadence with the rest of humanity, the accord of movement, the harmony of thought. Each of them their own person, but moving in synchronization. Perhaps the withering of the tree was a gift. To take with them into the world what the tree contained inside. The past was gone. Maybe in this changed world, there was comfort in that.

"Then the Virohi are in the universe now," she said softly. "The Virohi *are* the universe now."

"Yes."

"But then—" A horrible thought struck her, as she recalled the worst of what she had been. The worse of what humanity had been. "Their infection, and our hatred—did we harm—did we contaminate—" The words slipped from her. She couldn't complete her thought, horrified.

Iravan shook his head. "Infinity absorbing infinity," he said softly. "You didn't harm the universe. You could not."

It was perhaps deeply arrogant and presumptuous that she should think that *she,* this small insignificant thing, could hurt the universe, but Iravan did not laugh at her. He took her hand in his, interlacing their fingers, and squeezed. "Take comfort," he said softly. "They did this back in Nidhirv's time too. This was the purpose of an ashram. You did not change it. You returned the cosmic creatures to their home. Manav knew it, I think. *Awakening occurs beyond time,* he wrote in his poetry. He must have known of this true purpose of an Ecstatic. The Moment is repaired, or perhaps gone altogether, submerged into that ocean of awareness. I can't know, but I don't sense it anymore, neither that nor the Deepness. I think it is a sign—architects don't need to sense it anymore, much like the complete beings, because we don't need to manipulate those realms anymore toward our own unity. We have achieved that unity, and now birth and rebirth will occur as they always have. Human beings will continue to reincarnate. We will all of us finally be well and truly complete."

Iravan had spoken of Manav's poetry before, and she had her own memories of it, from a time she had held Bharavi's book. She could feel his wonder in his words, this man who had worried about Bharavi's rebirth too. If all he said was true, then she would be born again, this time with no need to traject or seek her yaksha, but complete, right from birth.

Balance is an unheard rhythm, Ahilya thought, remembering. *We continue to live, in undying separate illusions.* She had seen that poetry back when Bharavi's book had been in her care. Iravan had studied it, mentioned the lines to her long ago too, when they'd been trying to work together in Nakshar to save Nakshar. She understood now finally what the words meant. Manav had lamented the separation of people—of architects, non-architects, of all consciousness from the consciousness of the universe. Yet people were not divorced anymore from themselves and each other. Cohesion had come to an end, but their minds had aligned in amazing ways, human finally in all their humanity. Perhaps Manav had survived the planetrage.

If so, she would go to him. She would tell him they'd won. Perhaps he would be proud.

"Do you think Manav could have imagined all of this would occur?" she asked softly.

Iravan sighed deeply. "He could not have. So much of this occurred because of one slip, one monumental choice. But Manav is—has always been—more complicated than any of us could guess. He came to my rescue through his yakshas twice, and I imagined him to have more than one yaksha, but I never could imagine why. I think I understand now. Manav sought freedom from his capital desire too—a desire that had imprisoned him for lifetimes. It was that which split his yaksha into two in the first place, perhaps in a lifetime lived long ago. Instead of fulfilling one desire, he found a way to break the desire down. Architects have been defined by our need to control the world, but Manav tried to simply understand. I wish to be like that myself dearly."

"We lost so much knowledge," she said. "Because for some reason, they outlawed Ecstasy long ago. Because they upset that balance, and stopped returning to the universe what they had taken. If things had only gone that way, Manav would never have had to split his capital desire. The cosmic creatures would never have unleashed such destruction."

"They outlawed Ecstasy because of me," Iravan said. "Because of me and Manav, in a way. It was Nidhirv and Vishwam who envisioned a path of divergence first, away from the culture of their ashram. They could not have known where it would lead, and perhaps they were not the only people to think this way, perhaps there were other pressures of the time too. But the change occurred because of a marriage Manav and I shared once." His voice trembled, and tears filled his eyes. "It is a knowledge that will haunt me for the rest of my days."

Ahilya stared at him, shocked. To think that Manav had been associated with Iravan through lifetimes. To think that they had followed each other through so many cycles of consciousness. "If Manav is Vishwam reborn," she said in a low voice. "Does it mean you two were destined to be together?"

She could hear her own distress, but Iravan's hand clutched hers tighter.

"No," he whispered. "No, that's not how birth and rebirth work. Bharavi studied these things, as did Manav, as did I. Once in a different time, Nidhirv and Vishwam were married, they were lovers, they made vows—strong vows to each other, as strong as the ones you and I did. And perhaps Vishwam's desire to find Nidhirv was so great, carving such a deep imprint into Vishwam's own consciousness, that it resembled a capital desire. It is what led his future incarnations to always hover around Nidhirv's consciousness. Around my consciousness. That is why he protected me—one half of him wishing for freedom from everything, the other half compelled to keep me safe. It does not mean that Manav and I were destined for each other, only that we shared a past. Manav had a family, sons and daughter, and he was very much in love with his spouse. Vishwam—from another life—could not be allowed to dictate that. The dead should not be allowed to hold the living hostage." Iravan breathed in deeply. "It is another thing I have learned, no longer a hostage to my own capital desire. We are free, Ahilya. We are free."

The explanation reverberated in Ahilya's mind for long seconds. She squeezed his hand, and he returned the gesture, then the both of them fell still again.

"We've woken to a strange world," she whispered finally.

"One rich with possibility again," he answered, and she knew what he meant. Everdust had once been depleted, and with it possibility had left the world, but everdust had come into being when two halves became a whole. Not the half of yakshas and architects like they'd imagined before, but that of the Virohi and the universe. She'd worked this out herself in the last few minutes.

"We had it wrong," she said, nodding. "The architects who built the habitat, they didn't just stop the earthrages and trap the Virohi in the Moment. They must have released the Virohi into the universe. That is how they created everdust."

"Yes," Iravan said, sighing. "I think so too. That is why I never found another cosmic creature trapped in the Moment other than the one that you and I trapped. Those ancient architects and citizens understood and remembered what so many generations before them didn't. Perhaps they used a similar method to Cohesion. Everdust has returned to our world now, though we cannot use it. Trajection is finally over."

A strange emotion lurked underneath his words. Ahilya wondered if it was regret—he could have done so much with the manipulation of possibility—but Iravan's face was relaxed. His other palm curved protectively around whatever he was holding. The blade of stone around his neck was missing. He'd likely used it in his repair of the Moment.

"You said your past lives are cut off from you," she said. "Then is the falcon gone?"

"The falcon and all the yakshas were released with the Virohi," he confirmed. "For you it was an embracing. For me, negation, a release of all that I once was. In the end, it is the the same thing."

"Nothing," she said. "And everything."

He only smiled at this echo of his own words. The breeze lifted the shock of silver hair from his face, and he breathed deeply, closing his eyes. Ahilya looked to the city in front of her and the jungle beyond, and her heart began to race, in recognition of the great inevitability. She couldn't bear to see him now, in all his beauty and honesty. He had looked like this all that time ago when they'd married each other. This was the man she loved, and he was here now with her, finally. *Finally.*

"There is so much still to do," she murmured. "Cohesion has fragmented though I still feel a resonance with it." She saw him smile from the corner of her eye, and Ahilya smiled too, at her use of this word. "We are changed as a species in some profound way. I don't know in what form, but I think all of us understand each other better. If trajection is truly gone now, then we will need another form of energy. I suppose we can build something from all this."

She did turn to him then, and saw that he was smiling fondly. Iravan lifted her hand, his fingers still laced within hers, and kissed her softly.

Then, slowly, ever so slowly, he let go.

"Eskayra is waiting for you, I think," he said softly.

"Yes."

"And you want to go to her, don't you?"

Did she? Surely, if Eskayra was alive, she would be hunting the city for her, waiting for her. Perhaps the others too—Naila and Dhruv and Chaiyya, maybe even Basav. She thought of Esk's relief. She thought of the future they could now have. She imagined it was Esk's hand in hers, and then she saw Iravan. The high cheekbones, the curling hair, and his eyes that still leaked with intermittent tears. Everything she had experienced, and endured, and become, all of it had occurred with this man restored to her. If there had ever been any hope for them, this is where it all started. This is where it all returned.

"What do *you* want?" she finally asked.

Iravan grinned, soft and boyish, full of dry amusement. "Me?" he said lightly. "Ever the same thing, my dear. Children, and domesticity, and a life with you. If I could, I would live forever as your husband.

That is what I hoped to do with the blade of pure possibility. But I don't think you want that, and I don't think you should. I am not sure I should either. I have only come to an understanding of myself now. I need time to gather my pieces, examine which are from the past, which are really mine. It is something I should have done a long time ago."

So much had changed, but in some ways he had not. This was an Iravan answer, through and through. Ahilya was grateful. It could not be any other way, but she did not want to hurt him.

"You will be all right then?" she asked.

"I will."

"What will you do?"

Iravan lay back, his head resting on his hands as he gazed at the sunlit sky. She thought she could see the entire universe shining in his eyes, a kaleidoscope of stars.

"I think," he said softly. "I think I will lay here a time."

She stared at the image of this man, handsome and free for the first time ever. Her heart brimmed with so much love, that she thought she might explode. Before she could change her mind, Ahilya hurried away, descending the hill.

She was near the bottom when she heard his voice again, drifting on the breeze. A last question, one that caught her by surprise.

"Wait. I need to know. Do you regret it?"

Ahilya did not turn back, but she stopped. Images cascaded over her, of the many years, and the many seasons she and Iravan had gone through.

"Several things," she whispered finally. "But not you. Never you."

She heard a soft huff of laughter, part awe, part disbelief. He was there, a part of her now. Just as she was of him. Nothing would erase that.

Ahilya walked down the hill, toward her new beginning.

EPILOGUE
DHRUV

He tromped through the jungle, pushing past tall weeds irritably. Even in the worst of times, after Irshar had crash-landed, he had disdained the jungle, instead keeping to the Garden's solar lab. To have to come to it now, when there was no need to, irked him so much that he kicked a passing shrub, only to have it entangle his foot.

Dhruv let out a part grunt, part groan, hobbling away from the foliage, brushing past a thick swarm of mite-flies. What was he doing, responding to a summons here of all places? Kiana would be wondering where he was. He was supposed to meet her to discuss the future of sungineering and the city. Life had begun again with the constant rains. Some people had ventured far beyond the city and found the ocean. Fruit trees had been discovered, and a rudimentary form of agriculture was beginning, but with the loss of trajection they relied on fire and candles to light their evenings. It was a personal insult, after everything sungineering had once achieved. He should be back in the city with Kiana and the others, trying to cobble together a technology for the future of humanity. Instead, here he was, brushing spiderwebs from his face.

He had been so surprised to receive the message, he'd sat staring at it for long minutes before beginning his trek to the jungle. He hadn't even bothered to bring a coat, and that was unlike him.

Well? Could he be blamed? No one had heard from Iravan in months. Yet somehow the man had known which house was Dhruv's, and left a message unseen. *Typical,* Dhruv thought sourly. Reality had changed, but Iravan had remained the same. He could not tell if he was annoyed or relieved.

Dhruv was out of breath when he finally found Iravan kneeling in a clearing, his hands filthy, sleeves covered in mud though they were rolled back. The man was smiling as he studied his handiwork. The sapling he'd planted was small, barely a foot high, but wild and leafy, white buds nearly ready to bloom. Dhruv inhaled, and smelled jasmine. This again? He felt his annoyance grow. What was Iravan's plan now—to somehow seduce Ahilya again? She was happy now. Dhruv had been to her wedding, this one with a person he actually liked.

He loomed over Iravan, and crossed his arms. "And where have you been all along?" he asked, scowling by way of greeting.

Iravan laughed, then rose, dusting his hands. He reached over and embraced Dhruv, and it was so surprising, so awkward, that Dhruv froze. When Iravan stepped back, Dhruv took a few hurried steps back, lest Iravan do it again.

"Sorry," Iravan said, mirth in his eyes. "I should have asked, but by rages, it is good to see your face. Though I suppose, I can't really say 'by rages' anymore, can I?" He burst into laughter, and Dhruv's eyebrows rose.

What the fuck, he thought. Had Iravan finally cracked? Dhruv had never seen him this way, childlike, exuberant, mischievous. The man was practically bouncing on his toes. He was almost effervescent. A startling thought came to Dhruv that Iravan had never looked as charming. No wonder Ahilya had fallen for him once.

"Are you all right?" he asked cautiously.

"Yes, yes," Iravan said, waving a hand. Then he leaned in as if they were surrounded by a thousand people instead of alone in the wretched jungle. "Can you keep a secret?"

"What do you know about me?" Dhruv replied dryly.

That made Iravan chuckle again, but to Dhruv's great relief it was short-lived. "I found something," Iravan said. Dhruv's eyebrows climbed higher and higher, as the man related a tale of more ashrams he'd found, "—not ashrams, they don't call themselves that anymore—" and cities orbiting the earth, "—airships, perhaps—" from one of the other bands of society.

"Nakshar and the sister cities were just one band," Iravan ended, his eyes gleaming. "We fell from the skies, as did many others perhaps, but the highest bands—ones we never heard from are alive. They ascended the planet long ago, centuries ago, high into the edges of the atmosphere beyond the gravity of our planet. They ascended trajection."

Dhruv's eyes widened. "Then we are not the last of our species."

"No," Iravan said, grinning. "No, we are not."

Questions blinded Dhruv, too many to track. What had those cities experienced during the turmoil? Had they felt anything? Had they seen the planetrage from so high up? Why hadn't they helped? Why had they abandoned all the others? Iravan seemed to know more than he was telling, but didn't offer it. *Typical*, Dhruv thought again, but he didn't ask either. What would be the point?

"How do you know this?" he demanded instead.

Iravan looked at him. Then, with a wink, he rose into the air, hovering a few feet off the ground, before coming back down next to Dhruv.

Dhruv gasped. "You retained the everpower?"

"No—not that," Iravan said. "But something else. When the falcon and the others used the blade of everdust, they wished for each of their desires to be fulfilled. But all those desires were all demands of power, and they made their way into me, my body, fulfilling in their own way with the everdust my past lives used. And now, I have this—this new thing. This new life." He shuddered, his mirth temporarily forgotten. "I don't like to think of that time too much," he admitted. "Their presence was a violation. I am simply grateful for the gift."

Dhruv did not probe. Long ago, he had learned not to interfere where he shouldn't, and he had no desire to learn of Iravan's experience.

"Is this what you wanted to tell me?" he asked.

"No," Iravan said. "I wanted to give you something. When I was up there, in the higher atmosphere learning of these cities, I… I made something. I had one last sliver of everdust remaining. And I asked it to become this—a gift for you, and for the rest of them."

From his pocket, Iravan withdrew a small hard stone, the size of his fingernail. Dhruv accepted it, bringing it close to his eyes. The stone gleamed, not a stone at all but something else, latticed with a crisscross pattern. It blinked golden, and felt warm in his hands despite the coolness of the jungle. It almost looked like—

"The sun's energy," Iravan said, clearly unable to contain himself. "It works on the sun's energy."

Dhruv looked up slowly, from the stone to Iravan.

Iravan's eyes glittered, reflecting the strange stone. "You can really be a *sun*gineer," he said.

A slow smile crept on Dhruv's face. "You insane, wonderful man," he breathed.

Birds burst out of the foliage, squawking, and the jungle reverberated with the sound of both men's laughter.

GLOSSARY

- **Allvision:** The melted reality that shows the Moment, the Deepness, and any other extradimensional planes as a single sludge. An objective reality unlike the subjective reality of the Evervision.
- **Cosmic creatures:** Creatures from another dimension who cause earthrages. An earthrage occurs when a cosmic creature splits itself, and only stops when the split is complete. The split portions of cosmic creatures become trajecting architects and yakshas.
- **Conduit:** An extradimensional reality available only to those who can traject. Often visualized as a tunnel that connects the Moment and the Deepness.
- **Deepness, The:** An extradimensional reality available only to those who can traject Ecstatically. The Deepness is an infinite black space where the Moment can be summoned. One can move from the Moment into the Deepness using the Conduit.
- **Etherium:** A third vision of reality that manifests itself between an individual's brows. Unlike the Moment or the Deepness, this is available to non-architects as well as architects. Unlike the Moment or the Deepness, which are shared realities, each person has a unique Etherium personal to them.

- **Everdust:** Green dust of pure possibility that presents itself in select places as physical glittering green dust, and in the Moment as stars.
- **Everpower:** The power to manipulate the elements, consciousness, and any basis of reality through one's desire.
- **Evervision:** An extradimensional reality available only to those architects who have subsumed their counterpart yakshas. Within the evervision, one can view the Moment, the Deepness, and the Etherium side by side and simultaneously.
- **Excision:** The act of cutting an architect from their trajection, both in the Moment or the Deepness. Traditionally a punishment for Ecstatic architects. It has recently been hypothesized that excision cuts architects away from their counterpart yakshas as well.
- **Garden, The:** A location in the habitat, shaped like a garden.
- **Heartpoison:** A plant that grows in the jungle, poisonous enough to harm a yaksha. Fatal to humans.
- **Irshar:** The last ashram of humanity.
- **Mirrored chambers, The:** A place within the Etherium where one speaks to the cosmic creatures.
- **Moment, The**: An extradimensional reality only available to architects. The Moment is infinite, and contains the literal possibilities of all living things within it which are represented as frozen stars. Traditionally, architects are trained only to see the stars of plants in the Moment, which is how they manipulate them. Architects themselves enter the Moment as dust motes. As living things, they also have their own infinite possibilities represented as stars within the Moment, though most architects are not trained to see that.
- **Resonance, The:** The falcon-yaksha's form in the Deepness, the Moment and the Conduit.

- **Solarchamber:** A sungineering invention that looks like a room but is made of bio-nodes.
- **Supertrajection:** Ecstatic trajection.
- **Trajection:** The power used by architects when they build constellation lines within the Moment to connect different stars to each other, which in turn changes the form of those living creatures within normal reality. Trajection energy is different from Ecstatic energy. Trajection is also sometimes used as an overarching term to refer to trajection proper as well as Ecstatic trajection.
- **Virohi:** The cosmic creatures.
- **Vriksh:** A singular core tree for Irshar created out of the merged trees of the sister ashrams.

AUTHOR'S NOTE

Now that the story is over, I see how long it has lived in me. The seed of the idea for *The Rages Trilogy* came to me almost two decades ago when I had an identity crisis. As people do in such times, I turned to my heritage for answers.

For me, this was a return.

I was raised in a Hindu household where, though my family practised our traditions and pujas, we thought of gods and goddesses not existing as true historic people, but concepts that were personified. Mythology was everywhere—but more importantly, so was philosophy—and it is one thing I always correct when people ask me about the trilogy; that it is based on Hindu philosophy, not mythology.

In Hindu philosophy, the search for one's identity is ultimately a spiritual journey. In ancient India, ashrams were places of spiritual awakening and enlightenment—literally hermitages and monasteries, often within a forest or in the mountains, where seers called rishis would live with their disciples and train them in meditation. Through such meditation, one could achieve oneness with the universe.

The idea of universal oneness permeates Hinduism. In some schools of thought, one's personal consciousness is referred to as Atman—spirit, while the universe's consciousness, that which is infinite, aware, intelligent, and ever-watching, is referred to as Brahman. No matter how these concepts are dissected and discussed, one foundation is common—that both the individual consciousness and the universal consciousness are effectively the same thing.

In the Yogasutras of Patanjali, an academic treatise of the philosophies and practices of yoga, one which was compiled nearly three thousand years ago, this universal consciousness is called Isvara. Jiddu Krishnamurthy, a modern-day scholar, referred to the universe's awareness as a truth, which was a pathless land—which one could come to not through certain practices, but through simply opening oneself to such awareness. In the Upanishads—Vedic texts which speak to meditation and ontology—this concept is often a matter of self-realization. To rise beyond physical phenomenology to view the universe, while acknowledging that physical phenomenology is intertwined with the universe.

All of it one indivisible existence, if only a person could view it like that.

One approach of arriving to spiritual oneness that I came across is the concept of *Neti Neti,* which literally means "not this, not that." It is a concept that encompasses the limitation of the human mind to grasp the awareness of the universe in language and thought—and as a spiritual practice, it is the process of constantly separating oneself from one's surroundings, identities, environment, and objects in life—everything that defines oneself, including thought—so that one may transcend the limitations of labels and language, and ultimately become *Iti Iti,* "this too, that too." Or in other words, the universe.

This concept of two opposites intersecting and interacting, where one cannot know themselves without the other, where one completes the other—this is where Iravan and Ahilya came from, and why I decided very early in the work that they would be married.

Marriage in Hindu history and culture has always been a sacred tradition. This is not to say that relationships of love that exist outside of marriage are not important; in fact, stories of ancient India are rife with such relationships, Krishna and Radha being easy examples. However, marriage itself was understood as a deep bond. In ancient times, it was considered a bond that could hold a person grounded—to society, community, and civilization.

Spiritual awakening often existed in competition with such a bond. Hinduism is a culture of embracing several points of view (often simultaneously!) and while there are certainly texts and stories where spiritual awakening can occur in concert with these bonds, the journey of Iravan and Ahilya's marriage took inspiration from the texts which pitted the holds of society against spiritual awakening. One path needed to be abandoned to pursue the other.

Of course, this abandonment was not treated callously. In fact, many schools of thought believed that a person had to go through as many stages of life as were offered to them before seeking spiritual awakening—to become a householder, a parent, an artist, a trader, a politician, a leader—anything that held one committed to society, *before* leaving society to search for oneself. Services to community were important, and acceptance into a true ashram often took place after one had fulfilled their role to community; to do so otherwise was often sacrilegious. This thesis inspired the heart of Ahilya and Iravan's relationship—the conflict of a seeker wishing for more, while being tied to society. Both Ahilya and Iravan interpreted it in their own ways. From *Neti Neti* to *Iti Iti*. Both of them seeking.

In Hinduism, seeking that spiritual awareness is often considered a person's highest calling. It is a desire that lives within every consciousness—*soul,* if we are to use that word—to reunite with the greater whole. A desire that transcends lifetimes and manifests through multiple rebirths.

Birth and rebirth form a cornerstone of *The Rages Trilogy,* inspired directly from reincarnation being such a basic tenet of Hinduism. Reincarnation in Hinduism implies karma—the unfulfilled desires of a past life manifesting in the future—though, in the West, this concept has been appropriated and mutilated so deeply that the word itself holds no meaning anymore. People often think of karma as a balance of the universe for good to occur to good people, and evil to evil people—as if good and evil were not simply functions and definitions of the time period and society one lived in, but were unshakeable truths of the universe. The true understanding of karma is something more subtle that that—a strong desire containing an energy so deep it creates a memory imprint in the subtle states of consciousness that then cycle into birth. It is this energy of desire that inspired the relationship of a yaksha and an architect.

Ultimately, *The Rages Trilogy* is a work of speculative fiction.

It is peppered with many references, but I don't claim to be an expert of the philosophies it borrows from. While the heart of the series is inspired by texts, songs, studies, and stories spanning over four thousand years, I relied on my modern-day imagination, making plot decisions based on the fantasy world of the books. Seen in one way, the entire trilogy is a manifesto of attempting to reach universal oneness, the pitfalls and side quests, the dangers, the sacrifices, and ultimately the relationship such a journey has with real, breathing, everyday life. But seen in another way, it is simply another work of fiction—a rich, weird, fever dream of a series that provides entertainment and thought for the right kind of reader. For me, it is both.

In an SFF landscape rich with mythos and philosophies from the Western world, I am honored and humbled to offer a piece of my own culture for your interpretation.

ACKNOWLEDGEMENTS

Of all the books I've written, this one was the hardest to write.

Through critical burnout, pregnancies and birth, day-job hustle, health concerns, a cross-country move, multiple competing deadlines, and heaven knows what else... this book made it through. Still kind of hard to believe as I write these acknowledgments.

My deepest thanks to George Sandison, first and foremost. Dear friend, brilliant editor, and total nerd—thank you for consistently making me a better writer, for taming a wild, incoherent manuscript into this epic finale, for working late nights and holidays, for being so flexible with timings and schedules, and for just being an overall wonderful human being. This series that I am so proud of would not have made it without you. Thank you as well to the wider Titan team: Kabriya, Charlotte, Katherine, Rachel, Hannah, Kate, Adrian, Julia, and every other team member who has worked on this trilogy.

Thanks to Lucienne Diver and The Knight Agency for never losing faith in me through my own crises of confidence. For continuing to advocate for me, chasing up translations and admin work, and for being super communicative through this journey. It is a great comfort knowing there is someone so accountable, methodical, and professional watching out for me.

Thanks to my writing crew and The Sprint Server, Aparna

Verma, Elyse John, Chelsea Conradt, Gabriela Romero Lacruz, and MJ Kuhn. Your late-night commiseration through our writing sprints got me over the finish line. Drafting this was difficult, but I showed up because I had you for company. It is a gift to have such invested, brilliant authors cheering for you.

Thanks also to mom friends who are also writers. Shannon Chakraborty, Hannah Long, and Sunyi Dean—you guys know the pain of trying to work on a complex book during brain fog and with little kids. Thanks for your memes, your parenting advice, and your constant cheerleading. You reminded me to be gentle with myself. I didn't follow that advice very well, but I appreciated it all the same, and I'm working on it, promise.

Special thanks to Essa Hansen, for all the reality-breaking chats and brainstorming. No one else quite gets it the same way you do, and your help working out some of the weird stuff is so appreciated. You are brilliant and wise and so hecking creative. Thank you for your availability.

Thanks as well to Sharmila Devar and Pranshu Mishra, the audiobook voices for Ahilya and Iravan. Wow, did I get lucky to land you two. Not every author is so fortunate that their audiobook narrators become such fans of the book, really pouring so much emotional and creative depth into the work. I loved being able to nerd out with you two. Thank you for giving my book your voice.

Thank you, one thousand times, to my critique partner David Esarey, who came in at the last minute with a life-saving read that elevated this manuscript. Your astute comments, and throughline since the first book, were absolutely spot-on. Thanks for sticking with me for all these years, following the shenanigans of these two jokers.

To my readers who followed me through this series from the start as well, or new ones who came to it after other work—thank you for being here. I hope you enjoyed this book and that it fulfilled all the promises the series opener made.

To my family, Ishmish, Lulu, and Tate. You three saw it all! Writing on my phone while nursing, agonising over plot points during dinner, my distraction through the days when you needed me, and my tears when technology crashed on me… Far from being impatient, you gave me time and space to work this out. You are all incredible, and I love you.

And finally to my past self who was full of doubt about this. You did it, dude.

ABOUT THE AUTHOR

Kritika H. Rao is a *Sunday Times*-bestselling author of speculative and children's fiction. Whether writing for younger audiences or adults, Kritika's stories are influenced by her lived experiences, and explore themes of self vs. the world, identity, and the nature of consciousness. When she is not writing, she is probably making lists. She drops in and out of social media; you might catch her on Instagram @KritikaHRao. Visit her online at www.kritikahrao.com.